GARRETT & SUNNY

by

Peter Butler

1

2

Also by Peter Butler

Womanhood

Kinky

Buy Me a Dream

Published by: Peter Butler
ISBN: 978-0-9924417-3-9

Cover design by Peter Butler.

ACKNOWLEDGEMENT

I wish to extend my endless gratitude to Kathryn Butler for her tireless work on the manuscript of Garrett & Sunny.

Her efforts and encouragement kept me on-track from the first few pages and through the countless revisions until I could finally type "The End" and mean it.

Garrett & Sunny

Chapter 1

A bed can be used for sleep... for fun and recreation... for reading... for resting... for recuperating... Or in my case right now... for dying.

I hope I'm being melodramatic, but the honest truth is I feel absolutely dreadful. I have made this diagnosis without opening my eyes - It is actually my waking thought. Stomach like an explosive bubbling cauldron - head woozy going *thump.. thump..* as it orbits around my body - joints aching - a shadowy black-clad figure with a scythe in his hands overhead. That last part I imagined, but it wouldn't surprise me to find I was in a hospital bed hearing my mother gently weeping as an unfamiliar voice says, *'I'm sorry, there's nothing more we doctors can do. Please sign the Organ Donation form before your weeping becomes uncontrollable.'*

Hell no..! Don't do it mom, my imagination fights back against itself, *my heart is good for a lot more kicks, before you give it to someone else.*

I force my eyes open to prove my right to keep my organs, but nobody is actually there to notice - No mom.. no guy with a scythe.. no doctor.. although one of the three might be useful. The jury is yet to decide which one.

Now that I'm semi-roused I begin to analyze my symptoms again and realize that alcohol might be responsible for my depleted state. I have experienced the occasional blinding hangover in the past so I feel competent to make a diagnosis. But when I think about it a little deeper, today's symptoms have an added dimension that I've not experienced, one that probably rules out a hangover. The best way I can explain my problem is to compare it to a heavy fog draped over my brain, stopping vital information from coming out. Admittedly I have had only a minute of wake-time to make this observation, but already several thoughts have started, then seemingly just stopped or drifted off, as if my brain just lost the energy to go on.

Never-the-less, alcohol may still be part of the problem, and if it is, it would be useful to know what I drank.

What did I drink?

I search my brain but I cannot recall anything. Not just what I had been drinking - Anything! Where I went last night, who I was with, what I did, how I got into bed, even - none of that information is available - The more I search, the more I find missing. Now that is definitely weird. I've had memory slips in the past but never a total blank-out. This might be serious.

Maybe I've had a stroke... or developed Alzheimers... or - my thumping headache suggested to me - *contracted some exotic brain eating disease?*

I move my arms and legs and they seem normal - except for the pain in the joints. I remembered that a symmetrical smile is a good way to test for stroke and I grin like a monkey and use my fingers to measure if both sides are the same. I lock my fingers in shape having used them to measure the distance from the corners of my mouth to the corners of my eyes, then bring my hands together. The fingers and thumbs touch together perfectly. Symmetry. Rule out stroke. I don't know any tests for brain eating diseases or Alzheimers apart from loss of memory, so I quiz myself: *What is my name? Garrett Nixon.* So far so good. *How old am I? Thirty-two.* Ha! Doing okay here. *Now, something harder. What is my sister's name?* I don't even pause, it's there straight away. *Megan Cullen.*

Having aced all those difficult questions I conclude it is just my recent memories that seem to have disappeared, or more correctly, been erased - Logically, I was there when they were being created, so my brain had them, but now it doesn't. More than strange, that is a little scary. I swing my legs out of bed and sit on the edge waiting for my eyes and brain to sync up. My gut is still gurgling but, thankfully, I don't feel I'm in imminent danger of throwing-up. I take my time, sitting there with my elbows resting on my knees, my hands supporting my throbbing head.

My daily waking moment can often be very special, my brain is relaxed having had a whole night to devour any problems that were bothering me, and frequently it delivers some answers at this moment. These waking epiphanies are greatly valued and taken very seriously. Today - no epiphany, just a need to look-up a word. One that means the opposite of epiphany.

When I eventually feel replenished and strong enough to look around the first thing I see is my dresser, and my blank-canvas, memory-less world, suddenly becomes interesting. I love this beautiful piece of furniture; it is made of old oak that was given a second life, which is to say it's made of secondhand timber; a phrase the marketers quickly replace with words like *antique* or *historic* which miraculously lifts its value tenfold. If only the rest of business was that easy we would all be millionaires. In it's first working life this particular timber was part of a wharf for over a hundred and fifty years. I bought the dresser a few years back, not only because it looks great, but also because it reminds me that value and usefulness can be found in most things, sometimes you just need some imagination and hard work to reintroduce it to the world, not to mention a catchy marketing phrase at the end of the process. Besides, who else can say as a conversation starter: *Guess how many people have walked on my dresser?* It is a rhetorical conversation starter, if that is at all possible.

Given my current state I'm mildly impressed that my brain can recall details like these. But, what the hell happened to last night?

As wonderful as the dresser is, that is not the reason for my sudden spark of interest in it. It is nothing crazy like somebody is actually walking on it, but something unusual is sitting on it. Apparently, I have a handbag. My missing evening last night has just been presented with some potential answers.

It's a big, red leather bag, and I do mean big, not quite suitcase dimensions but definitely carry-on size. I don't think it's my type, so I can't imagine I would have bought it.

Or worse... stolen it.

This is really starting to piss me off.

Slowly, the obvious more likely option occurs to me, and a sly smile creeps across my face.

As quickly as my impaired condition allows I twist my head around to the bed, fully expecting to see a woman lying next to where I lay a minute ago. I should mention my bed is king-size and a Sumo wrestler could have been sleeping there beside me and I would, most likely, have been clueless about it. Once again I should explain - I chose the Sumo because he is a politically correct example of a very large person, not because I have a preference in that direction.

But back to my bed, unless I'm dating the Invisible Woman, it is empty.

I scan the room for some clues and I'm rewarded straight away when I see a scanty pair of pink panties on the floor at the foot of the bed. It gets better; there's a non-matching white bra a short distance away. From where I stand wobbling, they both appear to be quite small. That's to say, too small for me to wear. *Surely I wouldn't have bought them to go with the red bag? No..! Surely not...*

But I do have that gap in my time-line and, at the moment, only slightly freaky questions seem to be filling it.

'What the fuck did I do last night?'

I actually say this out loud, and startle myself as the words come back and land in my ears.

Or, more importantly... who?

I turn back to the dresser with the big red bag sitting temptingly on top. Very wrong thoughts enter my head.

This is potentially dicey, I've never been one for invading peoples private things, but this was different. It was unlikely the woman would have left without her bag, not to mention her underwear, so the only conclusions that I can come to are that I have slept with a woman, in my own bed - and that woman is still in my house. Minus her panties and bra.

I smile and raise an eyebrow at that last thought, and realize that in all the excitement of these discoveries the pain in my head has almost disappeared and my woozy stomach is less of an issue.

Had I just invented a magic cure..? Or was I just an easily distracted, horny guy?

I'm pretty sure I knew which side I'd put my money on.

I examined the outside of the bag while I listened as hard as I could. Apart from the madman still beating a slow, rhythmic drum inside my head no other sounds came to me. I held my breath to maximize my chance of hearing her. I had a choice at this point, I could go searching through the house and find the woman and attempt to feign some sort of familiarity about her - I had, presumably, slept with her after all. The other option sat within arm's reach of me.

Expediency... or moral correctness... Difficult dilemma. Which should I choose?

The first thing I noticed was that the contents, and there were many, were scattered randomly over the bottom third of the bag. I mainly recognized pill-bottles containing vitamins and supplements. The woman was clearly some kind of health-nut, or more to the point, a walking pharmacy. There were other more normal handbag items scattered amongst her pharmaceuticals, like some makeup and a mirror, lipsticks, perfumes, a hairbrush and a small packet of tissues, not that I was an expert on the subject of what women carried in their handbags. I couldn't see the metaphorical kitchen sink, but I'm sure there was one there... somewhere.

At least I had my first clue about her. My second actually; she wasn't Sumo large, judging from the underwear.

I felt around inside the bag, painfully aware of the noise I was making as I pushed my way through the rattling bottles. The side of the bag had a familiar bulge, secured by a zip at the top. I opened the pocket, put my hand in and was rewarded when my fingers felt the shape of a wallet. In spite of its bulging size it came out relatively easily. It was made of the same red leather and looked like a mini-me handbag; obviously a matched set. Or perhaps the bag was a complete entity and was reproducing, maybe even cloning itself. This wasn't such a crazy thought, given the size of the thing.

I held the wallet up and examined it. It had a little flap with a stud that secured its two sides. My fingers were poised to cross that final boundary and flip open that flap when I froze in horror. Out of the corner of my eye I caught sight of the handle on the bedroom door turning and the door begin to push open.

I didn't have time to replace the wallet.

I didn't have time to do anything.

I stood there like a rabbit frozen in a headlight beam. The evidence of the crime firmly clenched in my hand, and I gather, a look of total anguish on my face.

Her eyes locked on me the instant she entered. She stared at me.

Or was it glared.

My brain was refusing to help in any way. Under more normal circumstances words would have come rushing out of my mouth, hopefully with a combination of wit and humor. But not at this moment - the empty, blankness of last night had returned to paralyze me.

I stared, open mouthed, at her. She glared at me. Mouth tightly closed.

Stalemate!

Seconds, that seemed to me like hours, passed. My weakened state actually became an asset for the first time that morning when she was forced to speak first.

'Taking my virginity wasn't enough for you? You want my cash, too?' Her look hardened even more, becoming more like mock, over-the-top severity, than that of a really pissed-off woman.

I frowned at her, partly because my mind was trying to process the changed look on her face, and also comprehend what she had just said. But mainly because my mind-mouth coordination was still useless.

The other factor that was playing havoc with my normally confident manner was what I was looking at. She was in her mid-twenties, I guessed. Her hair still looked as it must have when she got out of bed. The fact that she had made little attempt to fix it ticked a box in my mind. Her powder-blue dress had wrinkles and creases from a night left anywhere other than on a hanger. Long, flowing wavy honey colored hair cascaded over her shoulders. She had no make-up on which only served to emphasize her natural beauty. High cheekbones with two big, perfectly shaped deep blue eyes either side of a nose that would most likely be considered a bit too big by classic beauty standards. But by my standards, which I like to refer to as 'flawed

16

perfection', she was bang on the money. My eyes swept down the length of her body confirming my first impression.

Typical of a woman who gets stared at a lot, she had instantly taken in my reaction and had already awarded herself a point in the game she was playing with me. That part I was pretty sure about - I was involved in a game. Memory-less and brain dead. What could possibly go wrong? She was still staring at me challengingly, and I realized that it was my turn to speak. I returned her look, trying to replace the previous look of horror with a half-ass smile. I had no mirror to check the result, but from her change in expression I probably managed to look more like I was in agony than what I was aiming for, which was a friendly guy, who just happened to have a wallet in his hand that didn't belong to him.

My mind must have been on some sort of time-delay mechanism, in a desperate attempt to cover my weirdness, I blurted out, 'You were a... *virgin*!' Accompanied with what I hoped was a look of shock.

As the words were toppling out of my mouth my eyes were already on their second trip around her body. They seemed to want to do their own thing, ignoring the command from my brain to look *shocked.* She was gorgeous, and even in my fragile state I reasoned that the question of her virginity must surely have been resolved many years ago.

So, she had a sense of humor. I award her another tick! And she's already miles ahead on the scoreboard. In fact, I doubt that my name is even listed on that scoreboard.

My problem is still real though. I have no memory

of last night and because of her untimely return I still don't know her name. And she says we made love. This thought really pisses me off, as making love to her is something I would want to remember, forever. I'm not saying that I've never been with a really beautiful woman before. I have, on many occasions, but I have almost always found them wanting in personality or sense of humor, or intelligence, or humility, or... something.

I hardly knew anything about this woman, but my instincts were screaming at me in a way that I'd never experienced. I trust my instincts. In importance they rate along with my waking epiphanies.

Still with that unreadable expression, and looking straight into my face, she said with emphasis, 'I was.'

Her answer wasn't specific, in that she didn't actually confess that the virginity loss happened last night. This strengthened the feeling I had that she was playing with me.

'I have some money here.' I held her wallet out in front of me. 'I'm happy to compensate you.' I smiled my best smile.

I was relieved to feel that my mind was coming out of its glue-like coma. Her attitude towards me seemed to be softening too, because she gave me a tight-lipped, half smile. So there was a small chance I might be able to partially retrieve this situation, so long as she doesn't rethink my last joke and decide I just called her a prostitute.

Then she counter-punched with the dreaded question: 'What were you doing in my bag?'

I paused a beat, then I smiled. It was a smug smile, the sort of smile that challenged her to call me on this. I said, 'I was just looking for some pain-killers. Thought you might have some, the bag looks like it's big enough to have one of everything known to mankind inside it.'

I knew this was far from a good response, but at least it sort of explained the unexplainable. I put the wallet back into her bag. Besides, everyone knows the best form of defense is attack. I hoped it would work.

She stared at me with a, '*I don't believe a word of it'*, look on her face, and then she slowly shook her head as if to say she was ready to move on. Did I finally have a point on the scoreboard? The crowd didn't go wild, as the sports commentators say, so I was left to wonder.

She turned and walked over to the bed with a floating grace that resembled a skater on a sheet of ice. I loved it. As she turned and sat I noticed she was carrying two cups of coffee. Strange that I didn't notice this before. In fact it was the coffee smell that wafted into my nasal passages that I noticed first. Seems my eyesight is the most easily distracted of my senses. Who would have thought that?

'Is one of those for me?' I said with a quizzical look, pointing to the cups as I walked over and stood in front of her.

'There's the problem,' She nodded as she replied, looking me straight in the eye, 'I didn't put any sugar in, so I don't think we'll need your help.'

'What?'

'With any stirring.' She added with a questioning, raised eyebrow, and she pointedly dropped her gaze from my face.. to my waist.

I followed her gaze and with horror realized that I was standing there... stark naked, and the *stirrer* she was referring to, was - well... straight in front of her face.

In my defense, from the time I had opened my eyes this morning until this very moment, I had been totally on edge and distracted; trying to solve problems with a brain that was barely functioning. And this had required all of my limited ability to concentrate.

'Oh, God!... Oh, Crap!... I, I.. didn't realize... I had no idea! So sorry.' As I said all this I made a ridiculous attempt at regaining my decency by thrusting my left hand over the relevant bits and pieces. It was too little and too late, and I don't mean that in a smug, bragging way.

She was enjoying my discomfort immensely, I could tell this by the huge grin on her face. She began to chuckle, which slowly grew into a laugh which then grew louder, to the point where her entire body started shaking uncontrollably.

She knew she was losing it and in desperation held one of the cups out to me which I took in my one available hand. But this wasn't enough to stop the spillage from starting, so with a very wobbly hand she urgently thrust the other cup in my direction. Instinctively I grabbed at it with my other hand.

Having to expose myself again only made her laughter even worse, which in turn caused a large splash of very hot coffee to land on my bare right foot during the handover.

Now, one of my feet was as red as my face.

She started rolling on the bed in fits of laughter, her hand thrust over her mouth was doing little to muffle the sound. I was left standing there in pain, trying not to hop, embarrassed, naked and completely devoid of any dignity. A low point in my life that I hope I never manage to best. But all of my discomfort was taking second place to the glimpse of pearly-white bare backside that I was given when her rolling around on the bed caused her dress to slide up to a dangerous level.

Eventually she regained control of herself and rolled back to the sitting position, smoothing and pulling her dress down as she did.

Damn!

She flicked her hair back to reveal a beautiful, natural blush on her face.

God, it was hard to think about anything other than her when she was in front of me.

She looked at me with deep intensity, and then, thank God, she smiled. It was a genuine smile, full of warmth. I guess she was seeing the situation from my perspective for the first time.

Wow! I love the smile she's giving me, it's just so... Well... just for me.

She eased herself off the bed and went to where her panties lay on the floor. She came back to me, knelt, and gently wiped the remaining hot coffee from my foot with them.

Maybe I'm reading too much into this, but this was probably the sexiest thing that any woman had ever done to me. I could only look down at the top of her head and think, *I really don't want to blow it with this girl. Whoever she is - she's something special.*

She left the panties beside my foot and sat back on the bed. She smiled at me again and said, 'I'm sorry about your foot.' She held her hand out and I passed back her cup.

Unlike her, I had no clothes lying around that I could put on. I considered her panties, but even brain-impaired as I was I realized that would be weird and dismissed the thought. I wondered where my clothes could be? As she was sitting on the bed linen I couldn't even use a sheet to wrap around myself. I thought of getting something out of the dresser, but it seemed a bit like shutting the barn door, after the horse had already bolted. I decided it was safest just to sit beside her.

I did, and we drank our coffee in silence for a minute or two. I was starting to feel almost comfortable being naked in her presence and it certainly didn't seem to bother her.

My impatience finally won out and I tentatively said, 'Last night was great.'

I hoped she would agree and elaborate, but she just nodded and murmured. 'Mmm...'

Eventually she said, 'It was lovely.' Then she qualified her opinion, 'Well, most of the night was.'

We drank in silence again. This was like being involved in a high-stakes game of poker - for me, anyway. Show no emotion, don't let on that you've got nothing.

'Are you feeling better now?' She finally asked when her coffee was finished.

'It's just a foot, I got another one.' I said, in a very poor attempt at a mafia tough-guy voice.

'No,' she chuckled, 'I meant after last night. Truf and I were very worried about you. The way you suddenly went all quiet and sleepy.'

Now this was the first really valuable clue I'd been offered. Truf is my best friend and if he was there he would never have left me if he thought there was a danger or risk. So I can assume he also approved of her.

I decided to subtly try and dig deeper. 'I don't

remember much of it at all.'

'Well, I can tell you that Truf was the one who carried you inside to the couch. If it was just me you'd be waking up in the garden or more likely, beside the road.' She laughed at the idea.

So, I was on the *couch*, presumably still fully clothed. How did I get undressed and into bed? Nothing was coming back to me about what she had just described. Even more frustrating, no memories at all were being triggered.

I tried again. 'What the hell was I drinking? My mind seems totally blank about all this.'

'We were drinking all sorts of things, mainly spirits though. Lots of toasts to your grandfather, Ed.'

At last a partial memory stirred inside my head; something concerning my grandfather was due to happen. I wonder what it was, and if it was happening today? I searched my few active brain-cells but nothing floated to the surface. Thankfully, I always write important things in my diary, so I'll check that later. Plus, Truf will be able to fill me in on last night. Things were looking up.

I was about to ask more, when I noticed her looking at the clock on the wall.

'Oh, God! I have to go,' she said, as she reached over and gathered up her bra and panties from the floor. She took the coffee cup out of my hand and moved them both to the dresser. The bra and panties were casually tossed into the bag on top of all the pharmaceuticals, and the kitchen sink. Then, in one fluid move, she draped her giant red, cloning, carry-on size suitcase full of pharmaceuticals over her shoulder. On anyone else the bag would have looked too large, but she carried it with so much confidence that it seemed to be a part of her own body. I also noticed that the color of the bag complimented her dress superbly.

I loved watching the way she did things. Everything about her was so poised and elegant, and at the same time so carefree and casual. Like most guys, I spend a lot of time looking at women and I can usually find things to love about most of them, but she was scoring points in ways that I had never even considered before. *Her bag complimented her dress superbly...What the..!*

She came over and stood in front of me. I stood too, and for the first time that I could actually remember, we were close enough and in a position to do damage. I was about a foot taller than her and I looked down into her face.

'Thanks for an... interesting night.' She offered as she gently cupped my face with her hands, then lightly kissed me on the lips.

She pulled away after the kiss and looked into my eyes intently, but it was too late, my arms were already folding around her back. I kissed her this time, a little harder than she had kissed me, and she responded with equal vigor. I felt her arms fold around my back, locking me in just as tightly. Neither of us seemed all that anxious to end this.

Finally, she released her arms and gently eased my shoulders away. She leaned her head back, 'Whoa!' She mumbled through heavy breathing. 'This is very different from last night.'

She moved just out of my reach and then she backed away towards the door, her eyes never left mine. I matched her step for step, but she kept just out of reach.

'I want to see you again... Soon.' I said.

'Then call me,' she countered lightly, her eyebrows raised in a questioning manner. Then she turned and reached for the door handle.

I was devastated and steadily building up to a mini anxiety attack. I didn't have her number, her name or any real memory of our time together. But she obviously thought I did.

I was about to blurt all of this out, but when I noticed the knowing look on her face my instincts kicked in and I held off. Her expression was challenging me. Or was it mocking me? She seemed to understand the turmoil that was going on in my mind.

She said, 'I left my number.' Then she gave me a sly grin and slid out the door. She turned back for a moment and waved goodbye, the way women do, wiggling her fingers.

My hand automatically waved back the same way as the door closed behind her.

She could hardly have missed noticing *Little Gary,* was also waving, but in a much more manly way.

***

Straight after the door had closed I pulled a pair of shorts out of my dresser and began my search for *the number.* It clearly was not in my bedroom, so I headed out.

I surmised it would be written on a post-it note or a scrap of paper, and my office would be a logical first place to try.

I entered the room that a large part of my normal day takes place in. It's a large area that was originally designed to be a lounge room, but I decided I could do my relaxing in one of the other smaller living rooms. There are three of us who work in this one office, so we have no secrets from each other. I call Sky and Sophie my right and left hands and my workday would struggle to get anywhere if they were not around to help organize me.

My desk is the first thing you see when you enter; it sits in front of the rear wall and faces into the middle. It is larger than the two desks occupied by the girls. This isn't an ego thing on my part, my work requires the use of two large-screen displays and they just wouldn't fit on a smaller desk. A huge bay-window sits behind my desk looking out to a leafy garden. I love looking out there because it's so peaceful and at the same time, vibrant. It is also the perfect distraction, which is why I sit with my back to it. This morning the curtains are tightly drawn.

I know straight away she has been in here because my chair is slightly askew, as if someone had just spun around, got up and left. I never leave my chair like that. In direct contradiction to my work, the rest of my life is very informal, although I have to admit some people prefer the word 'slob' to describe me. Unkind. Casual, is the one I use. The harsh truth is that I'm quite anal about my work area - a tidy desk equals a tidy mind, is the theory. My work is complex and finely detailed and I need to be able to get information as quickly as possible, hence the six filing trays laid out on the return. I call it my Hekyll and Jyde personality, I know that spoonerism is a bit too cute, and not many of my friends seem to get my little attempt at humorously explaining one of my many *charming* idiosyncrasies. It's most probably me who is off-target with that one, as I try hard to not surround myself with fools.

Sky, my right hand, mocks me endlessly about this little isolated neatness obsession and a quick look at her work area confirms why. Her desk is a disaster; papers are spread out all-over it, a calculator is half buried under an open book, both of which are casually placed on top of an open prospectus that she has been studying. And so it goes. There's even a computer buried there somewhere. I call Sky my right hand because her desk is to my right and I put up with her 'mess' because she is absolutely terrific at her job, which is to assist me with company research and analysis. Besides, she can find anything on her desk, blindfolded. I know this because I foolishly bet against her with real money, once.

Sophie, my left hand, is my accountant and office manager and the rudder that keeps the Nixon Fund heading in the right direction. Consistent with that area of expertise Sophie has her desk as sterile as an operating theater. Her idiosyncrasy is a love of plants, with which she has surrounded her work area. The one thing on her desk that looks out of place is the machete that Sky and I bought her as a joke, just in-case she needed it to get to her chair. We're a small team, I'm the boss, but you'd never know it. And I wouldn't have it any other way.

The only other noteworthy feature in the room is the bank of filing cabinets lined up side-by-side on either side of the door. Government regulations being the confused mess that they are, require us to keep a paper copy of just about everything we do. I haven't had a tax audit yet, but Sophie keeps telling me to expect one, especially now that we are starting to make some good money. But that will be her worry if and when it happens. I hope. Filling in forms and taxes are two things that I detest.

The Nixon Fund is a private hedge fund and we currently have nineteen high wealth investors who use our services. Hedge funds make informed, but often, quite risky investments. The term hedge refers to our use of financial instruments that act like an insurance policy to protect us from any abnormal ups and downs of the market. For example if we take a position in a particular company on the Stock Exchange, we will simultaneously use futures contracts or options that allow us to sell some of the investment at a set price in the future, which somewhat protects us from sudden, expensive, price movements. We manage these financial tools very closely. Getting rid of them when the market moves up and our investment is making money. Entering into them again when the market starts to drop away. All the time keeping the actual dividend earning stock as a base. Our income comes from the profits we make for our investors, so if we weren't any good at this we wouldn't be in business.

My fund is comparatively very small, but it is growing nicely. I am trying to shift our emphasis into actually controlling, or completely owning the companies we invest in. This has become necessary because the American banks and investment firms, are in the process of destroying the concept of individual investors being able to trade shares on any global market. They would not be able to do this without their government being totally on-board with it. Inside the financial industry it is called a "Carry trade", and it involves *printing* trillions of dollars, which are in reality just pieces of paper with drawings of dead people and large numbers printed on them, and in themselves only worth something as long as people trust and believe in them. I say printed, but I really mean virtual, because most of it only exists as a very large number on a computer screen. This so-called money is very quickly swapped for real assets that will still have value when the dollar eventually collapses. Noticed the Dow making consistent new highs lately? A very nice deal for the small number of people who ultimately gain from this. A terrible deal for the rest of us all around the world, but particularly for the average American citizen. When they eventually work it out all hell will break loose or, more likely, will have already broken loose. Until that day there is a mad scramble going on, under our very noses, to buy up everything of value - with cash. The amateurs are still using credit, not realizing they are ultimately just buying a house, or whatever, for the investment company - at a discount of however much they pay as a deposit.

The state of the financial world has forced me to become paranoid and prepare for a very different future. As a result, the Nixon Fund rarely makes paper copies of sensitive data, by that I mean trading decisions and strategies. This information is encrypted and kept on a hard drive, or more correctly, it is shared around many storage devices. I have created hidden 'virtual' drives on our computers and servers for this data. If someone looks at the system data they will see a displayed size for the hard drive that is actually less than the real amount available. This gives me enough space to have my sensitive programs and data included without any intruder even knowing they should be looking for them.

Naturally, I have a dummy program that updates

itself daily with false data that is visible to an initial search. The same data is backed-up on the externally located servers, but spread around many locations, so accessing just one server would only give up one piece of the jigsaw puzzle.

This is probably over-kill as the logging program that I created will, hopefully, alert me to an attempted intrusion very early on in the process. So if someone tries to get into my business they better be pretty good at it, otherwise I will know.

All of this data is secured by an encryption program that I also wrote and I'm reasonably certain that it's as good as any in the world. Self-praise is no recommendation, I know, but hey - it is good. Having said that, I have little doubt that the guys working with the NSA in the US are probably way ahead of anything I've come up with. Between them and the FED, investing has become a dirty business these days. For this reason I've recently had to minimize my reliance on stock charts and indicators and lean a lot more heavily on the fundamentals of the companies I'm investing in. Things like the amount and type of debt they are carrying, the valuation of their assets and their profit and loss numbers.

Sophie and Sky both know how to access all of the features of our system, but if either of them accessed the data from outside the office it would still initiate multiple emails and an SMS message to my phone. They both know this and on the occasions that this might happen they would call me first to stop a potential panic reaction.

Computers are my passion. I studied computer science at university and wrote nearly all the programs I use in my work. This gives me an edge over most of the other hedge-funds. If they are small, like mine, they usually buy programs off-the-shelf, or, if they are large they have a department full of computer geeks to do that work. Quite often the problem for them, is that the person who does the analysis has to try and convey to the geek exactly what he or she wants the program to do. Then the geek gives it his best shot. Then the analysis person tells him what it's not doing and the geek goes away and alters it, and so on, and so on. It can take some time to get it working effectively.

In my case I'm the analysis guy and I'm the geek, so when I talk to myself I understand exactly what I'm saying. Saves a lot of time.

These days it has become fashionable for Funds to employ "Quants" as specialist analysts. They are usually highly skilled computer scientists, mathematicians or "Quantum" physicists who are smart enough to work out that a career in the finance industry pays much better than designing rockets or teaching at universities. The funds put these collective, highly intelligent brains to work to design automated trading strategies and models. These are the group of people we have to thank for High Frequency Trading; an invention of craziness that allows certain companies to buy and sell millions of shares, all inside the space of one second. It's crazy and not necessary for what they claim: to "make" or create markets when trading is quiet. Quiet is as normal as frantic is in a free market. It's purely and simply Government sanctioned manipulation by a small number of chosen citizens.

The whole investment industry has changed so much since the USA, in particular the Federal Reserve, which is a privately owned business and not controlled by the USA Government, collapsed the global markets in 2008. The Fed's job is to print the USA's money. When too much money is printed it ends up going into rubbish investments that ultimately fail when they run out of idiots to on-sell to. You've heard of Junk Bonds and Sup-Prime Loans...?

Back in 2008 it was Sub-Prime housing loans made to people who could never repay them, which the USA banks bundled together and sold as "investment quality" bonds to organizations like European pension funds. When these financial instruments collapsed, so did Europe.. and America and the rest of the world. Thanks a lot, you jerks!

The GFC in 2008 wasn't a market collapse - It was a systemic collapse because it involved governments having to re-jig their basic economic models, and it hasn't been fixed, just 'wallpapered' over. One thing that America is brilliant at is best exemplified by what they do in Hollywood - making people believe in things that aren't real.

Because of this I'm really vigilant these days.

I'm not a quant, in fact, I'm not even qualified. My entire family were jointly surprised and pissed-off when I never bothered to turn up for my final university exams. The only family member who got it was my grandfather, Ed. He had been there and done that and understood me enough to know that if I was to have my own business it would be something I would need to commit to until I was successful. Having something like a career to fall back to would make giving up all that easier.

Besides, all I needed from the course was the

knowledge and I had that. Proving it would come if I succeeded, not with answering some questions for the academics. Ironically, some of the people who did answer those questions and went on to graduate are driving cabs for a living today. The other reason that I didn't want a "Certificate" was the overwhelming need to conform at that level of education. It was almost like a cloning process where everyone leaves with the same knowledge that they then try and sell to a prospective employer. I was much happier working on my own projects. Call me a Lone Wolf.

Not that I'm a quitter, either. Quite frankly, it was just arrogance. I knew I could do this. To be more accurate; by the time I was due to take my exams I had accumulated a share portfolio worth well over a million from my part-time trading of the share market. I was young and a smart-ass. Hard to imagine, I know.

End of story.

Well maybe not. In 2008 when the bottom fell out of the market, a sizable chunk of my bank balance went with it. Over the next year and a half I managed to make it all back and my plan to start my own Hedge Fund was once again back on track.

It also helped greatly to have a grandfather who was a retired legend in the Investment Banking industry in the City, and the source of most of my real knowledge.

I looked everywhere on my desk, but I couldn't see a note. I noticed my phone-charger was empty. That was unusual.

Maybe not, given that last night still didn't even qualify as a blur.

The disappearance of my phone happened in that mysterious blank stage of last night. I didn't notice it in

33

the bedroom, so maybe it is on the couch. I usually take it everywhere with me, so I almost certainly took it last night. Normally, the last thing I would do before going to bed is charge it. Hence, my surprise.

But then I don't even know where my pants are, so maybe surprised is too harsh.

I check the filing trays for a note. I check all of the desks, Sky's takes longer than it should. Nothing. But I do notice some of the papers in the trays on my desk seem to have been disturbed. I suspect my overnight guest has been snooping through my work.

My mind starts to wonder if maybe that was the reason she came here. Maybe she drugged me so she could have plenty of time to get some information she wanted.

Maybe not. After-all she had nothing with her when she came back to the bedroom, apart from the coffees. Perhaps she had a camera or a flash drive to record what she wanted, and she left it outside and collected when she left the bedroom. She did make a point of closing the door. I made a mental note to check if she had tried to access the computers.

No shit, Sherlock! Are these thoughts really coming out of my mind? From the very same idiot who just raided her bag, or at least attempted to. *What the hell am I thinking?* She probably just wanted to find out a little about me. I doubt I was very talkative by the time we got back here. I would probably have done the same in her place. I decided to drop that whole line of thinking. I had a note to find. And now a phone as well.

I move on and scour the lounge but without any success, but I do find my shoes, shirt and jacket from last night. I seem to have carelessly scattered them all around the couch. But no pants. Not my normal behavior. On impulse I go back to my bedroom and open my closet. My pants are there, hanging neatly from a coat-hanger. My underpants are on the floor beneath them.

I try and picture myself undressing and throwing my clothes all over the place, while a girl I just met stands there watching the bizarre spectacle. The other thought I have is far more appealing. I imagine she is the one ripping the clothes off me and throwing them on the floor. But why did I bother to hang my pants? Weird. A third alternative involves Truf, but this doesn't even get to the partially formed stage before I dismiss it. I decide it's definitely the second scenario.

I stop daydreaming and move on to the third most likely place to leave a note: the kitchen.

For a big house the kitchen is not a very big room, but it does have quite a lot of bench space. Clearly, it's meant for food preparation, but I use it more for dirty plate and pot storage. The dirty items only need to be scrapped and put into the dishwasher, but I still struggle with the scrapping and putting part. The obsessively tidy part of my persona starts and ends in my office.

I notice a freshly rinsed bowl in the sink and the open box of organic muesli she has left on the table. So she's definitely been here. But there is no sign of a note... or the phone.

I move on and search the three spare bedrooms, then the bathrooms and even the laundry room, but without success. The dining room is hardly ever used and has a *don't mess me up* aura that discourages people from casually using it. I never use it, and a quick look through the door confirms that she was not game either.

Then I hear it. A phone is ringing. My ringtone, my phone! And it seems to be coming from the kitchen. I run though the house and arrive there just as the ringing stops and the caller either goes through to voice-mail, or hangs up.

Damn!

The ringing seemed to be coming from somewhere near the refrigerator, so I check on top of it and the cupboards and benches around it, but I can't find it.

I open the fridge door and check the shelves thoroughly, it's quite lightly stocked at the moment as I haven't had much time to look after my domestic issues. I open the egg section, the crisper on the bottom and even the butter compartment. Nothing.

In desperation I even look in the freezer.

I start again, this time I shift bottles around and look behind tins and jars. Then back to the fruit crisper where I start rummaging through the oranges and apples.

Success! She had buried it under some apples. I say she, because even drunk and high on illicit drugs I would never do that to my phone. I think!

Fact number three: She's a certifiable psycho!

I realize this can't be an accident. It would have to be something like: she was getting herself an apple and the phone somehow slipped into the tray and the apples just happened to tumble over the top of it, and she never noticed any of this. No way. She hid it there deliberately and she had a reason. My short-term memory might still be shot, but my thinking was back up to speed, thank God. This was a game she was playing with me, one that was meant to continue long after she had left here.

Given the effort she had spent in hiding the phone I guessed that she has inserted her number into the address book. Maybe it was her who just called? I checked the voice mail. It turned out I had three messages so I played the most recent one.

'How's my favorite grandson? I was just calling to see if you can come around today, after your appointment with Gerald. I know what that meeting is about and we need to discuss some things. Seriously, I'd like to see you today, Gary.'

That was my grandmother Liz, and I'm not only her favorite grandson, I'm her only grandson, I think. Her voice triggers memories in me. My grandfather, Ed, died a few weeks ago. His death tore me apart, I loved the old guy more than my own father. That's not actually saying much as I don't get on with my father, and Gramps literally replaced him during my teenage years. Gran is a wonderful, loving woman and I also think the world of her.

Everyone in the family, with the exception of my father, would be keeping a close eye on Gran over the next few months, so it was a given that I would happily call around and see her.

The second call was from my mom. *'Hello darling, it's mom. Your father is not well today. I think Dads death has had a big impact on him. It would be really lovely if you could pop around and see him. He misses you terribly, you know. We love you.'*

I put the phone down. This was safer than holding it, as there was a good chance it would have been crushed or thrown through a window.

That's the way my father, Alex Nixon, works. The bastard. What a piece of shit! He's playing the *'poor me'* card' again. And using Mom to do his dirty work. Well stuff him. It's not going to happen.

I would have liked to be able to see Mom though, we get on really well, but it would end badly if dad was in the house. And he would be... he never leaves it these days.

I took a moment to cool down, then I played the last message, hoping it was her. It was Megan, my sister, '*Hi Gary. Why do you never answer my calls? I'm sure you check the Caller I.D. and let me go to voice-mail. I wanted to talk to you about our meeting with Gerald today, but hey, it's not important enough for you to pick up, it's only your sister.*'

Contrary to what she said in the message, I talk to Megs at least once every day. We are very close and she likes to 'take the piss' out of me, whenever she can.

I dialed her number.

'So you do know how to talk on the phone.' Was her opening line.

'I'm sorry, Megs. I had a really late night apparently, and I couldn't find my phone. It was in the fridge.'

'What are you talking about, Gary? Are you still drunk? You're certainly not making sense.'

'It's a long story, one that even I don't know, yet. But it involves a woman who hides phones in refrigerators. I'll tell you what I know when I see you.'

'She sounds like a psycho!'

'Ha!' I laughed at the similarity of our sibling thought patterns. 'That's exactly what I thought. But, she's really something, Megs. We connected. She's had a big impact on me.'

'Oh God! Are you in love?' She chuckled, '... again! What's her name?'

'I don't know. It's in this phone, somewhere, but I haven't had a chance to find it.'

'Gary, do you have any idea how lame you sound? If I didn't know you so well, I'd say you were doing drugs. Look, you're not fifteen anymore. You can't fall in love with every pretty little thing who flutters her eyelids at you.'

I didn't want to get into this right now, so I said, 'What did you call me for?'

'I wanted to know if you could pick me up, for our meeting with Gerald today?'

So Megs was going to the meeting, also. Normally, it would have made sense to do that, because Megan's house was only a mile or so away from here, but I had to see Gran after the meeting and she was on the other side of the city. But I still said, 'Sure, no problem. What time are we meant to be there?'

'Three, so you be here at two thirty, Okay? Don't get sidetracked and head off to the Registry Office to get hitched with your psycho girlfriend.'

I ignored her sarcasm, and said instead, 'What's the meeting about, anyway?'

'You were there when Gerald told us he needed to talk to us. At Gramp's funeral.'

Now a small memory came back to me. I remembered how both Megs and I were surprised by his manner and his insistence that the meeting take place on the thirteenth. Neither of us had any inkling of what was to be discussed, and he refused to elaborate at the funeral. We guessed it concerned Gran or Ed, as he is my grandparent's legal representative.

'Yep, I remember now.' I was anxious to start looking for the phone number, so I said, 'I've got to run, Megs. Lots of shopping to do before then... and I don't even know her ring size.'

I ended the call without giving her the last word. Small victories can be strangely satisfying.

I opened the "Contacts" list. It was arranged alphabetically, so I hoped her name wasn't Zelda or something similar. This was my only personal phone and I had all my friends and business contacts listed. It was a very long list. I scrolled down, thinking I could probably delete a lot of these names, but decided against it. You never know. I was looking for something that seemed new and I found it in the "H" section. *Heidi*. I do not know a Heidi. Well I didn't, until now.

I pushed the call button and waited.

'Hello.'

I tentatively asked, 'Is that Heidi?'

'No.'

Damn! It occurred to me that she had given me a false number. 'I'm sorry. I was given this number but it's obviously a mistake.'

'Yes,' she said, 'but it isn't a wrong number.'

'But you just said you weren't Heidi... Oh! I get it. You just answered her phone. Could I speak with her, please?'

'That's not going to be possible,' she replied.

Games within games. I was pretty sure that I was talking to the girl who was here. She sounded very similar and this bizarre, cryptic conversation certainly seemed to come from a mind like hers.

I decided I needed to try and gain some control, so I said, 'I'm sorry to hear that, I really wanted to talk to her about something she lost at my place last night. Sorry to bother you.' I quickly ended the call, guaranteeing that I would have the last word.

I replayed the conversation in my mind. *Obviously a*

mistake....but not a wrong number.

So Heidi wasn't her name. It was a test to see if I knew her real name. Oops! Failed, big time.

I couldn't see any way to improve my place in the game, so I decided to end the nonsense and just admit that I had no memory of last night.

I twisted the phone in my hand and my finger was just about to hit redial, when it started ringing.

'Hello.' I said.

There was a longer than normal pause on the other end, then she said, 'You have no idea what my name is, do you?'

'Well, I'm pretty sure now it isn't Heidi.' I answered tentatively. Then I added, 'But you did put that name in my phone, so I have to assume that you can't spell your real name. My first guess is that you're a Russian spy and your real name has about twenty letters, and it just wouldn't fit in my phone. Or, now that I think about it, my favorite theory is that you have multiple personalities and they all have different names. One would definitely be Sybil, of course.'

She chuckled. Maybe I'd just scored a point in her game. 'No. It's Sunny.' She thought for a moment, then continued, 'And yes, I do have a few different personalities, but they are all good fun, hopefully.'

I could tell from her voice that she was enjoying this, so I said, 'Nice to meet you Sunny. Let me take a stab at your full name. Is it Sunny... Lecter?'

'Ha Ha...You're starting to sound a lot like a guy I met last night.' She laughed. 'No, my name is Sunny McGuire, well actually it Sonya McGuire but I changed it in school because some creative little clown started calling me "Piss". Piss-on-ya was just stupid enough to

41

catch on. Now I only answer to Sunny.

I laughed, 'So you changed the name but retained the golden theme. Well played, nice touch.'

'You lied about your name,' she retaliated. 'You said it was Gary. Turns out it's a bit longer than that. You have trouble spelling the big word?' She deepened her voice as she said this, mimicking my earlier dig at her Russian name.

'We have something in common.' I replied. 'At school, some of the kids decided Garrett was too hard for them, and not nearly as amusing as their choices of "Parrot" or "Carrot". So I started using Gary. Now, even my mom calls me Gary.'

'Well, Garrett Nixon, you need to know that you failed the "Find the Phone" test and the sad thing is, it's not really designed for humans, it's more an animal test. They usually replace the phone with food for them. The average chimp will do it in under three minutes.'

'That's rubbish. You just made that test up. Besides, I would have aced it if you had put it behind the beer. I'm beginning to think that you really are related to the Lecter family.'

'You know that can't be true, because you're standing in your kitchen, hopefully dressed by now, talking to me,' she laughed, 'and not still in bed, trussed up like a turkey awaiting an appointment with a carving knife. Now, to important matters.' She changed the tone of her voice again. 'The contents of your fridge, in fact your entire kitchen, are pathetic. If that's what you eat then you really need to keep your medical insurance up to date.'

I replied, slightly defensively, 'It's not normally that barren, I haven't had a chance to...' I smiled to myself,

42

as I remembered exactly who I was talking to, 'The truth is, I've found that when I have *virgins* over, they're usually really hungry in the morning, and while I sleep on blissfully exhausted, they're consuming the contents of my fridge. It just became too expensive, so now I deliberately leave the kitchen understocked.' I paused, realizing that my attempt at humor could very easily be taken the wrong way. If she really was a virgin I had just added her to an imaginary list that was presumably very long, and if she wasn't, then I just sounded like a tight-ass. I tried to retrieve the situation a little, 'But I notice you only had a bowl of muesli, which makes you an unusual *virgin*.'

'Aw gee! Not special?' she laughed. 'I also had an orange... and both are long gone, so I can't give them back.'

I liked the way things were going, so many of the women I had dated in the past were overly keen to score any point they could. When I managed to put my foot in my mouth, and I usually did, they would happily place theirs in also. Almost like they were looking for ways to keep some distance between us. The fact that she had just laughed off an opportunity to do that was significant. I have never been very good at managing the subtle mood changes that women seem to go through in the early stages of a relationship. Sunny seemed to be the perfect woman, beautiful, playful, intelligent and easy going, too. Time to find out.

'You don't happen to own a pub?'

'No. Why would you ask that?'

Oh, she didn't get it... 'I've always wanted to meet a woman who owned one,' I chuckled defensively. 'It's not a big deal.' Clearly she hadn't heard about most guys version of the perfect woman.

'Well I'm sorry to disappoint you. I'll go and get one this afternoon.'

'Sunny, you do realize that I have very little memory of last night?' This was a lie, I still had no memory at all. 'Tell me how I got home and why my clothes are all over the lounge room.'

'You really don't remember? Pity, you were a lot of fun right up to the time you passed out.' She waited a moment, as if she was working out just how much she should say. 'I can't take all the credit for getting you home and inside. Truf half dragged, half carried you from the cab,' she giggled.

It was a beautiful little sound that I was fast beginning to fall in love with.

The fact that Truf came back here and then left us alone confirmed that he trusted Sunny.

More importantly, he could tell me everything that went on last night.

Truf is a very good judge of character, the sort of guy who can spot a phony from a mile away. He got his name back when we were kids together. For as long as I've known him he was fascinated with rocks and anything to do with the earth. He was always digging things up that caught his eye. When we were about fourteen I saw a documentary on TV about a Frenchman who roamed the countryside near his home with a pig, who used its incredible sense of smell to uncover buried truffles. From that day on Henry Stonewall had a new name. Not that I was really comparing him with a pig. It just seemed appropriate. He liked being included with a group of special people finding all sorts of valuable things just under the surface of the earth. Where the rest of us only saw dirt and rocks, Truf could see gold or silver or tin.

Truf's one of the country's top geologist's now, and has his own business. He works on contract for most of the big mining houses, preparing opinions on the value of their leaseholds and mapping out their best options for any potential mining. He works all over the world and does very well.

Truf is also a very big, powerful man. I'm over six foot tall, but he towers over me, so getting me from a cab to the lounge would not be all that difficult for him.

'Oh, look at the time!' She suddenly shrieked over the phone. 'I have to get to work. I'm sorry I stole a bowl of your muesli and an orange, all I can suggest is you come around to my place and you can have some of my muesli, I think you'll like it. I don't have any oranges, so we'll need to work something out to replace that. Are you up for that?'

I'm pretty sure she wasn't really talking about breakfast cereal; at least I hoped she wasn't, so I said, 'I think I'm up for that. What time suits you?'

I waited for a response... and waited, but the phone was quiet.

She had already hung-up.

Crap! At least I had her phone number, now.

I was still trying to work out if her last statement about the muesli was a euphemism. God, I hope it was.

Chapter 2

Driving along Megan's street is like being in a tunnel. It's lined on both sides with large Camphor Laurels with thick branches, heavy with leaves. The massive trees tower over the street, creating a darkened tunnel through which I drive.

I pull up in front of a neat white picket-fence with foliage spilling over and through it. Megan likes the green leafy plants and has filled her garden with varieties that create small forest-like pockets around her front and rear yards. There is a modest size open grass area in the middle for Chelsea and Livvy to play.

As I walk towards the front door I offer up a small prayer that Megan's husband, Tim, will not be at home. Just before I reach the first of the three steps that lead to the veranda my legs are simultaneously grabbed from behind. This attack is accompanied with squeals of delight from two little girls, who were clearly hiding in the bushes waiting to ambush me. Not to spoil their little game, I was expecting this attack, having spotted them as soon as I arrived; their attempts at camouflage were not quite the equivalent of a crack SAS team.

I allow them to drag me to the grass and they pile on top of me, still squealing and laughing. I start to growl and snarl like a dog at them and they squeal even louder. I manage to ease Livvy, who is the youngest at four years of age, off me, but Chelsea, who is one year older, seizes the opportunity to put me in a head lock and plant a big, sloppy kiss on my cheek. Not to be outdone by her sister, Livvy manages to slip away from my arm and copies her sister, giving me an equally sloppy kiss on my other cheek.

'Ooh... yuck!' I feign horror at being kissed by the girls and pretend to wipe their kisses away with my sleeve while I half-heartedly try and push them away - even though I love their affection with every fiber of my body. This just increases their screams and squeals, and the intensity of their kisses.

I give up and lay there with my arms stretched out in surrender, smothered in their beautiful kisses and infectious laughter.

Looking back over my head I see Megan standing at the top of the stairs, with her hands on her hips, laughing and shaking her head.

'Who needs a German Shepherd when we have these two little guard dogs?' She chuckles.

One at a time I lift the girls off me and sit up, but they won't be put off that easily and grab at my arms, until Megan says, in a slightly more serious tone of voice, 'That's enough girls. Uncle Gary has been subdued, you can go back to playing now. Well done.'

Reluctantly, but still giggling, they disentangle themselves from me and run off towards the side garden. Clearly the best area to hide bikes in. There is nothing quite like local knowledge to give you the edge.

Reaching the top of the stairs I give Megan a kiss and a hug. She says to me with a pained look, 'Do you have a jacket, Gary?'

'No. I thought the shirt would be enough.'

'Pity. You have a grass stain on your shoulder. Wonder where that came from?'

I looked over my shoulder and saw the top edge of

what she was referring to. 'Oops! That's going to look really inappropriate amongst the overly neat and expensive senior executive level of the Shawston Towers legal offices. Oh well, tough shit, I don't have time to change.'

'I'd offer you one of Tim's shirts but we both know they would be too small,' she smiled at her empty gesture.

The reference to Tim made me realize that my silent prayer could not possibly be answered. The fact that the girls were at home meant that Tim would need to be there to look after them when Megan left with me.

I looked around half expecting him to be standing in the doorway and was pleasantly surprised when I didn't see him. Tim and I don't hate each other; we just don't love each other. I struggle to deal with his constant bragging and annoying self-promotion. Strangely, the others in the family seem to accept it, even admire it, which pisses me off even more. The guy is an underachiever and a capital J jerk, no other word for it.

Tim is in middle management at a nameless toy importer. They bring in the Chinese plastic rubbish that you find in almost every store with a toy department, and definitely in every home with a child. Needless to say, Chelsea and Livvy have a pile of toys that they could get lost in. I don't approve of this concept of more than enough, is not enough, and have to bite my tongue on the subject. And it makes it damn near impossible to buy the girls a special gift at Christmas and birthdays. To Megan's credit she manages to keep both girls pretty well grounded.

The girls have managed to retrieve their bikes from the garden and are riding in circles on the grass, laughing and just being kids, so Megan and I head inside for her to grab her bag and say good-bye to Tim.

'How you doin, Gary?' He greets me just inside the door with a handshake, his other hand holds what appears to be some sort of toy helicopter.

'Fine thanks, Tim.'

I can't bring myself to inquire about his health, the fact that he's well enough to be standing there is disappointing enough, and the conversation takes on an awkward moment.

Megan stepped in to fill the void. 'I'm going to be a little longer than I said originally, Tim. Gran called me earlier and asked if I would come and see her after the meeting with Gerald. Gary's going too. So if you can get the girl's dinner ready that would be a big help.'

This was news to me also, as Gran hadn't mentioned Megan when she invited me. Intriguing.

I glanced at Tim and saw that he was not happy with this news. He was almost glaring at Megan and I instantly understood why she had waited until this moment to drop the news on him. He had always resented that her family had a connection to big money, when he himself had come from the poor side of town. Not that the calculating side of Tim couldn't see the eventual payday down the road, so I guessed he also bit his tongue a lot. We had something in common after-all. You've just got to love the dynamics and politics within an extended family.

Tim brought his feelings under control, grunted acknowledgment and decided to change the subject. He said to me, 'I want to show you our new range of remote control helicopters, Gary. I have a few at home to test and they're brilliant.' He held the one in his hand up, for me to admire. 'The top of the range are called Quadcopters and even have cameras, they use four, really quiet rotors and are able to hover for ages. I've been playing with them all afternoon.' He grinned and winked at me in a conspiratorial manner, then added, 'The blond over the back should get herself a bikini' then he chuckled. 'Well, on second thoughts, maybe not.'

Megan gave him a tight, forced smile, and said, 'Next time, Tim.'

'Yep, maybe next time, Tim,' I echoed. 'We need to go if we are going to make the appointment on time.'

We headed out the front door after Megan gave Tim a less-than-warm peck on the cheek and some instructions that included keeping an eye on his girls, and not helping the woman over the back look for her bikini. We got as far as the front lawn and then another, much longer farewell took place, accompanied with lots of kisses and squeals.

The drive in to the city normally takes about fifteen minutes and today the traffic is being kind to us. It's only a short time before Megan is onto me. 'So, tell me about your new girl. Have you found out her name? What was the problem last night? Why couldn't you remember much about it?'

I cut in to her never ending list of questions. 'Her name is Sunny and we are supposed to be seeing each other again tonight. At least I think we are, she hung-up before we could settle any details.'

Out of the corner of my eye I can see Megs rolling her eyes and shaking her head slowly from side to side. I know when it's said out loud it sounds weird, maybe even stupid, but there is something free spirited and different about Sunny that I find absolutely wonderful. Her hanging up on me before any crucial details are finalized is more of a challenge to me, than rudeness. I get her - I think. Or, maybe she really is psycho.

'When I woke up this morning I had a total blank in my brain about last night. I mean completely blank. In fact I still have it. Sunny has told me a little of what happened, but even when she talks about it, I can't recall any of it.'

'Is there any chance you were drugged?'

'You did hear me say I couldn't remember anything?' I shrugged my shoulders and gave her a smug, tight grin. 'I don't know. She said we were drinking all sorts of things, so maybe I had some sort of alcohol poisoning. The good news is that Truf was with us, so I'll be able to get a better picture of the night when I talk to him.'

'Truffle!' The way she said his name made me turn and look at her. She had a strange look on her face that didn't make any sense to me.

She noticed me looking at her, and said in a serious voice, 'How is Truf? I haven't seen him in a long while.'

The way she said *a long while,* made me look across at her again, and I think she blushed.

Weird.

We were on the edge of the city, stopped at a set of lights, casually observing the different types of people as they made their way across the pedestrian crossing when Megs gestured, excitedly, towards a rather plump girl with hair that was badly dyed and seemingly cut with garden pruning shears. She was wearing a miniskirt that was both too short and too tight, causing her midriff to dangle over the front of it. 'There she is

Gary! From what you've told me that's got to be Sunny crossing in front of us.'

I gave her a dirty look, which she laughed at, then became more serious, 'She sounds really interesting, Gary. I know you have high standards - that's been your problem all along. You look for perfection when it just doesn't exist. It's all about being prepared to compromise.' She smiled at me. 'You're just going to have to accept that Sunny comes with her own psychiatrist.'

I reluctantly conceded she could have a point.

I have been to the Shawston Legal offices on Lower Thames Street on a few occasions and I buzzed the receptionist to admit us to the underground visitor car park. The ride up to the twenty-fourth floor takes only seconds and the view of the cityscape behind the reception desk that unfolds as the lift doors open, is breathtaking. I tried to imagine how I could ever explain to my investors why I needed such an expensive location to conduct my business. Clearly, Gerald was at the top of his game. But seriously, as a client you have to know that *you* are paying for all this.

Thank God, I'm not one of Gerald's paying customers.

As you enter the reception area you are swallowed in soft ambient lighting and surrounded by rich, dark stained wood-panel walls on which hang wonderful works of art. Was that a Monet to my right? Surely not. But a print or reproduction in this environment would look as appropriate as a ham sandwich at a Jewish wedding. The impeccably dressed receptionist welcomed us with a big smile. I noticed her glance at my grass stain before suggesting we each take a seat in one of the thickly padded, expensive looking leather armchairs. She motioned me into the one in the corner, which ironically hid my grass stain from any other reception visitors. She's good, this girl.

Presently, Gerald came out and welcomed us both, warmly. As he led us back to his office he asked, 'Would you like a coffee or tea, maybe a cold drink? We will need about half an hour to get through what we need to do.'

We both decided on coffee, and Gerald relayed our order over his shoulder. 'Two coffees, Terri - when you have a chance.'

The slick, almost rehearsed exchange made me feel like we were entering an expensive restaurant. '*Madam and Sir will be sitting at table nine, Terri.*'

Gerald's office was impressive, his view was even better than the one at reception, taking in the whole length of the Bridge, and from our lofty height the cars crossing it look like toys. In the distance a jet left a contrail as it flew off to distant places, seemingly still at a lower altitude than us.

Our luck was in; Terri must have had a chance, because our coffees appeared, elegantly transported on a beautiful silver tray, almost before Gerald had time to offer us a seat in one of his dark-green leather-bound chairs.

'It's wonderful to see you both, again. You look lovely, Megan.' He made no mention of how lovely I looked, so I assumed the grass stain was not a good match with my chosen shirt - or his office, maybe my grassy-green clashed with his leathery-green. 'I'm sorry that I was not prepared to give you any information about this meeting at Ed's funeral, but that was hardly the time or place to discuss matters like this. I guess you assumed it was to do with Ed's death. I am his estate's executor and your grandmother's legal representative.' He shook his head sadly as he mentioned Ed.

I sat back and took a sip of my coffee. It was exceptional. Terri was, without question, a gifted barista. I smiled to myself at the sounds of words and their meanings. A barrister with his own barista.

Gerald continued, 'You have most likely guessed that Ed's share portfolio passed to your grandmother. She doesn't have the energy to manage all her affairs anymore and has given me Power of Attorney over that part of the estate. She still makes the final decisions, but I look after the day-to-day details for her. I'm not letting anything out of the bag by telling you she intends leaving both of you a major share of that portfolio in her will.' He looked at both Megan and me and nodded, knowingly. We both grinned like kids on Christmas morning. Then he continued. 'Ed's will has singled out one particular share in his portfolio, a mining exploration company called Plutarch Resources to pass immediately to the both of you. The company is based in Australia and Ed has owned these shares for a couple of years, I should add that Liz also owns an equal number of shares in that company in her own name. They apparently had sentimental value to Liz as she was the one who insisted on acquiring them. They are certainly not a stock I would have recommended. You might well know more about them than I do, Gary.'

I shrugged my shoulders and shook my head as he looked at me questioningly. I had never heard of the company.

'I had a quick look into the company's details and

found that they are a junior explorer with some exploration leases in Australia, mainly in the middle of Queensland, out past Roma and near Culgawinya. I did some quick research a few days ago and it seems the company has been looking for Coal Seam Gas. I don't know if they have been successful.'

He allowed us a moment to consider what he had said. When I first got into share trading speculative mining shares were my bread and butter trades. They are cheap to buy and if you get it right, capable of doubling, even tripling in a very short time. Get it wrong and the opposite can happen. Spec shares are not an area that my Hedge Fund deals in. We are into Blue Chips - solid companies that have a good cash flow and a long track record of profitable trading. So why the hell were my grandparents interested in this company? It made little sense. But still, it was their money and a few dollars invested in something a bit risky might have been their idea of buying a lottery ticket.

Gerald continued, 'Ed's will provides to each of you, five million shares in Plutarch Resources.'

'What the..!' Megs exclaimed, before she caught herself and stopped. Gerald's palatial office seemed an inappropriate place to drop an F-bomb.

My mouth was wide open, also. I was furiously trying to imagine how much those shares might be trading at. Gerald had a smile on his face at Megan's gaff, which I interpreted as meaning that the F word did get dropped inside these hallowed expensive wood panel walls.

Before we had a chance to comment, Gerald continued. 'When they made the purchase Ed was required to get permission from the Australian Stock

Exchange before they could legally take possession of the shares. Their holding breached certain Takeover Laws. For that reason I have advised Liz to retain ownership of her shares for a little longer. As you are all related parties we will most likely need to re-visit this issue with the Stock Exchange, but hopefully I can convince them that no breaches have occurred by the shares passing from Ed's ownership to that of his grandchildren.'

Gerald looked at Megs and noted the look on her face. He added, 'It's not quite as much as you might think, Megan, although it is still significant. The shares are currently trading at ten cents each.'

A half a million Aussie dollars... each. Giddy up Ed!

I was trying to look cool and collected, but my mind was racing. I looked across at Megs and saw that she was also doing mental arithmetic at a furious rate.

'You each possess just under five percent of the available shareholding of Plutarch Resources. The shares have never paid a dividend and the share price has been as high as twenty two cents. Sadly that was the price that Ed and Liz had been buying at. But over the past year the price has been steadily dropping. So there seems to be a considerable amount of selling pressure in the market. Because of the distance involved Ed never bothered to try and get himself elected to the Board of Directors, even though his shareholding would most likely have made that possible. I can offer no reason why Liz wanted him to buy these shares. She would not discuss it with me; said it was personal.' He raised his hands in a gesture of helplessness.

He paused and gave us both a moment to gather our thoughts.

I did some quick maths, 'From what Gerald has told us there must be about one hundred million Plutarch shares on issue.'

This Megs fully understood. 'Thank you, Gramps,' she acknowledged with a large, beaming smile.

I continued, 'But these small explorers are notorious for just stringing their shareholders along in the hope of eventually making a big discovery. Very few do, but they keep asking their shareholders for money by making what are called Rights Issues.'

'Oh! So it's not all wonderful?' Megan asked.

'If the company genuinely has discovered something of value that they can mine then it's usually good,' Gerald answered her question. 'But sometimes the Directors and Management just give themselves a nice pay rise with any money they raise.'

'Yes,' I said, 'the joys of dealing with the so-called "Penny-Dreadfuls"'

'I did some quick checking before you arrived here today, so you'd have some information to think about,' Gerald added. 'Ed and Liz's combined holding is the largest with 19.9% of the stock. Next comes a company called MienOne with 10.8%. It's Chinese held and operated by someone called Ling Mien. I checked the name out and he is the son of one of the many new Chinese billionaires. A fellow called Ong Mien.' Gerald gave us a look I couldn't quite work out. Did he think that was a problem? I needed to do my own research on this. He continued with his rundown. 'A couple of Hedge Funds in the States each have 5% holdings, and a family Trust in Australia has 4.5% of Plutarch Resources. The rest are small holdings, mainly Australian.'

I could see poor Megs was totally overwhelmed with all this news, so I suggested, 'I can go over the details with Megan later, if you'd prefer Gerald? I think we should get as much information as we can. I'll get Sky to do an in-depth analysis of the company.'

He nodded in agreement. 'We need to advise the Australian Stock Exchange of the share transfer, but because of Probate and so-on I'll be able to delay that for a little while. You never know, it might turn out useful to fly under the radar for as long as possible,' Gerald gave me a conspiratorial smile, which made me wonder if he was in possession of more information than he was telling us. 'You won't be in possession of the shares for some time, but you will have the authority to make legally binding decisions about the shareholding, just as soon as you sign these forms I have drawn up.' He handed each of us some documents, the pages held together with bulldog clips, which we read.

We both finished reading at the same moment and nodded to Gerald, who picked up the phone and asked Terri to come in and witness our signing.

We left the building in silence, both of us contemplating the abrupt change in our circumstances. Megan had never been all that interested in money, but I suspected Tim would be overjoyed at this development.

The traffic was chaotic now. Because I work from home I had almost forgotten just how big a bitch driving at peak-hour is.

After we left the inner-city area and I was able to concentrate on something other than the traffic, I said, 'I'm a little freaked out going to the house again after Gramps' death.'

Megan nodded in agreement. 'It was just so sad the way he died. Good in one way, as he obviously didn't suffer very much, but horrible for Gran to come home from her walk and find him that way.'

The police had determined that Gramps had been carrying a pot-plant down the back stairs, when he had fallen. The coroner had concluded that he had broken his neck instantly, and would have suffered very little pain. Liz's next door neighbor, Polly, had called in to have a cup of tea with them only to find Gran sitting on the ground, cradling Ed's twisted head in her lap, surrounded by the remains of the shattered pot-plant. With tears pouring down her face she had sobbed, "My beautiful Ed is dead, Polly."

We dragged on, seeming to make very little ground, but eventually we pulled into our grandparent's driveway.

Ever since I can remember I always got a kick out of coming to this place. They had lived here for about thirty years and the house had always seemed too big for the two of them. They had help in running it with a housekeeper coming in three days a week.

I drove up the fine gravel driveway, enjoying the crunching noise the tires made as they rolled along. The driveway curved gently around the numerous large trees that grew in front of the house and I looped around and parked near the front door, facing back the way we had just come in. Sitting on a half an acre of manicured land the double story Georgian house still looked timeless and majestic. Its brickwork was painted an off-white color with a gray trim around the windows and doors. A huge leafy ivy draped itself over various parts of the exterior. It looked amazing when its leaves started to turn orange and then gradually a brilliant red. Eventually it became a mess on the ground for the gardener to deal with. He complained to Liz that it needed to be cut back heavily for its health, but she would have none of it. She loved the way the ivy hugged at the house and softened its harsher angles. So they compromised and he got to trim it back each year. Just a little, to stop it blocking the gutters and covering the windows and doors.

By the time we had climbed out of the car Liz was standing in the open doorway to welcome us. We all embraced warmly.

'You look terrific, Gran.' Megan said, as she kissed her on the cheek and held her at arm's length to look closely at her.

Megan had been offered the right to call Gramps, Ed, at the same time I had, but she preferred to keep things the way they always had been - Gramps and Gran. I'd stuck with Gran for Liz, too, somehow she just seemed more like a *granny* than a Liz. But Ed and I had been working together on my special *education* since I was fourteen. He had taken me into his work quite a bit and as I grew older, and bigger, it seemed inappropriate to call him anything other than his name.

Everyone at his work called him Ed, even the part-time people who cleaned the offices at night. Ed was the sort of guy who remembered everyone's name and all of the important issues in their lives. He was universally loved, in spite of the fact that for most of his adult life he was the man in charge of one of the City's biggest Investment Banks and when necessary, he could be as tough as nails.

'How ya doin, Gran?' I said as I took my turn to do

the hugging. At seventy-eight, Liz Stratton was still in pretty good physical shape, but understandably, lately she was looking a little drawn, a little older and a lot more fragile than she had.

She smiled warmly, 'I'm doing just fine now that both of you are here. It brings back memories of many years ago, the both of you racing around those trees over there.' She pointed to a couple of large maples in the middle of the lawn. 'Mind you they weren't quite that big back then.'

Megan and I looked too. 'They were still big enough,' Megan said. 'I remember Gary talking me into climbing up that one on the right, when I was ten. And the resulting broken arm. And the month in plaster.' She punched me, semi-playfully, on the shoulder. 'Memories, eh! Gramps must have had so many good ones in his time here. He had a fabulous life with you, Gran. You were both so lucky.'

I noticed she had the beginning of a tear in her eye, so I said, 'Let's get inside. I'm keen to hear what you wanted to talk about. The meeting with Gerald hit us a bit like a lightning bolt.'

I led the two women into the foyer.

To say Gran's house is impressive would be an understatement. It was more than just the large size of the rooms and the color coordination, it was the overall impression it emitted. Everything just worked together. This was totally the result of the love and effort that Gran had put into the place, Ed's input started with a checkbook... and ended with a signature.

Gran had decorated the house in a tasteful homely way; there were many painting and lithographs on the walls, and even a prized Persian silk rug hung on the dining-room wall. Nothing Gran had used to decorate their home had been put there to impress visitors. If she loved a painting by an undiscovered artist, she happily displayed it beside a well-known piece worth many thousands. Her choice in furnishings was equally inspired, and I guessed that an awful lot of it was expensive.

I shuddered at that thought, Megan and I had been treated like little god's by our grandparents and, as young kids, allowed to run free and pretty much unchecked inside this place. I hate to think what damage we probably did.

We continued on into the main living-room and my eyes instantly went to the beautiful painting by the Australian artist Arthur Boyd that dominated the wall facing the door we entered through. The painting's sky was an incredible cobalt blue blending into a darker almost indigo blue. In the foreground a sparkling river, encrusted with giant colorful boulders, wound its way across the front of a large, rocky cliff with trees clinging on to any available foothold. It was huge and impressive; about twenty feet wide, and would have looked out of place in a room of smaller size. Gran loved to tell visitors that the artist used his fingers to apply the paint and only rarely used a brush. This room was Gran's favorite as she had made a point of only using works by Australian artists. Boyd was joined by other contemporaries like Storrier, Whiteley, Olsen, Blackman and so on. The reason was simple; Gran had been born in Australia and this was her way of connecting with her past.

Liz Shorrock had made the huge journey to England at the ripe age of twenty-one. The trip had been a gift from her parents in recognition of her outstanding academic achievements which had seen her accepted into Cambridge University. The family ran a 1000 acre pastoral property near the Victorian town of Ballarat and Liz was the first Shorrock to, not only graduate from high school, but top the state academically, at the same time. Being a female added even more weight to the achievement all those years ago.

Liz had taken her place with many other new girls at Newnham College and during the first week she and a small group of new friends had visited the famous Mathematical Bridge over the River Cam. This footbridge links both sides of Queens' College which was home to a young mathematics student called Edward Stratton. While standing with her friends on the apex of the bridge Liz had looked down to one of the punts which had stopped just below her and found herself looking at a young man who was staring at her with a large grin on his face.

'What exactly are you staring at, and why is it amusing you so much?' She had demanded in her sharp Australian accent.

'As it turns out,' he had replied, gleefully, 'I'm staring at the most beautiful *Australian* woman in the world.'

Liz had blushed and said, 'Thank-you... I think. But you haven't answered my question.'

He had laughed in a confident way, and said, 'I just love the irony. You see, it just *figures* that I should meet the woman I'm going to marry, on the Mathematical Bridge.'

The other girls had all groaned in unison at his line, but Liz had looked into his eyes and seen the intensity of his feelings.

They had rarely left each other's side from that day forward.

That all changed a few weeks ago.

Megan said, 'I'll get us some drinks.' She left Gran and me and headed out to the kitchen.

I had my arm around Gran's shoulder and she felt tiny and fragile as I led her to one of the comfortable sofas as Megan disappeared through the door.

'I was just thinking what a fantastic job you've done with this place. I'd never really noticed before. I suppose when you see something so often you take it for granted, but now that Ed's gone I'm looking at what you've done with fresh eyes, and I have to say it's really special.'

'Ed always liked to *finesse* whenever he could,' she laughed for the first time since I had been there, then she added, 'I'd always notice and tell him off... "Get your clumsy big paws off that Ed," I'd say. "It looks just fine where it is."' She shook her head, realizing the words sounded harsh and nothing like the playful banter between them actually was.

I joined in her laughing as Megan returned carrying a tray of glasses. 'That's music to my ears.' she said, as she placed the tray on the table in front of us. She handed Gran a glass of Sherry with a single ice cube inside it. It clinked musically as it was transferred from hand to hand. My glass of beer made no such noise, but the frothy head looked just perfect. We'll make a bartender out of this girl one day.

I had no idea what Megan had made herself, it was crimson colored and had ice in it. It looked suitably 'girlie', but without the straw or umbrella, or even a cherry. I've been to a few kid's birthday parties at

Megan's place and one thing I've learned is that the mothers of young children seem to take great comfort in alcohol. I'm not calling them drunks, on the contrary, they seem to do a great job, but it must be more stressful than my job, because at the end of the day I rarely think about having a drink to "take the edge off", as Megan explains it.

My inappropriate thought on the topic of mothers and alcohol was interrupted by Gran.

'I imagine you're both intrigued by Ed's decision to transfer those shares into your hands?' She asked, as it turned out, rhetorically. 'There are two components to the gift. The first is, that we love you both dearly, and want you to have something from my side of the family. Those shares were purchased with the money I inherited from the sale of my parent's farm. The second reason is more like a baton-change than a gift. I'll put it bluntly; it's a request for a favor.' She smiled wryly at both Megan and me. 'I'm a little embarrassed about this, kids. I had Ed buy those shares to help out an old friend of mine in Australia. I'm afraid to say that between the two of us we managed to do very little to help that friend. I'm hoping that your youth and vitality will be more effective. Obviously, that is if you agree to help out.'

Gran paused as if to gather her thoughts, took a sip of sherry and then put the glass back on the table.

'I will say, at this point, that if you are unable to assist I'll completely understand. You both have busy lives and responsibilities that must take preference over a second-hand promise that was made by a senile old lady, without your knowledge.'

I noticed Megan had put her drink to the side, so I followed her lead. She was looking at me in a way that I knew well.

'It goes without saying, Gran that we will help out any way we can. Especially now that we know you're senile.' I smiled broadly as I said it, hoping that the actual request would be something relatively simple. Megan was nodding in agreement.

'Thank you both,' she responded, returning my grin. Gran was about as senile as your average teenager and was deliberately being self-deprecating. 'It might make things easier to understand if I tell you some of the background. As you know I'm an Australian by birth. I still have many family members over there and until recently Ed and I visited at least once a year. Very early on I fell in love with some of the local art - it was so vibrant and fresh and it reminded me of my early years in that wonderful country. I began buying works and over the years met and became friends with a lot of the artists. One, in particular caught my attention. He is an aboriginal artist called Warra Goomagawa, and we became very good friends,' she looked up to see two very attentive faces looking back at her. She smiled.

'We have a few of his works scattered throughout the house, and I love them all. Maybe you have noticed the large one in the dining room opposite the Persian rug? All I know is that Warra is the aboriginal word for water, but I can't see any water in his painting.'

Gran reached over and took another quick sip of sherry to keep her throat moist.

I knew the work she was talking about. It was a large painting, but done in the style of dot painting that aboriginal artists have become famous for the world over. It's theme was very simple, a black to dark gray under-painting with a huge number of curved lines made up of white, to light-gray dots that gradually changed in size. This gave an effect of a wave within a wave. The curves run side by side only to be intersected with another series of curved lines of dots. And so on. The painting had mesmerized me on many occasions, but unlike Gran, I could see water in the painting. To my eyes the lines seemed to flow like water drops cascading over a waterfall. But who would know, these things are subjective.

'Warra Goomagawa lives in the middle of Queensland, the closest landmark is a small town called Culgawinya. His people still lead simple tribal lives staying mainly within their own community. I bought his art, not only because I love it, I wanted to spread goodwill throughout his community. They are the loveliest people you will ever meet.' She paused and shifted position slightly allowing her to make use of the armrest. She smoothed out the lap of her dress as she settled in to her new place on the couch.

'About two years ago, Warra made the trek into town and phoned me. He asked if I could come out and visit them, because they had a big problem. I knew that for Warra to make that trip meant walking for many days - not something he would do lightly. Ed was unwell at the time so I had to go on my own. What I saw broke my heart and also frightened me. Where there used to be, gentle free running streams there were evil smelling stagnant cesspools, with a horrid green sludge covering the surface. Needless to say the fish and yabbies' had all died, these used to be a big source of food for the aborigines.'

Megan and I exchanged looks of shock as Gran explained further. 'It seems a company had started drilling wells all over the land they live on. It wasn't the drilling that was causing the problem, it was the chemicals that they put down the holes they made. They were trying to extract Coal Seam Gas and the method they use has the dreadful name of "fracking". Apparently some of these chemicals had escaped, or maybe the miners just dumped them when they were finished. It's very remote country. The result was the same, they were killing the land that Warra's people live on. Quite a few members of the tribe had become ill, some had even died, but no one could prove a link between the illnesses and the fracking.'

I asked, 'Would I be right if I suggested the name of this drilling company was Plutarch Resources?'

'The very same one,' Gran nodded. 'So, you can probably see where I'm going with this.' She reached for her drink and we all took a moment to digest what she had said.

Eventually Megan said, 'I don't get it, Gran. What possible good would buying those shares do?'

Gran turned to her and shook her head. 'I had no idea how I could help Warra's people. I researched the whole issue of Coal Seam Gas, or CSG as they now call it. Anything that is really bad is converted to an acronym these days, to soften the impact on average peoples ears. It seems the local Government has turned a blind eye to the damage these mining techniques can do. Local farmers had had little success trying to stop the miners through legal means. So I thought I could buy some shares and maybe get some influence over the company. Sadly, the answer to your question is... not very much.'

Megan was looking to me to provide an answer, but

I didn't have one.

'Ed let me keep buying until just under the twenty percent limit. He'd received permission for us to buy that many shares. I had forced the price up considerably with my on-market buying, the broker I had used was a complete idiot. I was considering the process of nominating for a position on the Board of Directors. But Ed's death has put an end to that.'

I was thinking about the situation but I couldn't see any quick fix, either. 'Maybe we could get together with the other large shareholders and see what they think about the direction the company has chosen.'

'A Chinese fellow by the name of Ling Mein has a holding about the size of mine, or rather the same as the two of you now. I have looked him up on the internet but getting information about Chinese people is very difficult, compounded by the language difference, plus he's a pretty secretive character. He's quite young and it seems his father is quite wealthy. My guess is that he's out to impress his father and prove to him that he's the man to take over the family business when the time comes. But he has two brothers who might have something to say about that. Either way I don't think he has much empathy for the Australian countryside. He's a Chinese businessman and I suspect his shareholding would be solely for profit.'

Gran eased herself up and walked over to the solid, dark-wood bookcase that lined the wall beside the door through which we had entered. She searched for a second or two, then extracted a book, brought it back to the table and gave it to Megan. It was called, "Tribal Art" and she began to flip the pages. From where I was sitting I could see it had many pictures of aborigines doing bark paintings as well as hunting and preparing food. She put her hand out and stopped Megan when she came to a picture of an old man with a paintbrush in one hand and a thin stick in the other, standing in front of a large canvas that was stretched out on the ground.

Gran said, 'That's Warra Goomagawa. Golly, I must have read this book twenty times. Those people to the right of Warra are his family. The little girl sitting in front of them is his granddaughter, she's dead now. She developed a rare form of cancer for which the doctors had no cure.' She shook her head sadly, leaving the underlying cause to our imagination.

I moved over and stood behind Megs looking at the book over her shoulder. Warra seemed to be middle-aged, but the woman, whom I presumed was his wife, appeared to be a lot younger. The kids also seemed quite young.

Gran said, 'Take the book with you, it might give you some help in deciding what you want to do.'

I looked over at Megan and she was nodding agreement, even though no words had passed between us. Gran looked back and forth between us and smiled.

'We had better head off, Gran,' I said as I stood and moved over to give her a hug goodbye. 'We have some thinking to do. We appreciate the gift you and Ed have given us.'

I drove Megan home in silence. She was still in a state of shock in light of everything that had happened today. I was deep in thought, trying to get a grip on what I needed to do. As I pulled up at her house I said, 'I think the first thing I need to do is fly out to Australia and look at what Plutarch is actually doing.'

Megan looked at me questioningly. 'That's a pretty

big spur-of-the-moment decision, Gary.'

'Maybe. But it's essential that we have some facts before we can decide what we can do to help Gran, and as I know almost nothing about the running of these small exploring companies, I'll see if Truf will come with me. I'll get Sky started on researching Plutarch and Sophie can begin digging into the Chinese guy and the owners of the other big shareholdings.'

'Is there anything I can do to help?' Megan offered.

'Can't think of anything at the moment. We'll talk when I've got a bit more information to offer.'

She kissed me goodbye and I drove off.

In my mind I was making a list of things that needed to happen and the all important thing seemed to be the timing. I realized that Truf was essential to the whole process, but he had his own business to run and it was a big ask to get him to drop everything and do me a favor. But, that's what friends are for. I pulled over to the side of the road and dialed his number.

'So, you're alive.' The deep baritone voice announced into my ear. 'It was touch and go for a time there, last night.' He chuckled. 'I guess having Sunny there was enough for you to choose life. I'm damn sure I would have, in your position.'

'Apparently I need to thank you for getting me inside the house.'

'No need, I was just showing Sunny how strong I was. It backfired though, she decided to stay with the guy who had passed out.'

'Yeah, she's smart... and beautiful, but I need you to tell me all about last night. Seriously Truf, I have zero memory, it's almost like I was drugged.'

'Wow! Drugged? I hadn't thought about that, it's a

possibility you know. Sunny's boss bought us a round of drinks towards the end of the night and there was some confusion about who was supposed to get what drink. Maybe he was trying to drug Sunny and you accidentally got her drink... Or, maybe he fancied you,' he laughed. 'But you went all weird just after you had that drink.'

This was all news to me. I had a lot of questions to ask Truf about the night and the answers would take a lot of time. Time that I no longer had. So I said, 'I want to hear everything you've got about last night, but before that I need to know how busy you're going to be over the next week.'

'Next week? Let's see. I'm expecting the results of some trench samples to come in tomorrow or the next day and I'll need to write the report on that. At the end of the week I'm flying to Brussels for a conference. The rest of the time I'll be doing some catch-up office work.'

'Any chance you can do me a favor and ditch all that, and come on a little trip with me? I wouldn't ask if it wasn't super urgent and really important to both Megan and me.'

'Megan!'

Something about the way he said her name registered in my brain. What the hell was going on there? My married sister and my best friend. Surely not.

'Well if you need me then I can hardly refuse. What's it about? And where are we going?'

I pulled my face into a grimace as I said, 'Australia.... mate.'

'You weren't joking when you said, "favor".'

'A place called Culgawinya in the middle of Queensland to check out a company called Plutarch

72

Resources who have leases in the area,' I replied, relieved that he hadn't shot me down when he heard the destination. 'It seems that Megs and I are major shareholders in the company, thanks to Ed.' I shifted in my seat and changed ears with the phone and as I did the Call Waiting beep went off.

Truf said, 'Wow. How many shares has he left you guys? I do know a little about Plutarch. A penny dreadful with a track record that is dismal and a management that seems more interested in lining their own pockets, than bringing resources online. Shares trade around ten cents... Not to sound demeaning.'

The Call Waiting had stopped beeping and the call must have gone through to voice mail. Damn, I wonder if it was Sunny calling. I couldn't interrupt Truf anyway, having just asked him the biggest favor I ever had, and him agreeing to go along.

He continued, 'They are looking for CSG at the moment, but I think they would happily announce they were looking for pearls in the middle of the desert, if they thought people would give them money to do it.'

'You're saying they're shifty?

'That's the word on the street. How many shares did Ed have?'

I could almost hear his jaw hit the ground when I told him our shareholding. There was a pause in the conversation as Truf did the same arithmetic that both Megan and I had done. Eventually he said, 'I can see why you want to check them out. There are a few existing CSG wells out that way, but I don't think any are all that close to Plutarch's leases.'

'That's the thing, the shares have been steadily dropping in value for the past year or so.'

'You do realize that we don't have any legal right to be poking our noses into what's going on with the leasehold, even given that you're a shareholder. You can write and ask permission to see what they are doing, but that would take some time for the reply. So, we are going to need to sneak in, under the radar, so to speak.' Truf laughed out loud at the thought of being a law breaking renegade.

I explained the rest of the situation to him. The more he heard about how Gran had hoped to help the aboriginals, the more he became committed to the task. Truf was a lover of the mining industry, and he hated the rogue entrepreneurs and scam artists who gave his industry a bad name. Mining was a messy, dangerous business at the best of times, but the idea of wantonly destroying the ground and the water table, just to extract a commodity that invariably ended up going overseas to enrich a foreign country, was against every principal he held. There were safer, more sustainable ways to do it. I knew this because Truf had given me the lecture on more than one occasion.

He said, 'Okay, Gary. It's about 22 hours flying time, plus whatever time we loose with the stopover. We should try and leave tomorrow or early the day after. I need to be able to analyze any data that we collect. I want to get back by next weekend. You okay with that?'

'Sure, but we both need to use the morning to get whatever we are going to need. So, I'll come to your place around ten o'clock. And Truf, thanks mate, I know it's a big ask. I owe you. Just tell me one more thing. How did I meet Sunny? Please don't tell me I used some cheesy pickup line.'

'You really don't remember?' he asked. 'She was the

74

one with the cheesy line. We were sitting at a table when she came over, tapped you on the shoulder and said, "*Are you stalking me? Cos, if you are, you're being very obvious.*" I don't think either of us had even seen her up to that point and you said something along those lines back to her. Then you took a proper look at her and saw she was drop-dead gorgeous, and you said something like, "*You do look an awful lot like my mother, so if I was looking at you, I was most likely just wondering what my old mom was doing in a place like this.*'"

I found myself pulling a face as Truf repeated my words.

'She looked at you like you had just slapped her in the face. Then she walked away. You mumbled something like; you'd just royally fucked that up, and that you thought she was the best looking woman you'd ever seen. I didn't argue with you on either point.'

I had to agree; it didn't sound like my finest work.

'You looked over at her a few times and every time you did, a different guy was hitting on her. Then out of the blue, she tapped you on the shoulder again, and asked for your name. You asked why she wanted to know it. She said something like she needed it for the police report she was making on the stalking situation. So you said it was, Bruce Wayne and you asked her name. She asked why you wanted it, and you said it was standard procedure in the "Service". She said it was "Jo Kerr".'

That sounded more like it; seems I lifted my game, a little.

Truf continued his recollection. 'It went on like that for quite some time until you eventually offered to buy her a drink. Then one of her friends came and joined us and the night got interesting for me, too. We all had a great time, lots of laughs until her boss appeared out of nowhere. He was a total tool, talking about himself all the time, a bit like your brother-in-law, Tim.'

Something about the way he said Tim's name caused another red flag in my mind.

'Anyway, he went to the bar and got us a round of drinks. We were doing Tequila shots at that stage and when he got back Sunny just grabbed one off the tray and slammed it down. It was quite strange then, her boss looked like he was really pissed at her for doing that. Eventually, he said he'd just had a call and had to go. He just put the tray of drinks on the table and left. We all had our drink and....

My phone started a low continuously beep in my ear. I looked at the display and it was flashing, "Battery Empty"

'Shit... my battery's about to die.' I butted in urgently to Truf's commentary.

Truf didn't reply so I took the phone from my ear and checked the display again. It was completely blank.

I didn't have a charger in the car, so I was screwed.

I threw the car into gear and accelerated hard down the road. By now it was dark outside and I knew the phone would need a good couple of hours to recharge and I still had half an hours driving to get home.

Chapter 3

I made it home in record time, unbelievably, my driver's license was still a valid legal document. I raced into my office and plugged the phone into the charger.

As I had come through the front door I noticed a note on the table in the hallway so I went back to read it and give the charger a chance to work its magic. The note was in Harry's scrawl, which looks like a combination of abbreviated shorthand letters and unrecognizable squiggles, and could easily be mistaken for the work of a monkey, let loose with a pen.

Harry Buxton is my landlord and he comes and goes as he pleases in my home. To say we have a loose arrangement would be accurate. I have rented from this ancient Englishman for the past eight years and despite the difference in our ages, we get along famously. Harry is a smart guy. Not in the classical sense as he has no degrees or letters after his name. His years of life experience and his down-to-earth wisdom are what I enjoy having access to. He has a view of life that few people can hope to compete with. It's all a perspective thing with my mentor, Harry.

I see it like this: The rest of us are standing on the ground, observing and dealing with everything that is happening in our own little worlds, but the bigger objects around us stop us seeing very far ahead. Harry's viewpoint is different. It's like he is floating above us and looking down. His perspective might miss a lot of the day-to-day stuff that we are all involved in, but when it comes to knowing the "big picture" and seeing what is coming up around a metaphorical corner, then Harry has the unique advantage of years of experience. He has a special ability to sum things up and simplify the complicated, but without the cynical bitterness that can often be part of conversations with old people. Having said that, I have to say that Harry is losing his edge as the days go by; his hearing is poor and his eyesight very questionable.

Between Ed, who was well educated and worldly, and Harry, with his abundant life experience, I have been privy to an exceptional education over the past few years.

That's not to say that Harry's not an opinionated old fart. He is. He just has a happy knack of being able to laugh at all of the world's problems. He claims to know the answer to each and every one of them, but accepts that the world could care less about his opinions. Mind you, he uses his less than perfect hearing as an excuse to avoid having to defend some points of view.

Sadly, I think Harry has the beginnings of dementia. He delights in telling me nearly every chance he has: 'You should employ a teenager, Gary... While they still know everything!'

I laugh politely every time he tells me this. Not because it's funny, but because Harry is almost doubled up with laughter at his joke. Every time. One day I'll have to tell him he's told me the joke before, but that probably wouldn't help, because I think he'd forget that, too.

Harry's big thing is doing repairs around the house. He's still reasonably agile and doesn't carry any excess weight, so he can still do quite a bit. Coming from an age where self-sufficiency was a normal expectation, Harry will tackle just about any household problem, in spite of having eyes that send blurred pictures to his brain and hearing that, quite frankly, doesn't even know it's supposed to be sending information to his brain. For him, a ladder up to the roof to fix a broken tile or replacing a washer on a tap is no problem. Either is sliding under the house amongst the cobwebs and spiders to clear a drain or check a heating duct. The problem is, with Harry a ten minute job lasts at least an hour and a half and even then I need to help him find the bits and pieces he drops and can't find.

Occasionally he accepts his short comings and hires a qualified tradesman, but not until he has had a go at it himself. Because of this, I now have any electrical repairs done without Harry's knowledge. I couldn't live with myself if the old guy fried himself on a live wire. Besides, the rent I pay is woefully less than the place is worth. I suspect Harry is aware of this but is happy with the situation. I doubt that he's saving his money to buy a fancy car or take a girlfriend to Monte Carlo. I suspect old Harry is quietly loaded, but having been born just after a depression and schooled in frugality by strict parents, he never learned to accept the excesses that people today seem to take as normal.

Harry is one of the good guys in my world.

I think his note read, *"Gary. I have decided to paint the black horse... H"* Or it might have read, *"Gary. I have decided to paint the back of the house... H"*

I scribbled on his note. *"Fine by me, Harry. I'll be away for a few days. Try not to get kicked. See ya... G"*

As I finished my note to Harry the home phone rang. Hoping it was Sunny, I ran to pick-up.

'Hello.'

'Gary there's something wrong with your other phone. It's dead.'

It was Megan.

'Yeah, I know. The battery's flat, I'm charging it now. What's up?'

'I told Tim about what went down today and needless to say he's in favor of selling all the stock and living the good life. I told him to "get stuffed" and he's a bit pissed at me at the moment. The bottom line is, he insists on going with you to see what is happening in the mining leases.'

'Oh shit! That's a problem; I've already organized to go with Truf. What does Tim think he can achieve?'

'He wants to have a say in what happens. I've told him it's more a case of respecting Gran's wishes than a bequest of money, but he doesn't get it. I'm sorry to do this to you Gary. Think of the bright side, he might fall down a mine-shaft or get bitten by a snake.'

'Aw sis, don't you just know how to cheer me up. But truth be told, he's more likely to meet his end with Truf's hands around his throat.'

'We wouldn't want that,' she replied, with more intensity than was required. 'Again, I'm sorry, Gary. But he insists on going with you.'

'Tell him I still need to book flights. I'll text him the details. He needs to pack tonight as I plan on getting the first flight I can. One minute late and we leave without him.'

'I'm dying to hear about what you have planned with Sunny. How did it go?'

'Funny thing, that. You know that flat battery I mentioned? Well I haven't been able to talk to her, yet, because her number is only on that phone.'

'You can get the number off it while it's on charge.'

'I realize that, but I'm on my home phone, tied-up at the moment with a call from my sister who seems intent on destroying my day.'

She said, 'Oops...!' and the phone went dead.

The other phone still had a long way to go to fill the battery, but with the charger supplying the power I was able to flick through the "Contacts" list until it gave up the number for "Heidi". I wrote it on a sticky note and took it to my desk. I loved the game she had initiated and decided that she would always be listed as "Heidi" on the phone. Changing anything might be enough to upset the Gods that had brought us together and alter my instincts that had screamed at me the moment I first laid eyes on her. Well, I couldn't vouch for the first time, but definitely the second time I laid eyes on her.

Truf seemed pretty confident that we had some chemistry happening last night... and she did come home with me. These were all good things. Or were they? What sort of girl comes home with a strange guy after only a few hours together? I hesitated to go down that road, as I was aware of the double standard that males can get away with and even be labeled as heroes and studs, where women tended to be judged in the totally opposite way. I was not prepared to even let my mind imagine that Sunny might just be looking for a happy ending.

I knew the way I was thinking about this whole situation appeared more like the emotions that a teenager feels: That first time you encounter the dysfunctional emotional turmoil that females are capable of creating in a perfectly sound male brain.

Megan had spotted it, immediately.

But she was wrong to infer that it was something that happened to me frequently. Maybe when I was fourteen it did, but it didn't feel exactly like this. Back then it was all new, every single thing that I did with a girl was a first. Holding hands, the first clumsy kiss, the over-eager fingers delving into areas that had long been dreamed of, only to discover that there were rules and protocols to be followed. That things that worked to stimulate a boy, sometimes had the opposite effect on a girl.

Those days were long gone. I'd had a lot of experience with women since then and not all of it had been good. But I had gained knowledge from every single encounter, both the good and the bad, and the more knowledge I accumulated, the more I'd come to the conclusion that I would never find that one woman who just stopped me in my tracks.

Had that just changed?

I had my home phone in my hand, but I didn't dial, I sat there deep in thought. I wanted to clear up some of my feelings before I spoke to her and I wanted to find out a lot more about her.

I fired-up my computer, intent on booking three return airline tickets to Australia while I pondered my next move with Sunny. On a whim I quickly checked to see if she had tried to use the computer and was pleasantly surprised with the result.

I managed three business-class tickets on a Malaysian Air flight at 7:05 p.m. tomorrow. I was lucky to get business-class at this late stage, I was expecting to have to fly first-class, which would have really stung. Never-the-less Tim was getting a bill for his part of this little trip.

With that organized I returned my thoughts to Sunny.

If my instincts were to be believed then it would be devastating to find out that she was just playing with me. Much better to play it cool and keep things at a moderate level. We had apparently slept together, but somehow I think she was toying with me on that one. Surely, if I was incapable of remembering, then I would have been incapable of doing that. Surely? Maybe I'd just invented a new psychological disorder - Sleep screwing.

The more I thought about the missing hours in my memory, the more I believed that I had been drugged. When I was a teenager I'd had my appendix removed and I distinctly remembered the same situation. One minute I was lying on a bed with a doctor saying, 'I want you to count backwards from one hundred.' Then, the next thing I knew I was laying on a bed in a different room with my family looking down at me. I can still remember saying, 'When are they going to do the operation?' Only to be told it was all finished over an hour ago.

That blank empty nothingness between the two events seemed weird at the time, but I can remember being somewhat grateful that I'd missed all the action. This current situation was the opposite. I wanted to fill in every second of that time with Sunny.

I looked at the clock. It was nearly eight and I hadn't eaten. Then I remembered that Sunny said she owed me a bowl of "muesli" and that euphemism, made me hungry in a more urgent way.

I dialed.

She answered, 'Hello.'

'Is that Heidi?'

'Who is this?'

Here we go again. Game on.

Five minutes later and for the second time in one day I was driving like a man-possessed, because of a woman I hardly knew. To my credit it was not only because I believed that sex might be on offer, it was equally the desire just to be with her.

Wow! I realized that I had best keep that knowledge to myself. If I kept going on like this in no time I'd be watching daytime soaps and telling Truf how lovely he looked with his shirt collar tucked up on that angle. *Get a grip old son.*

I might be okay at the banter and bullshit that the pickup game requires, but the area I struggle with is the truth and honesty thing. I tend to be pretty straight-up when I think it's required, and I knew I was at risk of saying too much tonight.

Just relax, enjoy yourself, play a bit and... watch every bloody word that comes out of your mouth.

I was so out of my depth.

Her apartment was on the second floor and she greeted me at the door with a big smile, then a big hug, and then a kiss. At this rate we would be doing it in her doorway. And that didn't bother me one bit. She seemed to come to the same conclusion at that moment also, as she broke away from me and led me by the hand through the doorway.

Fine by me. Let's just get that bloody door closed!

The front door led into her lounge and I could see a balcony straight in front of me. A kitchen area seemed to be off to the right, there was another closed door beside that, which I guess is a bathroom and immediately beside the front door was another door that had to lead to her bedroom. I started to pull her in that direction.

She held her ground, and said, 'I need to eat something.'

She punched me on the chest when she saw that I had deliberately misinterpreted what she'd said and had a huge grin on my face.

'How do you feel about Sushi?' she continued, adopting a more business-like tone. 'There's a place just around the corner and all the staff are authentic Japanese.' She paused, then added with a grin, 'I don't really know that, they might be Korean or Chinese, but the food is good. I just want somewhere that we can talk and not be distracted by, err... distractions.'

'Unless we eat in different restaurants I'm guaranteeing you that I'm going to be too distracted to talk. Why don't we stay here and get the thing that's distracting us off the table. Then we can go out and eat?' I quite liked my little pun, but sadly she stuck to her guns.

'That's part of what I wanted to talk to you about. So. No. We need to eat, right now, and we need to do it somewhere other than here.'

As we walked, hand-in-hand down the street, I tried to think of where she could be going with the thing about us having sex, being part of what she wanted to talk about. I couldn't find anything good that started with those words.

We hadn't even began to go out together and this seemed like we were going to have a "Honey, we need to talk" conversation. Yet, she was hot for me, I could tell that much for sure, and if I was any hotter for her, I'd have flames coming out my ass.

We entered the restaurant and instantly, every pair of male eyes fixated on her. She did look sensational. In what I was beginning to believe was typical Sunny, she wore a simple mini-skirt and one of those singlet T-shirts that manage to hug every contour of a female body. The type that make it very hard to maintain eye contact.

'Arigatou!' I said to the waitress, and pointed to the two of us and then to the tables.

This is the one Japanese word I know, I like the way it trips off my tongue and I use it whenever it seems appropriate. I think it means "Hello", but whatever its translation is, it works. Our waitress shows us to a table and bows at the waist as we take our seats. She hands us each a menu and bows again. We bow our heads in response and she backs away, leaving us to do our reading. It's very tiring trying to be Japanese.

'Why did you thank her, before she did anything?' Sunny said, with a grin.

'I didn't. I said "Hello".'

The look on her face coupled with her raised eyebrows told me that I'd said, "Thank you", which made me worry about a previous incident a few years ago. I had turned a corner and crashed straight into a beautiful, young female Asian student. On reflection she must have thought I was some sort of creepy pervert when I uttered my only Japanese word to her.

We studied our menus and then the ever vigilant waitress came back and took our drinks order, in near perfect English I should mention. She returned with a chilled bottle of Chardonnay for Sunny and a beer for me. She brought two wine glasses, just in case I suddenly acquired some class during the course of the meal.

We ordered our food and after the waitress had left we looked at each other, both waiting for the other to set the course of the conversation.

I took a big drink and went first. 'I have to go away for a few days. I'll be leaving in the morning.'

She frowned, bit her bottom lip and rested her head on her hand with her index finger pointing up her cheek. She seemed to be weighing up what I had just said. It didn't seem to me to be that profound, but she was clearly pondering something that I wasn't aware of.

'Can I come with you?' She lifted her glass to her lips and took a drink. Her eyes never left mine.

I wasn't expecting that. Maybe I had misread this thing. This was definitely a bit too clingy. My face must have betrayed my thoughts because she suddenly broke into a broad smile and added, 'Huh! Got ya... You thought I was so totally into you, that I couldn't bear to be away from you for a second.'

I laughed and visibly relaxed. 'In my defense it happens all the time.' I pointed my finger around the restaurant. 'Did you notice how the people here just couldn't keep their eyes off me, when I walked in?'

She grinned. 'Yes, I did notice that. Very impressive.' She reached over the table and put her hand over mine. 'But they'll just have to wait their turn, tonight you're with me.' She withdrew her hand, then added, 'It did seem to be mainly the guys looking, though. Is there something about you my *gaydar* didn't pick up?'

Our meals came and we shared parts of our dishes, which she handled expertly. In my case a chili prawn proved too elusive for my chopstick skills and ended up in my lap, instead of my mouth.

Sunny grinned and said, 'Arigatou..?'

The next hour passed in a comfortable, relaxed way. It really amazed me how quickly we had assumed a familiarity with each other. Kudos to my instincts. I told her about the trip I had planned, but I skirted around the reason it was being undertaken, telling her I was honoring a request from my Gran.

Sunny told me that she was a TV Producer on a show called "Impressive People" which was in production and soon to air on the BBC, and that was her boss that I had met last night. I pretended that I knew who she was talking about, but apart from Truf's uncomplimentary description of him, I was clueless.

By the time we left the restaurant Sunny had finished her bottle of white, and I had gone through four beers. The extra wine glass would not need to be washed. We walked along the street hand-in-hand as before. I had a sublime feeling that the world couldn't get much better than it was right now. Then I remembered that we were heading back to her place and dropped my opinion down one notch.

Once again Sunny seemed to be thinking pretty much the same thought as me. 'Gary, I know we planned to spend the night together and it would certainly make it just about the perfect date, from my point of view.' She paused long enough for me to realize there was a "But" coming. 'But, I want to wait.'

That *but...* was the very worst one on the quick list I'd begun drawing up as she paused. My sublime feeling evaporated and was replaced with a combination of anxiety, anger and confusion. I could only stare at her, with my jaw open.

'It's not that I don't like you, in fact it's the exact opposite.' She studied the footpath as she spoke, afraid to meet my gaze. 'I had a terrific time with you last night and again tonight. I think we have a shot at being incredibly special to each other and I need to wait before we move to that level. I know that probably sounds stupid to you, but sex would really fuck-up my brain, right now.'

I think I knew what she was trying to say. As soon as we crossed that line, sex would become the main thing in our relationship. She wanted time to test the depth of her feelings before lust could take control and head the relationship off in a path resembling a skyrocket. All consuming, totally exciting and fulfilling, only to be followed by the inevitable big explosion, and then plateau and perhaps slide into oblivion. That's the way these things had gone in the past.

I wanted it to last this time, too. I wasn't sure that sex would be a bad thing at this stage - for me anyway. But then I'd never had the thing where "two become one"; totally lost in each other and inseparable.

Maybe I would, soon.

She didn't want me to come inside her apartment, but I had to. Four beers needed to go somewhere and I was as sober as a judge after her announcement. I went to her bathroom and when I came out found her standing near the front door. It was wide open.

There's a possibility she was telling me something, here.

I walked over to her and took her in my arms. 'I already know you're special. But I think I understand what you're saying... and I'll go along with it.'

We kissed and then we kissed again. My hands began to wander around the extremities of her miniskirt and she let them explore for a little bit, then she eased herself away. 'I'm serious, Gary. I need time.'

I slowly shook my head at her.

Then a thought occurred. 'This morning you told me that I had taken your virginity last night.' I raised my eyebrows in a questioning manner. It was more mocking than questioning, and she smiled back sheepishly and said, 'I might have lied a little bit about that.'

'Which part?'

'Both parts. You were pretty out of it when we got back to your place. You started to take your jacket and shirt off as soon as Truf got you off his shoulder. He thought it was a good time to leave, but I said I'd stay and look after you. As I was seeing him out you headed off to your bedroom. By the time I got there you were asleep on the bed.'

'Then, how did I get to be naked?'

She bit her lip and looked at the floor. 'I might have helped a little bit with that,' she looked back up and grinned an innocent little-girl look at me. 'I didn't want your clothes to get all crushed. I'm a very neat person, you know.'

She was absolutely not that person she described. I would call her classy casual, and I hadn't seen any evidence of obsessive neatness. Interesting.

'So you took advantage of me when you knew I wouldn't be able to resist?'

'No. At that stage I wanted you to wake up and I would have been there with you. I lay beside you all night.. waiting.'

90

'Aw, that's just wrong! You're going to send me off into the night with that thought in my head.'

'I promise I'll make it up to you. You just need to hold on for a bit longer. Time is what I need.'

Hold on a bit longer! I was going away for a week - at this rate I'd either be the size of a blimp or have already exploded. Cause of death - embarrassing.

She led me by the hand to the doorway. Her fingers combed through the back of my hair and she pulled my face down for one last kiss.

I walked slowly out, then I stopped, turned back and looked longingly at her. She stood, framed by the doorway and gave me the sweetest smile.

'You promised me muesli.' I shook my head in disappointment.

She laughed. It was sexy, dirty laugh. 'You'll just have to settle for a banquet, when you get back from Australia.'

Chapter 4

I woke-up lying on my back after a fitful sleep that definitely included a dream about Sunny. I knew this because the sheet that covered me resembled a tent. In spite of what I said to her I really couldn't understand her need to wait.

Women... Go figure.

I had a lot to do and the first thing I needed was a shower. The blast of cold water on my chest cleared away more than just the cobwebs. While I soaped myself up I started to make a mental list of what I needed to accomplish before Truf and I got together. Information on Plutarch Resources was needed so I was going to have to get both Sophie and Sky into research mode. That would piss them off as they valued their weekend free-time. They were both in-between relationships and hitting the dating pool pretty hard, so I determined to call them later. Hopefully the extra few hours' sleep would gain me some brownie-points with them - but I wouldn't put money on it. Most of the information they'd be looking for would be found on the stock exchange databases I paid handsomely to access, and they could Google the rest. I paid for their home internet connections for this very reason; it was a two way deal. By that I mean I got to get work out of them from home. Both girls were in their element rummaging through complex, esoteric web minefields.

I used both my hands to squeeze the last of the shampoo out of my hair and as I rinsed it all, one last time, I thought of the problem of communicating with everyone from the outback. I knew Truf had a satellite phone and I hoped I could use that to connect my laptop. The thought of being out of touch with the market for a few days is my definition of a nightmare. I would leave the girls with a set of instructions in case of a calamity. The first line on the list will be: call me on Truf's satellite phone.

The markets had been relatively stable for the past few weeks and I didn't expect any major moves, but who can predict something like an earthquake in a major US city or the actions of the idiots running the global economies. As I said, you need to be informed and in-touch.

I rubbed myself dry with a towel and contemplated the tension that Tim's presence would cause. Truf had a relationship with Tim that was cold and distant; much worse than mine with Tim. He was my brother-in-law and I had to be civil with him for Meg's sake. Truf had no such restriction and usually referred to him as the *weenie*. Now, it's fair to say that most people are weenies when compared to Truf's gigantic frame, but in Tim's case Truf is also referring to his character and personality. Tim has a talent for annoying people because he is totally self-absorbed, a trait that would be intolerable even if he was successful. Which he isn't. So, all my diplomatic skills would be tested over the coming days.

I knew Gran was an early riser, she is an avid gardener, probably already pruning her carrots or mulching her lawn, so I called her first. She answered almost immediately which made me happy as you can never be totally sure with early calls. People do occasionally like a sleep-in.

'It's Gary, Gran.'

'I know that, sweetheart. It is illuminated on my phone,' she offered in a cheerful voice. 'Are you calling to tell me that you can't help me with my dilemma?'

'Exactly the opposite, well at least hopefully. I'm flying to Australia this afternoon and I'm taking Truf with me. Tim has decided he needs to come along, also. We intend to find out everything we can about Plutarch and what they are doing. Then we'll see if we can come up with a plan to help your friends out.'

'Oh, Gary, I never intended to take up that much of your time. And Truf's also. I thought you'd be able to do it over the web.'

'It's just a quick visit, Gran, we'll be back in a week. It's essential to know exactly what we're dealing with.'

'You're the expert. I'll Direct Deposit some money into your account for expenses. Have you got a pen handy?'

'You don't need to pay the expenses, you've already given us the shares.'

She ignored what I said and began to give me a list of names and phone numbers of people who would be able to help with our visit. She ended with; 'Text me your final flight number and arrival time and I will arrange for a cousin of yours, called Sammy, to meet you at the airport in Brisbane.'

The way Gran got on-board with the organizing made me realize just how sharp her mind was. On a health level this made me happy, but regarding Plutarch it worried me: If she and Ed had no success then I was definitely not in for an easy job. I ended the call by giving her Truf's satellite phone number.

My next call was to my travel agent who promised a call back within half an hour.

Then I made a quick call to Truf to make sure he brought his satellite phone.

My third call was to Sky, and she wasn't at all happy to be woken so early. 'Damn it, Gary. I just got to sleep.'

'Sorry Sky,' I offered and started straight into an explanation, followed by a list of things I needed her to do over the coming days. I ended with a question: 'Did you get all that?'

'I'm sleepy, not stupid,' she replied with a definite edge to her voice. 'How long did you say you were going to be away?'

When I told her, she said, 'Great. Sophie and I will be able to run the office from the beach at Monte Carlo.'

I know she was joking - God! I hope she was. There was a hint of sarcasm there. As an afterthought I added cheerfully, 'I met someone last night. Her name's Sunny McGuire and we really hit it off.'

'Oh! Give me a break, Garrett.' She sounded pissed-off, not happy for me like I'd presumed, and the use of my full name was also a clue. 'You're talking to a woman who's alone in her bed and now also sleep deprived, thanks to your call.' She paused a moment and I think I heard her blow her nose. 'I'm thrilled to the back teeth with all your news this morning. Feel free to wake me anytime with your wedding announcement.' She ended the call without the usual pleasantries.

The jury was in: there was definitely sarcasm there.

Sophie was more agreeable, answering after a few rings with: 'Morning, Boss. You do realize it's early. I was just on my way out for a jog.'

I explained why I had called and could hear her

making notes as I spoke. After a minute or two I heard a distant voice behind Sophie, asking, 'Are you going to be long?'

'Have you got company, Soph?'

There was a rustling noise on the phone, like she had put her hand over the mouthpiece, then she answered after what seemed to be a way-to-long pause, 'Nah... It's just the TV.'

One of my girls is sarcastic to me, and the other one lies to me. Whatever happened to good old-fashioned respect for the boss?

As a means of payback I deliberately didn't mention Sunny to her and just before I said goodbye I added playfully, 'I hope your TV has a really long power cord... if it's going on that jog with you.'

With my twisted mind I realized after I'd said it that there was a double meaning there as well. I hope her sensible accountants brain doesn't register things like that.

I was happy that one of them, at least, was making headway - sharing a small office with two *sleep deprived* women was not a whole heap of fun.

With the main calls out of the way I settled down to some work on my computer. I made some preliminary notes on Plutarch and printed off the list of main shareholders and management, plus any other notes I thought might be useful.

Every so often my mind would wander back to Sunny. I needed a break so I decided to Google her. I couldn't find my girl amongst the listings. She was yet to make her mark on the world. I searched for Impressive People and found a small listing. The synopsis said it was "a close-up look into the lives of people who were shaping the world for the new generation". Simon Sexton was named as Executive Producer and a small picture accompanied his name. I didn't recognize him, but he looked like the tool Truf had described, so I penciled him in as the prick who drugged me - if you look like a bad guy, you must surely be a bad guy. I should have been a detective.

As I was having those thoughts it suddenly struck me: If he really did intend to drug anybody it had to be Sunny, and if that was true then he must have intended to be the one to take her home and, oh shit!... rape her. This realization hit me hard. I was about to fly off to another country and there was no way I could protect her.

I called her immediately, but got put through to her voice-mail. 'This is Sunny. I'm not available right now. Please leave a message.'

The beep couldn't come soon enough for me. 'This is Gary. I need to talk to you, urgently Sunny. I fly out in a few hours and I absolutely have to talk to you. Call me back the first second you get a chance.'

***

The three of us had checked our main baggage at Heathrow but I was holding off for as long as possible before venturing further into the airport system. If I had to, I was prepared to abort the trip and stay with Sunny. I still hadn't heard from her, despite leaving three messages, all saying the same thing. Tim had just wandered off to get some novels and magazines, leaving Truf and me alone for the first time since we had arrived at the airport.

'You're probably overreacting, you realize,' Truf announced in an effort to bring some sanity to my thought processes. He'd been watching my distracted behavior and was relieved when Tim's momentary departure finally gave him a chance to discuss it with me. 'We don't know it was a drug that caused your problem, you might have had a reaction to the grog or something you ate. It might have been a virus of some sort. There's probably a dozen different possible causes.'

'I'd love to believe that, but you do the math Truf and tell me what you come up with. Simon arrives and buys a round of drinks, Sunny grabs one - the wrong one...'

I stopped talking because my phone was ringing.

I grabbed it out of my pocket. 'Sunny?' I almost shouted into it.

'You've got it bad, little brother,' my sister's laughing voice said into my ear. 'I'm sorry to disappoint you... again.' After a momentary pause, she continued, 'Here's an idea, why don't you pick up another phone in Singapore just for Sunny, so the rest of us can have a small chance of talking to you on this one.'

'Give me a break, Megs. I was expecting a return call from her. And it's Bahrain not Singapore, and no, I don't need a special phone for her, besides you're talking to me right now.'

'You sound on-edge. Having some preflight nerves? Or was the "got it bad" statement right?' She chuckled down the phone at me. 'Don't answer. I don't want to talk to you anyway. Put Truf on the phone please.'

I held the phone in front of me, a look of surprise on my face, then I handed it to Truf, who had been watching closely as I talked with Megan. 'The call is for you, apparently.' He took the phone from my hand and annoyingly turned his back to me.

'Hello Megan,' he said in a cheerful voice, and he began to walk away. With my phone! The one that Sunny would be calling on any second.

I was tempted to walk after him, but my upbringing kicked in, plus I had also just been delegated as bag-watcher and laptop minder by the other two. Without either of them asking - Very rude.

I stayed put. What could Megan be talking to Truf about, I wondered? Maybe she was pleading with him to not hurt Tim. Whatever it was I wished she'd finish so I could have my phone back.

I could see Tim was at the register paying for his purchases. Truf's back was all I could see of him and that was unreadable. He knew how keen I was to talk to Sunny and he would surely answer if he heard the "second call" beeps sound in his ear, so I relaxed a little.

So far the tensions within our little group had been contained, probably by the never-ending list of things to do before we actually got on board the plane, but I suspected that would change when we found ourselves squeezed together in a small place for a length of time. Because of the last minute booking I could only get two seats side-by-side, the third seat was three rows away and Tim had been allocated that one for the first leg of the journey. Both Truf and I were quite open and clear to Tim that he wasn't necessary on this trip. He seemed to be comfortable with the decision and my description of him as *excess baggage.* I was deliberately blunt; well, actually rude with him. With his ego and self-importance it was necessary to keep him in line; otherwise he'd be trying to run the show.

'Got enough reading material for a few weeks,' Tim announced as he walked up beside me. True to his words he had a carry bag that contained two or three novels and at least half-a-dozen magazines. I noticed a glossy "London Real Estate" listings magazine amongst his purchases. Had he possibly came into some money, lately?

'Megan called when I was in the shop and wished us all a safe trip,' Tim said, much to my amazement.

My mind was racing; *Why would she make two separate calls?* I looked over at Truf who had turned around and was looking at the two of us. He laughed at something that Megan had said, then took the phone from his ear and walked back to join us.

I tried to think of a way to mime, *whatever you do, don't mention Megan's call,* but gave up. I doubt even a professional mime artist could have got that message across to Truf. I settled for a very small shake of my head in the negative, accompanied with a frown. It was more like a shudder, which was close to the truth about how I was feeling.

I need not have worried. Truf's an intelligent boy. He simply handed my phone back without a word, then said to Tim, 'Got enough "girlie" magazines for the flight?'

This was the first of what I suspected would be many such hand-grenades lobbed between them. I looked at Tim and he simply smiled at Truf.

'Oh, I'm sorry Truf. How inconsiderate of me. I forgot to get you any.'

This could only go downhill from here, so I put an end to it by saying, 'Looks like I'm not going to get the call I'm expecting and,' I pointed to one of the many overhead monitors, 'the Flight Departure Board is suggesting we get ourselves down to the Gate.' I didn't wait for them to agree. I extracted my carry-on luggage from the small pile beside me and walked off.

***

To say the room was lavish would be like describing Buckingham Palace as "quite nice". The house was located in Kensington and the owner reportedly had paid over thirty million for it. Like most places in that price bracket it was hardly suitable and required another fifteen million to be poured into it to make it *special*. And special it was. In this one room the walls either side of the huge ornate marble fireplace respectively contained a large oil painting by Van Gogh and a huge bright abstract by Miro. Each costing millions and yet still managing to look out of place in a room that was home to many different decorating styles. It was a visual feast and a testament to its owners loud, splashy version of good taste. Good taste that money seemed incapable of buying.

Two men sat facing each other in comfortable leather lounge chairs in front of a large real log fire. Despite the day being warm it added to the opulent aura the owner wished to convey. After-all, it was in the contract. A 4K camera stood, unmanned, on a tripod framing the two men side on, capturing the fireplace and of course the artworks. Beside each man, but outside the frame of the two-shot camera crouched two cameramen. Their job was to provide a variety of shots at different angles of the two men as they talked animatedly to each other. Large lights placed in strategic places completed the scene.

Below the line of the cameras dozens of assorted cables snaked their way back to a group of people standing behind a small bank of equipment about twenty feet away. A man and a woman, both wearing head-sets, stood looking at the monitors that showed the view from each of the the three cameras.

The man waited until the owner of this lavish room had finished making his point, then called, 'Cut!'

As he pulled his headphones down around his neck he looked to a second woman holding a large plastic case and a box of tissues and nodded to her. She scurried over to the two men and began dabbing the visible sweat off the owner. As she re-applied touch-up makeup to him she handed the tissues to the other man who began dabbing away his own sweat.

'I'd like to go over there and piss all over that fire, it's screwing up this shoot,' the director whispered. Carefully measuring his tone so his words didn't carry to the owner.

'I've read the contract, Brian, and there's absolutely no clause in it that allows "pissing on the fire", Sunny whispered back. 'Rumor has it that he spent half a million quid having that fireplace built.'

Brian walked over to the seated pair as the makeup woman moved across to repair the hosts makeup.

'Is there anything we can do to lower the temperature in this room, Ashleigh?'

'There's no fucking way that fire is going out, Brian,' he replied tersely. 'But you do have a point, it is getting a little warm in here.' He turned in his chair and waved at one of his assistants who came hurrying over. 'Grant, turn the aircon to maximum and direct it into this room.'

Turning his attention back to Brian, he said, 'I love

that fireplace. I designed it myself,' he smiled smugly as he said it, 'but without the flames it's just a beautiful marble surrounded black hole. Besides it has to make your job easier,' he looked at Brian like he was stupid, then added, 'having something as beautiful as that in the picture.'

'I was thinking of you, Ashleigh,' Brian responded in an even tone. 'The fireplace is superb, but sweat running down the face of the star of the show... not so much.'

Clearly the two men didn't like each other, but both realized that they needed each other's cooperation to make this program work.

'It's going really well, Ashleigh,' Sunny offered, having just joined the group sensing that tensions were reaching a dangerous level. 'We should be finished here in about fifteen minutes, then we'll set up in the backyard and get some shots of you looking unbeatable on the tennis court. Brian's a perfectionist, he wants the sun coming from just the right angle for those shots.' She smiled her most winning smile at both of them.

There you go, two gigantic egos nicely stroked in one sentence.

'Sunny, Sunny, Sunny,' Ashleigh said, with a disappointed smirk on his face. 'The girl of my dreams and the only reason I'm doing this show. There's antique French furniture all around the room and masterpieces on the walls - all insanely expensive, plus my incredible fireplace, but you still manage to be the most beautiful thing in the room.'

Sunny giggled like a schoolgirl and smiled, as she was expected to, at the compliment. *Bullshit, pal. You're doing the show for the exposure - to score a point with your uppity little group of billionaire buddies. And the only reason you keep trying with me is because I keep saying NO. You hate it when you can't buy something.*

Sunny was the line producer for a new television show called "Impressive People". The BBC had signed on for 8 episodes, with an option to renew. The one they were shooting at the moment on Ashleigh Thombartson was Episode 6.

Ashleigh was forty-two years old and the only son, and heir, of an exceedingly rich banker. He had been in charge of the family fortune for five years now, and contrary to predictions had actually managed to increase the family's wealth during his tenure. Ashleigh had seen the explosion of popularity of the mobile phone and predicted their ability to replace the PC as the most useful piece of electronic equipment. Having no actual knowledge on the working of these items didn't stop him making a modest investment in a group of people who did. Ashleigh provided the funds to allow hundreds of budding Phone App creators to do their thing. If successful the profits were spit fifty-fifty. Most failed, a few were moderately successful, but to date, nine were unbelievably successful, going on to sell tens of millions of copies and some eventually going on to become computer games and even movie franchises. Ashleigh used his newly found status in the computer industry to purchase some underfunded companies that his advisors had suggested had huge potential. Add some money and his acknowledged ability to pick winners and these struggling companies soon became household names. His luck had held

Ashleigh had taken daddies five-hundred million and turned it into over a billion. In the process he had become an even bigger tool.

Sunny had met him in an upmarket pub and had initially been attracted to him. He was reasonably good looking and very self-confidant and she said yes to an initial date. He turned up in his special, "one-off" purple Ferrari and drove like a manic imbecile to La Estrada, the most expensive restaurant in town, where he proceeded to treat the staff like they were a subspecies. It had only taken ten minutes in the restaurant before Sunny had lost her patience, and her temper. She had stormed out, giving a conspiratorial wink to the head-waiter as she flew past.

That hadn't dampened Ashleigh's ardor. He still phoned her at least once a week, promising to be a better man if she would only give him another chance. But for Sunny, you only get one chance to make a first impression and Ashleigh Thombartson was dead in the water.

***

I'd been trapped inside a large, shiny metal cylinder for four and a quarter hours, speeding away from the woman I desperately wanted to see, or more accurately, talk to. Sunny hadn't returned my calls and I was seriously beginning to worry about her safety. I had been trying to work on my laptop but found my mind wandering.

I figured the on-board phone system would be the best option to use in the air, but the results had been the same. Every call went through to her voice-mail.

I stood and began to edge my way past Truf's knees again, preparing for another chat with her voice-mail.

'At this rate they might want to charge you extra for

the wear and tear on the flooring,' Truf said, as he swung his large frame to the side to make room for me to get by.

'Screw their floor, I'm paying them a fortune to use their bloody phone,' I snapped back. I had tried to sound amusing, but it came out poorly.

Tim sat in a window seat three rows in front of us. Beside him an attractive young brunette was being bored to death by him. I say *bored to death* because I've been in that same situation quite a few times myself; self-obsessed Tim believes a good conversation is one where he talks non-stop - and you nod. He probably just told her how he found a cure for cancer one morning, then climbed Everest in the afternoon and, just to avoid boredom, got out his chemistry set that night and found a way to turn his excrement into gold. The look on the brunette's face was telling me Tim was lucky the airlines were no longer allowed to offer passengers metal cutlery.

With thoughts like this running through my head I decided I should go to the bar and have a drink before I call Sunny. Due to the last minute booking the cheapest seats available were Business-Class. That should have hurt, and it did, until I checked my bank balance and found that Gran had deposited thirty-thousand in there that very morning. Did I mention that I love my grandmother? To be fair Gran is wealthy and at an age where she no longer has any desire to spend money on *things*. And now that Ed has passed she most likely won't even be going on any more holiday trips. Depressingly for Gran, and for me, her only major future expenditure is likely to be of a medical nature.

I need that drink - my mind is in bad place.

I sit at the bar sipping a single-malt with ice when I'm joined by an elderly man who introduces himself as Hector. Uninvited, he sits beside me. Oblivious to the fact that I had come to gather my thoughts he proceeds to regale me with some stories from his past. Hector, it turns out, is a retired Aussie doctor, returning home after visiting his son in London for the past month.

After I had downed my second scotch I was glad Hector had developed a thirst at the same time I had. He was telling me yet another story about a patient of his, many years ago: 'She was a very elderly, fragile widow and I had to help her up onto the examination table,' he was saying. 'She was very nervous as she had come for an internal examination and a Pap Smear. I'd never treated her before and she explained that her husband had been dead for five years and she didn't see the point in having the test, but her daughter had been nagging her to get it done.'

Hector took a sip of his ice-cold beer, then continued. 'She was lying there on her back with her knees bent and her dress hiked up to her waist, when she timidly announced, "There are cobwebs up there." I had my back to her, as I was gloving up at that stage. I was keen to relax her so I joined in her joke and said, "Not to worry Mrs. Lindsay, I'll just brush them aside." I turned around only to see her pointing to a cobweb on the ceiling.'

We both burst out laughing. I imagine Hector had probably told this story a thousand times, but still got enjoyment from it. The more time I spent with certain old people, the more I determined, in my own mind, the type of old-bugger I should be in about forty years' from now. Hector had convinced me that I needed a strong repertoire of funny stories and I made a mental note to start writing them down from now on, just in case my memory starts to go... before my knees... or my heart... or my liver... or my...

We parted company with a promise to try and meet for drinks on the next leg of the trip. As I walked away I realized I had missed an opportunity to get information on date-rape drugs from the good doctor.

With familiar apprehension I punched Sunny's number into the planes satellite phone.

'Hi, this is Sunny.'

'Thank God. I have you at last. Didn't you check your messages?'

'Messages? No. This is the first chance I've had to take a break on this shoot. Who is this?'

'Sunny, this isn't the time to bring Heidi back. It's Gary, in case you really don't recognize my voice. I'm about five miles in the air and a few thousand miles away from you, so maybe I sound different.'

'Gary,' she said in a cautious, questioning way. 'Are you the Gary who waves goodbye to women in a peculiar manner? A way that would definitely get you arrested if you did it in the street?'

'Yes. That would be me. I like to put my heart and soul into farewells.'

'I'm reasonably certain it wasn't your heart that was waving at me, so it must be your soul we're talking about.'

'Sunny, as much as I love joking around with you I need you to be serious, please.'

My somber tone brought about the change I was hoping for, and she said cautiously, 'Okay... what's the problem?'

'I've given a lot of thought and done some internet research on what might have happened to me last night and it comes down to one thing. I believe I was given Rohypnol - it's odorless, colorless and tasteless, so it can be slipped into a drink without the target being alerted.'

'The date-rape drug?'

'Exactly. The symptoms are: sedation within half an hour of ingestion. Loss of consciousness up to two hours later. The symptoms last about eight hours and complete memory loss after all of that, is normal.'

'That does sound like a description of you.'

'And all of this happened just after your boss bought us a round of drinks.'

Sunny was incredulous, 'You're suggesting that Simon gave you Rohypnol?'

'Don't be daft,' I countered. 'I'm suggesting that Simon was trying to drug *you*, but I got that drink by mistake.'

'Oh, Gary, that's just silly,' she countered my serious tone with lightness. 'I've known Simon for a couple of years. He's a bit of a sleaze, but he's never shown any interest in me. Plus, he has a beautiful wife and a baby girl,' she paused a moment, presumably thinking of more ways to shoot my theory down, then added. 'And we're both up-to-our-necks busy with this TV show we're making.'

'Shit!' I exploded, just as an elegantly dressed middle-aged woman walked by. She gave me a scornful look, poked her nose even further in the air and kept walking towards First Class. I waved an apology to her back. I used my hand, the old bag didn't warrant the type of wave that I reserve for Sunny.

'Sorry Gary, I know you want to find out what happened to you. The drug idea makes some sense from your description of the symptoms.' She paused, then added cautiously. 'Did you have yourself tested?'

'No... I didn't even think about that.'

'Too late now. You need to do it within hours of it happening.'

She surprised me with her knowledge of the subject. 'How do you know about the testing procedure?'

'I don't live under a rock,' she laughed as she said it; like it was common knowledge. 'Besides, I'm a producer. I'm meant to be up to speed with things that are happening in the world.'

'You're very cocky, Miss Heidi,' I said, and smiled to myself. 'Would you humor me enough to at least keep an eye on Sleazy Simon and not put yourself in a position where you're alone with him?'

'You do realize we work in the same office and he's my boss. It just can't work. Even today, he drove me to this shoot and he'll need to drive me home.'

'I meant don't join him for a quick drink at the end of the day.' This wasn't going as well as I'd hoped.

'One date! That's all we've been on and already you're trying to tell me what I can and can't do.' She was laughing as she said it. Thank God.

'One date - plus we've slept together... and you've seen me naked. That's a stronger relationship than most of my married friends have.'

'Slept, being the correct word... and in reference to your last point - you have the nerve to call me cocky.'

'Stop it Sunny,' I conceded the game to her with a laugh. 'You have a way of making the blood flow out of my brain and into a part of my body where it can do absolutely no good, at the moment.'

'Is that your way of saying you're waving goodbye to me.'

I cracked up and laughed loudly, just as Mrs. First Class walked by again, giving me my second disdainful look. 'You should drink less, or use some of your money to buy yourself a new bladder, you haughty old cow.' I whispered to her back as she moved out of hearing range.

'Why do I need a new bladder?' Sunny asked in a confused manner.

'Sorry,' I chuckled. 'I was just talking to a woman who seems to be either incontinent, or planning on robbing me.'

'I believe you when you say the blood seems to have drained out of your... ' She stopped talking abruptly and I could just make out the sound of someone else talking to her. After a few seconds she came back. 'Sorry about that Gary. Brian, the director, has finished setting up on the tennis court and I'm required. Have a lovely trip. I'll give some thought to your suggestion.'

The phone went dead.

***

Sunny placed her phone back into her bag and hurried through the house and out to the tennis court. Phones were strictly banned from any area where shooting was being carried out except for Simon who kept his phone in his shirt pocket and set it to vibrate mode. Sunny took up her position beside Brian and nodded her approval of the camera angles he had set up.

Ashleigh was dressed in a black, tight fitting shirt

111

that had something emblazoned across the front and back that Sunny couldn't make out. His shorts were bright red and his tennis shoes matched the black of his shirt, the red laces matched his shorts. A baseball cap rounded off what was clearly a well-orchestrated human billboard. Ashleigh didn't miss many chances to advertise his companies.

At the other end of the court stood a statuesque, redhead dressed in the same outfit, but in reverse - her shirt was red, shorts black and so on.

David Delaney, the host and interviewer of *Impressive People*, sat in the umpire's chair. His earpiece carefully hidden from the cameras.

Sunny put on her headset, connecting her with David's ear and pressed the button to open the microphone. 'Brian says we'll most likely only use this sound as a guide, David. Ashleigh's not a pro so keep the dialog simple, we will need to overdub it.'

She walked out on to the court and strode up to Ashleigh, finally able to read the banner on his shirt - *Dimonty Electronics*. 'You bring new meaning to the word subtle, Ashleigh,' she said, gesturing to his shirt.

'Gotta let people know you exist, Sunny. There's no point in being a brilliant secret,' he retorted.

'I'm surprised you didn't have the name chiseled into the marble fireplace for the last shot.'

He looked at her like she had just said something profound. 'Bloody good idea. Can we shoot that scene again?'

Sunny looked at him with a frown and said, 'I wasn't serious, Ashleigh.'

He grinned at her and said, 'And neither was I - I just like to fuck with you.' The way he said this left little room for misinterpretation.

In an attempt at deflection, Sunny said, 'Play well and you might have a love-match with your tennis ace, in the other court,' she looked around at the matching billboard who looked striking. Literally - she was holding her racket like a club, and was looking back at Sunny with a little too much intensity.

Ashleigh noted the exchange between the women and gave a subtle grin. 'Georgina! She's an easy beat,' He focused his attention on Sunny and said, 'You're the one I'd like to play with.'

Sunny shook her head slowly. 'Not my game, Ashleigh.' She looked back at the redhead and realized if the woman's eyes were lasers she'd have been vaporized by them long ago. 'I came to tell you that we probably won't be able to use the sound from this shoot, we'll have to dub it later. Given that you're not experienced in lip-syncing you should keep the talking to a minimum.'

The irony was that as she said this, she realized that she'd forgotten Ashleigh was wearing a microphone and his lurid suggestions might have been overheard.

The huge grins on both the audio-guy and Brian's faces, gave her the answer.

***

'You can't do any more, Gary,' Truf said. 'She's a smart girl, she'll watch her ass - Sorry mate, terrible choice of words.'

'She said she'd "give some thought" to my suggestion of keeping out of reach of Simon,' I scratched my head in confusion. 'I don't think I've convinced her, Truf.'

'I repeat - she's a smart girl,' Truf said, his tone suggesting that the subject was becoming a little overdone. 'She's known him long enough to work him out. You're only going on my opinion of him and I'm notoriously bad at working people out. Look who I chose as my best friend...'

'Okay Truf. Sorry I've been a bit obsessed about this. It's just the uncertainty of what happened and the frustration of not being able to help her if she needs me.'

'I know mate, but she's managed to survive this long without your help, another week is not beyond her capabilities.' He said this in a flippant manner, leaving me in no doubt what he wanted to happen.

Truf having effectively closed the subject, left me with the choice of silently dwelling on it, or accepting I was powerless to help Sunny and move on. As I mentioned before, I try to not surround myself with idiots.

With two long flights to endure I let my mind wander back, evaluating my life so far. By most standards it would be considered a charmed life. I have a mother and sister who both have my love and gratitude for the role they've played in shaping me. As big sisters go, Megs is brilliant, providing both a mentoring role and a best-buddy role. Lately, she's moved more towards the best-buddy part as bringing up two small girls is a huge task.

There is one member of my family who has fallen to the wrong side of the tracks: My father, Alex Nixon. I have deliberately deleted him from my inner-circle; it's the only way I can deal with the situation. I wish mom would have the balls to divorce him, but she seems to be stuck in a world where loyalty takes precedence over her personal wellbeing. Megs feels pretty much the same as I do, but her feminine attributes allow her to be more forgiving in her dealings with him.

Alex Nixon has impacted on everybody in the family in a negative way, but none as much as me.

Back in 1995, when I turned fourteen, Ed, or Gramps as he was known to me then, took me aside on my birthday and said he was going to teach me how to make money. I was ecstatic, given that he had done that himself, rising from a penniless beginning to become a very rich man in the space of a few years.

My enthusiasm dropped a little when he explained that I needed to get a job during the school week and another on the weekend. I complained that I'd have no time for my friends, but he said; "You'll be surprised, Gary. The harder you work, the better you'll become at organizing your time. You'll find you have just as much time with your friends, but it will be better quality time."

He was correct, of course. I got a job delivering papers before school five days a week. On Saturday's I worked at O'hallorans Hardware. Both workplaces happened to be owned by friends of Ed, undoubtedly just a coincidence.

The deal Gramps made with me involved him 'lending' me my startup funds, with me paying him back a monthly sum from my jobs. One of the companies Ed was the chairman of was Nixon-Eagleby, one of London's top brokerage firms, and my money making practical course involved learning about the stock market from a group of that companies stock-brokers. Because I was just a kid my parents had to open the

Trading account and corresponding bank account for me. We chose Charles Halifax to be my brokers because they were one of the first London firms to offer online broking. Ed needed me to be at arm's length from his business and being able to trade through my computer was infinitely better than a squeaky-voiced kid calling a Trading Room to do a transaction.

Over the next few months I spent my early mornings working, my days going to school and my afternoons talking to Gramps on the phone or in his City office. Saturday was hardware day and Sundays were spent mostly in Gramps home office learning the business of trading stocks from the master.

Gramps had initially given me three stocks to purchase with the money he had lent me and they were doing quite nicely. The more their prices improved the more I wanted to learn from him. I found myself using charts and what they call studies as my preferred way of interpreting the market and individual stocks. This meant I was looking at where the investment community were putting their money. Gramps worked more with what are called the 'fundamentals' which meant he looked for financially healthy companies with great assets and little debt. We complimented each other nicely and he fed me a few nice tips which helped refine the process.

By 1997 I had not only repaid Gramps his startup money, I had managed to build my account to an amount that would have allowed me to purchase a brand new Ford Focus. I restrained myself on the car purchase, because at that stage I was in love with trading and my charts were telling me that companies involved with the internet were starting to become hot. I moved myself totally into those companies, much to Gramps dismay - He wanted me to stay diversified which would give me more security. But I was young; one of the kids that Harry Buxton, my landlord, wants me to employ, and, as luck or good management would have it, I managed to double my wealth in the space of about nine months.

Now I could afford a mid-range BMW, and I wasn't even eighteen.

At Gramps insistence I sold half my stocks and left the money in the bank. That turned out to be sage advice as the market had a mini-crash not long after that. This crash gave me a reality check as I hadn't seen it coming and, prior to that, I was beginning to think I was invincible.

Part of me really wanted to buy the car with that money that was sitting in the bank, but a section of my brain had become so hooked on trading that I only saw money as something you use to buy shares with. I compromised and bought a secondhand car for a few grand, as I was about to start University soon. I held on to the stocks that had crashed as I still saw a future for the internet companies.

Late in 1998 I was fully invested in my internet shares, again. I'd even convinced Gramps to lend me some extra money which had quickly gone in the same direction. With trading, timing is everything. Some say its all luck, but if you know what you are doing and it comes off - then you know what you're doing. Just like a pro-golfer trying to get the ball in the hole, when it comes off it can be spectacular. 1999 was my spectacular year. Internet stocks exploded and my wealth was now up to where I could purchase a top of the range Beamer. I was feeling completely bullet-proof. The feeling didn't last long. It wasn't that the market collapsed again, it kept on going and going, to the point where I could have bought a small fleet of Rolls Royce's.

The problem was: I wasn't in the market. All my shares had been sold. By my father. Without my knowledge. It seemed dear-old-dad had a gambling debt and no money of his own to settle it. But he did have access to a bank account, and my trading account was in his name. Problem solved. The bastard simply sold every share I had painstakingly built-up over the past few years and withdrew the cash.

He'd managed to save himself from having something terrible like having his legs broken by the gambling boss's thugs, or maybe even a bullet to the head, but I'll never know because I refused to talk to him from that moment on.

My father's standing with the rest of the family was terminally impaired by his callous action towards me. Not long after this he had some sort of mental breakdown which resulted in him becoming semi-vegetative. He's still in that state, today.

The really sad part is that if he had told me about his problem I'm pretty sure I would have given him whatever he needed. Blood is thicker than money.

Eventually the share market crashed after skyrocketing for the whole year in what became known as the dot-com bubble. I was studying Computer Science at Imperial College in London and was just as poor as nearly every other student. But I had an edge. I now knew how to make money. Gramps came good with yet another round of startup money and I began trading again. Before my course was completed, I'd managed to accumulate another sizable trading account.

This time in my name.

I'd been so deep in my reveries that I'd forgotten I was in a plane with Truf beside me. I looked over at him and he seemed to be asleep. A flight attendant walked by and I asked her if I could have a beer.

'Of course, sir. Which brand would you prefer?'

'Let's go with Fosters,' I said, with a smile. 'It's time to become an Aussie.'

She smiled and left me to get the beverage - or should I say, the grog.

She was a bonza lookin sheila, too.

***

Ashleigh Thombartson was not easily deflected. He had cornered Sunny after the shoot on his tennis court had finished. They were in the small, but well-appointed room that was used by those not required on the tennis court, to watch the game. This time Sunny had checked to make sure the microphone had been taken away before she uttered one word.

'Have dinner with me Sunny,' he almost pleaded. 'Give me a chance to apologize for last time. I cocked-up, I was nervous, I rarely date women as beautiful as you.'

She was almost going to accept his apology - not his invitation. But that flaky last line was just so typical of Ashleigh, she thought. She cast a glance towards gorgeous laser eyes, who was standing about thirty feet away, glaring at her, as usual.

'No thanks, Ashleigh,' she replied keeping her voice

as business-like as possible, 'I have to keep working with Simon.'

'You're a tough nut to crack, Sunny. But I'm not going to give up.' He gave her a long, ominous look, then added, 'The more you struggle, the more I'm going to keep trying.'

'Ashleigh, please don't. I'm not interested. And the truth be told, you're not interested in me, you're just pissed-off that I won't agree to what you want. You need to get over that and move on.'

'I'm not pissed-off, as you so eloquently put it, I'm turned-on by you. I intend to find a way to get through to you.'

'Ashleigh, what more can I say? I've tried simple statements. I've tried polite rejection. I've even pointed out that your tennis partner over there is all but waving her knickers in the air, for you. But none of it seems to be getting through your thick head.' She said all of this in a very even; almost gentle way, so the next part would have added intensity. 'STAY THE FUCK OUT OF MY LIFE... YOU REDICULOUS ASSHOLE!' she shouted.

Every eye in the room watched her as she walked away.

Simon watched her coming towards him with a mixture of emotions. He expected to see fury or embarrassment on her face. Instead he saw a thin smile that she hid from the rest of the room. She crashed into him and buried her face into his chest.

He seemed embarrassed by her actions, unsure what to do suddenly finding himself in the middle of something he had no involvement in. Eventually he patted the back of her head in a conciliatory manner.

'Is that the best you can do to console me?' she whispered to him.

'Apparently... I'm not quite sure what I'm meant to be doing. Are you distraught?'

'Hell yeah! I'm devastated,' she chuckled quietly. 'Trying to get that creep out of my life is worse than trying to scrape fresh dog shit off your sneakers. Just won't go away.'

'Well, I should at least thank you for waiting until we have the shoot in the can before you started scraping.'

'My pleasure, Boss. But you owe me a drink after we finish here.'

Unfortunately she couldn't see the look that eased its way onto his face, because her own face was still buried in his chest.

***

My Foster's was almost finished and I contemplated a second, but decided against it given the change in time zones, the pending jet-lag and the need to keep my wits about me in my role as referee. I realized I'd been a bit of a pain in the ass to Truf over my concerns about Sunny. I felt the need to make it up to him. I looked over and studied him but he still seemed to be sleeping.

'You freak me out when you look at me like that,' he said to me without opening his eyes.

How did he do that?

'Don't be,' I responded. 'Ugly bastards like you are totally safe around me.'

'I've been told I look serene when I sleep,' he said, as he straightened up in his seat. He sounded slightly offended.

'Get women drunk enough and they'll say anything. Especially when they wake to find themselves next to what surely must be a Mountain Gorilla.'

'Have we just passed into the "Let's kick the crap out of Truf!" time zone?'

'Sorry mate. I forgot you needed an hour or two after you wake up to get your sense of humor back.'

'A sense of humor is only needed when something funny is said.' He looked me in the eye and said, 'I heard you trying to hit-on the flight-attendant. How did that work out?'

'If you call asking for a beer, hitting-on someone, it worked out just fine. I got what I wanted.'

'I meant you pretending to be a bronzed Aussie,' He laughed at the picture that had formed in his mind. 'Take off that shirt and the reflection off your pasty lily-white chest would be enough to blind someone.'

I smirked at him figuring he was allowed one cheap shot, given that I'd apparently offended him. 'Tell me about Coal Seam Gas,' I offered up a bone to my friend, knowing how he loved to go on about any topic that involved holes in the ground.

'Put simply, they drill into the ground until they reach the layer of coal. Then they change angles and drill along the seam. The methane gas is trapped in amongst that layer. To get it out they pump in a cocktail of chemicals that essentially cause a mini-earthquake within the layer of coal; they call it fracking. This breaks up the coal, releasing the gas which is then pumped back to the surface and collected.'

Truf's face told me he had more on the subject if I wanted it.

'So, why would Gran's aboriginal friends be upset?'

'The problem is the chemicals that they use. There are so many different types and quite a few of them are seriously dangerous, some are known carcinogens that are banned in almost every other area of life and commerce. But certain Governments seem to be more interested in the export income they can get from this relatively new source of energy, than the potential damage extracting it, can do to the countryside.'

I nodded, not wanting to interrupt Truf's explanation.

'The first problem comes with the "earthquake" they create. Sure, they can map the coal-seam, but they can't predict the damage their underground explosion will cause to the surrounding rock material. If a crack forms that ultimately leads to the surface, the methane gas will escape unchecked and will most likely be unstoppable. You've probably seen it on TV where somebody throws a flame out onto the middle of a bubbling river and the air above the water bursts into flame. It's not only flammable, it's poisonous also.'

It was obvious to me that Truf wasn't a fan of this mining technique, so I added, 'I remember seeing footage of a guy with flames coming out of the cold water tap in his kitchen. Is that the same thing?'

'Yeah. The cracks can also let the methane seep into the groundwater or aquifers. That's a huge potential problem in the area where Plutarch is drilling. The Great Artesian Basin extends under a large part of the eastern half of Australia and most of the rural communities totally depend on it for their survival.'

'From what you've just told me, somebody would have to be a complete psychotic idiot to allow this type of mining to go ahead.'

'I'm just giving you the things that can possibly go wrong and the more that do go wrong, the more Governments put a stop to it. The U.K. Government basically suspended or banned CSG back in 2011.'

'But not the Australians?'

Truf shook his head. 'Governments get advice and opinions from all different sources, which is as it should be. Some of my fellow Mining Engineers can be very eloquent if enough money is stuffed into their pockets. It's not too difficult to make a case in favor of the process, and to find numbers that suggest the bad things I mentioned, rarely happen.'

'Rarely, doesn't seem like a word you'd want to bank on.' I suggested

'Governments love export money, so they have a natural bias towards keeping the practice going. The miners tell them that the coal is buried a long way under the aquifer and the chemicals and gas would never get into that water. They don't emphasize that the well they drill to get to the coal-seam goes straight through that water bearing material. Instead, they concentrate on the fact that the well is cased in concrete and the water is protected.'

Truf looked at me and gave a pained grin.

'They neglect to say that it's an industry standard that about 50% of all well-casings fail during their working life. You don't need much imagination to see a casing failing close enough to the aquifer one day, to create a big problem. The main aquifer in that area is called The Great Artesian Basin and it sits, pretty much, under the entire eastern half of Australia. It's vital, the rural communities all depend on it because rain is quite unreliable in most of that area. If it became poisoned and undrinkable, well... I'd hate to think what would happen.' He looked at me in a way that suggested he had actually thought about it and didn't like the conclusions.

'Shit! I own 10% of a company that's potentially going to kill people.'

'Plutarch don't have any producing wells at the moment,' Truf smiled at me, aware of the irony in my situation.

'But they are presumably pumping chemicals into the ground, otherwise why would the waterways be polluted? According to Gran the aborigines have had to move camp.'

'An accidental spill would be the most likely reason for the chemicals ending up in the billabongs - that's what they call those outback pools in Australia. The area being so remote means that the company could probably get away with an occasional transgression like that. The Australian aborigines have a lot of power as a group, but a small, isolated community like that one has virtually no say.'

'So my task is simple then. I need to find some way to shut down Plutarch's CSG activities, repair the aborigine's damaged water source and find some fish to put back into it. Oh, and try and keep Plutarch's share price from completely disappearing.'

Truf laughed. 'Yeah, that sounds about right. What plans have you got for our second day there?'

Chapter 5

Our plane tracked over what must have been outback Queensland. I'd looked down and seen earth and not water, and then I'd done some rudimentary math and concluded that the plane was traveling at about 600kph to 700kph and, according to the captain's last announcement, we were less than an hour from landing. Our flight route over Australia would take us a few hundred miles north of where we needed to go once we landed, but looking out the window made me feel dread. From 30,000 feet, the cloudless view of the landscape was yellow, flat and bleak. On the ground I knew that would become red, flat and bleak. I knew it was hot, and the cloudless sky reinforced that opinion. The terrain would be very similar where we were going.

I had been to Australia on three occasions, each time only visiting the cities of Sydney and Melbourne. As a result my idea of Australia was a lot like my idea of the States, which I had visited many times. Big, busy and noisy, and they speak a kind of English. That is being unfair, harsh even, as many parts of Great Britain could also be accused of that. As judges go, I take no prisoners

This trip promised to be an eye-opener as I was going to experience the famed 'Outback'. A dramatically beautiful land of extremes and hardship, fit only for snakes with venom in their giant fangs so vile that a single drop is capable of killing hundreds of people, crocodiles that can take down a buffalo the size of my first car and even plants like the Stinging Tree, that injects any unsuspecting animal or human that blunders into its branches or leaves with probably the most painful venom in existence: so painful that people have actually committed suicide rather than endure it. Witnesses have told of stung horses beating their heads against trees or rocks, one, reportedly even running over a cliff to end the pain. Must get one and bring it back for the yard. Even if it only ate one thief a week it would be better value than a pit-bull.

On a comparable subject, I had ended up with Tim beside me for this final leg of the journey down-under. I had the window seat and Tim had been nagging me like a little kid to change seats. I gave up and swapped, figuring I'd seen enough to guess what was coming. On the plus side, we were going far enough inland that I could ignore my fear of crocodiles, knowing they only populated the northern coasts. So, I only had to avoid stepping on snakes or bumping into trees and I'd be safe. The fear of Tim, not so much - death by boredom was an ever-present threat.

'Mind if I ask why you insisted on coming along with us?' I asked, mainly to end the inane, stream of utterances like: "Hey, look at that" and "Wow! That river looks like a giant snake," and *Gee! I'm a giant tool...*

He turned from the window and looked at me, seriousness written all over his face. 'Like you, Gary, Megan and I are now the owners of 10% of a listed company. I think it's my duty to know everything I can find out about it.'

'You do realize we only have that shareholding

because Gran is counting on us to help the local aborigines? It's not so much a gift,' I continued, with annoyance written all over my face, 'it's more a request for us to do what she isn't capable of doing.' I refrained from adding that the shares were left to Megan. There was no "and Tim" written on the papers I saw her signing.

'Of course we should do everything we can to help,' he replied, momentarily relinquishing the high and mighty attitude. 'I get it.' He shook his head, and I think I saw a hint of a smile appear. 'But there will most likely come a time when we have to accept that we probably can't do very much for them.'

Tool!...

I didn't say that, I just looked at him with what I hoped was a neutral expression. We had to spend quite a few days together and it was way too early to show him my, *you're a complete asshole,* face.

I decided to have a final pee before we landed, so I gratefully left Tim and his running commentary of the Australian landscape from 30,000 feet and headed down the aisle. Truf was six rows away and as I passed him I noticed the old lady seated beside him had fallen asleep on his shoulder. He's such a softie, just sitting there, reading a magazine and making every effort to not disturb her. I was going to make a visual joke, but he didn't look up. As I reached the toilet, the door opened and to my surprise my new friend Hector, the doctor, emerged.

'Well, hello, Gary,' he said, astonishment all over his face. 'Lovely to see you again. I should have assumed you'd be on the same connecting flight. Pity, we could have had another drink together.'

'Nice to see you. too, doc.' I replied. 'But I could only get an economy ticket for this leg, and us poor-folk aren't allowed to associate with you rich people.' I grinned at him, cheekily.

He smiled back. 'That's too bad. I'd have liked to hear some more about your investigation into Pluto Resources.'

'It's Plutarch,' I laughed. 'Yeah. I enjoyed our chat, too.' I opened the door and went inside the toilet waving as I did, 'Bye, Hector.'

Inside, I looked into the mirror and a tired bloke looked back at me. Puffy eyes and his hair was a mess. He had a fashionable day-old growth on his face that managed to make him look more like a homeless person than a cool guy. I splashed water on my face and did my best at restoring my beauty then I headed out the toilet door only to find Hector standing there waiting for me. He held out a card which I took and read. It was one of his old appointment cards, presumable no longer usable for that purpose. He'd written an address and phone number on it.

'If you get a chance when you're done checking out the mine give me a call. I'd love for you to pop over for that drink,' he said with a welcoming smile.

'That's very kind, Hector. I'd love to, but I'm traveling with two other guys and it's literally a flying visit.'

'Well the offer is also good for them,' he responded. 'If I don't get to see you again, good luck and have a fruitful trip.'

I studied Hector's card as I made my way back to my seat. This time Truf was looking when I got to his row and I managed to give him a wink and a lurid, *like your girlfriend,* look. He smirked back.

Just as I reached my seat the captain made the announcement that we were beginning our decent into Brisbane and the weather was a cloudless, balmy 29 degrees Celsius. Who'd have guessed.

***

The bar was crowded and noisy, but Simon and Sunny had managed to take possession of a table for two that nestled next to a concrete pillar. They had to contend with people squeezing through the narrow gap between their chairs and those surrounding the neighboring table but that just added to the vibe and buzz of the place. The Thombartson shoot had finished and they had left the crew to pack up the cameras, lights and audio gear while they discussed how they would edit it. That was the plan, but so far editing hadn't been mentioned once. Both of them seemed tense and in need of that first relaxing drink.

'I can't believe Ashleigh's cheek,' Simon was saying to Sunny. Their heads close together so that he could be heard over the loud ambient noise. 'What an arrogant, pushy, privileged prick.'

Sunny smiled back in a way that made Simon realize that this wasn't an unusual thing for her to have to deal with. 'Why don't we edit his story to make him look just like that?' Sunny offered, knowing full-well what Simon's response would be.

He shook his head, disappointment showing on his face. 'The show is called Impressive People, Sunny, not Arrogant Assholes. But maybe you've hit on an idea. We should pitch that to the TV Execs.'

'They would buy it, for sure,' she laughed. 'They'd expect to be the stars of the first series.'

Simon reached over the table and rested his hand on Sunny's. He hadn't crossed any boundaries by doing it, but he was very close. He looked intently at her and said, 'With your looks and quick wit you should be in front of the camera, Sunny. Gorgeous and funny is an unbeatable combination. We should work together and see if we can make that happen.'

'We already work together, Simon,' she said as she slid her hand out from under his and used it to lift her glass to her lips. Up till that moment she had used her other hand for that, but she needed a way to extract herself from a potentially embarrassing situation. 'Besides,' she continued, 'I doubt I'd be very good in that role. I don't suffer arrogant fools lightly and quite frankly, most of the people you feature in your programs have caused me to bite my tongue.'

He looked at her incredulously, and grinned, 'You think!'

She gave him a look that conceded she'd said something obvious.

Simon continued. 'That's the thing, Sunny. I seem to mainly work with males. Beauty can take the edge off an aggressive comment when you have the sexual interplay happening between a man and a woman.'

'Sex does seem to be at the heart of it all,' Sunny agreed. 'Ashleigh has certainly worked that out.' She smiled, and then added to qualify her statement, 'He could just as easily have had a buddy lined up to play tennis with, but no, he goes for a silicon implanted "Bunny" who has never had anything complex, like a tennis racket, in her hand before.'

'There you go, Sunny,' Simon laughed at her summary of the situation. 'I rest my case. With your looks, humor and a hint of sarcasm combined with my contacts, we could go a long way - together.'

Sunny was picking up mixed messages from Simon. They had worked together for a while now and they had never had a conversation as personal as this in all that time. Maybe it was just him relaxing, finally feeling more comfortable with her. Or, perhaps he misread the hug she had given him after her incident with Ashleigh. No. It couldn't be that. Simon was an intelligent, successful man. He had a beautiful wife, Suzie, and a baby. He couldn't possibly think she was coming-on to him? Surely.

It was time to find out.

She dug into her bag and retrieved her cell-phone from the side pocket. She quickly scanned the list of messages. Most were from Garrett. She had already listened to the early ones so she guessed the rest would be of the same nature - stay away from Simon! His concern was touching, but way-too repetitive. Action was required to correct the balance of that relationship, also.

She slid off her chair and moved over beside Simon. She put her head close to his and held the phone at arm's length. One selfie coming up.

'Say cheese, Simon.'

***

Clearing customs took longer than I expected mainly because Tim's luggage got a more thorough than normal check. Seems I'm not the only one who thinks Tim is a shifty guy. Eventually, they let him through. I'd hoped they'd at least do a cavity search, but they settled on just looking in his bags.

'The bastards don't even tell you what they think they are looking for.' He spat the words out, clearly offended by the treatment. 'At least in America, they say, "Enjoy your stay, sir," at the end of something like that.'

'They're just doing their job, Tim. It's most likely random. What did they say at the end?' I asked as he was clearly pissed at the whole process.

'He said, "Fuck off, Pommy bastard".'

I looked surprised. 'That's a bit rude. Do you want to complain to his superior?'

'Nah...' He shook his head and twisted his mouth, clearly uncomfortable discussing it with me. 'I might have said something to him, first.'

'Shit Tim! If you get into trouble on this trip you're on your own. Truf and I never signed up to be your baby-sitters. You do realize you have to pass through here again in a few days? You can bet he's flagged you in their system.'

Truf, to his credit refrained from wading into this mini argument, and stood quietly waiting until we were done.

I turned my attention to him and said, 'Somehow we need to locate my cousin - a guy called Sammy who I've never met, or even heard of before this trip.'

We began to walk towards the waiting area, each of us pushing a luggage trolley.

'I've got our transportation under control,' Truf said to me with a grin. 'I've already located Sammy, *he's* a really good looking fellow.'

133

'Great. Point him out?'

'Here's a clue, Gary. Look for a cardboard sign with your name misspelled on it.'

Amongst the large group of friends and relatives waiting for our flight's arrival, I saw the sign. Garrett had become Garrot. At least Nixon was correct. As was Truf, with his opinion of *good looking.* Sammy stood holding the sign in one hand, waving with the other at Truf who was waving back. Sammy was wearing the shortest pair of shorts imaginable. Two tanned, well-shaped legs completed the visual feast all the way to the ground. As the sign moved around Sammy's perfectly shaped breasts wobbled into view.

Our trolleys seemed to suddenly accelerate and we rounded the aisle and moved through the crowd of greeters towards her.

Sammy ran to Truf, reached up and gave him a hug and a kiss.

'Welcome to Australia, cuz...' she said with a giggle.

She was considerably smaller than Truf and probably in her early twenties. She had long auburn hair that was tied back in a pony-tail, her skin was flawless and her smile and bubbly personality, infectious.

'Thank you, Sammy. In more ways than one,' Truf responded with a big grin, after she had unwrapped herself from him. 'But I'm not your cousin, I'm his best friend.' He extended his hand to her. 'Call me Truf,'

Sammy blushed, but took his hand and shook it vigorously. 'Nice to meet ya, Truf.'

I was standing beside Truf and I said, 'Hi cousin, I'm Gary. Lovely to meet you.' I closed the small distance between us and gave her a hug in the hope of covering any residual embarrassment.

She quickly recovered her composure and gave me a kiss on the cheek. In control again, she said, 'Hi Gary, great to meet you as well.'

'And, this is Tim,' I said, pointing to him. 'He's a step-cousin or second cousin or something. Tim's married to my sister, Megan.'

'Hi Tim,' she said, and he too, got a small kiss on the cheek.

'Well hello, cousin,' said Tim in his normal leery fashion. 'It looks like the Australian side of the family has grabbed a big handful of the available *good-looking* genes.'

Sammy just laughed at Tim's lame statement, and I could see in her eyes that in one sentence he'd managed to convey to her that he was a dick-head. Nice work, Timmy.

'It's incredibly nice of you to come and meet us, Sammy,' Truf said.

She turned to him and gave him a big smile. 'No worries, mate. Gave me a chance to legitimately get my head out of the books.'

We were making our way out of the terminal and as the automatic doors swung open the hot Queensland air hit us for the first time. The three of us simultaneously slowed as if we had walked into something tangible. Having come from cool London, to air conditioned plane, to air conditioned terminal, to the warmth of Brisbane was quite a shock. Sammy realized we had slowed. She looked back and laughed. 'If you think this is hot, you're going to absolutely love Culgawinya. It's so bloody hot out there the hens lay hard boiled eggs.'

That brought a round of laughter. I was really liking my cuz.. Sammy was my type of girl; great looking and a sense of humor, although I guessed that was an old Aussie joke, but perfect to drop on three newly arrived Londoners. I looked over at Truf and I know him well enough to see he had arrived at the same conclusion. And Tim. Well, that's a no-brainer; she was young, female and breathing. Enough said - his tongue was hanging out of his mouth like a dehydrated Doberman. And I don't think it was because of the heat.

Sammy led us to a Toyota Land Cruiser and we piled our luggage into the rear and headed off. Sammy drove and Truf sat beside her. I could make out the remnants of some pink paint on the windscreen in front of Truf's face and I said to Sammy, 'What was written on the windscreen in the pink paint that has been mostly scraped off?'

She glanced at me in the rear-view mirror and said, '$29,950' I saw her smile at me as she said it.

'Did you steal it just for us?' Tim chipped in.

'Sort of... It's yours for the trip. It was on dad's used car lot and it seemed perfect for you. Nan said to give you anything you need, and last time I looked it was a bloody long walk to where you want to go.'

'Glad it's got a GPS and an air conditioner,' Truf entered the conversation. 'It's perfect,'

'Actually it's six years old, so not perfect anymore. By the way, dad said to tell you - You break it, you've bought it.' She grinned again.

'We'll treat it like it's a girlfriend, lots of love and TLC,' Tim said, and I saw Sammy's eyes roll in the mirror. Mine did the same. Maybe I'm being too critical, but everything the moron says is either corny, saccharine-coated or just plain stupid.

'What books did we drag you away from?' Truf said,

in an attempt at getting Tim to shut up.

'A fascinating little piece on the macromolecular structure of an organic polymer that I'm interested in altering, to improve its light emitting qualities.'

'Ha! I'm pretty sure I've read that one,' Truf said as he pulled a face. 'Don't want to spoil it for you, but it's the ex-wife who did it.'

Sammy took her eyes off the road momentarily, looked at him and said with a raised eyebrow, 'Your ex-wife?'

'Couldn't possibly be. Don't got an ex, or even a current one, for that matter,' he grinned at her.

She grinned back, clearly getting the answer she wanted.

I could see this developing nicely so I sat back and watched the scenery flash by and listened to the two of them subtly run a checklist against each other.

Tim, who is as perceptive as a dead tree, kept trying to impose himself into the conversation only to have the door politely shut in his face, every time.

It turned out that my little cousin was doing her PhD in Molecular Biology on Organic Light Emitting Diodes, or OLED's which were fast becoming the video screen of choice. Her actual thesis escaped me, but I'm sure Truf memorized every word she said. So, I could find that out if I needed to.

We drove for about a half an hour and eventually turned into the parking bay of "Roger's Executive Used Cars." We piled out and Sammy led us through the yard to the office. Roger had about one hundred cars on his lot, I guessed, mostly late model Mercedes, BMW's, Audi's, Jag's and Volvo's. I imagined they were secretly grateful to have the Land Cruiser leave the lot as it seemed a little outclassed by the other marques.

Roger saw us coming and jumped up to greet us. 'G'day boys, great to meet ya. I'm Roger Gregson,' he said enthusiastically, as he offered each of us his hand. Sammy gave him our names as he shook each hand. It was a bit like the Queen greeting her key troupes, moving down the line shaking hands and nodding, "lovely to meet you." Roger was about fifty, a slight, wiry man with a pleasant face and a healthy crop of pure white hair. I think I could see a resemblance to Gran in his features. His age difference to her more likely meant he was probably my cousin, which made Sammy, his daughter, my second cousin. I think. I'm not good with family trees, although the branch I was currently getting to know seemed like nice people. Prior to this I'd adopted the approach of not looking into the extended family. Lets be honest, there'd be nothing worse than finding that you were related to a long list of convicts.

I'm kidding.

'I wish you'd have given us a little more notice that you were coming,' Roger was saying. 'Marge and I have a couple of spare rooms we could have let you use. Sammy moved out years ago and her brother Greg, decided he wanted to study in Melbourne. Go figure?'

'Thanks for the suggestion, Roger,' I said. 'It's just one night and we're booked into a hotel in the city. But, why not join us for dinner? It would be lovely to get to know you and Marge.'

'I wish we could, but Marge an I have an APEX dinner to go to. Been booked for months, so we can't get out of it.'

'I'm free,' Sammy chipped in, causing Roger to give

her a strange querying look.

'Wonderful,' I said. 'We can get to know your family through Sammy's eyes.'

We talked for a while longer, mainly small-talk about Ed and Gran, or Nan as she seemed to be known in the Southern Hemisphere. I just hope we were all talking about the same people. Then Roger excused himself to go do a deal with a customer who was giving the salesman a hard time and wanted to only deal with the boss.

Sammy said that she would make a restaurant booking for the four of us somewhere nice and pick us up from our hotel at 7:30. I was glad to go along with her local knowledge. Truf seemed particularly happy with the way things were turning out.

Me, not so much. I could see my dinner turning out to be mainly spent with Tim. I almost pulled Hector's card out of my pocket to invite him, but decided against it. Given his advanced years and all the traveling he'd done over the last couple of days, he'd most likely be tucked up in bed already.

I glanced over at Tim and I'd swear he was having the exact same thoughts about spending time with me.

After I had settled in to my hotel room the first thing I did was check my emails. Both Sky and Sophie had provided some more background material for me to study on Plutarch Resources. I had lots of time to read the details later so I just glanced at what they had provided then went back to my inbox. I found an email that somehow had bypassed my spam-filter. It was from someone called "heidi1691" and it was a gmail account - and it had an attachment. Normally, I would immediately delete a rogue email like this if it managed to get this far through my security system. I made a mental note to check how it got through my filters, but took a chance and eagerly opened it. I liked the name - it sounded awfully like someone I knew.

Dear Paranoid Amnesiac.

Don't want to sound needy, but I miss you. (Maybe you've forgotten me again. I should explain. I'm the one you slept with - but didn't... Coming back to you now?)

I regret leaving things in a way that caused you to head off Down Under clearly frustrated. But, I now have my head around that issue - and frustrated has become MY middle name.

Heidi Frustrated McGuire. It sucks :-)

BTW. You are wrong (see attachment) - I survived.

I opened the attachment and a picture of Sunny appeared. It was a selfie, taken in a bar. It was her with her arm around Simon, their heads squeezed together to fit in the shot. Both of them smiling cheesily.

Shit!

Even from the other side of the planet this girl could push my buttons. Big-time. Okay, I should defer to her knowledge of Simon over my quickly formed assumption that he was a Rohypnol rapist. But to make the point with a picture like that. Well, that's just cruel.

I hit "reply"

Dear Frustrated. I need more clarification. Which night did we not sleep together? And, are you the one on the left or the right in that picture? Garrett... and frustrated "Little Gary".

I hit "send" and then took a moment to ponder her email. She wasn't too far off with her paranoia jibe, but my insecurity was totally based on wanting to keep her safe. I could take the high-ground here. But my desire

140

wasn't totally selfless, I seriously wanted to get to know that girl. Every part of her, including her wonderful crazy mind, if that was at all possible. She did more than push my buttons, she made things pop - Little Gary would attest to that.

It felt good to have a shower and a proper lie down on a flat bed and I was so exhausted I almost did a Hector and slept through dinner, but something woke me from my nap just in time. Maybe my left and right hemispheres were working in concert together, again. Maybe I have a guardian angel. Or more likely, a siren went by outside and woke me.

I needn't have rushed because our *taxi* - that would be Sammy, was fashionably fifteen minutes late.

She pulled up into the drop-off bay at the hotel in a black Golf GTI. She hopped out and the three of us all did double takes. She was wearing a simple black mini-skirt that barely covered her incredible backside. She was totally aware that her legs and backside were features to flaunt if she wanted to impress guys. Job done. Six bulging eyeballs would have told her the three of us were on-board with her plan. Getting on-board the Golf was a different matter. It was a two door model which required some gymnastics from the two unfortunates who were allocated the backseats. Truf claimed the seat in the front because his long legs would be too cramped in the back.

Come to think of it, Sammy was the one who suggested that.

'Nice car, Sammy,' I said, massaging my legs from the contortion-like experience they had just endured. We sped out of the hotel driveway and quickly blended with the city traffic. She was driving a lot more aggressively than she did from the airport.

'It's not mine,' she shook her head. 'I don't own a car. That's one good thing about having a dad who has about a hundred of them. I just grab one from the lot whenever I need a ride.'

'Nice deal,' I replied. *What the hell would have been the problem with grabbing a big Merc or Beamer, then?*

We ended up at a nice French Restaurant called Beauforts. The food and wine were exceptional and after an hour or so I even found myself actually enjoying Tim's company. The more Australian wine I drank the funnier my English brother-in-law became. Just as well, because Truf and Sammy had withdrawn into their own little world, as I had feared would happen.

Tim and I had ceased to exist to them.

I have a vague memory of singing Waltzing Matilda and even having my arm around Tim's shoulders as we departed the restaurant. Thankfully, Sammy had stayed with Perrier water for most of the night. No doubt aware of her father's rule: You break it - you've bought it. Or, maybe she had some other compelling reason.

Back at the hotel we went through our gymnastics routine again, this time in reverse, to extract ourselves from the little Golf. The hotel Night Manager was particularly amused by my performance as he held drivers door for me.

'Thank you for a wonderful night and everything you did for us today, Sammy,' I announced on behalf of our little group. 'You are, without doubt a national treasure and when you next come to London I insist you look up me.' I was slurring my words and Sammy was grinning at my pathetic attempt at chivalry.

'Thank you Garrett, I promise to look up you.' She gave me a hug and kissed me twice on the cheek. Tim got similar treatment, which hardly seemed fair, as I was the one who gave the speech.

'Away we go, my merry band of men,' I said, to rally my troops. 'We need to let this incredible woman get to bed as she has books to devour in the morning.'

Truf held his ground. 'I'll join you two in a little bit,' he said. 'I have a question or two that I'd like to put to Sammy before we say goodbye.'

'Does it involve electrical biomechanical dynamics, or whatever she's studying?' I slurred.

'Hopefully not,' Truf said, as he literally pushed me towards the hotel entrance.

Truf and Sammy were still standing close together beside the car as Tim and I were standing outside the elevator, both examining our hotel swipe cards for some indication which floor we needed to go to. Eventually the manager came over and suggested we try Level 6. Rooms 615 and 618. What a clever chap to know that.

Travel and time-zones make a mess of me. Add too much wine and things get properly screwed up. I woke at 5:30, according to my bedside clock radio. I checked my phone, which I had deliberately left on London time - 7:30 p.m.. Perfect for calling Sunny, but not perfect for me, my head felt very second-hand.

I knew only one way to clear it quickly; I decided to go for a run for half an hour, then have a quick shower and call Sunny when I was refreshed. I consulted a map which showed a large park nearby. I changed into my jogging gear and left.

The first ten minutes of pounding the track that wound its way through the park were hell. The next ten had me feeling almost normal and the last ten brought me totally up to speed. Metaphorically. At this hour of the morning the streets were eerily quiet, but the weather was perfect. I had barely built up a sweat as I pounded my way up to the front of the hotel. I slowed to a walk as I reached the doors.

I had my hand poised to punch the up button when the elevator light lit up and made a little "ping". The doors slid open and Sammy came striding out, turned and almost bumped into me.

'Oops!' she said, with a cheeky grin.

'Hey, what are the odds?' We both laughed to cover any potential embarrassment.

'What can I say?' she said, 'We really hit it off. He's a great guy.'

'You don't have to sell me on that, Sammy. He's been my best friend since before we became teenagers. I'm really happy for the both of you.'

She gave me a long, hard look, then said, 'Have you got time for a coffee?'

I was hardly dressed for a social situation, but I still said yes.

We made an interesting pair as we entered the hotel's 24hr restaurant. Me, all sweaty and wearing a T shirt and joggers. She, dressed as she was the night before, looking sensational, but more than a little overdressed for breakfast. The staff were just setting up the Buffet Breakfast but the waitress was happy to get us two coffees.

After we settled into our booth and made small talk for a minute or two before our coffees arrived. I took a sip and felt another piece of my recovery fall into place.

'Ah, that's good,' I said. 'You probably didn't notice,

but I had a little too much to drink last night.' I grinned at her.

'Really!' she said as she gave me a wry look. 'Couldn't tell.' She shook her head.

'Are you mocking me, young lady?'

She smiled. 'You looked like you needed to be mocked...'

'What did you want to talk about at this obscene hour of the day?' I asked, trying to not give the impression I wanted to leave.

'We didn't get much of a chance to get to know each other, yesterday. I thought we could make a start this morning.'

'Okay,' I agreed. 'You go first.'

'I'm easy,' she said, and rolled her eyes when she realized what she'd said. 'I'm twenty-six and working on my PhD. Dad lets me work at the car yard three days a week selling cars to guy's who seem to like dealing with me,' she grinned, and shrugged her shoulders. 'I'm pretty good at the job, apparently, and make a terrific living. I'm hoping to finish my thesis in the next six months and if it's well received I've been promised a grant to continue working on my process with an option to take a 5% royalty of any future profits or, if I wish, a lump sum, the amount to be determined after the results are finalized. I'm pretty sure it will all work out so things are looking good.' She paused and looked me in the eye. 'And now I've just met a guy who I think has the potential to play a big role in my life.'

'I should stop you there, Sammy,' I said with a grin, 'and warn you I'm pretty sure I'm taken, already.'

She shook her head and laughed again. 'I like you Gary, you're good fun, but we're cousins and I couldn't risk having children with problems.'

'That's all crap. We're second cousins and the chances of deformities or other problems are about the same as any couple. Hell, you're the scientist. Why am I telling you?'

'I know all that Gary, I was just trying to let you down.. gently,' she smiled at me. 'And what do you mean, "you're pretty sure you're taken already"? What are you waiting for? Is she meant to take out a full-page ad, or something?'

I briefly explained the newness and complexities of my relationship with Sunny.' She laughed when I said her name.

'Sunny and Sammy. Why don't Truf and you change your names to Donny and Danny? We could be a soap opera.'

We talked some more and a crucial point in time must have ticked over because a steadily increasing number of patrons started to fill the restaurant. Buffet Breakfast is open for business. We decided we had been subjected to enough judgmental looks from the new arrivals and left the restaurant. I walked with her to the hotel entrance.

'I'm really glad we met, Sammy. I want to stay in touch with you.'

'We will. But just how much, depends on that big buddy of yours, upstairs.'

'You mean, God?' I said, with a smile.

She absorbed what I said, and then answered, 'Yes... You could say that.'

She kissed me and walked out the door.

Sunny had spent the entire next day at Bang-On Cutting. A small editing company that Simon employed to handle the piecing together of each show. Dougie Dunn was in charge of the process. A veteran with over thirty years' experience, Dougie had worked on major films and TV shows and his experience and touch were invaluable.

Sunny's role had been to mainly let Dougie know which "take" of each scene had been her and the Director's choice to be included in the show. This was important as many of the scenes had numerous versions shot, some with different camera angles, some with stuff-ups that made them ineligible and some that were just plain boring, or bad. The majority of each day's work ended up on Dougie's floor. Well, metaphorically speaking, as these days everything was digital and nothing actually ended up on the floor or was even actually erased. They kept everything because it cost almost nothing to do that, and you never knew when a small part of something might be useful.

To say nothing ended up on the floor was not correct. Dougie was a relentless note-taker, constantly marking in-points and frame numbers on the pad he kept beside him. In moments of inactivity at his computer desk he drew doodles. These were the times when Simon and Sunny discussed ideas on which he had no input to offer. The pages filled quickly and were discarded just as quickly. Whilst Dougie could cut a scene frame perfectly, those same hands lacked the ability to hit the waste-bin with any level of consistency. The result of twelve unbroken hours of editing was that the floor near the bin had turned white with countless balls of scrunched up paper.

This wasn't the only area where rubbish had piled-up. The desk that Sunny was using had become the resting place for the cardboard coffee cups that the four people in the room had no further use for. The fourth member was Robbie, the audio engineer. He was a quiet, almost invisible type of man who patiently sat at his console and, on-cue, performed his tasks with the consummate ease of someone who was more comfortable with knobs and dials, than people. If Dougie required a sound-effect of the most obscure thing, like a snail sliding across a bell, Robbie would have something appropriate within seconds. Robbie's console had become an extension of his personality. He had the annoying habit of punctuating actual conversations, the other people in the room were having, with sound-effects. If someone said something profound they would all hear a *Ta - Da!* trumpet out of the massive overhead JBL speakers. The punchline of a joke would find that an audience of many hundreds had enjoyed hearing it, also.

The first few times Robbie did these things were amusing, but after twelve hours Sunny found herself actually contemplating if it might be worth doing the jail time she'd incur from permanently shutting Robbie down.

She was saved by Simon.

'I say we call it a day Dougie,' he said. 'Good work, everyone. We'll pick it up again at 9 tomorrow morning?' He looked at Dougie for confirmation.

'That sounds like a plan,' Dougie agreed, the weariness showing through in spite of his best efforts to hide it.

Sunny and Simon began to gather up their personal items. Sunny checked her messages and turned her phone off for the night. Dougie and Robbie began shutting down their consoles and turning off monitors.

'I'm taking Sunny for a quick bite to eat. Anyone want to join us?' Simon said.

'Thanks Simon, but I can't. I still have some office work to do,' Dougie answered with a glum look.

'No thanks,' Robbie quickly said, fearing he'd be involved in an uncomfortable social situation that would see him completely out of his depth.

Half an hour later Sunny and Simon where unwinding over their second drink while they waited for their pub meals to be served.

'I gave some thought to your suggestion that I might be able to move to an on-camera role in the future,' Sunny said. 'I enjoy being a line producer, but it's a lot of work and the money isn't terrific. Plus the thought of waiting for you to retire, or stoke-out, to get your job doesn't seem all that attractive.'

'For me either,' Simon chipped in.

Sunny smiled at him, then continued, 'I guess you could say that I'm... interested.'

Simon looked at her with an intrigued look on his face. After studying her for some time, he said, 'It's not easy getting that first break, you know... How badly do you want it?'

Was something being implied with that question? Sunny wondered. She eventually decided it was reasonable to ask. If Simon was going to introduce her to the people who matter, with regard to these things, and by doing so, endorse her, then he had a right to know if she would turn her back and walk away at the first sign of things getting tough.

'It's not narcissism or even a monetary thing,' Sunny answered after thinking it through. 'It's being able to have a say in things, and have it matter, and to be a part of popular culture. That is something I want very much.'

'I wouldn't have suggested it if I didn't think you'd be wonderful. Whenever you walk on set and the camera catches a glimpse of you I find myself staring. Even when there's some serious eye-candy competition, like on Ashleigh's tennis court. When you walked up to him, Brian had his camera set up in a position that had Ashleigh, the bimbo and you, all in shot. I looked at both Brian and the audio guy and I could see they were both focused on you,' he raised his eyebrows and nodded to her to emphasize his conclusion. 'When you stand in front of a camera, every guy wants you.'

Sunny was uncomfortable with the direction this had gone. 'Just having a guy *want* you, isn't that great an achievement for the average woman,' she said. 'I'd happily wager you that any woman in this bar could stand on the table and say to the room - "Any guy who would like to come home with me tonight should line up here." and she'd get that line almost immediately.'

'That's different, Sunny. It's a direct offer to have sex. The camera is not like that, because it takes the offer off the table, to borrow your example. But it still creates the want. A want that *can't* be satisfied, which makes it even stronger.'

Sunny was about to make another point but their meals arrived and the waitress had to interrupt them to ask who had ordered what. That broke the rhythm of their discussion and their hunger soon took over and they found themselves ravenously attacking their food.

Sunny replayed the conversation in her mind as she ate and decided she'd been overreacting with her concerns about Simon. He was a pretty serious guy and his career meant a lot to him. It was just coincidental that sex had been the topic, two days in a row. The conversations had to have been purely academic.

***

Back in my room I showered and dressed in what I thought would be acceptable outback attire. I wondered if I should make sure the others were awake before I called Sunny, but decided they were both responsible adults.

I used the hotels phone knowing international calls were as common and as easy to make as calls to someone in the next suburb these days. I had arranged with my phone carrier, "Three", to be able to use my own phone in Australia, but I guessed it might be cheaper using the hotels facilities. I'd find out if I was correct when I got back to London. Very handy.

I dialed the international numbers for London and then her number, a complete sequence of numbers that I now knew by heart, and waited for her to pick-up.

'Hi,' her cheerful voice said. 'This is Sunny, please leave a message after the beep..'

Shit...!

I waited for the beep to end, hoping that my frustration would remain in-check when I eventually left the message. 'Hi Sunny. It's Gary. I was hoping to actually talk to you, but that never seems possible. Would you do me a favor and allow my new best friend,

151

your phone, to have dinner with me when I get back to London. You can tag along, too... if you're not too busy.' I laughed, to hide my sarcasm, but did a pathetic job. 'I'm about to head off to the middle of Australia and bravely do battle with the wildlife and the trees, and my phone won't have reception out there. I'll email you Truf's satellite phone number. Please call me. I'll be thinking of you. Stay safe.'

I hung up.

Crap...!

Chapter 6

I decided to drive the first leg of our mammoth journey into the wilderness. Before we left the city we needed to stock up on some amenities. I had already told our GPS where we wanted to go and I think I heard the voice inside the machine actually groan at the prospect of hitting the outback. Truf was busy searching its database for a camping store as I gingerly made my way through the unfamiliar streets.

Truf diverted us to a store where we bought three tents and three sleeping bags, just in case we had to rough it. I hadn't bothered to book rooms at a hotel in Culgawinya, in fact I didn't even know if they had a pub. Stupid statement - this was Australia: First, you build the *pub*, then you can start on the town. Whether the pub, or pubs, had guest rooms, I didn't know. Did they even have phones? Electricity? A sheriff? A blacksmith? I'm being harsh, we were only traveling to the country not back in time.

I hope.

We bought things we thought we might need; a hotplate, a couple of torches, a cooler, a first-aid kit, a lamp and so on. I asked if they had anti-venom. The salesman thought I was joking, I wasn't, but to cover my rookie gaff I laughed along with him. It was a long list of purchases, but as none of us were campers, or even hikers, we most likely forgot some essentials. Next, we went to a supermarket and stocked up on food for the trip. We bought a few cases of bottled water; I remembered the description of the local billabong. Plus, some bags of ice for the cooler. I wondered how long that would take until they became bags of warm water. As we were leaving, I noticed a toy store next to the supermarket and my mind flashed back to the photograph of Warra's family in Gran's book. I remembered the little girl who had died mysteriously and I quickly made a diversion.

Tim saw me heading for the toy store and he peered at me like the heat must have effected me, but he still came along; toys are his business, after-all. When I explained what I was doing he actually took control of the purchasing, which I was more than happy with. I didn't have an exact tally of the number of kids, so we also bought some footballs, basketballs, badminton sets and other games that could be shared around.

I made a point of hiding the toys in the back of the Land Cruiser so the kids wouldn't see them. I have no idea of the political correctness of buying total strangers kids presents, so I intended to ask Warra first before we handed them out.

Gran had pointed out that the aboriginal communities are "dry". She wasn't referring to the lack of water, but the problem of alcoholism, so that scuttled my original plan to buy Warra a gift. In the end I decided to go empty handed to the elder members of the tribe. I absolved myself of guilt by reinforcing in my mind, that we were trying to give Warra back his land. And, from what I could gather, that would be the ultimate gift.

We gradually left the built-up area of the city behind us, houses and shops were replaced with paddocks and trees, and began our trek to the great beyond. I could tell each of us felt like a modern day version of Columbus in our air conditioned four wheel drive, with our snacks for the journey by our side. The map we purchased at the camping store suggested that we actually weren't trekking very far into the Queensland outback. Our journey across the state only took in the first third of its width. Then, if we continued on, there was the Northern Territory and then Western Australia.

In perspective, we were barely leaving the coast. Did that bring crocodiles back into my calculations of things to feed my paranoia? Things that would undoubtedly try to kill me?

Culgawinya is about 500 kilometers from Brisbane so we'd be driving for most of the day. The sun was relentless and well and truly in control of the temperature, but thankfully it was at our backs and the air-conditioner was keeping us cool as we sped along the smooth bitumen surface. I wondered how long we would have the luxury of a bump free ride.

The three of us were wearing sneakers, jeans and long sleeve denim shirts when we entered the camping store. A serious conversation with the salesman had seen the three of us exit the store in solid boots, fawn colored shorts and short sleeve shirts. We each had a Crocodile Dundee hat on our head, complete with a row of plastic croc teeth around the band. Kind of cliché; Englishmen go outback, stuff - but at least the hat should strike fear into any crocs we encountered.

Assuming they had seen the movie.

'Where are we stopping for lunch, Gary?' Tim asked.

'Geez, Tim,' I snapped at him. Some paranoia tension finding its way to the surface. 'We've only been driving for fifteen minutes. I was planning on going for as long as we could, then stopping for coffee or maybe a beer, then driving some more before lunch came into the equation.'

'I wasn't complaining, Gary.' His tone suggested hurt. 'I was just checking the map and we should be able to make it to a place called Roma for a late lunch. It's actually a big dot on the map so it must be a reasonable size.'

'Okay. Sorry I snapped, Tim. A table for three at Roma's best restaurant. It might be our last decent meal for a while.' *Maybe ever?*

I turned and looked at Truf, who had been conspicuous by his silence so far. 'You okay?' I asked.

'Yeah' he nodded. 'I'm fine.'

'Did you have a late night?' *A loaded question - I know.*

'Nah.. I was in bed not long after you two buffoons worked out how to use the elevator.'

Damn... Wrong question.

'Think you'll be seeing Sammy again?' *I can be relentless - like a terrier with a bone.*

'I'd say there's a 100% chance of that.' I sensed his eyes boring into the side of my face. I looked around at him and when I did he gave me a wink. He used the eye that was hidden from Tim. I grinned.

That made me feel better. For a moment I thought he was trying to exclude me from his good news, but it was merely Tim he was trying to exclude.

The miles began to build up, unlike the scenery which had become more and more desolate and flat. The paddocks and fields still had a greenish tinge to them so we were still a long way from what could be called the real outback. We could make out distant rocky ridges; they were more like hills than mountains, but the famous red color began to feature in the rocks. I began to get excited.

Local radio stations were no longer an option this far from civilization and we had forgotten to bring any CD's. The Land Cruiser's radio didn't have an auxiliary jack to play music from our phones through it. I was at the point where I decided to start singing those ridiculous songs that people sing along to in situations where boredom is the only other option. Songs that I remembered my ancient uncle constantly singing to keep the good 'ol days fresh in his mind. Simple lyrics and a memorable tune - how could it fail? I began tentatively with a quiet rendition of a well-known chorus; so well known that I didn't know the songs title or the main verse. I should have paid more attention when Uncle Charlie was in full swing. I got some looks from the other two; the "kill me.. NOW!" type, but I pressed on, hoping the catchy stuff would eventually gain some momentum. Tim saved the day by rudely interrupting and introducing a game for us to play. He called it, "Would you rather...".

Truf agreed with him instantly. Yes! He'd rather.

'Here's the scene,' Tim said, 'You're on a first date with a girl who you really like. You've been trying for ages to get her to go out with you and she has finally agreed. You are going all-out to impress her. You take her to a nice restaurant, and one of the two following scenarios happen. You have to choose which one you'd rather happen.'

Truf and I nodded that we understood.

'The meal is nearly finished and you excuse yourself

to go to the bathroom. Sadly, a malfunctioning water tap causes a large splash of water to fall all over your inner thigh, leaving a wet patch on your trousers looking exactly like you've just peed your pants...'

I grimaced at the thought. Truf seemed to be considering it carefully.

Tim continued, giving us his second scenario. 'The waiter has just presented the bill to you and in an effort to impress your date you call him back to give him your Gold Card immediately. In your haste to get the card out and show her it's a "Gold" card you not only manage to make a condom fall out of your wallet and land on the table in plain view of both her and the waiter, but along with it a well known blue, diamond shaped Viagra tablet goes bouncing across the table and stops just in front of her.' He grinned at the two of us. 'Which would you rather, gentleman?'

'Sounds just like every date I've ever been on,' I laughed. 'I think I'd choose the first option. I reckon I could talk my way out of that. I'd even make a point of getting the manager out and complaining about his faulty tap.' I smiled to myself, confident I'd aced it.

'I'd go with B,' Truf announced. 'At that stage of the date you'd have to have a good idea of where you stood with her. If the magic wasn't there, it makes no difference - there wouldn't have been any "After-dinner mints" for you anyway. On the plus side, you've just shown her you have money and a deep interest in making things extra enjoyable and safe for her.'

'That's the biggest load of horse-shit I've heard in ages,' I said, laughing out loud. 'The only girls who'd accept that logic are paid by the hour.'

Truf joined in the laughter. 'I know... but you pushed

in and grabbed the first option, so I had to make a go of the second one.'

Tim was smiling and laughing in the back seat. Smug bastard. He knew his game had trumped my Sinatra impersonation.

Laughing chews up miles on a road trip faster than anything I know, and it was good that the three of us were all doing it. My task as moderator between Truf and Tim was looking to be easier than I'd thought. We were, as the psycho-babble set would say - *bonding.* Who'da guessed.

'Okay, give us another,' Truf said.

Tim thought for a moment, then smiled. 'Same deal as before. First date, girl you really like and don't want to cock it up. This time you arrive at her door and just as you ring the bell your stomach goes into spasm and you fart, uncontrollably. You pray that the door won't open mid-fart and luckily it doesn't. But that's the total extent of your luck. Your bodily expulsion is loud and long but there's a chance the noise of the doorbell has covered it. Then you're engulfed with the smell - it's positively awful - and no amount of arm waving is moving it on. She opens the door and gives you a wide smile. That quickly fades when she is confronted with you standing, with a look of horror on your face, in the middle of an aroma that you'd get if a five day old corpse stepped in a fresh pile of dog shit.'

'Ouch,' Truf squirmed.

Tim just grinned, raised his eyebrows and went straight into his alternate scenario. He was enjoying being at the core of our interest. Why wasn't that a surprise? 'Okay fellas. This time when you ring the bell you're suddenly struck with a fit of sneezing. You feel something moist touch your face just as the door opens. She looks at you in shock. You have a giant gooey slimy greenish lump of snot, about six inches long, dangling from the end of your nose. As you lift your head to look at her it drapes itself against your lower face, covering your mouth and chin.'

'Where the hell did you find these... *things*! Tim?' I laughed. 'I can't even think of a word for them.'

'Ha Ha... The girls have a kids book that's full of mildly embarrassing, slightly risqué situations for under-fives. They love it when I read it to them at bedtime. All I did was ramp it up to an AO rating for you boys.'

Truf and I pondered our choice as the miles continued to flick by. The countryside was mainly flat and dry, trees were thin on the ground and we hadn't even seen a kangaroo yet. We were comfortable and sweat-free inside our air-conditioned car. I got the impression that ten seconds outside would be enough to change that.

'Well, I think your chances of getting laid that night are about the same as getting a pig to fly,' Truf said. 'But I'm going to go with the snot problem. Maybe you could make a case for hay-fever. The first scenario only leaves you explaining you have stomach issues, possibly diarrhea, and I've got nothing to make that acceptable.'

I agreed with Truf on that one.

Our childish little game continued for another half an hour or so, at which time we began to see scattered houses start to line the road. This was just as well because we had run out of ridiculous scenarios to entertain ourselves with. The ones that Truf and I added were pretty lame given that we had to devise them on-the-run, so to speak. Tim had clearly been preparing his, but good on him for trying. He seemed to be a different guy at the moment.

We still had quite a way to travel so I decided it was time to give them a paradox to ponder: 'Okay boys, let's see you chew on this little mathematical problem for a while. Three guys check into a hotel for the night, they plan on saving money so they decide to share a room. The receptionist tells them it will cost them $300 which they pay and head off to their room. After they have left, the receptionist realizes he has made a mistake; the hotel has a promotion on at the moment and the room should have only cost the men $250. He takes $50 out of the till to refund them the overpayment. On the way up he realizes he can't equally divide the $50 by three so he comes up with a solution; He puts $20 into his own pocket, leaving each of the men $10 which he reasons they will be happy enough with. The men each paid $100 for the room, with their $10 discount it became $90. 3 times $90 is $270, plus the $20 the receptionist pocketed comes to $290. What happened to the missing $10?'

I loved the looks on their faces as they did grade school math and couldn't find out what was wrong.

Tim folded first. 'Okay, I give in, explain it Gary.'

I gave him a superior look and said, 'No Tim. I want you to work on it, it will help fill in the time.'

I'm pretty sure I saw him mouth *asshole.*

We arrived at Roma around 1:30 and, ironically, settled for a couple of pies each for lunch. I say ironic because the heat was tangible and our shirts soaked in sweat and a hot pie would have been my last choice. As it was, it was our only choice: all the restaurants and pubs had shut down their lunch menus. We consoled our rotten luck by each having a beer or two to counteract the heat of the pies. We decided to keep our lunch break short before we attacked the bitumen again - in our air-conditioned car.

By 4:00 we had arrived at Culgawinya and were in luck as the local pub, called the Drover's Dog, had rooms available for us, giving us a reprieve from becoming campers.

I was wrong about the countryside, it wasn't red at all. They had had some rain a few days ago and grass had begun to poke through all over the place. George Jenkins, the local publican, assured us that without follow up rain the grass would be dead in a day or two. The weather forecast for the area read: Grass will be dead within two days.

My first floor room was acceptable and very welcome after the long road trip. I bounced on the bed and decided it was almost okay. It was surprisingly cool in the room, given the heat outside. Two ceiling fans did their best to keep the air inside circulating, which simulated cooling. An air conditioner poked invitingly out from one of the walls. I turned it on only to be greeted with a blast of air that seemed hotter than the air I was standing in. The unit made as much noise as a 747 on take-off, so I gave up and switched it off.

To compensate me for the faulty air conditioner, the hotel had provided a balcony. No privacy here - it was the same balcony that was shared by all the guests, as it ran around the entire front of the hotel. Each room had a deck chair sitting beside the window-door and the veranda looked like it would be a nice place to watch the sun go down, with a beer in my hand. The deep roof-line ensured the balcony remained in shade for a large portion of the day. All the guest-rooms accessed it through an identical huge sash window that was also each rooms main source of light, except for the single light bulb that dangled from an ornate ceiling rose. The shadeless bulb hung at arm's length over my head in the middle of the room. All the guests shared a bathroom, which was at the end of the hall.

Everything considered, our accommodation was good enough.

We had arranged to meet in my room at 6:00 and then go for a walk around the town. The heat was still stifling even though the sun was fast approaching the horizon, so our walk didn't last long. The flies were getting ready to make way for the mosquitoes and moths so we were able to walk with a reduced need to wave our arms to keep the insect life off our faces. The shops we strolled in front of all had overhanging verandas providing shade to the footpath. As soon as we ran out of shops on our side of the street we crossed over and walked back under different verandas to the Drover's Dog. We still managed to see most of the town in that minute.

To the left of the main entrance of the pub, in the shadow of the upstairs veranda, stood a bronze statue of a dog. Actually it sat; it was life-size and the dog weirdly wore a hat. The hat was polished brightly unlike the rest of his body which was coated in dust and a greenish patina. To a casual observer he looked just like a real pooch sitting outside the pub waiting faithfully for his owner to emerge through the double saloon doors.

We all deduced that the pub must have been named

after him, and as we walked beside him each of us automatically reached out and patted his hat, which explained why it was polished. Something about a dog sitting with its head at hip height invited patting. Especially when the risk of being bitten was small. The dog statue was doubly comforting for us as our hats seemed to be very similar to his, giving us the impression we'd fit-in seamlessly with the locals. And, seeing that we were here to snoop, that had to be a good thing.

We slipped into the bar invisibly, like three cold-war spies, and I studied the room. I estimated there were about fifteen patrons, spread out in small groups around the room. Only four of them were women. That part I did count. The room buzzed, and not just from the flies that still swarmed in here, it was filled with loud conversations and raucous laughter. A jukebox played a song from the Fifties, I think it's called Rock Around The Clock.

I was wrong about us being able to blend in. The "buzzing" noise level dropped noticeably as we entered, then rose again just as quickly. The men certainly all wore hats like ours, even though they were inside and the sun had basically finished work for the day. The difference between their hats and ours was that theirs were dirty and work-sweat stained. They looked like they had been bought when the song that was playing in the background had been first released, and the family dog regularly chewed on them. Ours looked a lot like the one on the dog outside; kind of shiny and new - and unchewed. Our sweat-stains didn't measure up either. In short: we couldn't be more obvious if there was a spotlight focused on us.

George, the publican, took our order for three beers, which he delivered to us with practiced ease. 'There you go, fellas. That should hit the spot.'

'Thanks George,' I said and took a large gulp of the icy cold liquid and felt better almost immediately. 'Are we the only strangers here, tonight?'

'You're the only Poms,' he laughed. 'The rest of them are strange in their own special ways. Most of 'em are nice, though.' He glanced over to the pool table where a stocky man in filthy clothes was lining up his cue to sink a ball into a side pocket, then added with a sneer, 'most of 'em.'

'We bought the hats hoping to blend in,' Tim added.

'No hope of that in a small town like this,' George offered. 'Everyone knows everyone - and everything about 'em, too.' He gave an accepting shrug of his shoulders.

Truf picked up George's inference about the man playing pool. He had his back to us and seemed to be playing by himself. 'I was thinking of having a game of pool. Do you think that chap would like some company?'

'I'd prefer it if you didn't do that,' George said. 'He's a mean son-of-a-bitch, that one. His name's Felix, he lives in the room beside yours, number five.' He shook his head. 'Every time someone plays pool with him it ends badly. If he wins he wants to keep playing, but for money. When he gets rejected he usually starts a fight. If he loses he usually starts a fight then, also. Either way I end up with broken cues and smashed glasses and it takes half a dozen of us to pull him off his victim.'

'If he's such a bad-ass why do you let him stay here?' Truf asked.

'Stupidly, I rented out the room to his company for six months. Took the money up front. That was a mistake. Now it's gunna take a team of lawyers to get the bastard out. I'm stuck with the prick for another two months. My wife and I just give him minimal service and keep as far away from him as possible.'

'So, pool is out of the question,' Truf said, and he took a long drink of beer. 'What about dinner? Is he going to start a fight if we eat near him?' He grinned at George, clearly not concerned about Felix and any threat he might pose to us.

'You're probably safe, as long as you don't make eye contact with him. You know what they say about wild animals, they take that as a threat or a challenge.' He grinned at the three of us. 'Bev, my wife, does a damn fine steak and chips. Or if you Poms prefer, sausages and chips.' The cheeky bastard had us stereotyped. 'I'm afraid we're fresh out of lobster and caviar,' He said, covering his ass by going up-market. 'Sold them all to the same bloke who bought my last bottle of vintage Bollinger.' He laughed at his joke. 'In 1959.'

We looked at each other, then simultaneously nodded and said, 'Steak.'

'Three steaks it is, gentlemen. Medium or rare?'

Three voices said, 'Medium,' in unison.

We were beginning to sound like The Three Stooges.

**

Sunny and Simon had endured another day of editing and the program was looking very slick. Ashleigh was even looking quite acceptable, Sunny had

166

to admit. They had left a lot earlier than the day before as Simon had some calls to make and Sunny needed to work on her computer.

The production company they worked for was owned by a now retired veteran of the television industry, Julian Peg. Simon ran the place, unchecked, these days as Julian had succumbed to the ravages of old age. Their offices were located in a fashionable section of London. It was a two story single-front building with an ornate bright yellow door and a brass plaque beside it. It sat amongst many similar buildings on busy King's Road in Chelsea, but double-glazed windows created a blissfully quiet aura inside, only penetrated by the occasional emergency vehicle siren or the odd blast from a car-horn.

Sunny played soft, laid-back music through the speakers on her desk. She adored Dido and had been to every concert she had played near London, in the past six years. Dido was subtly inviting her to, "Let's Runaway" and she hummed along as she typed out a request to film some sequences of a shoot, scheduled to take place three weeks away. Regulation were the bane of her job and she hated all the red-tape and hoops she had to jump through, just to get a junior level Government employee to regally grant them approval to do their job.

'You look frustrated and somewhat stuffed, if you don't mind me saying so,' Simon said, beside her. She hadn't heard him approach and she jumped as he spoke. 'A little tense, also,' he added, noting he had startled her.

She turned to see him holding two glasses, both containing a small quantity of a clear liquid. She raised her eyes, questioningly.

'Time to knock-off, Sunny,' he said, as he held one of the glasses out to her.

'What am I drinking?' she asked as she took it from him and sniffed it.

'Vodka.' He gave her a quizzical look. 'You're acting like I might try and poison you.'

Sunny's mind had immediately flashed back to the night she had met Garrett and his consequent conclusion that Simon had been trying to drug her. It was nonsense of course, but she had still subconsciously reacted to it. 'Just a reflex action. I thought I could answer the question myself. But, seeing it's Vodka it's odorless.' She took a sip and felt the alcohol warm her mouth and slightly burn her throat as she swallowed.

'I like that song,' Simon said as she sipped. 'You're crazy about her, aren't you?'

'Crazy, is a bit strong. I'm closer to enthusiastic. I've found another I like, also.' She clicked on to her media player and scrolled to the top of the playlist until she found the song she wanted. She double-clicked and a similar haunting voice floated out of her speakers.

'Very sweet,' Simon agreed.

'Her name is Kate Miller-Heidke. The song's called, Share Your Air and I've nearly worn it's little digital signature off my hard drive by playing it so much,' she laughed, and sipped again.

'I like it when you laugh. It's very... sexy. Hang-on a moment,' he said, as he walked back to his office.

Sexy..? Sunny thought it was a little inappropriate to use that word. Just another act of strangeness to come from Simon recently. Before she could give it deeper thought he returned carrying the bottle of Vodka.

'I noticed you had almost finished,' he said, and

topped up her glass before she could stop him.

What to do? He was her boss, the person who paid her and a mover and shaker in the industry who could be a bad enemy to make. She really couldn't afford to start anything. Even if he *was* coming-on to her, he could just deny it and claim she had misinterpreted what he had said, and she would look like an idiot. No. She would have to wait for something more conclusive before she raised the subject.

'We should do this more often, Sunny,' Simon said as he moved behind her as if he was looking over her shoulder and reading her playlist. 'Your taste in music is heavily biased towards women. Have you got a thing against us fellas?'

'Not at all. I just find the girls voices more relaxing and that's usually what I need to do at the end of a day when I use this computer.'

'So, I was correct about you being a little tense?'

Suddenly Sunny felt his hands on her shoulders and he gently began to massage the taut muscles in her neck. It felt wonderful and she would normally want it to continue, but Simon had too many question marks building up against him in her mind. And, he had just crossed another boundary. As she was trying to find the right words to use to ask Simon to stop what he was doing with her neck she realized she was having difficulty concentrating; the words she wanted were not there, the sentence just hung, unfinished in her mind. She blinked her eyes because the computer screen seemed to become fuzzy. She felt herself begin to rock in her chair, his massaging was making her whole body sway. Weird...

Sunny's last thought before she passed-out was: *Oh*

shit... He's just crossed another boundary.

***

Still in a timezone confused state I woke early, so I headed down the corridor to the bathroom for a shower. Despite it only being 5:00AM. someone had already been there and had left the bathroom a mess. Two towels were lying in the middle of the floor and the shower rose was dripping profusely, a cake of soap sat in the drain hole. The shower only had a cold tap and I turned it off, even though I was going to be using it in a few seconds. I knew how valuable that resource was in this parched part of Australia.

I also knew Truf would never have left the tap like that and I strongly doubted even Tim would. That narrowed the list of potential culprits down somewhat.

I stripped off, entered the shower stall and turned the tap back on. The pressure that came from the shower-head was pathetic. I suspected it would be due to the limited water supply. I quickly washed and shampooed. The rinsing-off was the difficult part, but I eventually got the suds out of my hair.

As I turned the tap off I heard the door rattle. When it didn't give there was a polite knock.

'Nearly done. Give me thirty seconds.' I yelled.

It had to be Tim or Truf, so I quickly dried myself and wrapped the towel around my waist. I opened the door. In front of me stood a woman in her early thirties dressed exactly like me.

'Oh!' I said in surprise, gripping the flap of my towel even tighter to prevent any accidents. 'So sorry, I thought it was one of my friends wanting to use the shower.'

'No worries, darling,' she answered. 'You take as long as you like.'

In spite of having just woken up and having that early-morning, disheveled look about her, I could tell she was a fine looking woman. I knew that because I was really staring at her. Her face was clear of blemishes and naturally pretty. Her crowning glory was a head of bright orange hair - a sure sign of madness, according to Aunt Maude, an elderly relative of mine. The towel hid any bumps and curves that she possessed, but I could guess they were there. Her hair was tied back in a tight ponytail and fell between her shoulder-blades.

I realized she would be correctly thinking I was ogling her, so I deliberately concentrated on her face as we passed each other. I said, somewhat defensively, 'That mess on the floor was there when I arrived.'

She smiled sweetly and said, 'I know. It's there every morning.'

I raised my eyebrows and said, 'Felix?'

She nodded and gave me a surreal half-smile. 'He wastes the water dreadfully, too.' As she spoke she bent down to pick up the dirty towels. This caused the towel around her to ride up to her waist and gave me a perfect view of everything a man wants to see. I noted Bev's collars matched her cuffs, so to speak, adding even more evidence if Aunt Maude's madness hypothesis was true. My fine upbringing told me to respectfully turn away, but my eyes would have none of that nonsense, and remained fixed on that one tiny part of her body.

I'm not stupid; I realized this was anything but accidental on her part.

She straightened up and tossed the dirty towels on the floor outside the bathroom door. Then she extended her hand to me, and said, 'I'm Bev.' An enigmatic smile eased its way onto her face. 'I live here.'

I realized what she was doing. By offering me her hand she had created a situation whereby I had to try and use my left hand that was holding my shampoo and soap, to also hold my towel together.

I tentatively released my right hand to shake hers. As I took her hand I prayed my poorly gripped towel would remain closed. A big ask as it was now under threat from the inside as well.

'Nice to meet you. I'm Garrett.' I'm sure my voice quavered as I said my name. I used my full name to try and regain some formality between us

She grinned at me and said, 'By the way, Garrett, It's not a good idea to lock the door. What if you had an accident? I don't take the risk. I always leave it unlocked.' She looked at me, knowingly, released my hand and stepped back inside the bathroom. As she did she let her towel fall to the floor, giving me the complete, uncensored version of the tease I'd just enjoyed.

Then she gently closed the door.

I stood there with my mouth open staring at the doorknob. "Little Gary" had fought his way free and was frantically pointing at it also.

Indecision.

Mad Bev was obviously George's wife, and he was a nice guy. I was a nice guy - a nice guy who didn't knowingly *do* married women. But... there was only a door between me and, unquestioningly, an invitation to a helluva good time. And Little Gary was quite adamant about which way his vote was going.

As it turned out, I was *not* a nice guy. I would argue it was a shortage of blood that caused the problem. Little Gary gets his supply it seems, directly from my brain.

She also lied, she did lock the door... after I joined her.

Actually, that might have been me. Mr. Paranoid.

***

It was now 7:30 and the three of us Poms were sitting around our Aussie breakfast table. The heat had already built up and we were all sweating slightly. The overhead fans did their best, their motors whirred in acceptance that they were fighting a losing battle. I had Gran's mud map of the location of Warra's campsite that she had emailed to me after I'd made the decision to come to Australia. She had marked Culgawinya and the main roads that spread out from it. Warra's current camp was marked clearly with a big X, just like an old pirate treasure map. Because it was hand drawn the scale was non-existent, but I knew from what I'd been told that it was at least a half an hour from where we sat waiting for our waitress to appear.

We were the only people in the room and a noise alerted us to the arrival of another person. We all turned to see Bev walking towards us. She looked sensational, she had a glow about her, a freshly scrubbed look, which I could personally vouch for. We had a clean waitress.

'Morning, boys!' she said with a grin on her face as she strode up to our table. 'I hope you all had a good night's sleep and any stiffness you had from your big trip yesterday has gone away.'

At that point I had to look away from her. I just knew her eyes would be focused on me.

'I'm Bev and I'll be preparing your breakfast.'

'I'm Truf. Very nice to meet you, Bev. This is Tim and this is Gary,' he said, pointing to each of us in turn.

'Tim and I said, 'Hi.' Then Truf continued, 'That was a superb steak you cooked for us last night.' Clearly he was impressed with Bev and intent on making an impression. She was that type of girl, outgoing and cheerful, some might argue a bit over-friendly even, but clearly stifled and bored by the constraints of living in a small country town.

'Thanks Truf. I try and make people welcome to our little pub, and meat is a kinda specialty of mine.' She turned her attention to me when she said the word "meat", and said, 'Gary... You look familiar. Have we met?'

'I don't know, Bev,' I replied, trying to give the impression I was thinking it through. 'I've only walked up the street once. Then into this bar, then into my bedroom. Oh, and I've had a shower this morning. Is there any chance we bumped into each other in any of those places?'

'Mmm,' she mused with a thoughtful expression on her face. 'You do look very familiar.' She paused and looked closely at me, then she added, as if suddenly enlightened. 'Like a boyfriend! That's it, you're the spitting image of a guy I once had in my life.'

'I hope it ended well,' I said.

'Hard to say... I believe we left it kinda open ended, now that I think about it.'

174

'Bit late now,' perceptive Tim added. 'With husband George on the scene, that must have closed down things like that.'

'Yeah... You'd have to think that,' she conceded.

'Bev, you know your way around here,' Truf said. 'Would you be kind enough to have a look at our map and give us some help on how we get to X.'

'Sure,' she said as she leaned over Truf's shoulder and studied the piece of paper. 'So, this is where the treasure is buried,' she said with a chuckle. Bev studied the map for a second. 'Okay, now I know where you're going - the aboriginal camp,' she announced triumphantly. 'This is meant to be the main road out of town,' she pointed to a line Gran had drawn. 'This is Deadman Creek... and the next one is Wombat Creek.' She traced the pen line with her finger. 'They're both pretty dry at the moment, so you'll need to keep an eye out for the white poles beside them that mark the water level during a flood. That will be your best and only clue that it's a creek you're crossing, not just a ditch. After Wombat Creek you need to drive for about another ten minutes, then the road makes a sweeping right bend, the track you need is just after that. It'll be a little overgrown as hardly anybody uses it. It takes you to the new aboriginal camp. The poor buggers had to move cos their water went sour at their main camp. What do you need to visit them for?'

'Gary's grandmother is old friends with one of the elders, called Warra,' Truf told her. 'We're on a short outback holiday and she asked us to call in and say hello.'

'I know Warra. He's a local artist. He came here once a while back, after their water went bad, actually, and asked if he could make an overseas call. George wasn't keen to let him until he waved a hundred dollar bill at him. George even dialed the number for him after that.' She laughed at the memory. 'We never knew it for sure, but we think he walked all the way from his camp to make that call. George offered to drive him back, but he said he was okay. He's a funny old bugger.'

'He must make good money from his art. My Gran has a big painting of his in her house.'

'You'd think,' she said, 'but they're not very good negotiators. Duh!' She chuckled. 'A hundred bucks for a phone call,' she shook her head in amazement. 'All I know is, some guy comes up here every couple of months and buys his paintings. He usually stays with us, but he keeps the paintings wrapped in brown paper with bubble-wrap all around them. He drives a big closed-in 4 wheel drive truck and he locks them in the back, so I've never actually seen any of Warra's work.'

'Thanks for your help, Bev,' I said. I gave her my best smile. 'Where's George at this hour of the day?'

'George is still asleep. That's the way we run it - a bit like ships in the night. I cook the restaurant meals at night and then leave him to look after the pub until he closes. I get up pretty early, usually before 5.' - She looked at me when she said that, 'and get some things straightened out, while he works on his beauty sleep.' She grinned at me. 'Which reminds me, I need to clean your rooms. Which one are you in Truf?'

'I'm in three.'

'Who got the one with the dicky air-conditioner?'

'I think that's me,' I said, getting a very strong feeling that there was a message being sent to me in all of this.

'Number two is Gary, then,' she said. 'Sorry about that noisy aircon - might have to see if we can give you a discount or something.'

'That's not necessary, Bev. I love it here. I think I'm getting value for money, you're doing a terrific job.'

'Great to hear. If you leave here satisfied, you might come again.'

I almost blushed at how literal her message was. To me.

I looked at the other two and, thank God, they were clueless - just listening to small talk.

'Okay, boys' she said, smiling at the three of us as she pulled a small pad and a pen out of the front of her apron. 'Breakfast! What can I get for you, fellas?'

***

Wombat Creek had been crossed about ten minutes earlier. I was very grateful for Bev's directions as the creek itself had no sign, just a chest-high white pole with black lines around it, on each side of the depression that apparently occasionally had water in it. Without her help we probably would be well on our way to Darwin or whatever existed out there at the end of this road.

'Which side is our turn-off on?' Tim asked. He had been made designated driver for this leg. I'd been pleasantly surprised at how well we had all been getting along. Obviously, both Truf and I had found some distractions to divert any pent-up frustrations into. But to Tim's credit he had been trying to fit in and be one of the boys, not king of the boys. Maybe the trick was to get him away from his home ground.

177

'The left,' said Truf.

'I think this is the bend she was talking about, up ahead,' Tim offered as he slowed the car down to a speed that allowed us to examine the edge of road for any hint of a track.

Just for added coverage I scanned the right side of the road in case we'd got it mixed up.

'Up ahead, just after that scrawny tree,' Truf said, 'looks like it might be the track.'

We all focused on the patch of bush he was referring to. There was no obvious opening or tire marks, but the bush did seem to be further from the road than the bushes on either side. Tim pulled to a stop and we all got out and walked to the area in question. The bushes did have a gap between them wide enough for a vehicle to pass through, but the sand colored grass was at least knee high and gave little hint that it may be covering a track.

I flattened down some of the tall grass with my boots, ever wary that one of the murderous snakes might rear up in front of me and stab me with its poison-laden fangs. And then club me with a Stinging Tree for good measure.

I would have made a crappy early explorer.

As I pushed the grass down I could make out two parallel depressions in the earth, that were very likely tracks from a vehicle. 'What do you think?' I asked the other two.

'I'd say this is it, but how the hell do we follow a track that's completely overgrown?' Tim said.

'I think it's the track, too,' added Truf, 'but I reckon we should drive along the road for another mile and make sure, before we commit to this one.'

That made good sense, so we all climbed back into the Land Cruiser and continued, slowly, along the main road. Ten minutes later we were back at our original track and began to cautiously make our way forward. It was tough going because the ground gave virtually no indication where previous vehicles had gone, because the grass was as tall as the side of the car. The ground we were crossing was, thankfully, flat with uninspiring bushes and trees scattered sporadically throughout. About a mile ahead of us stood a rocky red ridge that seemed to present us with an impenetrable barrier, but without a proper track to follow we had no option but to keep going straight for the ridge. It was the only landmark of any note. At least we could retrace our own tracks if we needed to get back to the road.

'This is bloody crazy,' Tim said in frustration. 'This grass is so tall we could drive over a ravine and not know it until we were crushed to death at the bottom.'

'Just keep your eyes on the road, driver,' I said, with a nervous laugh. 'From what I gather termite mounds are more likely to bring us undone than ravines. But they are mostly taller than a man, so you'd need to be drunk to hit one of them.'

As I said that, Tim yelled, 'Shit!' as he simultaneously jammed on the brakes. The car was only traveling at walking speed but still skidded to a stop on the loose dirt.

'What did we hit?' I screamed from the rear seat.

'Nothing,' said Truf.

He looked at Tim and continued, 'I saw it, too, Tim. Couldn't believe it.'

I was frantically trying to work out what the hell they were talking about, when I looked over the bonnet and saw it too.

A small black head was poking out above the top of the grass, which in this particular area was level with the Land Cruiser's door handles. The head seemed to be floating on the thick sea of grass, which swayed gently in the slight breeze. It was looking directly at us. The small head had a layer of tight curly black hair on top, jet-black skin and was grinning with a mouth full of huge white teeth that looked more like the shiny white wall tiles in my bathroom, from where I was sitting.

'What the...' I said, as the three of us rushed to get out of the car.

Truf was the first to reach the boy. 'Are you lost, son?' he asked as he knelt in front of the boy, who had a tan colored dog standing by his side.

'No bloody way, mate,' he replied arrogantly, which sounded inappropriate when delivered in a squeaky little voice.

I had joined Truf and was looking at the boy carefully. He must have been about ten years old. He was aboriginal, barefoot, thin, but quite muscular for a kid, and was wearing only a pair of torn red Adidas shorts. In his right hand he held a stick that had been sharpened at one end and blacked with fire to give the pointy tip added strength. A comparatively large bag, made out of woven dried grass, hung over his left shoulder. The small tan-colored dog sat patiently beside him.

'What are you doing out here in the middle of nowhere?' Tim asked incredulously, joining in our mini-interrogation of the child.

'I'm on my way to McDonald's, for lunch,' he laughed as he said it. He was clearly playing with us.

Rather than regarding us as his rescuers, he was actually mocking us. The cheeky little bugger.

'Do your parents know where you are?' I asked.

He looked at me like I was retarded. 'Of course they don't bloody know where I am, mate. How could they? They're not here, are they?'

We were clearly getting nowhere with the subject of him being lost, and given that we were also lost, I changed direction. 'Shouldn't you be at school?'

I got that look again from him. 'School!' He shook his head at me. 'It'd just be a bloody waste of time, mate.' He shook his head at the thought.

'No,' I replied in my most earnest voice. 'Everyone needs to go to school. It's important to get an education so you can get ahead in life.'

'Did you go to school?' He asked with a grin on his face.

'Of course.'

'And you're here in the middle of bloody nowhere, mate... Lost? Was ya school any help?' He actually laughed at me. He stopped laughing but retained the cheeky grin as his eyes locked on mime, then he added, 'Besides, the school is shut, it's bloody school holidays, mate.'

I couldn't help but grin back at the little bugger. My jet-lag and time zone confusion had brought me undone, but he'd played me like a pro. 'My name's Gary,' I said, and offered him my hand. 'What's your name?'

His small, bony hand had a disproportionate fierce grip.

'Joey,' he answered, and then pointed to his dog. 'This is me mate, Nine. He's a dingo' The scrawny dog wagged its tail at the mention of his name. I presumed from my estimate of Joey's age and the dog's name that dogs only lasted about a year, up here. A new dog every year? It was feasible - snakes..? trees? spiders? Or, maybe I was wrong. In the past when I've admitted that I usually add in a smart-ass way... I was once. But since I've been in this country I've been wrong more times than right, so that little joke has been benched until I get back to soggy, cold London.

'Great to meet you, Joey. We're looking for a fella called Warra,' I said, trying to emulate his style of talking. I left out the *bloody,* it didn't seem appropriate. 'Do you know him?'

'Yep.'

'How can we find him?' Truf interjected, clearly unhappy with the way I was handling things so far.

Joey pulled a face, like he was pondering the question, then said, 'I don't think ya could, mate,' he grinned cheekily at Truf. 'Better if I show ya.'

'Great,' Truf said. 'Climb in.'

He led the way back to car and held the door waiting for Joey to climb in. When he looked around he saw Joey had already climbed up on the hood and was sitting with his legs poking through the bull-bar on the front.

'Okay, Joey. Do it your way,' Truf said, with a laugh. 'But hang on tight,'

In return he was given Joey's "are you retarded?" look.

'Rabbit holes all over the place,' Joey said, shaking his head, as if we should have known that. 'Go where I point.'

The three of us grinned like idiots. It was total role reversal. In this part of the world Joey was the *in control* adult and we were the ignorant novices.

Tim set off at a very slow pace and Joey turned us in a wide arc to the right. Every so often he would indicate with his arm that we needed to make a sharp turn, I guess we had to avoid a rabbit hole or a rock.

'Judging from all the twists and turns we've needed to make, we must have had blind luck on our side not to end up with a broken suspension before we came across Joey,' Tim said.

'I don't think so, Tim,' I said with a chuckle - I'd had a rethink. 'I'm betting the little bugger is just playing with us.'

Ten minutes later we entered a clearing about 150 feet in diameter and saw aboriginal men and women sitting around in the shade of the few trees. They began to stand as we drove in to their camp and slowly made their way in our direction. About six kids came running towards us and other people emerged from bark huts that we could now make out. I heard a thump at the back of the car and looked around to see a pair of skinny black legs disappear up on to the roof. The Land Cruiser had a solid roof-rack so I relaxed a little knowing our new passenger had plenty of things to hang on to. It was academic, anyway, as Tim pulled to a stop after another ten feet and we all clambered out and stood amongst a group of about twenty people, who were looking at us suspiciously.

'Hello, everyone,' I said, smiling as I waved to them in my friendliest way, not quite sure what to expect. Some of them had spears. Did they even speak English? *Of course they did - Joey certainly did.*

Tim and Truf smiled and waved a greeting, also.

Joey had already jumped off the hood and was

standing with the others, looking back at us. I felt like Captain James Cook must have felt when he first landed on this continent. Unsure, vastly outnumbered, surrounded by flies and sweating profusely, having just left his air conditioned boat. Nine had joined Joey and was sitting proudly at his side with his tail wagging. He may not be in for a long life, but he certainly seemed happy. The people around him were harder to read.

I cast my eyes around the campsite trying to get a picture of how they lived. It was very basic; a few scattered campfires were spread around the open area. They were not being used at the moment. Maybe they would be soon, now that lunch had arrived. I'm joking - my nerves have kicked in. The huts were mostly made of scrap roofing-iron, supported by spindly tree branches, trimmed of any excess material. A strong gust of wind would most likely be enough to render the occupants homeless. On the far-side of the camp I noticed two dilapidated cars parked under a shade tree. They were both the same color: rust-brown, and I had my doubts that they even ran. Maybe they were used as houses. Numerous dogs played together, watched on by a group of toddlers who had clearly given up trying to keep up with them.

Eventually, an old man moved out of the group that had formed around us and walked over. 'Gidday... I'm Warra Goomagawa,' he said. 'Welcome to our camp, fellas.'

At last a friendly smile appeared. We introduced ourselves and Warra, in turn, introduced a few of his family members who had stayed close by and were regarding us with interest. All the men and the women were bare-chested and one woman was breastfeeding a baby, supported on her ample hip, as she waved hello to us. Some of the very small children were naked. Warra suggested we move to the shade of one of the bigger trees and sit down. A dead tree branch about fifteen feet long lay on its side and we were offered a seat on its most comfortable section, which turned out to be the most shaded - the tree was the same hardness its entire length, I think.

It was quite a culture shock for the three of us to see the way they lived, but everyone seemed happy. Eventually the women drifted off and continued working on some food they seemed to be preparing. Maybe they were making things for the camp members to use, like the bag Joey had over his shoulder. Everyone seemed to have tasks to do. The place clearly worked like a well-oiled... campsite?

Not to be excluded in any way, Joey stood in the middle of our group and thrust his hand into his bag. He pulled out a large dead lizard, about eighteen inches in length. I noticed it had blood oozing from a puncture wound at the base of its head. Joey held it up for all to see and grinned proudly.

'Bloody good, Joey,' Warra said. 'Take it to Mumma.'

As Joey scampered off, Warra asked us, 'What brings you to our camp, fellas?'

I began the lengthy explanation of the purpose of our visit and when I got to the part where I told them it was all at Liz Stratton's instigation Warra's face broke into a big smile and he clapped his hands in approval.

'She a bloody fine lady,' he said, nodding his approval. 'A good friend.'

'And a terrific grandmother,' I added. 'We can't make any promises that we can fix the problem you have with the mining company. We mightn't be able to do anything, but we're sure going to try.'

We continued talking with the men of the tribe while the women prepared hot coals to cook Joey's lizard on. Warra invited us to stay for lunch and we agreed, reluctantly. After all, who in their right mind could turn down freshly charred lizard. It turned out I had underestimated my new friends ability to put on a banquet. Our lizard, which turned out to be a goanna, was accompanied with a nice tasty serving of snake. The look of horror on our collective faces at the news that snake was being served caused the men to laugh at us. One of Warra's sons, aptly named Bully, explained that it was a harmless python we'd be eating and he'd caught it himself this morning. The other item of interest on the menu were some big fat whitish grubs

Given that I'd soon be eating some of the things that I had feared would be eating me I took the opportunity to ask the men about my other great fear. 'Are there any Stinging Trees around here?'

'You mean Gympie-Gympie? No, mate, we don't have him around here,' one of them answered. 'Need to go closer to the coast for him. Nasty bastard, though,' he added, with a respectful nod of his head.

'Well then, what about the snake with the really bad venom?' I cautiously worked my way through my list.

'Oh, we love those snakes,' Bully answered. Then he grinned, 'They're bloody beautiful.' He licked his lips to indicate his particular meaning of beautiful.

I realized I was being sent-up. To the aborigines these dangers were no more threatening than a speeding taxi was to me back in London.

'We don't have too many Fierce Snakes around here,

186

mate,' Bully continued. 'They're big buggers - fifteen to twenty feet long, and as fat as a bloke's arm. Some fellas call 'em Taipans. They're quick like lightening, but the boy, Joey, caught one a couple of weeks back.' He nodded his approval and reiterated his culinary opinion. 'Bloody good tucker, mate.'

I was still reconciling the fact that a boy Joey's age was allowed to wander the countryside alone with just a sharpened stick for protection. Well he did have Nine's help, but he'd not exactly tried to rip out throats out when we had suddenly presented in front of them. I wondered how the two of them would go about killing something as dangerous as a snake. I couldn't imagine Meg letting her girls get anywhere near a harmless spider, let alone any of the animals Joey apparently encountered on a daily basis.

Our meal was served to us by the women and I licked my lips in anticipation. Actually, I mean in fear. I willed my taste-buds to tell my brain it was just chicken - that is what everyone seems to say these exotic animal things actually taste like. My plate was a large leaf on top of a section of tree-bark. A selection of the meats were placed on top of it. The meat had been cooked on the open fire and was charred black, which strangely gave me some comfort. I could try and pretend it wasn't what it really is and in my non-scientific assessment, the intense heat might kill any poison that remained.

I bit into one of the pieces and chewed cautiously. *Yum... Chicken...y.*

Around me, our hosts were gnawing away at their food as if there was a prize for whoever finished first.

I tried another piece, this one a different shape so I assumed it was a different animal. I chewed again.

Chicken.

Tim and Truf were having similar experiences and I grinned at them both as I showed-off and boldly took a large bite of my chicken. *Mmm, delicious...*

The one item I just couldn't try were the grubs, I muttered, 'No thank you,' and shook my head when one of the women offered it to me. She grinned and popped it into her own mouth before I could change my mind.

After the meal, which we had all managed to keep down, Joey ran off to play with his mates. I took the opportunity to asked Warra if he minded if we gave the kids some presents. I gave him the choice of keeping them himself to give out when he felt it was appropriate, but he said we should do it.

There was pandemonium for quite some time with footballs landing in the middle of camp fires, sending sparks into the air, and basketballs crashing off unsuspecting heads, accompanied with lots of yells and swearing, and corresponding squeals and laughter. One of the balls became lodged in the fork of a tree and the inventive little buggers formed a human totem-pole, with a tiny toddler at the pointy end, who used a stick to dislodge the precious ball.

While the kids worked out what to do with their new stuff Warra showed us some of his art. They were very similar to the big painting in Gran's house, but considerably smaller. The roof and sides of Warra's home were made mostly out of scrap corrugated iron roofing material and some flat pieces of weathered plywood. The roof was supported by straight tree branches, and the various parts of the structure were secured together with strands of the long grass. I doubt it was rain-proof and suspected special precautions were needed to protect his valuable art when the weather turned bad. Maybe he stored them in the cars, but there was no guarantee that they were weather-proof either.

'I'm too bloody old to do the big ones now,' he explained, when I mentioned Gran's pride of joy. 'And the white dealer guy who buys 'em, pays me the same for each one.' He smiled proudly. 'A hundred bucks each.' He raised his eyebrows as he said it, clearly impressed with the remuneration he was receiving.

I wasn't so sure and neither were Truf or Tim. We all exchanged frowns of surprise. Warra had about ten finished paintings waiting for his dealer to collect.

'They are really beautiful paintings, Warra,' Truf said as he leafed through the works that were leaning against the main roof supporting tree-trunk inside Warra's lean-to home. 'You might be able to get more for them from a different dealer.'

'No mate,' Warra shot him down. 'My dealer, he a good bloke, a bloody art *expert*. He say the market is shit at the moment. He doin me a big favor buying them from me.'

'Have you been selling to him for a long time?' Tim asked.

'Yeah mate. Years and years. He's made me a rich man,' Warra said as he led us to a grass bag similar to the one Joey had, only a lot bigger. He held it open to show us inside. It was packed full of hundred dollar bills. Hard to estimate how many but certainly many tens of thousands of dollars. Clearly, Warra had little use for the comforts money can buy.

'Maybe you should put that in a bank, Warra,' I offered as a suggestion, but he shook his head as I was saying it. Obviously I was not the first to suggest such a radical move.

'Safer here, mate. No bugger's gunna pinch it - they'd get a spear up their ass, real quick.' He grinned. 'The only danger is bush fire. But I'd just dig a bloody big hole and bury it until the flames have gone.'

I couldn't find any obvious flaws in his logic, so I just nodded.

'We should get going and have a look at the poisoned billabong and check-in on the miners to see what they're up to,' Truf said.

'I'll send Joey with you boys, I reckon you'd be lost before you reached the edge of the camp.' Warra and Bully both laughed at his joke at the expense of three stupid, hapless white guys.

But he did have a point. Without Joey we'd still be driving aimlessly around the countryside. Three English Alice's looking for a rabbit hole to fall into.

Chapter 7

Joey was stationed in his now familiar place at the front of the Land Cruiser. His bag draped over his shoulder and his spear was wedged near his right hand, he looked like a modern day miniature warrior. As hood ornaments go, he was on the large size, but when you included his radar and GPS capabilities he was a welcome addition to the car. Nine trotted along beside us, clearly capable of maintaining that position all day, if required. Twenty minutes of driving brought us to the billabong. We could actually smell it before we could see it, and that was with the windows closed and the aircon on.

The water was putrid: a thick, deep green sludge sat on top and absolutely no aquatic plants grew in it, or around it. Even the large, well established trees nearby were all dead. A big part of the smell was coming from the many dead animals that lay around the edge of the pool. The best way to describe the area was like the rings of a tree trunk. The oldest victims were just piles of bleached bones, then a row of dead animals whose skin still remained partially intact but stretched tightly over their framework of bones. The internal organs had shriveled and disappeared leaving the skin depressed to the extent that the top layer rested on the bottom layer.

The most recent corpses were bloated like balloons as the gases inside had expanded in the heat and the process of decomposition. There were kangaroos, wallabies, rabbits, frogs, birds, even a couple of dingoes, all in these three repulsive states. It was as if any animal that touched the water or fed on the animals that had died from drinking it, also died. This had to be one of the most vile places on the planet and it was clear to all of us that mother-nature was in no way responsible for this outcome.

We were reluctant to get too near the water, but we needed to get a sample for analysis. We hadn't had the foresight to buy some plastic gloves, but Joey's ingenuity came to our rescue... again. He attached a plastic Coke bottle to a long stick, using some strands of tough grass to tie it securely onto the end. At full stretch Truf was able to half fill the bottle and safely retrieve it. We found an old rag in the car and wiped the bottle dry and then cut the grass away with a knife Joey carried in his bag. I screwed the cap on tightly, using the rag to prevent any residual poison from getting on me. I tested it to make sure it was leak-proof and then wrapped it in the rag a stowed it beside the jack in the back corner of the car.

Joey wanted to show us something that he thought we'd be interested in and he led us to the drill hole that the miners had made.

As we approached, Truf said, 'It's a dry hole. They've capped it and moved on.'

The top of the well had a square concrete lid, or slab, that had been poured over it. A metal pole, about the width of a man's hand protruded from it and it too had been filled with concrete, effectively sealing the hole forever. Joey kept going straight past the well and after a short distance it became obvious where he was taking us. We walked over a large mound of dirt and saw that the miners had dug a pit and simply rolled the drums that the chemicals had been stored in, into the depression. They were beginning to rust, but still seemed to be intact. I picked up a rock and threw it at one of the drums. It made a solid clunk sound instead of a hollow ringing sound. It was full.

But why hadn't they bothered to fill it in?

I hadn't noticed until then, that Tim had been busy with his phone taking numerous pictures of the two areas. There was some hope for him, after all.

'Can you send me copies of those pictures, please Tim?'

'Of course, Gary. I'll email them to you tonight.'

Tim had been the big revelation to me on this trip and I was gradually changing my opinion of him. That was up to this point in time. Now I had a new "biggest" revelation when I saw with my own eyes the disgusting way some people are capable of behaving. To say I was pissed at the people running Plutarch Resources was an understatement; a bit like calling a mass murderer a naughty boy.

'You make sure you all stay well away from this area,' Truf said to Joey. 'It's very dangerous. No playing, no investigating and under no circumstances should you pick-up or even touch any of these animals.'

'You think, boss?' He said to Truf with his now well-known cheeky look, covered with a huge grin.

'Okay. It's pretty obvious,' Truf replied, remaining serious. 'But I had to say it, just to guarantee there was no confusion. Anyone who touches that water might well die. You make sure you tell the other kids, Joey.'

'We know,' he agreed, momentarily becoming serious. 'My sister... she already died, mate.'

'I'm sorry, Joey. We are going to try and find a way

to fix this for you,' I said with more confidence than I felt.

'We should take a look at where they're drilling at the moment,' Tim said, and I noticed an attitude had crept into his tone. Similar to me, he was rightly pissed at the company he and Megan owned 10% of. I was warming to Tim; hence I'd elevated him to co-ownership rights. Hopefully my new found esteem will continue.

'Can you show us where that is, Joey?' Truf asked.

Such a question didn't deign an answer, but it still drew one of his looks. Joey tuned and headed back to the car. We followed, like three small children being led into class by our teacher.

I marveled at the arrogance in one so young, but I had to concede he only showed it when someone questioned his ability to command things within his own areas of expertise. The cocky little bugger had my respect. He was going to grow up to be terrific asset to his people - or become one of the great assholes of this world. Possibly he could become both, simultaneously. I'd be watching.

As we reached the car and Joey was climbing to his seat on the bonnet, I said, 'We don't want the miners to know we are looking into what they're doing, Joey. If it's at all possible can you get us close to them without them seeing or hearing us. We don't mind if we have to walk the last bit.'

'No worries, mate. There's a ridge nearby, we can hide behind that.'

The drill site was not very far and Joey indicated that we should drive slowly when we were close. Eventually, he turned around and gave Tim the stop sign with his hand.

We climbed out of the car and closed the doors quietly. Joey led us a little further and then he ran ahead to scout the site. We followed and found him lying on his belly looking over a rocky ridge.

I crawled up as stealthily as I could and joined him, belly down on the hot parched earth. The heat that radiated though my body from the ground was almost painful. How Joey could go barefoot over terrain like this was beyond my understanding. Then I noticed he had chosen a sizable tuft of grass to lie down on. The stupid guy with him hadn't thought of that.

Tim and Truf joined us at the rim of the ridge and we found ourselves looking down into a small compound that was cordoned off with a temporary wire fence about eight foot high.

Inside the fence stood a large truck with a huge drilling rig attached to its rear-end. The truck's motor was bellowing and blowing puffy black smoke out of its exhaust. So much for our need to be quiet. I counted four men working the rig. A pile of long pipes was stacked beside the fence and as we watched two of the men walked over and took one of the pipes from the stack and carried it back to the truck. On the far side of the compound I could see two dingy caravans and a couple of cars. In a far corner sat about ten drums that looked very much like the ones we had just been looking at a few minutes ago.

'Why would they just discard the other drums, when they clearly need them at this drill site?' I asked Truf.

'Search me. It makes no sense at all. The chemicals are expensive. The only thing I can guess is the other containers were damaged in some way and too risky to transport. Obviously there are procedures that should be followed if that were the case. Dumping them in a hole in the ground is not one of them.'

As we watched two of the men had attached a chain to one end of the pipe they had brought over to the truck and it was being hoisted up to the top of the rig. One of the men jumped up and worked the suspended pipe over the one that was just sticking out of the hole they were drilling. His mate joined him and they began to thread the two pipes together, the top one acting like a nut being screwed onto a bolt. When they were satisfied with the join, one of them gave the man at the control panel the thumbs up signal. The motor revved loudly and the pipe began to rotate and slowly drilled its way further into the earth.

'They must all live in those two caravans,' Tim suggested.

'Nah,' Joey chipped in. 'The big boss bloke drives back to town every day.'

'Have they drilled any other holes, Joey?' Truf asked.

'Nah, just these two.'

Truf looked at him questioningly and was about to query his tiny local expert, when he noticed the look on Joey's face. 'That doesn't make any sense,' he said, turning his attention to me. 'They've been working this lease for over two years. Even if they were drilling through solid granite all the way they'd have more wells to show than just these two. Something stinks here, and it's not just the billabong.'

Joey watched the two of us with interest. He had picked up that when any technical questions needed to be answered we directed them to Truf.

Down at the drill site something was happening. The

motor had suddenly been shut down and we could hear yelling. A fifth man had appeared and was giving instructions to the other four. He was stocky and wore a broad hat which covered his face. He must have been working in one of the caravans and was clearly unhappy with something the men were doing.

He went to the man who was working the control panel and grabbed him by the shirt and pulled him away from the machine. He leaned in and examined the dials and tapped one to check it wasn't stuck. Then he turned and yelled at the operator he'd just attacked. The worker slunk away and joined his mates. They were all obviously fearful of the man and stood in a bunch and watched him as he adjusted knobs on the panel.

The boss had clearly worked up a sweat with his sudden burst of anger and activity. He took off his hat and used his sleeve to wipe his sweat-soaked brow. Then he turned to the men and yelled at them once again. They quickly headed off to one of the caravans.

The boss turned back to the panel and as he did we got a glimpse of his face. We all looked at each other, wide-eyed. We knew that face.

It belonged to Felix the pool table hogger and fellow guest at the Drover's Dog.

As we walked back to the Land Cruiser Joey walked beside Truf. 'You the boss man, here?' he asked.

'No Joey. Nobody is the boss here.'

'But these two fellas always ask you what's goin on with those blokes who make holes in the ground.' He pointed back to the compound where the workers were in the process of getting another pipe ready.

'Remember when we were saying how important school is, Joey?' Truf said, giving his best impersonation of a teacher addressing a student.

Joey nodded.

'Well, the school I went to taught me all about what those men are doing with their drilling equipment, and all about the things that rocks contain that are valuable.'

'Rocks are good - I like 'em,' Joey said with enthusiasm. 'Sharp ones are really good. I can get baby wallabies with 'em from about thirty feet away. Dong 'em right on the bloody head and he falls over, then I grab 'em and stick 'em in the chest,' he held up his pointed stick and grinned, showing his pearly-white teeth. 'My dad taught me that.'

The three of us showed our appreciation of his talents by nodding to him. It sounded brutal, but we all realized that we, city dwellers, had long ago been desensitized from the actual capture and preparation of the meat we ate. The process was just a variant of Joey's method, but took place behind closed doors. All we saw was the nicely packaged piece of meat in the supermarket or butcher shop.

'I have my two lucky rocks in here,' he said as he reached into his bag and brought out two jagged rocks, both about the size of an apple.

I'm no expert but I could tell from their off-white, opaque color they were quartz. He held them up so we could see the crisp, sharp edges. I imagined them crashing into the skull of an animal and could see how effective they would be. I decided I was more than happy to have this ten year old kid as my protector in this harsh land. I wasn't sure if he actually was ten but for simplicity sake I had settled on that number. Nine was taken after all.

Joey stopped suddenly and instinctively we all did,

too. Joey held his finger up to his mouth, indicating that we should be quiet. Then he held up his palm to make us stay put. Nine had seen the change in Joey and knew what this meant. His ears pricked up and he scanned the area around him, sniffing as he did. Joey eased his way forward. The only thing of note that I could see was a small tree about ten feet tall. It was suffering from the drought and had hardly any leaves. I could see nothing that would be of interest to Joey. The three of us exchanged glances, clearly we had no idea what was going on.

Nine had been given no instruction but he knew instinctively to pad gently beside his master. Knowing he would be given the command to spring into action when the time arrived. The tree was Joey's focus apparently, as he headed straight for it in a quiet, stealthy manner that would be the envy of any professional hunter. He held the two rocks that he was showing us when he had suddenly spotted his prey. Prey that we still couldn't even see. He slowly raised his right arm and held it poised at the apex of his throwing arc. Suddenly the base of the tree exploded in a cloud of dust accompanied with a loud scratching noise as a small animal darted into the nearby grass. Before it had reached the cover Joey had launched his missile at it and it made a dull *thwack* sound as it crashed into the earth. Before the rock had even landed Joey had transferred the second rock into his throwing hand and was in the process of delivering it in the direction of the animal. An animal that none of us useless city boys had even seen, let alone identified.

The second rock crashed into the ground in almost the exact same spot as the first and Joey leaped into the air. 'Got the bugger...!' he yelled as he pumped the air in victory. Nine charged across the ground, covering it in less than a second. He barked once and growled as he reached the area where all the activity had taken place. He kept going a short distance into the grass before returning with a large lizard in his mouth. It was black, with a thin white lacy diamond shaped pattern all over it and much larger than the one Joey had delivered for lunch. This one was almost three feet long and nine could only carry it by biting onto one of its front legs. Its tail made a sharp line in the soft earth as he half-carried, half-dragged it back to Joey.

How the hell could I have missed seeing something that big?

Nine was given no praise for his retrieval work. Joey simply nodded and the dog dropped his prize to the ground. I noticed the poor lizard had a large gash at the base of its head and another half way down its back. The blow to the head had been enough to kill it. I had no idea which rock had been the killing one, but I suspected that Joey's skill would almost guarantee that it was the first one. Never-the-less I made a conscious decision to never cross my little protector. I now understood why he was allowed to roam the countryside alone. Joey was a pint-size Arnie - Sylvester, come Jackie Chan and I would seriously fear for the safety of any would-be nut-job, abductor who decided he'd found an easy prey in little Joey.

He picked up his capture and held it for us to admire. His pride and glee evident for all to see. 'He's a beauty, eh? A Lacie.. bloody good tucker. Lots of meat.'

My Google searches of things that should be included in my paranoia list, had brought up goannas.

As a result, I knew that Joey had caught a Lace Monitor Lizard. I hadn't added it to my list of killers, because it wasn't a killer. If it bit you you'd need antibiotics for sure, and if you managed to grab one in the wrong way, its lethal three inch claws would give a doctor a lot of practice at stitching. Google had not advised me that they were "bloody good tucker".

Lacie wouldn't fit in Joey's bag, so he draped it around his shoulders as he went to retrieve his two favorite rocks. He found them and used a tuft of grass to wipe the blood off them.

Truf was watching him intently.

'Could I have a look at your special rocks, Joey?'

He handed them over, clearly a little concerned that Truf might try and steal his favorite weapons.

I watched Truf as he turned them over in his hand, his eyes were wide with surprise and I could see why. I'm not a geologist, but I didn't need to be, the thick seam of bright yellow material that ran through both of them was enough of a clue for even me to know it was gold.

These are very special rocks, Joey,' Truf said, casting a glance at me.

'I know. Bloody good sharp rocks,' Joey concluded.

Truf looked questioningly at both Tim and me. Tim was also aware of what we were looking at. I gave a gentle shake of my head to Truf and I think he got the message I was sending. Tim, I wasn't so sure about, so I said. 'Remember how Warra looks after his booty from his art works? We have totally different values.' I'd hoped the use of the word *booty* was code enough to slip by Joey. I hoped the same wasn't true for Tim. He looked at me and looked about to say something so I gave him an urgent little shake of my head. I think he finally understood he should shut up.

Joey was watching us suspiciously. He'd seen the head shakes and had picked up something. He just didn't know what.

'You're right, Joey. They are bloody good rocks. But only when *you* throw them. I don't think any of us would even be able to hit the tree, let alone get the monitor lizard smack on the top of his head. You must be the best thrower in your tribe.'

Joey was pleased at being recognized as a great hunter and smiled proudly to me. 'Me dads pretty bloody good, too.'

I think what I'd said had deflected any suspicion that Joey had harbored that we were thinking of stealing his rocks, so I moved to the question we were all dying to ask. 'They are very pretty rocks. Do you remember were you found them, Joey?'

He looked at me with his now familiar "*of course.. are you stupid?*" look, and said, 'Yep.'

Truf couldn't contain himself any longer. 'Would you take us there, Joey?'

Suspicion returned to his face. He sensed he was missing something and he seemed to be trying to work it out but he was too young to make any sense out of it.

'I tell you what, Joey,' Tim interrupted his thought process. 'If you take us to the special rock place, we'll have a quick look around and then we'll go back to your camp and I'll show you how to kick that football. It takes a lot of practice, but I think I can have you kicking it at least a mile. Maybe two. What do you say?'

It was inspired of Tim to remind Joey that we had brought gifts with us. It did the trick.

'C'mon then,' Joey said, as he began walking back to the car. The Lace Monitor hanging over his shoulders looked more like a fat fur collar than a lace necklace. He carried it expertly, with the same nonchalance as a seasoned shopper returning from the supermarket with armfuls of grocery filled plastic bags.

***

Sunny tried to open her eyes but they seemed to be glued together. She moved slightly and her body complained; pain shot through her joints and her muscles went into spasm. She became alarmed. Slowly, she forced her eyes open and blinked repeatedly to clear them. The room was dark and yet there was light, she knew it because an unfocused dull glow persisted just out of reach of her vision.

She shook her head, slightly. It helped a little, so she shook her head again a little more vigorously. A few more blinks and, slowly, she began to make out her surroundings. She was in Simon's office. She had been sleeping on his couch.

Why?

No recollection came to her. She didn't wear a watch and she used her phone to tell the time, but it was nowhere to be seen. That, she knew, was unusual as she rarely left it more than an arms-reach away. She tried to sit and put her feet on the carpet but multiple stabs of pain caused her to stop and regroup. She searched her mind for answers but nothing came. After another minute her eyes had cleared considerably and she tried sitting-up again. This time she fought through the pain and succeeded.

She was sitting in Simon's office, on his couch, totally confused. Sunny looked out his bank of windows and saw the distant buildings lit-up in multi-colored lights. It was nighttime. But exactly what time? She needed her phone.

She wiggled forward on the couch until she was propped on its very edge. Slowly she stood. Her head swirled and she blinked trying to focus her eyes again. She began the slow journey to her own desk, groping her way using the furniture and walls for support. As she walked she became aware that her clothes felt wrong on her. Uncomfortable and twisted. She stopped and adjusted her bra that had been pinching the lower portions of her breasts, then she hitched up her skirt and, using her fingers, realigned her panties. She shook her head in wonder at what sort of crazy movements she must have done while she was asleep to cause her underwear to shift so much.

Her phone was on her desk and her computer was still turned on, the monitor had gone to sleep and she moved the mouse to start it up and see what she had been doing on it before she had miraculously ended up on Simon's couch. The screen showed a spreadsheet that she used to plan the forthcoming shoots in analogue order. Her MP3 player was still playing although she had turned the speakers off. That was strange, usually she would shut them off at the same time. Her phone told her it was 3:24a.m.

Her mind was starting to clear a little but she still felt quite unwell, overall. She had nausea, and pain in her joints and her bladder was full. She made her way slowly to the ladies room and looked closely at her face in the full-length mirror. She was a mess; her hair looked like a bird had nested in it, her mascara was smudged and had run down her face and her lipstick was smeared well past the edge of her lips. She soaped up her hands and washed her face as best she could and then dried herself with a few handfuls of paper-towels. She made her way to the cubicle and shut the door. Silly, she thought, *I'm the only person in the building.*

She lifted her skirt and dropped her panties to the floor, then she sat on the toilet. The change from standing to sitting brought with it a wave of nausea and she bent forward and closed her eyes, trying to relax her body and give the nausea time to dissipate. She began to breathe deeply and slowly. In through the nose, out through the mouth. Repeat until symptoms are relieved. But, she became aware of something unusual as she breathed in for the third deep breath. A smell. It seemed to be coming from her body. She sat back up and sniffed the air in the cubicle and the smell had gone away. She bent forward again and it came back. It was coming from her vaginal area and it was not a normal smell. She knew the smell, but in her groggy state couldn't pinpoint it so she used her fingers to probe the entrance to her vagina. She brought her fingers to her nose and sniffed. Instantly her eyes flashed open wide as realization set in. Her mind finally remembered what the smell was. The unmistakable odor of the lubricant that condom makers use to keep their products moist.

Oh! Fuck! No...!

***

Joey took us in the direction of the red escarpment that we had been heading straight towards when we had

205

first ventured off the main road. When we were close he turned us and we drove parallel to it for a couple of minutes before he gave the signal to stop. We eagerly piled out of the car and looked around keen to see if any mining presence could be detected. The place he had chosen was indented into the line of the low cliff. It was almost as if a large chunk of the earth had been dug out and smashed up. The main material that the cliff was formed in was a type of red or yellow sandstone. Not very strong or stable, but this area receives so little rain it had resisted erosion for millions of years.

The heat was intense and our shirts quickly became wet again with sweat, but none of us noticed. We were on a mission. Truf opened the back of the Land Cruiser and grabbed the medium-size pick he had purchased in Brisbane. He had bought two smaller ones which he handed to Tim and me.

Joey left the lizard wedged in between the bull-bar and the front of the car and had already started walking to the indentation in the cliff-face. When we caught up to him he was standing with his bare foot on a rock the size of a watermelon. 'Here's one of the white rocks ya like,' he said as he lifted his foot off the boulder. I could see the sparkle of the thin seam of gold from where I stood. 'But it's no bloody good, ya can't throw one that big.'

The three of us were speechless. I looked around and saw there were many others like it scattered around. Truf had already walked all the way into the deepest part of the indentation and was examining the rock-surface carefully.

I joined him and saw the euphoric look on his face. He looked at me and shook his head in disbelief. 'Never seen anything like it,' he said. 'It looks like the sandstone has been covering a layer of quartz for a long, long time. Wind erosion is the main thing that attacks it, but that is reasonably slow and takes a long time to do the job. The small amount of annual rain probably only helps hold the soft soil together, rather than erode it.' He picked up a small lump of the sandstone and crushed it in his hand to show me how soft and crumbly it is.

'But something has taken this large chunk of sandstone out and exposed the quartz in this one section.' He panned his arm around the mini amphitheater we were standing in. 'Thank God it did. Might have been another million years before the quartz became visible.'

The quartz he was referring to stood in front of us and it was plain to anyone who looked that it was full of hundreds, maybe thousands of veins of gold. Most were very thin like the veins of a leaf, others were incredibly wide - in places as much as 5 mm.

'There's no way of telling how far these seams go, is there?' I asked. 'Without doing test drills.'

'You're right. But I've seen plenty of potential sites for a gold mine in my time, but I've never seen anything as remotely obvious as this.'

Truf began to climb up the face of the cliff. Every few feet he would stop and chip away at the surface, check the rock he had dislodged and then climb higher.

'Tim!' Truf called out.

'What's up, Truf?' Tim answered from about thirty feet away, where he was busy sifting through an assortment of rocks.

'Would you go back to the car and get that large plastic drink cooler-box we bought and bring it back here, please?'

'It's full of ice and water bottles.' Tim said.

'Take the bottles out and ditch the ice, old boy. I need a strong container and that's the best we've got.'

'You're the boss,' Tim said and headed off to do as he was asked.

Joey wandered up to me and said, 'I'm gunna go hunting. Ya take too long to find ya bloody rocks.'

***

Joey and Nine followed the contour of the escarpment. He hoped he'd be able to find a scorpion hiding under a rock, or maybe a small lizard. The sun was fierce and even the ants had the good sense to stay out of it. But not those crazy white blokes. Just find a bloody rock and go back to camp, so I can learn how to kick a football. That was all he wanted them to do, but they seemed to want to find a special rock.

He stopped every few paces and rolled back any rocks he could manage to move. But the cool earth under each one he shifted was empty. Nine had run a short distance in front and was doing his bit sniffing the ground for any trace of food and peeing on any likely landmark that needed to be claimed as his.

Joey used his stick to probe any crevices he came upon and he finally got lucky when he stuck it into a deep crack in the red earth that ran all the way from the ground up to his head height. His stick had gone in at chest height and plunged into something soft. The end of the spear suddenly became alive with an animal that he'd managed to spear. A loud hiss came from deep inside the crevice and he fought to hold on to the spear as it danced in his hands.

Nine had heard the sound that told him Joey had found something and he ran back and stood at his masters feet, mouth open, teeth ready, waiting for a chance to be involved in the kill.

Joey was pretty sure it was a snake, probably not a goanna because he didn't hear any violent scratching sounds. But it was definitely strong and most likely big, and was giving him a good fight. He pulled the spear back, intending to plunge it in again but when he did the spear just hit solid rock at the back of the crevice. He plunged it in again with a similar result.

Suddenly all hell broke loose at his feet and he realized what had happened. The animal had been on a hidden ridge deep inside the crevice when he had speared it. When he had pulled the spear out, it had fallen down the crack to ground level, where it had decided to come out of the crack and face its tormentor.

And it was as mad as hell.

He looked down just in time to see the snake lunge at his leg. It happened too fast for him to jump out of the way and his spear was uselessly stuck inside the crevice. He watched as if in slow-motion, both fascinated and horrified at the same time as the snakes head sped towards him. Its fangs were clearly visible; he could even make out a tiny drop of venom that formed on the point of one of them as it caught the light. In his adrenaline charged state he even identified the snake as an Eastern Brown. Not the deadliest snake in Australia - just the second deadliest.

Nine darted into the fight, snarling fiercely and moving equally as quickly as the snake. Instinctively he went for its head, but his timing was slightly out and the snake's head punched into his face with such force that Nine's head crashed into Joey's leg and caused him to tumble over backwards and land on his backside.

The snake's fangs embedded deeply into Nine's cheek and delivered a load of venom into the side of his snout, then, just as quickly it recoiled and readied itself for another lunge.

As Joey fell backwards his spear came out of the hole with him. He kept hold of it, even though his eyes were fixed on Nine who had also hit the ground, but the dog's fall had ended on top of Joey's legs, pinning the small boy down. Nine lay there on Joey, his body trembling, slowly beginning to convulse. Behind him the snake knew it had won one battle, but it was badly injured from Joey's stabbing and hell-bent on destruction. And Joey was the only one left to punish.

It was a huge snake, maybe fifteen feet long and it reared up, towering over Nine's body. It formed the familiar S shape that usually was only used as a bluff to any potential threat. But Joey knew this was not a bluff and it was about to deliver a deadly strike at him. It was all happening too quickly. Joey still held the spear but it was harmlessly pointing at the sky. He looked into the deep black, completely round eyes of the beast. They were the eyes of death and they were focused on him. The snake seemed to peel back its upper lip in a type of macabre grin, or snarl, and hissed - its forked tongue flicked excitedly, tasting the air for hidden dangers. Either side of its tongue its long, thin white fangs protruded threateningly, glinting in the bright sunlight like steel daggers.

It began its lunge at Joey.

Once again he watched what was unfolding in slow

motion. Everything that was happening between the two combatants was now being controlled by instinct, there was no time to think or plan. The deadly fangs raced down towards his legs that lay prone and pinned. Joey had no awareness that his hand was propelling the spear down. The stick crashed, side-on into the back of the snakes head and Joey watched as the head appeared to snap up and go backwards. It wasn't of course, it was an optical illusion brought on by the spear driving the snake's body down faster than its head. The spear had snapped the beasts spine just behind its head, effectively rendering the top of its body paralyzed, but not removing the deadly threat of the venom filled fangs.

The direction Joey had brought the spear down had pushed the snake to his left and it hit the ground only inches from his thigh. Its body was as thick as a man's forearm and lay like a fat pale-brown hose, draped over Nine's still twitching body. Joey kicked out at the dogs body to free himself as quickly as possible. The snake's head was incapable of controlled movement, but the rest of its body was still thrashing around in a spasmodic frenzy, which was making the head flick from side-to-side. Joey knew that even the slightest scratch from those deadly, needle-sharp fangs would mean death to him and he pushed away from it as quickly as he could.

Joey stood at a safe distance and plunged the spear repeatedly into the snake's body. He kept stabbing even after the beast was completely still. Then he dragged its body off Nine's and threw it to the side. He sat beside Nine and gently lifted his head onto his lap and gently stroked his ears. The dog's mouth had begun to froth and the edges were coated in a white creamy foam. His breathing began to crackle and slow, until it finally faded to nothing... and stopped.

Joey continued to gently caress and pat his head, watching vacantly, as his tears silently splashed on Nine's lifeless body.

***

We lugged the rock filled cooler back to the car and the three of us managed to get it into the rear of the Land Cruiser. It weighed a lot and presumably was worth a considerable amount. But that was to be determined. It was, in fact the very reason Truf had collected the samples.

We did have one small problem: You can't just turn up at a laboratory with some rocks and have them analyzed. There are laws governing the ownership of minerals and metals contained in the earth and you need a lease to mine or even explore for these things. I'd heard stories of how an eccentric person had buried his wealth in the backyard of the house he owned. Sadly, the lease to the mineral rights of the area he lived in were owned by a mining company. How they found out about his buried wealth is a mystery, but find out they did. A court later ruled in the favor of the leaseholder as the items were buried deeper than nine inches. Leases are important legal rights and clearly, we did not have one. Technically we could argue we had 20% of one, but the last thing I wanted to do at this stage was share the news of this discovery. A idea was beginning to hatch in my brain.

'The boy's been gone a while,' Tim said, 'I think I'll take a walk and see if I can find him.'

He was correct so I offered to join him. In the end

all three of us went in search of Joey.

We found the little guy almost immediately and I could only begin to imagine what he had just gone through. Tough little bloke that he is, the sight of his tears tore me up.

I could hardly believe the size of the snake and it reinforced in my brain that I was correct about how many things could kill me out here. Its head was only partially attached to its body as Joey's stabbing had been thorough. We left the carcass lying there. Joey had no interest in it as food.

The little guy insisted that he would carry Nine back to the car. I walked beside him, ready to help him if he needed it. He didn't. The only thing he could have used was a box of tissues and I didn't have one of those, either.

Truf drove and Tim sat beside him. I shared the backseat with Joey, a dead lizard, and a dead dog. Joey gave Truf rough directions that eventually got us back to the camp.

Bully wasn't impressed that the dog had died. 'Stupid bloody animal,' he said when he saw the boy carrying his lifeless body towards him.

Joey stood in front of Bully and glared at him. 'He is a stupid bloody dog. The silly bugger stuck his head in the way of a brown snake and got bit - instead of me.' The tears flowed down his face.

Bully dropped his head in shame and said gently, 'Sorry boy. The dog's a bloody hero. We'll give him a Chief's burial.'

I left Bully and his son to discuss the arrangements and went to talk with Warra, who had stayed in the shelter of gum-tree.

'I don't want to get your hopes up too much, but we found out some pretty useful things today,' I said to him and he smiled at the news.

'Did you see what they did to our billabong? They shit, those people,' he spat on the ground in disgust.

'You're right, Warra. They're shit,' I agreed. 'The poisoning problem with the billabong is way out of my league. I'll make some calls tonight and see if there are people able to clean up places like that.'

'Thanks, Gary. You're like your grandma. You're a good person.'

I grinned at him, appreciative of the compliment, but worried that I wouldn't be able to live up to the praise.

'No promises, Warra. But we're going to give it everything we can. We'll be back tomorrow. We need to check out some more sites around here. Is that okay?'

'Of course.'

***

The sudden awareness of what had happened to her had made Sunny almost totally symptom free. She pulled up her underwear and left the toilet, completely forgetting she had a desperate need to pee. She had a massive gap in her memory and she knew from Garrett's description of his symptoms, a few nights before, that she had been "date-raped" under the influence of Rohypnol. Her mind was clear enough to make the connection that the common factor in both cases was Simon - her piece of shit, boss.

She returned to his office and began a systematic search. His desk drawers were not locked and she carefully checked them. Her long-term memory was coming back strongly now that she had become motivated. She remembered the program they had made on date-rape drugs had shown Rohypnol came in both liquid and tablet form. The tablets were easily dissolved and were odorless and usually colorless. Ironically that same program must have been when Simon obtained his supply of Rohypnol.

The desk was clear. The filing cabinets were locked, but she knew Simon kept a spare set of keys taped under his desk, hidden at the back of the drawers.

She began to check the filing cabinet drawers, first going quickly through each one, and when that preliminary search turned up nothing, each draw was investigated in detail. Rather than flip between all the pages inside each file she reasoned that pills or a bottle could be felt, so she lay each file on the desk and ran her flattened hand over it. The search had been underway for about ten minutes before she was rewarded with a bulge that deserved further investigation. She flicked her fingers through the sheets of paper to locate the lump. She pulled out a plastic zip-lock bag and looked closely at it. It had a gray-green plant material inside it which she assumed was marijuana. She placed it back where she had found it and returned the file to the cabinet. It was labeled "H". A thought occurred to her - If Simple Simon keeps his hash or hemp under "H" then maybe...

She had already been through the "D"- for "*date-rape*" file, so maybe the "R" file was worth jumping ahead to. It was a bulky file and she lay it carefully on the desk and began feeling for any tell-tale signs.

Success! She opened the file and found the source of the lump. This time it was a blister-pack, like any other pharmaceutical prescription product. It was filed correctly under "R" for Rohypnol.

You piece of shit, Simon...

Sunny sat in Simon's chair and put her feet up on his desk. The blister pack in her hand had three pills missing. She could only account for two. Simon must have another victim out there, somewhere. Maybe he tried one himself to judge the impact. Maybe he slipped one to Susie, his wife, to observe her reactions. One thing she could be sure of, Simon was a highly intelligent, calculating bastard. She had no idea why he would do something as criminally risky as raping her. *And, why her?* All she could come up with by way of an acceptable explanation, was, life had become boring and predictable for him and he needed to do something on the other side of the "edge".

Maybe she could find a way to help him with that...

***

The trip back to our hotel was subdued. Truf was driving and I sat beside him. The GPS had stored our days activity and we reversed it to make our way back to the road. Once we had located our original track in, it was easy to follow as the car had flattened a clear path through the tall grass.

I had lots to do when we got back to the Drover's Dog. The time difference between here and London meant that I could comfortably call people knowing that 6 p.m. for me was 9 a.m. for them, and we were both on the same day. My mind drifted to little Joey. He's quite a kid and I knew he'd be doing it tough for some time, after what happened today. That thought made me sad.

I liked the aborigines I'd met. Their world was a lot smaller than mine, but, in its own way was just as complex. I dealt with virtual things like money and perception, where they dealt with the reality of feeding and sheltering themselves. It made me realize that we were all fighting the same battle, but in my case the Government had put an artificial layer between me and the harsh reality of survival. That layer was called money and it allowed us to exchange goods and services without the need for like-to-like transactions. By that I mean, if I needed milk I wouldn't need to find something the farmer wanted to swap his milk for.

Money was a great invention when it was linked to gold, but letting the Central Banks of the world determine how much money they can print is an absolute disaster of an idea. Money would only remain a viable means of exchange as long as we all had confidence in it. Lately, I'd been steadily losing my confidence, given that my Government was printing the stuff like confetti. As was America, Japan, China. In fact pretty much all the nations that are party to the current economic system that we blindly follow are printing currency like mad. Inflation, maybe hyperinflation, depression, maybe systemic collapse, something is going to give and pretty soon.

I was preparing - I no longer actually counted my personal wealth in dollars, I used assets, and our discovery today fitted perfectly into my preparations.

The evils of money were responsible for Warra's troubles, too. The civilized world can only exist at its unreal level with liberal access to power. And oil was at the heart of it, and it was becoming depleted, which was driving the need for different sources of power. Hence,

CSG wells were popping up all over the world and with them the potential for massive destruction was increasing with every hole drilled.

'What are you going to do with the rocks you collected, Truf?' Tim asked after we had eventually turned back onto the main road and finally got up to a decent speed.

'Not much,' he replied. 'I can't get an accurate grading of the gold samples without milling the rocks and refining them. But I don't need to. I know it's gold, and it's the richest bunch of seams I've ever seen, judging by what we can actually see.'

'I've never seen gold in its natural state,' Tim said. 'Is that how it normally looks?'

Truf burst out laughing. Finally, he said, 'Oh Tim, if you only knew how far from normal those rocks actually are, you'd be laughing with me. A *normal* gold bearing sample of quartz would have a few thin specks, maybe the size of a grain of sand, or perhaps a thin vein about as thick as the line a pen makes on a page. Occasionally, a sample will have a larger showing. What we picked up in fifteen minutes is close to a mother-lode. I'm blown away by it. My guess is we have between $20,000 and $30,000 in gold in the cooler behind you.'

'This is sounding better by the minute,' Tim said with a sly chuckle.

'Don't get any ideas, Tim. Technically, we've stolen that gold. It belongs to Plutarch, so we have to just sit on it. If I put it in for processing, I'll be getting the results forwarded to me in jail.'

While the other two discussed their lives of crime I'd been wondering about how we needed to proceed.

'What do you need to do tomorrow, Truf?' I asked.

'I'd love to start mapping and drilling the area to find out a rough idea of how large the gold-bearing seams are. That process alone can take a year or two. We only have another day or two.' Truf looked around at me and shrugged his shoulders.

'So the best you can do is just look for surface gold in the surrounding area to get an idea of its extent?' I asked.

'We!.. old boy. The three of us need to spread out and scratch away. Bearing in mind that we can't do anything too obvious to the ground. We don't want to alert, what's-his-name - the CSG vandal?'

'Felix.' I offered.

'I think I should have a chat with that chap. Get a feel for what he's about.' Truf said.

'You heard George, Truf. The guy's to be avoided,' I offered.

Truf ignored my comment completely. 'You know, around a hundred years ago most discoveries had ore that averaged around 100g/ton of gold. Today, its under 2g/ton. All the easy to find gold has already been discovered.' Truf paused to allow that to sink in. 'What we've found has the potential to be a big deal.'

Both Tim and I liked the sound of that.

'Assuming the gold bearing rock continues deep into the earth, or spreads out over a big area. Preferably both,' Tim added, with a hopeful smile.

'Yeah,' Truf agreed. 'What I'd like to know is why this area has been ignored, especially seeing there are mining companies already working here.'

'They're probably just fixated on finding gas. And from what I've seen today, these clowns couldn't find gas if you led them to a BBQ gas bottle,' I said.

'Maybe,' Truf acknowledged. 'But I still intend to do some research on this area and see what's going on. It has never been a recognized area for gold. The main thing to remember is not to mention this find to anyone. Wives, lovers, workmates, grandmothers, psychiatrists,' he looked in the mirror at Tim and then across the car to me. 'Anyone!'

'Got it,' we both said in unison.

'Do you think I have a psychiatrist?' Tim said, offended at the suggestion.

Truf just grinned at him in the mirror. 'I said, psychiatrists - plural.'

We continued to discuss and plan the next few days as we drove on through the uninteresting, hot desolate countryside. I watched through the side window and thought of a ten year old boy wandering through that environment, all alone now. The landscape flicked by as I drifted into my deep thoughts and then suddenly I was looking at a picture of Australia I'd seen in books, many times. I shouted, 'Hey! Look over there.' I pointed through my window and the other two turned quickly to see what all the excitement was about. 'Kangaroos,' I said. 'I've finally seen some.' A group of five was bouncing their way across an open area, not far from the road.

'Afraid not, Gary,' Truf said. 'They're Wallabies.'

'Oh shit. How can you tell?'

'Wallabies are gray, Kangaroos are a red color.'

Chapter 8

We parked outside the Drover's Dog and Truf went to the back of the Land Cruiser and made sure any tools, that might give a hint that we were something other than tourists, were covered with the large picnic blanket that had come with the car. Sammy's idea I assume, as not many used cars have that accessory. The cooler had the lid closed and looked innocent enough. After that he double-checked that the car was locked by yanking on every door handle, then we headed to the hotel, patting the little bronze dog as we filed past him. In my mind he had become a monument to the tough, brave little Nine who had epitomized the characteristics needed to live in this harsh pocket of the world. Not that it had worked out well for him.

'G'day boys. Get up to anything interesting today?' George, the publican, called out when he saw the three of us walk in covered in sweat. Not that we were alone with that, everyone walked in bathed in sweat.

'Nah,' I said, as we headed towards the bar. 'Just the usual stuff. Getting lost in the bush, tripping over some rocks and having to deal with an Eastern Brown snake as long as a truck.' I grinned at him. 'Same crap we get to deal with every day in London, although I think the snakes back home have a different name and wear sneakers,' I laughed at my silly joke. George just smiled politely. 'Could have stayed in the UK and saved our money... We'll have three of your coldest brews, barkeep.' I added, in my finest British accent.

The light banter with a guy whose wife I had banged that very morning should have caused me some stress, but strangely it didn't. I guess some marriages are destined to end in the garbage bin. She had been 100% responsible for what happened. I was merely her weapon of choice. I felt sorry for the guy, for sure, but he married her - I only screwed her. And, I had every intention of *showering* again tomorrow morning. A thought that had been in and out of my brain repeatedly, throughout the day.

The three of us enjoyed our beer, letting the cold liquid linger in our mouths a little longer than usual. The conversation was football, and how Tim intended to teach Joey how to kick an Aussie football when he had never kicked one himself. Gold didn't get a mention. When our glasses were drained Truf and I headed up to our rooms to make some calls and send off emails. Tim decided to stay and have another beer as he wasn't needed for this work. He told us he was planning to call Megan before he went to bed.

The good news about the Drover's Dog was that it not only had electricity and the telephone connected, it also had access to the internet. I was totally impressed. Global communication from the middle of nowhere. Then I understood why. The enemy we had come to do battle with had taken hold of this area. Culgawinya was near a huge underground gas-field, an area called the Surat Basin and it was inundated with CSG wells, all owned and operated by corporations. Corporations who need to be connected. And Governments adore corporations.

Based on the gold I had seen at the site I had already made the decision to buy as much Plutarch stock as I could. That amount of visible gold would easily double the stock price, probably a lot more, when the speculators got wind of it. I fired up my laptop and scrolled down the mail in my inbox. Sky had sent me an updated list of Plutarch's major shareholders. The good news was that Megan and I weren't on it, and I silently thanked Gerald for delaying the paperwork. Hopefully he could stretch it out a little longer. The Chinese owned company, registered in Australia, called MienOne Pty Ltd, held 9.5% of the shares. Sky had made a note that they had acquired Plutarch shares about the same time Gran and Ed had been buying. This was the holding controlled by Ling Mien that Gerald had mentioned, and he was losing money. Billionaire Daddy would most likely be unimpressed with honorable son. I filed that information away in my brain.

Sky had included information about my competitor businesses in the USA - the Hedge Funds who were the other major holders of Plutarch shares. They were Samson-Jonkins, and Ambic Leveraged Investments, both were known to me and neither was usually a longterm holder of stock. They took positions in companies they considered *ripe* and waited for a takeover to be announced. Then negotiated a nice pay-day for themselves, by playing all the interested parties off against each other. Neither company had owned the stock for very long and the price was near where they had bought in at.

They were highly leveraged speculators and I knew they would be hot for a deal - at the right price. Which would not be the current price. If they were warehousing the stock for an anonymous buyer, then that would all be wrong. But, if they were warehousing there would most likely have been some increase in both their holdings of Plutarch, and also the share price. Neither of those things had happened. The first scenario seemed most likely.

The other large holding that interested me was registered to: Mackintime-Overly Family Trust. It was based in Sydney and controlled by Dr. John Mackintime. The trust owned 4.5% of Plutarch.

I pulled out the sheet I had printed back in London with all the information on Plutarch that I had found. I saw it immediately. MienOne held 10.8% just a week ago. Now they had 9.5%. Ling Mien was a seller. Excellent news.

I had lots to go over with Sky and there was no way it was going into an email. Even a digital phone connection is not secure these days, but time was vital here and what are the odds of someone being interested in me. Or Sky, for that matter.

I read Sophie's email which was detailed information about the main shareholders financial situations. MienOne was a private company and information about it was almost non-existent. But I guessed it was very capable of causing me big trouble if they found out the true situation with Plutarch Resources. As I had guessed the two hedge funds were leveraged up to their eyeballs. The Mackintime-Overly Trust was solid and had no debt attached. Dr. John was apparently a straight arrow, just adding a little speculative action to his portfolio of shares.

I used my own phone to call Sky, not knowing the phone setup in the hotel and not wishing for anyone in this part of the world to hear my conversation. It seemed safer.

'Good morning, Sky,' I said cheerfully.

'Hi Gary. Or should I say Good Evening?' She replied, mindful of the time difference.

'As long as you say it nicely, I don't mind.'

'Hey, I'm sorry I snapped last time. I slept badly that night. The idiots next door had a party and, well...'

'I understand. Forget about it,' I said. 'How's your mind today?'

'Razor sharp and keen to hear all about this Sunny.'

'Sunny is just great. I hope. But I need to talk to you about work. Do you have a pen handy?'

'I've had one surgically attached to my hand, for this very call and the many others I assumed I'd be getting.'

I laughed. 'I've been too busy to call. But I've been getting plenty of texts from the work computer telling me both you and Soph have been logging in from outside computers. I appreciate the work you've both done. I'm onto something big here and if it works out you girls will be heading for a big bonus.'

'Now, you have my undivided attention. The pen surgery is about to pay-off,' she chuckled.

'I need you to step up and do my role while I'm in Australia. The Nixon Fund is going to take a sizable position in Plutarch Resources. I want you to open negotiations with Ling Mien to purchase his entire holding, off-market. Firstly, confirm that he hasn't sold any more of his shares on-market and that his holding is still 9.5%. That's important Sky. I want you to offer him 9.5c a share, not a penny more for whatever his holding is at the moment. I know that's very unusual and normally we would need to offer him a premium well above the current market price to buy such a large parcel of shares. But I've had a psychic flash occur to me, I think he'll be calling you to accept in two days time.'

'Gary, You're clearly up to something that you won't talk about. You do realize he's probably going to just hang up in my ear when he hears your offer of 9.5c.'

'Just make sure he knows who we are and get his email address. I doubt he will hang up, though, he'll just assume you've come in with a low first offer. And Sky, I want you to send him an email right after the phone call, confirming the offer in writing. Give the offer an expiry time of close of business, say 5:30 p.m. two days from now, Aussie time. You need to stress it is an unconditional cash offer and will be withdrawn after that time. Get our lawyers to draw up the official offer and courier it to him.'

'You're certainly not making this easy for me by being so secretive, Gary. I've never handled the negotiating before, I've only ever sat-in on your deals.'

'Many, many times Sky. You're a smart girl - that pen surgery to your hand proves that. Ling has already started to unload his stock, so he's a definite seller. Oh, and by the way, check on who bought the 1.3% he just sold.'

'Oh! I can tell you that. He sold them on-market in small parcels over the whole week. He averaged between 9.5 and 10.5 cents for them. They were picked up by about thirty different investors, or speculators, more likely. Can you at least tell me why this is so urgent?'

'Can't say over the phone, but it has to do with a gift that Gran gave me, or wants to give to me. I need you to phone her legal rep. His name's Gerald Muggleton. He's the Senior Counsel at Shawston Legal in the city. I'm sorry, I don't have his number, and the receptionist might be reluctant to put you through to him; these boys charge everything in 6 minute blocks, at a million bucks per block,' I laughed at my sarcastic dig. 'So give Gran a call and ask her for his private number. I need you to give him this message. "Please delay any transfers for as long as possible." If it's at all possible, Sky, I would prefer him to tear up the forms we signed in his office the other day. Stress it is incredibly important. Email me his answer, ASAP. Make the text as cryptic as you can. Refer to him as "the guy" and the forms as "stuff".'

'This sounds very cloak and dagger, Gary. Is it all above-board?'

'Good question, Sky. I'd need a Law degree to give you an answer. A lot depends on how far Gerald has progressed, he did say he was going to proceed slowly so we could fly under the radar. I'm going to have Sophie get up to speed with how quickly we need to advise the Australian Stock Exchange of any relevant changes to Aussie stock holdings. If you get a chance can you remind her to get on to that? It might keep me out of the clink.' I laughed to take the seriousness out of what I'd just said. But deep down I wasn't totally sure of where I stood, English laws and Australian laws have the same common base, but are not identical.

'If we can do a deal with Ling Mien he'll want some cash pretty soon. Where are we getting that?'

'I want you to sell the Fund's holding of Apple shares. I did a quick conversion to Aussie dollars and that should give us about $1.2 million. More than enough for your deal with Ling.'

'Wow,' she said. 'You should go to Australia more often, things really start to happen,' she paused, then added. 'Tell me the truth, Gary. You're actually stretched out on a beach somewhere and this conversation is just to impress the Aussie chick on the lounge beside you, who you want to jump on.' She giggled, tauntingly. 'You'll be calling back in a minute and telling me to forget everything.'

'Just do as I say, woman, or I'll fire your ass and make sure you never work in this town, again.' I laughed back at her.

'Ha!' She laughed dismissively. 'I've never been to Culgawinya and I don't think I'd really want to work there, anyway.'

'You don't. It's a little too warm for us pasty white Poms,' I conceded. 'I appreciate what you're doing Sky. Good luck with your first solo negotiation. Oh, and one last thing, make all of these calls from your cell phone. Don't use the work phone.'

I checked my phone's battery and it was still strong, so I dialed Sophie. The call went through to her voice-mail. Sophie must still be in bed. Must have been a decent jog she went on to tire her out so much.

I called Sunny's number.

I think her voice-mail is starting to really like me.

***

I knocked on Truf's door.

'Come in. It's open.'

He was sitting on his bed with his laptop open, typing furiously into it. The scene looked funny to me. With giant Truf a normal size computer looks more like a toy on his lap and I wondered how those huge fingers managed to only strike one key at a time, especially at the speed they were working at.

His room was identical to mine, except his air conditioner was on and reasonably quiet. As a result his room was bloody comfortable mate, to describe it in Australian.

'What ya' working on?' I inquired.

'I think I have the answer to that little question we were asking ourselves about, today. The one about why things had remained unknown for so long.' He looked at me and tilted his head to the side and raised his eyebrows. Subtly asking if I understood what he was talking about.

Of course I knew that he was talking about the gold bearing rock we'd found and I fully agreed with his abstract way of introducing the subject. Not that I would imagine our rooms were bugged, that would just be silly. But the walls were thin and who knew who could be listening.

'Yep. I've been thinking about that, too. What's your guess?'

'I wonder if you remember seeing on the TV news the big floods that hit Brisbane back in 2011, in January actually? I can remember seeing boats and pontoons that had been washed away, racing along on the fast flowing water and crashing into bridges,' he said and shook his head at the memory.

'I remember,' I said, nodding in agreement. 'An awful lot of the city went under, too'.'

'Well, some of that flood water started its journey to the coast from the ranges North-West of here. In fact a huge amount of this actual area went under, too. You know the power of water, Gary,' he said with a chuckle. 'Remember when we were at the beach with your family, when a little wave collected you and catapulted you, ass-over-tit onto the beach, a few years ago?'

'It was more than a few years ago... and it was a bloody big wave,' I defended myself. 'And I was only fourteen. Give me a break.'

'Not my point, Gary,' he mocked my over-reaction. 'Water has the power to move mountains. You only need to look at what the Colorado River has done to create the Grand Canyon in the USA. That, I think, is what we we're looking at, here.'

I just nodded in case the spooks were all holding their stethoscopes to our walls and noting every word we uttered. What Truf had worked out was the answer for sure. The big flood of 2011 had cut a section of softer rock away that had been covering the gold bearing quartz for millions of years. Its time to come to the surface, and greet the sunshine, had arrived with that flood. And we were lucky enough to be the first people to stumble upon it. Well, not actually the first. Little Joey gets that award. But we were the first to understand what we had actually found.

I hope.

'I did some checking on our vandal friends,' Truf continued, still in code-speak. But then he lost patience with the game and gave it to me straight in a quiet voice. 'According to documents they have submitted to the Stock Exchange, they've drilled five dry wells, and are currently drilling number six. Joey and Warra say this current one is only their second,' He looked questioningly at me. 'We need to check that out. I can't see any way that the aborigines could get that wrong. This land is their life, they know where every bird roosts and every kangaroo rests. Where every drop of water can be found,' Truf offered up his list of analogies. He was on a roll and continued. 'For them to miss four wells being drilled so close-by is comparable to us missing a boil the size of a lemon on our butt.'

'Got it Truf. You can give the similes a rest now,' I laughed at his attempt to colorfully explain what he had discovered. He was right, though. There was no way Joey, Bully and the others wouldn't be all over that, especially after what the miners had done to their billabong. But why would Plutarch management deliberately lie to the Exchange? You can go to jail for that. I know this because I was treading very close to that same line at the moment. But nowhere near as seriously as these bastards seemingly had.

I moved close to Truf so we could continue talking. I had even less desire to be overheard than Truf had.

'I'm making a play on Plutarch Resources,' I whispered to him. 'I'm confident I can buy the Chinese guy's holding using Nixon Fund within the next day or two. Sky's working on it as we speak.'

He looked at me in a way that suggested he knew that is what I'd be doing. 'There's virtually no downside for you,' he offered with a grin. 'Even if you have to pay double, say 20c a share, the value of just that gold that's poking out of the ground would probably cover the purchase price.'

'That's kind of what I was thinking. The problem I have, Truf, is that I don't want to trigger an on-market takeover. I'm going to get Sophie to give me an exact reading on the laws here in Australia as to how much of the company I can own, or nominally control, before I am required to make a formal takeover offer.' I made a face at him, then added, 'That is, when I can get hold of the girl. I can only get her voice-mail so far.'

'I'm pretty sure above 20% will trigger the need to make an offer for control of the company. But you're not an Australian citizen, so possibly the laws are different for you.' Truf said.

'Yep. That's what I'm thinking, too,' I concurred. 'You're a vital part of this little expedition, Truf. I want you to be a big part of the future plans, one way or another,' I said.

He nodded in agreement. Like, that was a given; there was no way to keep him out.

'Now, the big question.' I smiled and raised my eyebrows questioningly. 'How much money can you get your hands on... quickly?'

Then I laid out my plan for Plutarch - and for him.

***

We sat at our table in the main bar, which was also the restaurant at the Drover's Dog and the three of us simultaneously wiped our mouths on our paper napkins. We had thoroughly enjoyed our thick, juicy Porterhouse steaks that had been perfectly cooked and served by our extremely flirtatious waitress, Bev. A side serve of chips and even a bottle of tomato sauce were available to drown any part of our meal that we wished to alter the taste of. Salad was the only thing missing. I enjoy a salad with a steak, but lettuce, cabbage and other leafy foods, strangely, don't do well in these warm parts. Boiled peas, beans and carrots were our vegetable accompaniment. They also struggle with the heat, but, in their favor, they transport very well in frozen form.

None of us were complaining, Bev had done a fine job. She was quite a woman, and I watched as she cleared our plates from the table. At least I think she was clearing our plates. I was looking at her backside and momentarily I had X-ray vision, just like Superman. Actually, it was probably a memory of a vision, but I marveled at my brains ingenuity. Being able to remove her clothes like that was a big plus. If I could just keep this skill and take it with me everywhere I'd be one happy guy. And Little Gary would also be a happy guy.

As Bev disappeared back into the kitchen with her arms piled high with our dirty plates I tested my new talent on the only other woman in the room. She was rather large and quite muscular. I guessed her age at about fifty. She was standing with her back to me and talking to George, who stood behind the bar pretending to be busy. I looked at her with the same intensity that I had been applying to Bev, but her clothes remained in place.

So much for my new skill. Although, now armed with hindsight I reconsidered and was a little relieved - some mysteries are best left as secrets.

I turned back to rejoin the table conversation, only to see Truf walking away. He was heading straight for the pool table. The one that Felix was in the process of deftly lining up a side-pocket with his cue-stick.

'What the *fuck* is he doing?' I whispered urgently to Tim, whose mouth gaped open in surprise. He clearly had nothing to offer.

Felix wasn't a tall man, but he had the solid, bull-like features of a man possessed of great strength. Truf was huge and in great trim and I knew from personal

233

experience that he was also incredibly strong. I wondered if Culgawinya had a hospital. A doctor. A morgue, even. Maybe those jobs were handled by the barber...

Truf tapped Felix on the shoulder as he lined up his shot. He was the only person playing the table, as all the locals had been warned of the consequences of engaging him, just like we had. Truf must have missed the memo, although I'm pretty sure he was there when it went out.

Felix turned on him and glared. 'What do you want?' he said very deliberately, in a thick German accent.

'A game of pool,' Truf said in a cheerful voice. 'You seem to be playing with yourself...' He let the inferred taunt hang in the air, then added, 'in need of someone to test you out.'

Felix had been at the pool-table the entire time we had been there. He had had a meal also, taking mouthfuls of food and a gulp of beer, between shots with his cue.

'I don't need to be tested, I know I'm the best,' Felix replied, dismissively.

'I beg to differ,' Truf countered. 'I've seen you cock-up numerous shots.'

'You're English, yes?' Felix said the word, English with a menacing little hiss on the end. Suddenly this local confrontation had become a thing of national pride. '*Cock-up*, is a phrase you English need to use all the time.'

'Mainly when referring to Continentals,' Truf smiled humorlessly back at him. 'You're Italian I gather.'

'You know well I'm of German heritage,' Felix sneered.

I could just make out the conversation from where we sat and I turned to Tim and said, 'I don't know what the hell he's up to, but I wish he'd given us a chance to vote on it before he charged off.'

'He mumbled something about testing the water. Then he got up and went over there,' Tim said. 'He said it to you, but you were staring at the woman at the bar and ignored him.'

Oh crap! I could have stopped this happening if I wasn't so busy thinking about... other things.

'They only seem to have one cue-stick,' Truf said to the German, 'and I don't fancy sharing it. It would be a dull game anyway, I fancy. So I withdraw my offer to play.'

'Perhaps, this is just as well, Englishman. I'd hate to have to break it over your thick skull.'

'From what I've seen of your skill, I imagine you'd most likely miss,' Truf said. He turned towards our table and fired a parting shot at the German. 'Either way, it would be a dreadful mistake.'

I watched as Felix's grip on the cue tightened and he began to lift it. Then he changed his mind and returned his attention to the colored balls on the pool table.

I'd been concentrating on the potential situation so intently that I hadn't realized the ambient noise in the bar had dropped to zero. This was why I could hear what the two men were saying. I looked around the room and saw every pair of eyes had been locked on Truf's exchange with Felix. Even Bev had picked up on the altered mood and had reappeared from the kitchen. She watched Truf every step of the way back to his seat. George was glaring at Truf and shaking his head from behind the bar.

Slowly, the room began to buzz again and Truf calmly sat back down at our table.

I looked at him with my eyebrows raised, and said. 'Why?'

Truf grinned. 'I had to know.'

'You must have missed it, but George already told us,' I replied, sarcastically.

'He couldn't tell me what I just found out.'

'What? That he didn't want to play pool with you?'

'It was in his eyes, Gary.' Truf looked at me intently and nodded, knowingly. 'I saw it. I now know how Felix will react when he's cornered.'

***

My short time in Queensland had taught me that the sun goes to bed early and gets up early in these here parts. In London we most likely would have just been going out for the night, but here in Culgawinya when they talk about nightlife, they are talking about the animals that come to life when the temperature drops to a semi-reasonable level.

I wasn't about to engage with any of those critters, and I wasn't ready for bed just yet. I took the time to compose an email to Sophie with the few details of the phone call that we still hadn't had. These were very general, non-incriminating details that I was okay with sending in an exposed manner. As soon as I'd hit the send button I picked up the phone and tried her number.

She answered giving me her best "Goldfinger" impression. 'Ah, Mr. Bond, I've been expecting you.'

It was a terrible impersonation, but good on her for having a crack. 'Keep your day job, Sophie,' I laughed along with her.

'So, what's with all this secretive, hush, hush, stuff? I've been talking with Sky and she thinks you might have gone bonkers.'

'Well, that is possible,' I conceded. 'But, I still want you to take it seriously. Very seriously. From now on nothing sensitive goes in an email and all calls need to come from your cell phone. I gather Sky has told you that we're buying into Plutarch Resources and that I need all the information about takeovers of Australian listed companies. I want the information just as bullet points, Soph. I don't want reams of technical stuff. How much I can nominally control without having to go all out and bid on the whole company? Who do they regard as associated parties? Their definition of warehousing shares. That sort of stuff. I want to fly under the radar for as long as is legally possible. That's your first assignment and I need it in the next few hours.'

'I think I can manage all that. Trying to not leave a paper trail, eh? It wont work. If it hits the fan they will access all our phone records.'

'All they'll get is the three of us just keeping in touch. Any internet searches you make will be consistent with the work you normally do. Except maybe for my next job for you. I need you to check around as many Australian art galleries as you can, and find out about an aboriginal artist called Warra Goomagawa.' I spelled his name for her. 'Pretend to be a buyer. I need to know how widely his art is being sold, so you'll need to call, or check websites of some English and European galleries as well. And if you have the time, some in the USA, too. Try New York first, then L.A. and Miami. I want the name of the distributing dealer. There may be more than one, but the primary Australian dealer is the main name I need. I've put all that in an email that you should have by now.'

'Do you actually want to buy a painting?' She sounded confused.

'Not at this stage. It's all tied in, though.' I heard her exasperated sigh. 'I'm sorry I can't tell you exactly what's going on. You know I would if we were face to face.'

'So, is that the end of our business, Mr. Bond?' She inquired, returning to her spy theme.

'I guess it is... Miss... What should I call you? Miss... Golddigger?'

'That's a little unkind - Golddigger? Couldn't you just give me the *finger* extension?'

I burst out laughing, 'If only you knew - I was doing that every time I called you and was sent straight through to your voice mail.'

She laughed, but it was more polite than hearty and boisterous, as I had hoped. Maybe, I'd offended her. *Women! Can't live with 'em - Can't shoot 'em.* So the saying goes.

'What's the name of your jogging buddy?' I asked, hoping to shift the balance of guilt back to her.

She was quiet for a moment, obviously considering if she should open that door to such a rude, insensitive bastard. The jury must have come down in favor of me, because she eventually said, 'Alan.' Another pause. 'I met him a few days ago at the market. We were both looking for cucumbers. Potentially a bit embarrassing if he was someone like you. But he isn't, thank God, (*there you go - payback,*) and we kinda hit it off.'

I ignored the gibe. 'I'm really happy for you, Soph.

Hope he turns out to be a good guy. And thanks for the great character reference.'

She chuckled. 'Sky mentioned that you've found someone you're interested in.'

We continued talking and sharing wisecracks for a few more minutes, comparing the two new people who had just entered our lives, and how much things seem to change after that initial innocent meeting. Innocent for Sophie, who knows what for me. Then my phone started its now familiar beep, advising me it was running out of juice.

It seemed as if everything was telling me the same thing - it's time for bed.

***

I mentioned that the sun gets up early here, but 4:30... Really! - That's just wrong. It's hard to sleep with a bright light shining in your face not to mention the rise in temperature that accompanies the light. Who can I complain to? Then Little Gary reminded me that mornings came with a bonus in this town and I changed my mind. Thank you, sun.

I jumped out of bed and unlocked the door. I even left it slightly ajar. If I had a neon sign saying *Please Come In*, I would have hung that on the door as well.

While I waited for Bev to arrive I checked my overnight emails. Messages from Sky and Sophie were listed in my inbox.

I opened Sky's first. She had done as I asked and kept it cryptic and vague.

The guy still has the stuff available at his place. But he's not keen about giving them up and wants to talk to your sister and grandmother first.

I made a call to your other friend and he seems keen to meet us for dinner, but he's expecting us to take him to a very expensive restaurant. He mentioned his favorite is called something like 125. He's available this week.

BTW, don't be mad, but I ate your apple.

So, Ling Mien will sell his holding for 25% above market price. Good luck with that. And she has dumped our Apple stock. Good girl.

I composed a reply for Sky:

I've been to that restaurant and it's overrated. My favorite restaurant will be a lot cheaper... keep him waiting for our invitation. You never know, he might change his mind.

Let's see the NSA spooks in the USA make something out of that, not that they'd give a shit about what I'm doing, unless my eating habits have somehow become a threat to US security. It pisses me off that they take and store a copy of everyone's emails. That's just illegal and morally wrong. The sort of stuff that Hitler would be doing if he was around today.

I made a quick call to Gran and asked her to call Gerald and cancel her gift - for the time being. She was keen to hear how I was doing, but had to be content with: *things are coming along, but it's early days.* I hope she understood I was in stealth mode and not just being a melodramatic dick. I was confident she would be cool with it, Gran's a fan and has rose-colored glasses on when she thinks of me, and also Megan, of course.

It seems Australia has made me paranoid on just about every level. I worry about the killer animals, the attacking trees, the early sunrises and sunsets, the NSA, the eavesdroppers hiding behind the walls, the phone hackers who listen in, and now thanks to Truf's heroics last night, the German living down the hallway.

I called Megs. She answered almost immediately.

'Gary. Lovely to hear from you. It's really exciting news. I'm thrilled it's...'

'Megs!' I cut her off, my tone was urgent. 'Shut the fuck up - Right now. Not another word.'

I had a terrible feeling from what she had just said that Tim had told her about our gold discovery. In spite of both Truf and me drumming it into him that nobody, outside the three of us, could know.

'I want you to answer my next questions with either yes, or no. Did Tim call you and suggest we had made a *big* breakthrough?'

'Yes,' she answered cautiously.

'Did he specify what the breakthrough actually was?'

'Sort of..' She dragged the words out, like she didn't sound totally sure about the answer.

'Have you told anyone what he told you?'

'No.' She hesitated, then added, 'I was planning on letting Gran know.'

'Don't! It's imperative that nobody else knows. There'll be plenty of time for that later. Promise me, Megs. Not a word to anyone.'

'You're scaring me, Gary,' she said tentatively. 'But I promise I won't mention anything to anyone.'

'Okay. I'm sorry I yelled. But it's a really sensitive situation and Tim had no business blabbing to you. Who knows who might have been listening?'

'I understand. Bloody MI6 constantly have that van outside my house. One day I'm just going spill the beans and let them know which brand of detergent I use,' she laughed, mocking my OTT reaction. 'But, I am pleased things are going well for you in Australia, Garrett.'

'Thanks,' I said, grateful we had moved on. 'Megs, I need you to call Gerald and tell him you are happy for him to tear up the papers you signed recently.'

'Why would I want him to do that?'

I sighed loudly down the phone and said very slowly, 'Because it will be helpful with my *sensitive* situation.'

'Oh! I understand, now - I think. Sort of... Sorry. I'm a bit slow at the moment. I'm not used to my brother telling me to *shut the fuck up.'*

'I'm sorry about that, Megs. I had to stop you saying anything inappropriate.'

'Apology accepted, Gary. I'll give Gerald a call and do as you wish. But only if you promise not to take it out on Tim. He was just excited and wanted to share what he had.'

'Okay. Deal,' I agreed. 'I have to go Megs. Got a lot to do. I'll talk as soon as I can.'

'Bye..' she said, but before I'd had a chance to hang up, she added, 'Gary, are you still there?'

'Yep,' I answered, hiding my annoyance.

'You're very wound up at the moment,' she informed me. 'You need to do whatever it is that guys do to relieve that situation.'

'Ha,' I half snorted, half laughed into the phone. 'You're a grudge holding cow, little sister.'

She chuckled back. '*Big* sister. And don't you forget it.'

I was still as mad as hell with Tim. The useless bastard can't follow simple instructions and risked tearing the whole plan apart. Not that he knew even a small part of the plan.

I'd promised Megs I wouldn't take it out on him. I assume she meant not beating the shit out of him, which was exactly what I had intended to do, up to that point in time. But, I could still yell at him and call him a stupid prick, which ironically was something I'd been dying to do ever since I met him. He'd managed to change my feelings about that during this trip. But in typical Tim style he'd been able to erase my warm, fuzzy feelings towards him with one simple conversation.

I wanted to get this nasty business behind us, so we could move forward - all of us on the same page. I didn't want to accidentally run into Bev at this exact moment so I went to my window; my entry to the shared balcony and climbed out. As luck would have it, Tim's window was wide open, so I charged over to it and climbed straight in. I planned to start yelling as soon as I was inside. But I couldn't. My mouth refused to work because it was gapping open.

I was greeted with the sight of two naked bodies lying back on the bed. Two sets of eyes were drilling into me. From the way they were stretched out I concluded that any business they were involved in had already been dealt with.

Bev recovered her composure first. 'Good morning, Gary,' she said cheerfully, as she slipped off the bed. 'I was just on my way out.' She picked up her towel, wrapped it around her body and walked out the door as if she had just come to deliver breakfast - or something. 'I'll see you boys for breakfast a little later on.'

I glared at Tim and shook my head. He had taken Bev's exit as a good time to throw on some shorts and was standing beside the bed looking at me. His expression was more than a little worried.

He should be. I charged at him, expecting he would run, but he just stood there and watched me come at him. It was almost as if he wanted to be punished. *Have it your way, old son,* I thought as my right fist plunged into his face. His head snapped back and his body crashed to the floor with a loud thud and skidded into the wall.

I massaged my fist, which hurt like hell, which made me wonder what his eye must be feeling like.

Tim shook his head in an attempt to clear any fogginess, then brought his hand up and felt around his eye socket.

I guess he was checking if any bones had broken. It was a good hit, but not that good.

'I'm sorry about what you just saw, Gary,' he said, eventually. 'You had every right to do what you did.'

'Megs is too fucking good for you, Tim,' I said with as much venom as I could muster.

'I know... I know... I know,' he almost wept to me. 'I'm so sorry. I didn't know what to do,' he said as he climbed up off the floor. 'I woke up to see Bev standing at the end of my bed. Naked. She was wiggling my toe to wake me. Before I knew it she was climbing on the bed and coming towards me.' While he told his story he moved back to the bed and sat on it, still massaging his swollen eye. He looked up and continued his explanation. 'I love Megan more than you can imagine, Gary. I hate the thought of hurting her.' He stared at me through his one functioning dopey eye, shook his head, and said, 'What would you have done, Gary? If it had been you? She practically raped me.'

I was fast loosing this argument and I hadn't even uttered one word. I knew damn well what I'd have done. In fact I'd already done it. But I wasn't giving up my advantage. This was a time to score points.

'I'm not married, Tim,' I answered, feeling thoroughly guilty for taking the pious, I'm better than you, approach. 'And I don't have two beautiful little girls that I'm responsible for.' I looked intently at him and shook my head. 'But I love Megan, too, and I can't see anybody gaining from her finding out what just happened. So we'll put this behind us and move on.'

He nodded in agreement.

I could see gratitude in his eye. I think the other one would have been showing resentment. Instead, it was turning a pretty shade of purple and swelling up nicely.

'When we get back to Brisbane the first thing you're going to do is have some blood tests at a sexual health clinic.' *Me too - but Ill be going to a different clinic.* 'And you're not going near Megs until the all-clear is given. Agreed?'

'Agreed.'

There was an awkward pause between us after all the dirty linen had been aired. It seemed appropriate.

'Megan is the reason I came barging into your room just now,' I said to him after a suitable period of reflection. 'I just spoke to her and she said you told her all about our big secret.'

'What?' He sounded shocked at my accusation. 'I didn't tell her anything about *that*. All I said was we'd found something that we should be able to use to get something good happening. I kept it really general. She doesn't know anything, Gary. I'm not stupid. I know how important it is to keep a lid on it.'

I left Tim's room the same way I entered. Well, not exactly. I was feeling angry and superior when I entered. On the way out I was feeling guilty and embarrassed.

Megs was right... I was bound up tighter than a baby in a blizzard. I needed a shower. Urgently. But I restrained myself until Culgawinya's public access vagina had finished with the bathroom.

Aunt Maude's theory was gaining credence.

***

I felt better after my shower. There's nothing like a good scrub to freshen a fella up. I had been in the middle of checking my emails when the Tim distraction had occurred so I went back to my laptop and and re-read the stuff from Sky.

Then I opened Sophie's email. It was in bullet points as I had requested.

A holding greater than 20% triggers a requirement to make a takeover bid.

But, under the Foreign Acquisitions Act, non-Australians may be required to bid if a holding exceeds 15%. Decisions are made for each individual case by the Takeovers Panel.

Warehousing - parking shares with a friend - Banned.

Working in concert with other shareholding parties constitutes an Associate arrangement. Will trigger the need for Takeover offer.

Takeovers Panel is for resolving disputes. If nobody disputes, they stay out of it.

I could see from that information that I was in for a

tough time if anybody disputed the way I planned to go about this takeover. The definition of related parties was a key. I could argue that I had no influence over what Gran, and Megs did with their shares, and I would be correct. But a half decent lawyer can have people swearing that black is actually white, in no time at all. And I didn't want it to get to that. I needed to avoid having the Takeover Panel brought into the equation and that required some fancy footwork from me. I needed a nice clean kill - wham, bam, thank you ma'am, I'm the new boss of Plutarch, and have everybody okay with that, even the current bosses.

A big ask, but I had a plan.

My email inbox was getting clogged so I spent the next half an hour clearing it. When it had been reduced to a small number I noticed the emails from Sky and Sophie that I'd only glanced at last night were still there. I read them properly.

The body of Sophie's email was about the financial status of the major shareholders of Plutarch, but her final paragraph had some interesting information about Warra's art.

Warra's paintings are sold exclusively in six galleries around the world. In London. Paris, Rome, Los Angeles, Miami and New York. Each gallery has its own principal dealer. But I dug deep, Gary. Really deep - as this was never intended to be found out.. All the galleries are ultimately owned by one man, hiding behind numerous holding companies, scattered around various tax-haven countries with non-disclosure rules. Oscar Barrymore. He is based in Sydney, Australia. His business is called Barrymore Fine Art. Ironically he has galleries in Australia, but they don't sell Warra's paintings. (fishy??)

Warra must be a rich man as his works sell between $10,000 - $50,000(US). How many do you want me to buy?

The Bond Girl.

Fishy, didn't begin to cover it. But... useful. I intended to do some more research myself, on Oscar Barrymore when I had emptied my inbox.

I composed a quick email for Soph:

Dear Goldfinger (NB - extension willingly added) Brilliant work. Need one more thing. Pls. send me a list of every Warra painting currently for sale in every location. ASAP. Incl. list price and total retail value of whole package.

M

After I had dispatched my reply to Sophie I opened Sky's email and read it. She had mainly given me the same information about Plutarch that I already knew, only in more detail. I found the money being spent on exploration and drilling rather large given what I had witnessed and I definitely intended to get Truf's opinion on that. The company was low in current assets, which means money for wages and rent and so on. It was going to need to raise some funds from its shareholders, soon. There was no way a bank would be willing to lend it money in the financial shape it was in. As a final note she had copy/pasted the remuneration packages of the Executives and Directors of Plutarch Resources. At the head of the list, with the title of Managing Director, was the name Felix Geyer. Annual income $350,000.

***

248

Truf kept looking at Tim and then at me across the breakfast table. The look on his face told me he had done the math and worked out that Tim's black eye was a present from me. The question he was dying to ask me, was why? Sorry, old boy, that one was on a need-to-know basis.

He'd already probed Tim about it and been told, 'I slipped in the bloody shower.'

He could hold back no longer and turned to me and said, 'You popped him, didn't you, Gary?'

I looked at him like he was insane. 'He told you.. He did it in the shower.'

'Yeah! Sure..'

It wasn't like Truf to delve this deeply into other people's lives, to actually call someone a liar meant he wasn't going to let this go. I could see his point, if there was trouble between the three of us he should know. But the trouble was behind us, so I said, with an exasperated look on my face, 'Okay! You've got us Truf. Tim and I were in the shower... together,' I rolled my eyes for dramatic affect. 'And, well, things got a little overheated and he went down and banged his eye.' I grinned at him. 'Is that what you wanted to hear?'

He looked at me with what was almost a glare and was going to take it further when our mad, orange haired waitress appeared at the table. She had her pad and pen ready and seemed to have little interest in flirtatious small-talk this morning.

'Morning.. What can I get you, today?'

Truf was the only one of us who responded to her greeting before giving her his breakfast order. Tim and I gave her our respective orders and then she turned to leave.

'Bev, wait up a second, please,' I said.

She turned back with a worried look on her face.

I returned her look with a solemn face and said, 'I have one small question for you.'

She bit at her bottom lip, and waited.

'Could you tell me the name of your German guest?'

She almost sighed out loud with relief, and said, 'Felix. Felix Geyer.'

'Thank you.'

After she had gone back to the kitchen and we had the room to ourselves I said to the other two, 'The Managing Director of Plutarch Resources is a fellow called - Felix Geyer.'

Truf looked surprised. Tim, not surprisingly, only looked half surprised.

'That's pretty unusual, isn't it Truf, that a company MD would be supervising the actual mining operation?' I asked.

'If it was a small private company, then sure, it would be normal. But, unheard of in a Stock Exchange listed company. The big bosses sometimes pay a visit to see how the money is actually being spent, that might be what's happening here.'

'I don't think so,' I said, 'George told us he'd rented the room to Felix for six months.'

After a delicious breakfast of bacon, eggs and a few other heart stopping ingredients we headed off through town on our way back to the aboriginal campsite. I noticed a sign on a battered old shop that said, "B. Smith - Solicitor" and I quickly asked Truf to pull over and park in front.

I opened the car door and said, 'Give me a minute, fellas. I need to check something with this guy.' I slammed the door shut before either could complain about the wait. They had no reason to, they were the ones in the air conditioning.

The entrance to B. Smith's office was a wooden door with flaky paint and a loose, rickety old doorknob that would have been unsuitable even for an outdoor toilet. I assumed from this low to no security approach, that crime in Culgawinya was not rampant and we needn't have panicked about someone stealing our car. I turned the knob, pushed the door open and entered the single room to find B. sitting behind his desk with a look of mild intrigue on his face.

'G'day mate. I'm Bryan Smith. What can I do for you?'

I introduced myself and explained what I needed. Bryan turned out to be a very nice fellow, even more so, when he explained his fee for the services I wanted performed. Unlike Gerald's million for every six minutes, Bryan's fee was well within my budget. We parted company having arranged a loosely timed appointment for later that day.

I climbed into the car and into the middle of a conversation. I was the subject apparently, as Truf was saying, 'Nah.. Definitely a will. He's scared of everything out here and Nine's untimely departure, yesterday, has done him in.'

I had missed Tim's opinion but guessed it would be way off the mark, too. I decided to cut them out of the loop for their rude behavior. I said, in my most superior voice, 'All done - Take me to the wilderness. Drive on, my good man.'

As we moved away, Tim asked, 'Well... What was that all about?'

'I'll tell you later,' I said. I wasn't ready to get back to buddy status with him, just yet. 'It might have been a waste of time.'

We entered the campsite and there seemed to be a lot more people here this time. Many had painted lines and dots on their bodies in various colors and a large fire was raging in the middle of the compound.

'I hope they aren't pissed at us for something,' Tim said, half-jokingly.

Apparently not, as about five kids immediately launched themselves at the car and climbed up to wherever a seat could be found. One sat right in front of Truf and rested against the windscreen, making driving next to impossible.

Truf pushed the button on the end of the wiper lever, which caused a jet of water to spray all over the window and the little guy, who immediately screamed and jumped off the bonnet in a fit of laughter.

We pulled up under a shade tree and made our way to where Warra, Bully and a group of men sat. All the men except Warra had paint on their upper bodies and faces.

'Morning boys,' Warra said as we approached.

'Morning,' the three of us chanted in unison. We smiled and nodded to the other men.

'What's with the painted bodies?' Tim asked.

'Chief's burial for the boy's dog,' Bully answered. 'It's a big deal, all the cousins and nephews come from all over. The bloody dog's a hero.'

'He certainly is,' Truf agreed. 'Where's Joey?'

'He resting, over there,' Bully said as he pointed to a tree with a small body curled up beside its trunk in the shade. 'Pretty torn up about the dog.'

We stayed with the group for a few minutes and then I asked Warra if we could talk to him about what we needed to do today.

'Sure boys,' he said, as he slowly got up from his seat on the tree-trunk. I could tell from his knobby-knees and the knuckles on his fingers that he had arthritis. Not a good outcome for one who's talent is painting.

We walked over to his hut where his works were stored. 'I have some bad news, Warra,' I told him. 'But first, I want you to look at this, and tell me if you know this man.' I held my phone in front of him. It had a picture of Oscar Barrymore that I had transferred over from the man's website.

'Hey. That's Aussie. He looks pretty neat in that picture,' he joked. 'When he come here he got his big-ass shorts on and a big hat.'

'His name is Oscar Barrymore, Warra, and he's stealing from you.'

'No way, mate. He's a good bloke,' Warra said with total conviction.

I hadn't told Truf and Tim about Sophie's discoveries and they were looking at me questioningly.

'He's selling your paintings all around the world, except Australia. And the markets not quite as *shit* as he told you, Warra. Your works are being sold for between $10,000 and $50,000 each. You are somewhat of a celebrity in the art world.'

'What the fuck you sayin? $10,000 to $50,000 for my paintings?' Warra exploded. 'The bastard give me $100. Shit! $50,000! You sure?'

'I'm positive.'

Warra was too stunned to talk for a moment and I

could tell all three men were keen to find out more, so I told them what I knew about Oscar's setup. When I was finished all three were shaking their heads in amazement.

'The bloody audacity of the man,' Truf said. 'Knowing full well that Warra would never travel overseas and find out what he was up to. And not selling them here in Australia makes it almost impossible for any other art dealers to poach Warra away from him. I bet his sales people tell buyers that Warra lives in remote Western Australia or somewhere far, far from here.'

'Wow!' Tim said. 'That's one hell of a scam.'

'It certainly is. The rest of his business seems legitimate,' I added with an ironic smirk. 'He deals in high priced works from reputable artists all over the world. Warra is the icing on his artistic cake, so to speak. People trust their art dealer to tell them if works are good investments and Oscar has managed to build a market for Warra's paintings over the years. A market, that he alone controls.'

'The bugger's gunna get a spear up his ass next time he comes here,' Warra said, and I knew from his determined expression that he wasn't joking.

'That's one way to deal with him, Warra,' I said, not wanting to sound like I was lecturing him. 'But I think I have a better way.'

I explained how I thought we should handle it and all three agreed it would most likely provide a better outcome for Warra. Plus, it would avoid the need for Warra to do jail time. A win-win. Hopefully.

With that agreed on, Tim, Truf and I drove off to our gold zone - the mother-lode, hopefully. We could smell real money in the air as we approached. Not the Central Bank crap, this money was going to need extracting and was of a finite supply. The small escarpment that held our fortune seemed to sparkle to our eyes. It didn't. It was just our collective imaginations filling in some details. I helped unload the equipment for Truf and Tim and watched as Truf began instructing Tim about what he needed to do. They were only going to get a very rough idea from this work, but we were all keen to see what extra information we could uncover. My work done at the escarpment I drove back, on my own, to the aboriginal campsite.

Nine's Chief's funeral had apparently just concluded as I saw most of the visitors were leaving. They had cars that were similar to the two belonging to this campsite. They were even the same color. Rust. I watched as they drove off in the opposite direction to the one we had driven in by.

My plan to deal with Oscar involved "B. Smith - Solicitor" and Warra, getting together. Warra was happy to make the trip with me. In fact, I think he would have made his bare feet and arthritic legs do the journey, if that was what was required. Such was his desire to punish Oscar Barrymore.

Warra seemed very proud to be seen driving off in a shiny, only six year-old, car. Even if it was a weird white color. His head was held high and he waved like royalty to his people as we drove by.

'Why don't you blokes use the road?' he asked, as I turned on to my familiar track.

'I thought this was the road.'

'No bloody way, mate,' he said with a grin. 'Turn around and I'll show you.'

We headed back and I found myself driving in the same direction the visitors had. It was a proper track and was free from rabbit holes and termite nests. Very civilized, all it lacked was a white line down the middle. The track was about half a mile long and then we turned on to a real road. It was still made out of dirt, but had been made by the local council, I gather, rather than a few local cars and trucks forcing a passage. Before long we were on the now familiar road back to Culgawinya. Ironically, the three of us had only missed seeing the real side road by about a quarter of a mile on our first day out here. It seems luck is a finite thing. Mind you, I wasn't complaining about my luck, so far, on this trip.

I discussed my plans in more detail with Warra on the drive to Bryan's office. I thought he might have some reservations about one of my requirements, which was the necessity for Warra to open a bank account, but he was so pissed at Oscar he was putty in my hands.

Bryan was very professional in the way he dealt with Warra. He understood that Warra was his client and wasn't educated about what he was actually doing, and he went to great lengths to explain it all. Part of the paperwork for my plan involved giving me "Power of Attorney" over his works. And Bryan pointedly asked Warra if he trusted me as this paper gave me the right to spend his money as I saw fit. I was both offended and impressed at the same time. He managed to dumb it down in a nice way, so Warra understood completely, and gave him every opportunity to withdraw if I was, in some way, forcing him into this arrangement.

Warra said, 'No bloody worries, mate. He a good bloke. His grandma a good lady, too.'

I worried that Warra wouldn't have a signature. Then

I remembered he was an artist and artists always signed their works. It was a security thing. Bryan had marked with an X where Warra needed to make his mark. His way too big artist's signature dominated the page, and the nice lady from the cake shop next door witnessed everything. Then, the three of us walked down the road to the local bank and opened an account for Warra. He didn't have any money with him so I offered up $10 to start the account. We opted for a savings account as ATM's were a little thin on the ground where Warra lives.

The Bank Manager accepted a copy of my Power of Attorney and set up Warra's account to be operated through my computer. Warra's address was listed as Bryan's office address. Street numbers were hard to find on Warra's front fence and letter-box. Go figure.

I transfered Bryan's fee, a total of $350, directly into his account. He had my details for any last minute extra charges that might occur. And with that, Warra and I were done with our business in Culgawinya. Well almost, I popped into the cake shop and bought a dozen of Judith's cream buns to thank her for her trouble.

I wondered how much of Gerald's lawyer time $350 Aussie dollars would have purchased. *Hello Gerald...* I'm sorry, Garrett. Your time is up.

A we dove off Warra attacked the buns. He was thoroughly impressed with the air-conditioned comfort that was much more effective at cooling than the cranked open side window of his own vehicle.

I dropped Warra back at his camp amongst his people and he grabbed the bag of eight cream buns off the seat to share with his family and waved me goodbye.

257

Truf and Tim were working at opposite sides of the gold zone as I pulled up. I walked to where Truf was working and Tim strolled over to join us. Truf explained what he'd discovered so far.

'The main seam of gold that I'm following is still quite strong all the way back here,' he said, indicating and area where he had scrapped some sandy, topsoil away to reveal the beautiful quartz with its specks of gold. I noticed that he had back-filled any earlier digging to, hopefully, conceal it from accidental discovery. 'There is absolutely no way I can check the depth without involving what is called a trenching study. For that, I need a backhoe and approval from the Authorities to dig a series of trenches that follow the gold seams. They usually give approval to dig about a meter down and and across and take samples along the way to get an idea of the inferred resource and the ore grade in the area.'

'I'm still getting gold showing where I'm working,' Tim added, giving us more reason to be happy and we all grinned like kids in a candy shop.

'Given that Tim and I have just picked one gold vein each and followed it to where we are at the moment, I think it's safe to say this is a big find. There are numerous other gold veins snaking off in different directions, but it wouldn't give me anymore actual information at this stage to investigate them as well.' He wiped his brow with his sleeve and smiled. 'My professional *guess,* Gary, is that there will be enough gold here to cover the cost of any takeover. Your downside is around zero. Your upside is unlimited.'

Tim looked at me with his working eyebrow raised. 'Takeover?'

'Trust me, Tim. If it works out, it will be good for Megan and you.'

We spent the next half an hour walking around the area. Each of us carried a section of bush in one hand and a clump of grass in the other. We systematically brushed the area clear of any evidence of digging. Back at the original site where we had first picked up the *special* rocks, we made a point of removing any rocks we could find that showed obvious gold. We carted them to the crevice where Joey had fought with the brown snake and tossed them into the darkness.

The dead snake had disappeared from what was meant to be its final resting place. Food is food in this part of town. I wondered if dingoes or some other small carnivores had dispatched it to their respective intestinal tracts. Maybe a tree had eaten it? But, surely the pointy end with the venom was still dangerous? I'd read that in my research: It's a tough land where even dead animals can still kill.

As a final gesture of covertness Truf and Tim walked backwards behind the Land Cruiser which I drove at walking pace, and they brushed away any footprints and tire marks.

Our job here was done. I drove back to Warra's camp and explained to him that we were going back to the city to work out our next step in our quest to help him and his people. As a parting gesture we unloaded most of the items we had purchased for the journey and hadn't used. The three tents were particularly popular as were the torches and spades.

'When do you think you fellas will be back?' Warra asked quietly. I got the impression he was a little saddened by our departure.

'I can't say, Warra,' I gave him a smile and a shrug of my shoulders. 'This is where it gets complicated.'

As we left Warra, Tim said to Truf and me, 'I still have to teach Joey how to kick his football.'

'You can use the time to learn how to kick one yourself, Tim,' I added with a chuckle.

***

Sunny had arrived a little late for the day's shoot. Simon didn't comment, in fact he barely spoke to her all day. She caught glimpses of him looking at her when he thought she wasn't noticing. It was as if he was assessing how well his "clueless victim" rape business was going. *If things go to plan, he's going to find out just how clueless this victim is.*

During her lunch break Sunny had driven off and returned just in time to help Brian, the director, set up his next shot. Sunny had been at pains to appear as normal as she could. It was difficult and uncomfortable talking to Simon and she kept the few conversations she had with him short, light and reasonably cheerful. At one stage of the day she was talking to David Delaney, the host of their show, Impressive People, and she caught sight of Simon in a mirror; he was staring at her with a fixed expression from the side, totally unaware that she could see him. It freaked her out, witnessing the intensity of his gaze. She was definitely an object to him. To test her theory, she laughed at something David said and put her hand on his shoulder in a warm, inviting gesture. The frown that appeared on Simon's face confirmed her theory; in his mind she was *his* object.

As they were packing up at the end of the shoot Simon came over to her. 'Do you have any work to finish up at the office tonight, Sunny?'

'Unfortunately, I do. What about you?'

'Yes. I have some calls to make.'

'Good. I was hoping to have a chance to talk to you in private about that subject you raised the other day.' She looked at him but he seemed unsure what she was talking about. 'The career opportunity you mentioned,' she added.

'Yeah, okay,' he agreed, with an unreadable smile.

It was important for Sunny's plan that Simon should not get back to the office before her. If he did there was a chance he would go to his filing cabinet and find something was missing in the "R" file and would instantly know she was onto him. For this reason she left immediately, even though she was meant to stay around and help with the packing up.

She was sitting at her desk when Simon turned up fifteen minutes after her. All the other office staff had been packing up to go, just as Sunny had arrived back at the office. They were grateful as that meant they didn't need to lock-up for the night.

'Brian's a little pissed at you for leaving so early,' he said, as he walked towards her. 'What was that all about? I didn't hear any fire-alarms go off.'

'I'm sorry about that. I'll apologize to him tomorrow,' she said and mustered up a smile. 'I remembered that I needed to call Barry Jenkins, the standby camera guy we need for a shoot next Tuesday and his number was back here in the office. He was catching a plane and I had to get him before 5:00. Anyway, it all worked out.'

Simon nodded.

Sunny swiveled in her chair towards him. She was holding a bottle of wine. 'I need the advice of a man who knows his way around a good bottle of red, Simon. Are you up for it?' She already had two wine glasses sitting on her desk in anticipation of his answer. She knew him well enough to know he'd be unlikely to reject the offer, especially when he saw the wine. She had spent 55 pounds on the bottle and knew it was good - well, at least the guy at the store said it was.

'Domaine de Chevalier Rouge, 2009,' he said, with a sly smile. 'What's the occasion?'

'I met a guy a week or so back and I quite like him,' she said, as she took the bottle from Simon and began to pour it into the glasses. 'He's been away on business and he's getting back tomorrow and I thought I'd cook him a special dinner. If you say this wine is good I'll get some for the meal.' She put a little extra in Simon's glass for two reasons. It would help dissolve the white powder she had already put carefully into the base of the glass, and it would avoid the possibility of mixing up the glasses.

'Sounds like this new man is going to have a special night, tomorrow.'

Sunny ignored the innuendo and she made a point of swirling Simon's wine as she handed it to him. She was pleasantly surprised to see that the Rohypnol left no visible trace at all. She made a point of sniffing her wine, like a proper wine taster would do. Simon did likewise. She grudgingly, had to admire the way Simon was playing things. The bastard was certainly cool and in control.

'That's assuming he survives my cooking. That's

why I need a nice wine, so at least part of the meal will be tasty and memorable,' she forced a laugh and held her glass for Simon to clink his against, then they both took a sip.

Sunny commented first. 'Well, to my laywoman's palate, that seems to do the job. Delicious.'

Simon nodded in agreement. 'Excellent. I must remember this one.' He held out his hand and Sunny passed him the bottle so he could study it.

'Drink up, boss. I plan on getting you drunk and getting a commitment out of you about this on-camera career you suggested yesterday.' She took another sip and noticed a spark come into Simon's eyes as he sensed an opportunity was coming up.

'We would need to work a lot closer if we we're going to pull that off,' he said as he took another mouthful of the wine. 'I mean, I would need to know you a lot better, to find the position that would suit you; to give you the best chance of success.'

'I think you know me very well, already,' she countered, trying hard to not give her words any subtle inflection. 'I think a position as co-host would be ideal. On a show that was light, but not stupid or silly like so many of the shows around today. I'm happy starting on cable, but if one of the main channels became available, all the better.'

Simon emptied his glass of wine and she hoped there wasn't any residue of the chemical still on the bottom. If there was he didn't notice as he poured himself another glass, keen to get as much of the liquid as possible. Then he topped her glass up, as well.

'You certainly have the looks... Sunny. And you have a nice... voice. And you're smart... and sexy,' he said, talking in a staccato manner as the drug took hold of him. 'And... you have a nice... voyzzz... too.' He looked at her with a confused, worried look and his upper body began to sway.

Sunny smiled at Simon. She was amazed at how quickly the stuff worked. 'Let's go into your office.' She put her glass down on her desk, stood up and gently led him, wobbly legged, through to his office, where she sat him on the couch. The same couch she must have been led to the night before.

Deja vu... All over again. She smiled tightly, and took the wineglass from his hand.

Simon sat there, his eyes seemed to be spinning, his lids began fluttering, then his head slumped forward and he slowly fell onto his side, his head coming to rest on the armrest.

Sunny pressed her fingers into his neck at the point in his jawbone to check his pulse. It was weak, but steady. Then she peeled one of his eyelids back and saw his pupil was twitching from side to side.

She left him and went back to her desk, picked up her wineglass and sipped it as she went to the office front door. She bolted it closed and turned off the lights in the reception area. Anyone looking in would assume the staff had all left. She knew the cleaners would not be in for another two nights and it was unheard of for any of the office staff to come back at night. She and Simon were the only ones in the office who did that. They had the place to themselves.

The equipment Sunny needed lay waiting where she had hidden it just before Simon had arrived. She retrieved it and carried it into his office. It didn't take long to set it up. Then she went to Simon and lifted him back into a sitting position. She slid off his jacket and then unbuttoned his shirt and slid it off him. He sat on his couch, bare chested with his head slumped forward, his chin resting on his chest.

Then she untied his shoes and removed them. Then his socks. Next, she unbuckled his belt and slipped open the button on his pants, then she slid down the zipper on his fly. He only needed the gentlest of pushes to make him fall sideways again. Sunny worked his trousers over his hips and then his boxers quickly followed. She pulled at the cuffs of his pants and wiggled them out from under his body until the pants came completely off. Then came his boxers. She threw all of his clothes onto his desk.

He was totally naked.

She looked at him, unimpressed, and thought of the sport he must have had at her expense last night. She had a sudden urge to punch him in the face, but restrained herself.

The equipment she had brought into his office was her 35mm Nikon Digital SLR camera and a tripod. She set it up in what she thought would be the best position. She propped her makeup mirror behind the camera allowing her to see the viewfinder when she joined him on the couch. When she had him framed the way she wanted she moved to the final part of her plan.

She took off all her clothes, removed her watch and her necklace and put on her one prop. Sunny became one of a million young women.

Sunny climbed on top of Simon's comatose body and imagined how he must have done much the same thing last night. His weapon had been a condom sheathed penis, her weapon was a wireless remote to control the camera's shutter. She angled his face so the Nikon could make him out clearly. She checked her mirror as she positioned her thigh to hide his sex organs, but still giving the impression he was inside her, even though his penis was totally limp and incapable of the act. Her own head would be turned away from the camera and the shoulder length blond wig she was wearing would give no hint that it was Sunny on top of him.

She fired the shutter off repeatedly, after every few shots she moved his head or his arm or leg, giving a variety of positions to create the image that he was an active participant. She even pretended to kiss him on the mouth for some of the pictures.

She climbed off him and played back her work through the viewfinder. Some of the shots looked staged, but quite a few were believable. She smiled to herself, she really only needed one. Job done.

Simon lay on the couch, naked and exposed. She didn't care if he woke in the middle of the night and made his way home, or the office staff found him like that in the morning. Either outcome suited her plan.

She quickly dressed and packed her camera gear back into its bag. She drank the remains of the wine in her glass and re-corked the bottle which was still a third full. She turned off all the lights and went to the office door. As she began to lock the door, she stopped and withdrew her key from the slot. That was nearly a tactical mistake. She left the building with a grin on her face; it occurred to her that she had just done her first, and more than likely last, porn shoot. And it wasn't too hard at all. She laughed out loud as that thought passed through her head.

No animals had been harmed in the making of this production. That was coming tomorrow.

Chapter 9

Truf and Tim were impressed that I had found the correct entrance to the camp, and sarcastically pointed out my timing was impeccable. Our mood was cheerful and light as we drove back to the hotel. It was early afternoon when we pulled up and we had collectively decided to drive back to Brisbane that afternoon.

Both George and Bev were working in the main bar when we entered and told them we were leaving.

'It's a shame to see you go, boys,' Bev said with an enigmatic smile. 'I hope you all enjoyed your stay here.' She glanced at Tim's purple eye and her smile briefly widened.

Truf, fortunately, spoke for all of us. 'We've had a wonderful time, thank you both for everything.'

'It's been a pleasure having you fellas,' George added, unaware that it was really his wife he was speaking for.

I wanted to add something complimentary along the lines of - *especially you Bev, your concept of customer service is way beyond what guests expect.*

From the look on Tim's face I guessed he would have liked to add a similar comment.

We packed quickly, settled the bill with George and hit the road. Tim and I were anxious to put the amusements of this little one whore town behind us. Truf seemed unusually keen to get to Brisbane.

We made it by 9:45 p.m. and checked into our city hotel. Truf had intended to give Sammy a call when he arrived, but was just as stuffed as Tim and I were from the drive. I was pissed-off with Sunny's complete lack of concern regarding returning my calls, so in a mini-tantrum, I punished her by resisting the urge to dial her number. *Was my new relationship falling over at the first hurdle?*

All three of us crawled into our lovely soft beds and slept like Sleeping Beauty. Without the beauty part.

In the morning I woke refreshed and invigorated. I was keen to see what communications I had received; maybe Sunny might have found the time to write a word or two, so I fired up my laptop. Sunny hadn't, but Sophie had sent me the list of Warra's paintings currently for sale.

My jaw dropped when I reached the bottom of the list. 67 works for sale. Total ask price $1.85 million in US dollars.

I had a shower and dressed in my normal *work* clothes. That is, Chinos and a colored or patterned business shirt and tie, with a jacket on top. Neat, with a hint of casual, I'm aiming for the "I'm a successful entrepreneur who doesn't need to try hard by wearing an expensive suit", look. I felt almost normal again. Something about wearing shorts makes it impossible to maintain a "please take me seriously" attitude. Today was going to get serious; I needed my uniform.

I met up with the other two at the breakfast buffet. As we ate I laid out my plans for the day.

'Tim,' I said, 'I need you to change into work clothes after breakfast. You and I are catching a plane to Sydney in an hour and a half.'

He looked at me, somewhat confused. 'I was planning a day of sight-seeing and...' he raised his eyebrows at me, 'maybe getting a medical check-up.

Why do I need to go to Sydney?'

'I've set up a meeting for you with Frank Spiller, an old mate of mine,' I said. 'Frank is a public relations expert. He's the guy celebrities go to when they get caught with their pants down doing something with someone else's spouse, or calling a cop a bigot and having it caught on tape.'

Tim glared at me. I realized he thought I was taking the piss out of him for his step from the path of righteousness with Bev.

I grinned at him. 'You are going to show your pictures of the poisoned dump site and billabong to Frank and have him work out a way to leak them to the media. But not until the middle of the afternoon... tomorrow.'

Tim relaxed and I watched his face - waiting.

It only took him a moment and his face suddenly changed. 'But, that will kill Plutarch Resources,' he said, with a look of horror. 'The share price will fall out of bed!'

I smiled broadly at him. 'You think?'

My mocking of him caused a rethink. To his credit, he almost got there.

'You want the price low, so you can buy it cheaply,' he announced with a triumphant grin.

'Not exactly, Tim. That would be illegal. I'll explain everything, later. Today is going to have to come together like a well-disciplined military exercise. If too much goes wrong then I'm likely to end in the toilet.. or more correctly, in jail.'

Truf had been looking on in quiet amusement. 'What role does General Nixon have for Private Truf.'

I smiled at him. 'I think we can do better than

Private for you, Truf.' I laughed at the fact he picked up on my my military description of the day ahead. 'Your job is the best of all. You get to play with Sammy. You have to store our rock collection at her place anyway, and I figure we'd have a hard time getting you back from that assignment - so you might as well have *most* of the day off, Corporal!'

'Corporal? I was expecting something at least higher than Captain.' He gave me his unhappy face, then continued. 'What do you mean... "most" of the day off?'

'I've emailed you a rundown of Plutarch's stated mining expenses. I'd like your professional opinion of how well they sit with the actual work they have been doing at the drill sites.'

'I'll definitely try and fit that into the schedule.'

'And, of course you have that important phone call to make to a certain cardiologist. Make sure you follow up with an email stating exactly what you discuss with him.'

Truf nodded knowingly back at me.

Ten minutes later I was back in my room. I made a call.

'Barrymore Fine Art. Julie Ickx, speaking.'

'Ms. Ickx, this is Garrett Nixon from the Nixon Fund in London. I need to speak with Mr. Oscar Barrymore, please.'

'I'm terribly sorry Mr. Nixon, but Mr. Barrymore is in a meeting and cannot be interrupted.'

'What I have to say to Mr. Barrymore is of the utmost importance... to him! I hate to be pushy, Ms Ickx, but I'm about to get on a plane and fly to Sydney for the sole purpose of meeting with Mr. Barrymore this afternoon. I need to verify that I'm not wasting my time.'

'You're flying from London in an hour, and you are expecting a meeting this afternoon?' She sounded incredulous.

I wasn't taking any crap from a secretary. I said, 'Don't be stupid, Ms. Ickx. I've already flown from London. I'm waiting in Brisbane for a connecting flight to Sydney. Please put me through to Mr. Barrymore.'

'Like I said Mr. Nixon, he's in a meeting.'

This was dragging on too long. I cut her off, by almost shouting down the phone, 'Enough of this nonsense. I'll put it to you as simply as I can, Ms. Ickx. Put Barrymore on the phone immediately, or he will not have a business by this time tomorrow, and you, Ms. Ickx, will be looking for another job, protecting somebody else's over-inflated ego.'

There was silence over the line for a second, then she said, 'Hold the line, please.'

I waited at least thirty seconds before he picked up the phone, and said, 'What is all this melodramatic nonsense about, Mr. Nixon?'

'What I told Ms. Ickx is one hundred percent true and accurate, Mr. Barrymore. I will be in your office in approximately three hours. You need to clear your appointments so we can deal with our business.'

'And that business is?'

'Saving you and your company, Mr. Barrymore. I will say no more over the phone. Please understand that I do not fly half-way across the world for a prank. Do I have that appointment, Mr. Barrymore?'

'Well, I guess so. But, I'd....'

I hung up on him before he could complete the sentence. I knew that would piss him off and put him just that little bit more on edge.

Truf dropped Tim and me at the airport an hour later and continued on to deal with his first arduous task for the day. The lucky bastard.

On the flight I gave Tim an overview of what was happening and his role in the plan. I believe I saw some respect in his eyes when he looked at me.

***

Tim and I parted company outside the airport. Two different taxi's heading to different locations took us away. We were both booked on a 6:35 fight back to Brisbane.

Barrymore Fine Art was located in the city proper in George Street. My cab pulled up in front of a large windowed area that featured numerous, expensive looking works of art. Some were suspended near the glass by thin wires connected to the ceiling, others, on large artist's easels, were strategically placed on angles and lit by hidden lights, giving a passer-by a fine visual experience from every vantage point.

The name "Barrymore Fine Art" was emblazoned over the double-doors in large gold block letters. It was also painted in gold on each window at the front, it looked very classy. The taxi had pulled into a Loading Zone to drop me off, half of which was already taken by a late model soft-top Bentley Continental. I notice it had a parking ticket stuffed neatly under its wiper blade. I hope it belonged to Oscar. If it did, the ticket was going to be the cheapest part of his day.

I pushed my way through one of the doors and stood in a vast area which featured many different pockets of brightly lit areas. Numerous maze-like walkways fed through the room. On the side walls small simulated rooms had been created with only three walls. Each wall contained various artworks, all were lit expertly by concealed lights. The rooms contained sofas and club lounges consistent with the type of art that was being featured. I presumed the seating served a double role in allowing a sales assistant to casually sell the surrounding works over a cup of coffee, or maybe a glass of single-malt, if the would-be buyer looked like their bank balance had some extra zeros in it.

A beautiful brunette approached me from out of one of the maze-like passages. She too was a work of art dressed in clothes that do not come from department stores and a body that would have a similar price tag, metaphorically speaking.

'Can I help you, sir?'

I'm damn sure you could... No flirting here, Gary. Time for business.

'I'm Garrett Nixon. I have an appointment with Mr, Barrymore.'

'Ah! Mr. Nixon. I'm Julie Ickx. Mr. Barrymores Personal Assistant. I believe we spoke on the phone earlier in the day,' she said, as she offered me a thin smile and her hand in greeting.

'Indeed we did, Ms. Ickx,' I said in my best British businessman voice. Superior, with a little Public School thrown in for good measure. 'Thank you for your assistance.'

'Mr Barrymore is waiting for you,' she said, as she led me through the maze of artworks towards the rear. 'He's keen to find out what *catastrophe* you are bringing to him.'

She was mocking me, making light of my visit. 'That

is very apt,' I said to deflect her attempt to feign casualness.

'Which part is apt?' she countered. 'The catastrophe or that he is waiting for you?'

'Both,' I answered with a shrug of my shoulders. 'If we can't agree on how to fix the *catastrophe*, then I fear he will have lots of time to wait for his occasional visitor in his new accommodations.'

That shut her up.

She knocked on a very nice, dark-stained ornate wooden door and without waiting, proceeded into the office. I followed.

'Mr. Barrymore. This is Garrett Nixon.'

'Mr. Nixon,' he said with a curt nod of his head, as he offered me his hand.

'Mr. Barrymore,' I said and did exactly the same back to him.

Oscar was a man in his mid-fifties. His waistline was an advertisement for the fact that lack of money was not one of his problems. He had an aura of one who partook of the good-life as a matter of course and he regarded anyone who didn't fit that social class as unworthy of his attention and definitely unworthy of his respect. From the way he was looking at me he had already made up his mind about my unworthiness.

'Can I get anyone a drink?' Julie said, as she backed away towards the door.

'No thank you, Julie,' Oscar answered for both of us in an attempt at putting me in my rightful place.

As the door closed behind Julie, the polite, niceness ended. 'What the fuck do you want, Nixon?' He bellowed in a booming voice to me.

I'd met this type many times. The illusion of power

was all a facade, a collection of props and big ideas expressed to the people who were most susceptible to bragging. It was all as fake as a three dollar bill. I was now convinced that the Bentley out front was Oscar's - a prop. As was the five thousand dollar fine-wool suit he wore. Props and distractions, necessary for a fat little man who had managed to get to a certain elevated financial level in life, not through brains, not through strength of character, but by bullying and luck. By finding someone, who had an actual gift that he could manipulate at will.

Up until this moment.

I stared at him, not saying a word and keeping my face totally expressionless. Then, I slowly opened the shoulder-bag I was carrying; I bypassed the laptop and pulled out a copy of the Power of Attorney that Warra had assigned to me. I stood. I was a good half a head taller than Oscar and I loomed over him as he sat behind his expensive mahogany desk. Another prop. He was trying hard to look like he was still in control but I could see his eyes were wavering. They wandered to what I had retrieved from my bag. I slid the legal document in front of him so he could read it, then I sat back down.

'By the way, Oscar,' I said. 'That little outburst just cost you an extra quarter of a million dollars. May I call you Oscar? Or do you prefer... *Aussie*?' He glanced up quickly at the mention of Warra's version of his name. 'What you are reading is your copy of a legally registered Power of Attorney document, relating to Warra Goomagawa, giving me unchecked power to deal with Warra's affairs. We have a thorough understanding of the theft and corruption you have been undertaking for many years against Mr. Goomagawa.'

He looked up from the document, his eyes had regained some fight. 'Who the hell is Warra Goomawhatever?'

'Oscar, you're doing this all wrong,' I shook my head at him, a look of disappointment on my face. 'That lie just cost you another $250,000. We've only been at this for a minute and you've already wasted a half a million dollars, that I was originally prepared to allow you to keep.'

I reached into my bag and pulled out the list Sophie had compiled of Warra's paintings in Oscar's six galleries. I put it on his desk in front of me but didn't give it to him, I left it taunting him.

'There are two ways we can handle this nasty affair, Oscar,' I said, as I fixed a challenging look at him, with one eyebrow cocked.

Oscar was returning my look, except his eyebrows were more in frown mode. We were playing a game of charades - guess which mood I'm trying to portray? He was going for impassive with a hint of "don't fuck with me", I think. He must still believe he could get out of this. I wondered what he had in the way of trump cards to play. Bluffing certainly wasn't going to cut it.

'The first way is that we go public,' I said. 'Call in the Fraud Squad and go through all your sales records for the past twenty odd years. Then bring the Taxation people in to pick over the bones of whatever is found. Oh, and don't forget the Cultural Heritage Laws you have broken by exporting paintings over the value of $10,000 without getting approval. Then we take you to the Civil Court and sue for what you have cheated Warra out of and then double it for lost interest, plus penalties. In the meantime I will personally mount a publicity campaign across Europe and the States pointing out what a fraudulent asshole you are. There go your six galleries around the globe. Poof! Oscar goes broke. Oscar goes to jail.' I paused to take a reading of his expression.

He didn't like my first option very much. I could tell because I was getting good at seeing past his manufactured expressions.

I continued talking, never once taking my eyes off him. 'I can see from your expression that you're not too excited by option number one. I understand. Jail is the last place you want to find out you've just become a sex-toy. I'm not totally in favor of it either because of the time it will take. You might be dead before it got resolved. By the way, dead was Warra's first choice. I managed to persuade him to let me try doing it this way. Which brings me to option number two: You make a very, very big cash payment to Warra to make up for his lost profits over twenty odd years. The means of that payment will be determined by me.' I grinned at him for the first time.

He glared back at me; his expression was still stolid and unbending. It was time to bring him into line.

'Oscar,' I said, 'snap out of it, man. Option number two is time sensitive. If you plan to accept it you have to do so right now.' I slammed my hand down on his desk to emphasize my point and the noise seemed to break through a barrier. He shook his head; just a quick little shake, like he was casting aside something annoying. Was it denial finally being abandoned? Or was he scheming a way out of this mess? The look in his eyes had me momentarily wondering if he was going to pull a gun out from under the desk and shoot me.

'How much money are we talking about?'

Bingo!

Short, succinct, to the point. Oscar liked option two. My preferred one, also.

'There are two aspects involved here, Oscar. The first one is, and you'll find this funny, Warra doesn't give a flying-fart about money. So, in retrospect, had you been fairer, or more correctly less greedy, and paid him maybe $500 or $1,000 per picture, this little scam most likely would never have come undone. That said, the thing that Warra values more than anything else is the land he lives on. And that land is under threat from a mining company.'

'So?' Oscar said. His expression once again, indifferent.

'To make up for your wrongful treatment of Warra, I want you to buy the mining company for him, Oscar.'

His mouth gapped open, a look of horror spread over his face.

'I might have overstated that a little,' I smiled and continued. I was enjoying his discomfort. 'I want you to buy him 10% of that mining company. It's called Plutarch Resources and it is listed on the Australian Stock Exchange. How you do that and how much it costs you is dependent on your negotiating skills. Sadly, the people who own the parcel of shares I want you to purchase - the one's you'll need to negotiate with, aren't uneducated aborigines, but hardened, highly educated managers of two American Hedge funds.' I paused for him to absorb what I'd just said. The look on his face told me he accepted that he'd be the one getting screwed on this deal.

'The shares are trading at about 10 cents each at the moment and you'll need to buy about 10 million of them. That should require over $1 million to purchase the shares as they will ask for more than 10c. The Funds are not interested in ownership of the company; they will sell to you for the right price.'

Once again I studied his face. What I saw told me that the number I'd just quoted didn't concern him. This was good news, the last thing I needed to find out was that Oscar was leveraged up to his eyeballs and had no ready access to cash.

'But... you need to consummate that purchase by 3:00 p.m. tomorrow afternoon, or the deal is off. So pay the premium they ask and get the deal done.' Once again I paused to allow him to digest his instructions. 'You buy the shares and immediately transfer ownership to Warra Goomagawa. You will need to get your stockbroker to do that for you.'

'And that's it?'

I laughed out loud at him. 'Oscar, you need to sharpen up if you are going to get any good at this,' I berated him. 'Of course it's not all. Warra needs to be paid his rightful share of the profits from the sale of his paintings. $1.5 million dollars is what we require. A cash deposit into his bank account.

'He doesn't have a bank account,' Oscar said with a smug sneer.

'I guessed it was you who talked him into storing the cash you gave him in a bag in his hut,' I nodded at him, acknowledging the benefit to him of not having the Taxation people aware of what was going on. 'Anyway, he does have an account now,' I said as an aside, annoyed at myself for accidentally subtly giving Oscar a compliment. 'By the way that payment from you was only going to be $1 million until you became belligerent and rude.' I gave him a broad grin as I played my trump card.

'So, that's the lot?' He asked, seemingly relieved that I'd only asked for such a small amount.

I would never know how much *free* money Warra had provided Oscar over the twenty or so years he'd been fleeced by him. But, I was prepared to let Oscar keep some of it, as he had made a market for Warra's art. And that was no mean feat given that there are probably well over a million artists across the globe...

'The final requirement we have is that you return ownership of the 67 paintings you currently have in your galleries in Europe and America to Warra.' I pushed the list over the table for him to study. 'Or, if you want to buy them and save bringing undue attention upon yourself you can just pay the total retail value into Warra's account. An extra $1.85 million. That's US dollars, but for simplicity sake we will take it in Australian dollars.'

'You can have the fucking paintings back,' he sneered at me. 'I'll need two to three weeks to arrange it.'

That last demand made me realize Oscar had a way around the customs people. That made total sense and explained how he had been able to avoid the strict laws about selling aboriginal art to overseas buyers.

'67 paintings in good condition, Oscar. Or, $50,000 to replace every one that is missing or damaged. I will advise you where they are to be sent.'

'Are we done, now?'

Finally, I saw the defeated look I'd been waiting for.

'Almost,' I said, delving into my bag for the final time. 'I've taken the liberty to write down every demand we have. Just replace that $1 million number with $1.5 million. I've included Warra's bank details, plus the name and number of his lawyer. You should know that I have access to his bank account through my laptop. I'll know if you do anything stupid. Plus, my phone and email details are listed if you need to contact me. You will also find the names and numbers of the American hedge funds that each hold about 5% of Plutarch Resources. I want you to insist that they advise me of the transfer immediately it is completed. This is vital, Oscar. If you miss the deadline, which I repeat is 3:00 p.m. tomorrow, we instantly move to the first option. The "go straight to jail and don't pass go", option. Do you understand?'

'Yes,' he answered flatly as he glared at me.

'You have some small advantages. The time difference between here and the US will benefit you if you need to transfer funds. I suggest you start calling the Hedge Funds from about 9:30 tonight to catch them bright and early in their morning.'

I got up from my chair and stood over him. He looked very different from the man who had yelled at me just after we met. I had no sympathy for the man. He had been a fraud, a thief, a smuggler and who knows what, for a large part of his business career.

I left him without saying another word.

I made my way through the gallery, admiring the works that surrounded me. Julie approached me from the side. A look of concern on her face.

'He can be pretty tough,' she said to me. A look of

genuine concern covered her face 'I heard him yelling, I hope he wasn't too hard on you.'

I looked at her and laughed. She was beautiful and self-confident. If the business went under she would find another job very quickly. Beautiful people always do.

'Goodbye, Julie,' I smiled. 'Nice to meet you.'

As I waited out the front of Barrymore Fine Art for a passing cab to pick me up, I strolled over to the Bentley, to admire it. It was a beautiful dark blue color. The canvas top was the same blue color. Inside the seats were a luxurious rich tan. It was a magic looking beast. The only things that looked out of place, were the three parking tickets on the windshield.

As I lusted over the car a rather lovely mottled eggshell-gray pigeon landed gracefully on the Bentley's canvas top. I waved my arms to move it along - even assuming who the owner most likely was I could see the car was an inappropriate roost for the bird. It took flight in alarm at my gyrations. Unfortunately the phrase "scared the shit out of him" came into play and it left a large dollop of pure-white poo on the canvas roof in its haste to depart.

Oh dear, someone was definitely having a bad day.

***

Tim's cab took him to a small worker's cottage in Millers Point. It was within walking distance of the City. Lower Fort Street ran beside the on-ramp for the Sydney Harbour Bridge and actually sheltered in its shadows. From where Tim stood he could make out the length of the bridge. He examined the front of the house and marveled at how something that was once the basic possession of a humble workman had, over time, become a prized piece of real estate, valued in the millions.

The brass plate beside the front door said, "Frank Spiller Enterprises". Tim rapped on the door, using the solid metal knocker that had provided that service for well over a hundred years.

The door opened and a smiling face greeted him. 'Hello. You must be Tim,' he said, warmly. 'I'm Frank Spiller. Nice to meet you.'

'Tim Cullen. Lovely to meet you, Frank.'

Frank showed him into a reasonably large sitting room, that had been converted to an office. He pointed to a large, comfortable looking lounge and suggested Tim take a seat.

'What's your poison, old boy? Scotch? Gin? Wine? Please don't ask me to make coffee or tea. I'm rubbish at it and Jeremy is out at the moment.'

From his accent and his attitude, Tim concluded that Frank was an ex-pat Londoner and quite gay.

'I'd love a beer. Or is that a stretch?' he said with a cheeky grin.

'Touché, old boy. I'm actually not quite as useless as I made out. Your brother-in-law taught me how to open a beer bottle many moons ago, when we were in school together.'

Frank poured himself a liberal shot of scotch and added some ice from a chest fridge. Next came Tim's beer which he gave to him without a glass.

'I couldn't help noticing your eye, Tim. Don't tell me you forgot to duck?'

Tim felt the non-purple part of his face color slightly. 'Nah. Slipped in the shower at the outback pub we were staying in.'

'I can't tell you how many times something unexpected, like that, has happened to me in the shower,' he laughed, then got down to business. 'I gather from Gary that you have some damning information about a mining company.'

Tim nodded. 'Plutarch Resources. They're a Coal Seam Gas explorer, drilling in the middle of Queensland. Sadly, they have no regard for the environment.' Tim pulled his phone out of his pocket and showed Frank the pictures.

Frank pulled a face and said, 'Oh hell! That's not right. The bastards.'

'Exactly,' Tim agreed. 'We want you to get these pictures out in the public domain, Frank. Along with the name of the company and its Managing Director, Felix Geyer. But we don't want to be seen to be associated, in any way, with the release of this information, and we don't want your name to be connected, either. Is that achievable?'

'Timmy, my friend, anything is possible if you know what you're doing. Fortunately, I do. Thanks to the internet we can generate some social network noise, then help it build to a crescendo. We do that by knowing the sites the journalists monitor. They love a scoop, particularly one that comes with pictures.' He looked up from the ones he was examining on Tim's phone, and said, 'And blow me down. We have some.'

'So, you'll help us out?'

'I'd like to know why Gary wants to sink the boots into a company on the other side of the planet from where he lives? Tell me about that, Tim.'

'It's very simple, Frank. Our grandmother, she's an

Australian by birth, is good friends with the aborigines who live near the drill site. They've been driven off their land and Gran asked us to see if we could help them.'

'You are both incredibly doting grandchildren to go to such lengths,' Frank said, his sarcasm and suspicion obvious.

Tim knew he'd have to say something to end Franks probing questions. Thankfully Gary had foreseen this outcome and they had devised an answer. 'What can I say, Frank. Gran's getting-on,' he grinned at him, then added, 'and she's kinda loaded, if you know what I mean. If she says jump we don't just do it, we ask her how high she'd like us to go.'

Frank seemed to understand this line of logic. He nodded to Tim. 'Got it.. But seeing you're both in it for the money, then I have to bypass the favor I was going to do for Gary and make this a commercial engagement. My fee is $5,000.'

'That seems like a lot of money for a few comments in Facebook and Twitter.'

'Oh, it's much more than that, Tim. Anyone can rant and rave on these sites, but its the same as standing on the top of a mountain and slandering every rich person on the planet. Nobody knows, nobody cares. But if a celebrity says something, even something mundane, it will most likely be re-tweeted to infinity. It's knowing the right voices to use, and in this case, because you require anonymity, it's knowing the "back-door" way to get the *right* voices on board. So to speak.'

Tim pretended to give this some thought. Eventually, he said, 'Okay, Frank. $5,000. The one other requirement we have is that the campaign must not start until after 4 p.m. tomorrow.'

'Great,' Frank said. A pleased smile spread over his face. 'I'll expect a direct deposit before that time. Gary knows my details.' He slapped Tim heartily on the back. 'Now, I'll get one of the anonymous prepaid phones I keep for situations like this, and we can transfer those pictures across to it.'

***

As Tim and Gary were flying back to Brisbane Truf was on hold on the phone. He had called Dr. John Mackintime's office earlier in the day, but the doctor was too busy to take his call. Truf explained it was a business call and had been instructed to call back at the end of the day. Around 7 p.m.. The doctor kept long working hours.

He held the phone to his ear, forced to listen to a dreadful single note, pinging version of Greensleeves. Abruptly the pinging ended and a relaxed, confident male voice came on the line. 'John Mackintime. Who am I speaking to, please?'

'Hello, Dr. Mackintime, my name is Robert Stonewall,' Truf said. He felt more than a little awkward using his actual name which all of his family and friends had stopped using back when he was in school. 'I'd like to talk to you about purchasing your family trust's holding of Plutarch Resources.'

Mackintime laughed when he heard Truf's plan. 'I think you've called the wrong office Mr. Stonewall. Dr. Davis, the psychiatrist, is one floor below me.' He chuckled some more. For him this a rare and monumentally funny quip. 'I'm sorry, excuse me. It's been a long day. Those shares have been going nowhere but down Mr. Stonewall. Forgive my bluntness, but why would you want to own them?'

'I already have a small holding in the company Dr. Mackintime and I too am very disappointed in the share price. I blame the current management. They're a bunch of fools. I need your share parcel to give me enough leverage to get voted onto the Board and change things. I'm a Geologist and Mining Engineer, doctor and I know I can run the company better than this German idiot, Felix Geyer.'

'Presumably, there are other parcels of shares you can purchase, Mr. Stonewall. From your enthusiasm for the project I suspect I might be better off holding on to my parcel and waiting for you to work your wonders.'

'I'm afraid you are my only chance to do this quickly, Dr. Mackintime. If I try and accumulate a sizable holding by buying at market, Geyer will be forewarned. The other similar size share parcels are being held by long-term investors who have many cross holdings within the Coal Seam Gas industry. Quite frankly, they are waiting for Geyer to bankrupt the company, so they can have first option on taking over Plutarch's leases.' Truf wasn't comfortable telling these lies, but he was confident that the company would bankrupt itself in the near future the way it was going. So, it was only a partial lie.

Mackintime said nothing on the other end of the phone. Truf did likewise, giving him time to ponder his options. Eventually Mackintime spoke, 'What is your offer, Mr. Stonewall?'

'I'm prepared to pay 10 cents a share for your entire holding. I will email you a formal, binding offer after I hang up. The offer will only be good until 4:00 p.m. tomorrow. That is my deadline. After that, if you haven't accepted, I too will be a seller, and will walk away from Plutarch Resources.'

***

I had slept well after my quick trip to Sydney. Needless to say my call to Sunny last night when I arrived back in Brisbane had gone straight through to my new friend; her voice-mail.

Aside from my Sunny problem, everything was in place and the day ahead of me was looking quite empty.

Waiting... Waiting... and then some more waiting. Time goes so slowly when you are watching the clock.

Truf had explained the way he had handled Dr. Mackintime and I approved of his tactics. We might make a share trader out of this boy, one day.

The first thing I had done in the morning was to get Sky to email Ling Mien and remind him our offer to purchase his 9.5% holding in Plutarch Resources at 9.5 cents a share would be withdrawn at 5:30 p.m.

By late in the afternoon, Frank's negative publicity campaign should become active and if I was correct Ling Mien would be calling Sky within seconds of it hitting the news. By 6:00 p.m. tonight I'd be in effective control of a company.

I hoped.

I planned on visiting my new friend Hector, the retired doctor I'd met on the plane, to kill some time and also get him to suggest where I needed to go to get some anti-Bev blood tests done. Tim was also planning on visiting a doctor as part of our agreement.

***

Sunny had spent a good portion of the night working at her home computer, until she had completed the necessary tasks. She had some missed calls and messages on her phone.

In the morning she played Garrett's message a second time and detected frustration in his voice. She felt bad about how she was ignoring him but this business with Simon had messed up her mind and she didn't want to say the wrong thing or snap at Garrett. It was better this way. Cowardly, but better. She vowed to herself to make it up to him when he got back to the UK.

Today was about getting even with Simon. She wondered about that - what could possibly even the score? Simon had raped her, entered her body without her permission - without her knowledge. What could possibly balance that ledger? The only way she could come up with would be for him to go to prison and experience the indignity and brutality himself at the hands of hardened criminals. The thought brought a shudder to her. No, she couldn't wish that upon anyone, not even Simon. She would have to settle with what she had originally planned. What she had in her bag right now.

Sunny parked her car and braced herself for the coming confrontation. She headed towards the office noticing Simon's car space was empty as she passed.

Damn! He must be still at home recovering from the drugs.

Sunny entered the office and immediately knew something was up. The five girls who shared the office duties were huddled in a group around one of the desks.

She walked up to the girls, who hadn't noticed her up until this point, and said, 'What's up, guys?'

'Oh my god!' said Claire, one of the accounts girls. She was about nineteen and still prone to outbursts of "girlie" statements. 'Laugh out loud, Sunny. Bree came in first this morning and found the office unlocked and Simon stark naked on his couch.' All five girls giggled at the retelling of a story that was going to do the rounds for some time to come.

Bree couldn't contain herself; it was her story after all. 'He was totally nude,' she giggled as she spoke, 'his thing just sitting there in front of me.' She made a face as she continued the laughter. 'I thought he might have been hurt, you know, mugged or raped or something. I called out to him but he didn't answer me, so I went over and poked his shoulder with my finger.' She grinned to her audience. 'He opened his eyes and he looked really weird. He looked at me like he didn't know me.'

'Did he have any cuts or bruises?' Sunny asked, laying the grounds for a defense in case it was ever required.

Bree just shook her head, not ready to give up the spotlight just yet. 'I said, "Simon... are you alright? Are you injured or sick?" He just stared at me. He looked confused. Then he realized he was naked and he yelled, "Oh shit!" and tried to stand up, but fell flat on his face on the floor. I tried to help him up, but he pushed me away.' She grinned at Sunny. 'He was crawling on his hands and knees towards his desk, where he'd left his clothes. I thought I'd better get out of there and let him get dressed, so I left,' she giggled to the girls and made a gesture with her finger and thumb, suggesting something small. The girls erupted into even louder laughter. 'A couple of minutes later he came storming out of his office. He was dressed, but I could see he'd made a bad job of it. He went straight out the front door without even looking at me. He looked furious.'

'Wow! I wonder what the hell he was up to.' Sunny said, placing herself in amongst the shocked and confused office girls.

Gradually the conversation about Simon began to run out of steam and everyone gravitated back to their own desk, and slowly the office took on its normal buzz.

Today was a no-shoot day for Sunny so she settled in to a routine of budgeting for the upcoming scenes they needed to create. Her job meant she was involved in just about every aspect of the pre-production, shooting and editing. The only area she had no involvement in was the selling and marketing, they were the areas Simon looked after and the way she had decided, to best punish him. She had concluded that to continue working with him was impossible after what he had done. She could never trust him, never allow herself to be alone with him and she quite simply didn't like the man. He was a pig.

She knew he should go to jail for what he had done, but the process of getting him there would be too horrendous for her. She doubted Simon would be capable of physically overpowering a woman; violence seemed to be out of his range of capability, he needed a cowards way to commit rape. She had his Rohypnol and she doubted, or hoped, he wouldn't be able to get any more. With that as her reasoning she had come up with the plan to blackmail him with the embarrassing pictures, to force him to get her a better job with some other company.

On-camera would be the ideal area for her to move to, but she would take anything half decent just to put Simon Sexton into her past.

Bree's description of him being "furious" was not a reaction she had expected. She was banking on reasoning and capitulation, two characteristics she already associated with Simon. Bad tempered and furious suggested Sleazy Simon had another side to him; one that he kept well hidden throughout a normal day. Hidden right beside his rapist personality.

She hated the idea of her pictures wrecking a family, especially one with a young daughter, but she reconciled that with the thought that Simon wasn't a fit person to bring up a child of any sex. Simplistically, she had managed to convince herself that she wouldn't need to show the pictures to Simon's wife, Suzie, just the threat should be enough to get what she wanted. Time would tell.

Sunny also had an alternate plan if Simon rejected her suggestions. She planned to scatter the pictures all over London, anonymously putting them in the letterboxes of people who did business with Simon, his friends, and especially any enemies, in the hope of destroying his career.

Do not mess with this girl. You might win a battle, but the war will be long and hard, and fought on many levels.

***

My morning with Hector turned out to be a lot of

fun. He is a nice man and not only suggested we have lunch at a lovely local restaurant, he actually insisted on paying for the meal. That wasn't the end of his largess. It seems the retired doctor had kept his Medical Registration up to date. He claimed all his friends still needed prescriptions by the hundreds and it was the least he could do. I suspect it was more a reason to keep his rather good brain, active. Either way, Hector himself drew my blood.

While he prepared his needle and tubes I told him my one and only doctor joke: A fellow goes to see his doctor. He says, "Doctor, I'm a kleptomaniac. Do you have something I can take?"

Hector laughed politely as he removed the needle from my vein, but I could tell he had heard it already. I told the joke more to distract myself as he jabbed me, not that I needed to, Hector was very good at his job and I barely felt it go in.

He promised to email the results to me in a day or three, when the pathologist had had a chance to do the blood-work.

To reciprocate his gesture I broke a cardinal rule and subtly suggested if he had a spare dollar or two he might want to pick up some Plutarch shares. I might even have suggested he should wait for a day or so before he did it.

I told myself it's only Insider Trading if you're actually on the inside. Denial is a cloak that is beginning to look good on me.

It was now 2:45 p.m. and Tim, Truf and I were taking coffee on the Terrace, trying to relax while inside, we were all in turmoil. We each had our laptop in front of us, open on our email accounts. Our phones were sitting only inches away.

Truf was the first to bag a winner. He opened an email and announced to us with a grin as big as a boomerang on his face, 'The Mackintime-Overly Trust has accepted my offer to purchase their 4.5 million Plutarch shares at 10 cents each.'

'Well-done, you,' I said and shook his hand.

Tim clapped Truf on the back. 'Great news. Congratulations Truf.'

A few minutes later my phone began to ring. The screen advised me it was an "Overseas Call". I refused to get my hopes up on that alone as all calls at the moment came with that announcement. Never-the-less I raised my eyebrows and grinned nervously at the boys as I said, 'Garrett Nixon speaking.'

'Indeed it is, I'd recognize that voice anywhere,' came a laid-back Yanky drawl over the phone. 'Wonderful to talk to you after such a long time. This is Johnson Noble from Ambic Investments, Garrett, You may not remember me but we met at a convention on a Mississippi paddle steamer, called the Robert E a year or two back. You managed to get me quite drunk on some Pommy concoction you were hot for at the time.'

'Hey Johnson, I remember you. You wanted British grog so we tried Pimms, it was all I could come up with, which is a bit of a girls drink,' I laughed. 'We must have been really smashed that night.'

'I think it might have been the scotch we did before that, that caused the damage. But I can still remember the night, so it can't have been totally devastating,' he joined in my laughter.

'Just giving you a heads-up courtesy call, Garrett. We've just unloaded 5 million shares of a little Aussie stock called Plutarch Resources to a guy by the name of Oscar Barrymore. He stipulated that you needed to be advised that the transaction had been consummated. I'm not going to ask what you're up to Garrett, but good luck with it.'

'Thanks, Johnson. Can I be nosy and ask how much you made the jerk pay?'

'He paid 25 over. Seemed very keen to get 'em.'

'Next time you're in London give me a call Johnson and I'll buy you a drink or two for that. Thanks for the call, old boy.' I disconnected and grinned at Tim and Truf, who were keen to hear the other half of the conversation they had been trying to piece together.

'Barrymore has secured the 5% holding that Ambic Leveraged held,' I gave a big grin. 'They made him pay 12.5 cents a share.'

'Things are going well,' Truf said. 'Only the 5% Samson-Jonkins own to go before Warra is a major shareholder.'

Tim cut in. He was looking over my shoulder at my computer screen. 'Gary, check your inbox. That name has just come up on your screen.'

I double clicked to open the email. It was from Meridith Jacoby, Director of Trading at Samson-Jonkins. I read the email out loud. '*Mr. Nixon. This is a formal advice to you regarding your client Mr. Oscar Barrymore. We have transferred 5 million shares in Plutarch Resources N.L. into his name this morning. Regards, M. Jacoby.*'

***

Simon never returned to the office, leaving Sunny

wondering if she should start delivering the sixty photos she had in her bag. In the end she decided to give Simon more time before she made that decision. She knew that the local bars would be abuzz, tonight, with the story the office girls would be telling to every single person they knew, so her job was half done already.

Nobody had actually put it together, yet. The consensus in the office was that Simon, either had hookers come in and he got too drunk and passed out. Or he was into some weird masturbation thing and passed-out. They were leaning towards the latter as there were no empty bottles or dirty glasses found in the office.

They had looked. Even in the rubbish bins.

He would be back in the office tomorrow Sunny decided and packed up for the day.

As she drove home she had the thought of randomly throwing out handfuls of the pictures as she drove through London. She discarded the idea as wasteful and she didn't want any little kids picking them up.

Sunny knew she had trouble when she pushed her key into her front door, only to have the door push open from the pressure her fingers provided trying to find the keyhole. The lock had been forced open with a jimmy. She could see the indentation in the door and the splintered wood around the inside part of the bolt-hole now that the door was open.

She stood in the doorway and pushed it fully open. Her instincts told her to call the police and wait outside, but there was a problem, the sachet of Rohypnol pills was inside in her filing cabinet. If the police searched and found it she would be in a lot of trouble, and not able to easily explain why she had the drugs.

She peered cautiously into the semi-darkened room. She could see it was a mess. Someone had turned her furniture upside down and scattered the contents of her cupboards and drawers over the floor. Was it a random robbery or something more personal? She noted that nothing seemed to be smashed, so it wasn't just vandalism it had been a methodical, thorough, but very messy, search.

That seemed to narrow down the list of suspects. Simon must have worked out that she had drugged him using the Rohypnol and would have been unlikely to put it back in his filing cabinet. Therefore, there was a good chance it would be here in her home. He had come looking for it and she could see he hadn't been able to open the filing cabinet.

She had to get it before she called for help.

She hadn't made any noise so far. The door had opened on well lubricated hinges and she hadn't been stupid like some people, and called out something lame, like, 'Is anybody in there?'

She scanned the room again from the doorway but couldn't see anyone hiding.

There was no other way. She edged slowly through the doorway, ready to bolt if he suddenly appeared. The bathroom door and her bedroom door were both shut. This was a cause of great worry.

Sunny poked her head around the door, ever conscious that a fist could come at her any second. Thankfully, nobody was hiding behind it and she let out a sigh of relief.

She needed a weapon and she had one - a baseball bat she kept for that very reason, but it was propped up beside her bedside table in the same room as her intruder might probably be searching right now. She thought of getting a knife from the kitchen but she doubted she would have the strength and determination to actually use one in anger. No, she needed a club long enough for her to swing from beyond arms-reach. She scanned the room and found her best available weapon, her aluminum camera tripod. It was lying on the floor next to her desk and she made her way to it.

She felt better when she had it in her hands. The slightly awkward three-legged metal device was about as long as her arm and effectively doubled the distance from which she would be able to attack. Or defend.

She continued on towards the bathroom and silently turned the door-knob. She held the tripod beside her head ready to crash it down on any intruder who rushed at her.

She pushed the door open and tensed herself for action. The door gently bumped against the doorstop on the wall, revealing an empty room. The shower curtain was open making it impossible for anyone to hide there. That just left the bedroom.

Sunny tip-toed towards it. She had heard no noise from inside her apartment and she was confident she hadn't made any so far, so the element of surprise was on her side. Although, she reasoned anybody who broke into an apartment would almost certainly be in a constant state of heightened awareness.

She stood at the bedroom door and listened for the sound of someone rummaging through her things, but no helpful clues penetrated the closed door. As she had at the bathroom she stood again and slowly turned the handle and pushed the door. It swung open.

She gasped when she saw him. It was Simon. Sunny

stood in the doorway, the tripod raised ready to strike and assessed the situation. He was lying on his back on the bed with his head resting against the bed-head.

He was naked.

***

Tim had been alternately checking online news sites and social media sites for most of the afternoon and nothing relevant had come to his attention. He began doing Google searches for "environmental disasters" and "chemical spills+ Australia" and any other combination of words he imagined might produce a result.

At 4:16 he struck a vein. Twitter had a tweet from @earthpartisan#1: "Be disgusted by this - death and destruction from CSG vandals. Get very mad, this is your earth they are killing." Underneath one of Tim's pictures showed numerous decomposing animals scattered around an outback waterhole. He expanded the tweet and saw it had already been retweeted 35 times.

He twisted his laptop around so Truf and I could see what he'd found and we all grinned.

I checked the Facebook page of a well-known Australian TV reporter, Robert Doran, who was a passionate advocate of environmental protection, and sure enough he had posted yet another of Tim's pictures, and had added an equally acidic comment. A long list of friends had already commented on the vile nature of the picture. The ball was rolling...

I could see the way Frank was handling this - it was masterful. No mention of Plutarch Resources had been made and judging from the comments on Facebook people were getting ready for a good 'ol hanging of whoever was responsible for all of this. I suspected the next tranche of postings would mention Plutarch. By not mentioning the company, Frank had intentionally forced people to do their own research, causing the Google search-engine to become very aware of a growing story of interest.

Half an hour later the internet was alive with the story. All of Tim's pictures were freely available for people to examine and sure enough Plutarch Resources' name was tightly linked to each and every picture. I jumped on to the news sites and went straight to the "Latest Headlines" and Plutarch Resources seemed to be everywhere as was the name of its Managing Director.

I had been waiting for the call. Expecting the call - but I still jumped when the phone actually rang. My built-up tension from an expectant day of largely waiting seemed to evaporate with that one little shudder from my body. I knew the final piece of my puzzle had just slipped into place.

'Good day, Sky.' I said, to a woman who was ten thousand miles away, but who could still *see* my smile.

'Good afternoon, Mr. All Seeing Mighty Prophet,' Sky said, and her smile was visible, because she actually laughed. 'Well played, boss. I gather you already guessed that Ling Mien has just called confirming he had just couriered to us his acceptance in writing of our offer of 9.5 cents a share for his 9.5% holding of Plutarch Resources?'

'I did kinda guess, Sky. Congratulations for the way you handled your part in all of this,' I said, keen to include her in the list of honors. 'I don't want you to be too alarmed when you hear there has been some very recent news over here about Plutarch. Seems they have caused a lot of environmental damage at their drill-sites. It has been disastrous timing from my part in offering to buy those shares,' I laughed loudly down the phone.

'I'm not even going to try and pretend I understand whats going on,' Sky said. I could imagine her head shaking from side to side as she said it. 'You've been completely on top of it, so far, so I'll go along with your interpretation that, that terrible information is hilarious, even though it will make your purchase at 9.5 cents look embarrassingly stupid. The market is closed over there at the moment, I gather, what are you expecting your shares to open at in the morning?'

'I think, less than half that price,' I chuckled, and then added, 'Sky... Be a love and email our friend Ling and formally ask if we can rescind our offer. Mention that we are willing to compensate him for the inconvenience we might have caused. Offer a payment of 10% of the purchase price if he is prepared to cancel the deal.'

'You're the boss,' she said, sounding like she would love to ask me what the hell I was up to. 'Unless he's overdosed himself on stupid-pills, that offer has a snowflakes' chance in hell of being accepted.'

'That's my grave fear as well,' I said with a laugh, 'but from a commercial perspective I think it is correct that we try and get out of the deal.'

'Gary, this is impossible for me. I want to know what you have done, I can't wait for you to get back so we can talk face to face. When is that likely?'

'Things are pretty much wrapped-up over here, now. I think by tomorrow I'll be heading back.'

'Can't wait... bye bye.'

I sat back and mused. To the world at large the company I nominally controlled was, at this point in time, being compared to Chernobyl and the A-bomb tests at Bikini Atoll.

Oh dear!

At least I wasn't the one who pushed the button.

**

Sunny didn't move from the bedroom doorway, fearing that if she did he would pounce on her. She began to study Simon more closely. He didn't look normal by any interpretation of that word. His body hadn't moved in all the time she had been there, he hadn't spoken and to the best of her recollection he hadn't even blinked.

'Simon! What are you doing? Simon! Answer me.'

He didn't react. His eyes were open but he didn't look like he was awake. Sunny took a step forward, her tripod still held threateningly for him to see. She never took her eyes off him as she advanced slowly towards him.

Then she noticed it. His right arm had a flesh-colored rubber tourniquet tied around the bicep, a hypodermic needle lay beside him. She moved to the end of the bed and looked over his body, a small medical bottle with a rubber section in the top - the type designed for syringes to dip into without needing to be unscrewed, lay next him. It had rolled into the depression his body had made in the mattress and rested against his upper thigh.

She moved alongside of him, still not trusting that he was incapable of hurting her. She prodded him with the tripod. His body moved from the pressure, but his eyes remained fixed as if he was staring at a fly on the back wall. Sunny leaned over and tentatively felt for a pulse in his left arm. It took a few tries before she found a pulse, it was very weak and irregular. His right arm was slightly swollen and had turned a reddish-blue. She undid the tourniquet, but the arm remained swollen and colored.

Simon was clearly close to death and time was important, whatever drug he had injected must be a serious one. But Sunny had some important thinking to do first. *Why had he come here to do this? Why had he searched and trashed her apartment if he had intentions of raping her again?* She made that assumption because he had undressed. Clearly in preparation for something. If he was just interested in getting his Rohypnol back he wouldn't have taken his clothes off. *But, wouldn't it make more sense to ambush her and knock her out, and then undress? Maybe he had shot-up to get high to give himself the courage to do all of that, but had misjudged the dosage and passed out.*

Every way she looked at it, added up to the conclusion that Simon had intended to hurt her very seriously, possibly even murder her. *Why? Up till last night she had never done anything bad to him, she'd never indicated they were more than workmates and friends. And he never flirted or tried to touch her. It made no sense. Something bizarre had been going on in Simon's head. Something very sick, and he had hidden it well.*

Given that Simon was intent on hurting her, Sunny decided on her course of action. She would give priority to her requirements before she worried about his. Her first action was to go to her computer, which he had tried to access but failed without her password. She knew this because it was powered up which was not how she had left it in the morning. Thankfully he hadn't smashed it. She quickly permanently deleted all the photos she had taken of him in the office. Then she went to her camera to remove the memory card, but he had beaten her to it. She moved to his pile of clothes and searched, eventually finding the small device in his trousers' coin pocket.

Sunny checked Simon's pulse again before she eventually called for an ambulance and the police. With revenge on her mind she had some other crucial things to do before they arrived. All of them required any fingerprints she left on the things she touched, be wiped away, and replaced with imprints from Simon's fingers.

Two minutes later Sunny was outside, she dropped the packet of pictures into a neighbors rubbish bin, making sure they went between the bags of rubbish as deeply as possible. As she waited, listening for the faint sound of sirens in the distance, she carefully hid the tiny black, coin size SD memory card from her camera in the thick bushy base of one of her next door neighbor's pot plants.

**

Truf, Tim and I were booked on a flight back to London that left in the middle of the afternoon. Our business here was almost done. Tim had confided to me that he'd had his blood tests and would have the results emailed to him in a couple of days. I wasn't too worried about Tim's results, as my results would be the same as his, so I had him where I wanted him.

The very last thing I needed to do was phone Gerald in London and have him instigate a few things while I was incommunicado on airplanes. Surprisingly, Terri his receptionist, put me straight through. Get the cash-register out and start the stopwatch, girl.

'Hello Gary, lovely to hear from you. Are you still in Australia?'

'Hi, Gerald. I'm just about to board a plane for home,' I said in clipped language, hoping that would be enough small-talk at fifty quid a pop. 'I need you to organize a few things for me while I'm in the air, if you'd be so kind. Firstly, I no longer have any problems with you going forward with Ed's bequest to Megan and myself. Including those shares, I have managed to get nominal control of around 45% of Plutarch Resources and I intend to mount a full take-over of the company. With that intention, Gerald, I would like you contact the Chairman and initiate an extraordinary General Meeting of the company as quickly as possible, using Gran and Ed's holding as your authority. If you need more leverage to do that, the Nixon Fund owns 9.5% and a Power of Attorney document gives me another 10% voting stock. Due to the total incompetence of the current Board I want to nominate three new Directors with myself as Chairman of Directors, Robert Stonewall is nominating as Managing Director and my brother-in-law Timothy Cullen will nominate as a non-executive Director.'

Gerald laughed down the phone. It wasn't a mocking laugh, thank God; there was a hint of admiration in there somewhere. 'You certainly don't mess around, do you, Gary? I guess you have heard that Plutarch

Resources is in the news at the moment?'

'Yes, Gerald, I'm well aware of what is going on. Incredible that I should be visiting at the same time that all came to light.'

I think Gerald picked up my subtle inference, but he still asked the question: 'You are not worried about it?'

'Well, of course I am. It's going to cost a lot of money to repair the ecological damage, not to mention any fines that come with it. But we have some resources and some options up our sleeve that will help.'

'I'll be honest with you Gary, if it was anyone else telling me this I'd be more than skeptical, I'd be worried. But I can remember having a conversation with your grandfather a few years back and he told me that you had the best brain he'd come across in a long, long time and he trusted your decision making skills even over his own. And I trusted and admired Ed's decision making skills. So you can see where I'm going with this.'

I was stunned into an expensive silence on the end of the phone. Ed had never, in his entire life, so much as complimented me on something. This was a full-blown recommendation. 'Wow,' I said, 'I appreciate you sharing that with me, Gerald. It means a lot.'

'Yes, I know it does. You have Ed up on a pedestal; it's only fair that you should know he had you on one, also.' Gerald chuckled down the phone line. 'This call is costing you money, Gary, and from what you've just told me you're going to need as much as you get in the near future,' he laughed at his joke, and in doing so reminding me that I had just paid for it. 'I'll act on your instructions and advise you when the current Board of Directors of Plutarch agrees on a date. Is there any other business we need to discuss?'

'Nope. That's the lot. Thanks again for everything, Gerald.'

'I'll see you when you get back. Bye, Gary.'

I was so pleased with what Gerald had told me I completely forgot to listen for the "*Cha Ching!*" as he closed his cash register.

***

'You are quite adamant, Miss McGuire, that you and Mr. Sexton were not involved in a sexual relationship?'

'Of course we weren't. I told you, he is my boss and nothing more. He has never even flirted with me.'

Inspector Brice had been questioning Sunny for ten minutes and she suspected he was just about done, because he was going back over the key points in his notes, presumably to clarify them. Simon had been taken away, still unconscious, by the paramedics a few minutes earlier.

'Do you have any suspicions what he might have been looking for in your apartment?'

'I can only guess, drugs, judging from the needle lying beside him.'

'Are you telling me you are a drug user?'

'Hell no!' Sunny shouted at him. 'I didn't even know *he* was a drug addict. I hate bloody drugs. You can check my apartment, you won't find any illegal drugs, I doubt you'll even find any Aspirin. I'm a health food nut, I live on vitamins, mineral supplements and organic food. The thought of using hard drugs, like Simon obviously puts into his body, is beyond repugnant to me.'

'Are you giving me permission to search your

apartment, Miss McGuire?'

Damn, I shouldn't have said all that. Sunny looked the Inspector squarely in the face, her expression was benign. He was a man in his forties and in reasonable trim, he had a pleasant face which was half-smiling at her. *The smug bastard is congratulating himself for tricking me into this.* 'I have no problems with that at all, Inspector. Perhaps you can help me tidy up as you go?'

As far as paybacks go it was pathetic, but as it turned out, unnecessary. 'That won't be required. But I will note that you offered us the right to search.'

'Thank you, Inspector Brice. Does that mean I'm on my own with the cleanup?'

'Afraid so, Miss McGuire. My wife expects me to help out at home and I find the joy involved in helping her is more than enough to satisfy any urges I have in that department.' He grinned at her.

'What will happen to Simon?'

'He is being taken to St Mary's Hospital in Paddington,' He fixed his look on her and shook his head. 'The paramedic said he may not survive the overdose, but if he does we will be charging him with breaking and entry, and possession of illicit drugs. I suspect it will be Heroin residue in the needle and the empty vial. And,' he paused and fixed his gaze back on Sunny, 'aside from the tire iron we found under his clothes, we also found some Rohypnol in his pocket.'

Sunny frowned and gave him her best look of concern mixed with surprise, not that it was news as she was the one who had taken the Rohypnol from her filing cabinet and put the tablets into his pocket. 'The date-rape drug! Are you telling me he was planning on drugging me and raping me?' She gasped. 'And if that didn't work, bashing me over the head with a tire iron?'

'He was naked and on your bed,' he shook his head slowly, as if he was still pondering the question. 'I've seen a lot of burglaries in my years in the police force, Miss McGuire, but I can't recall any where the perpetrator has done something like that. We will have to get a complete psychiatric work-up done on him before we contemplate any extra charges. Even if he intended to rape you he never actually tried, so we can't even charge him with Attempted Rape.'

'But that leaves me in a terrible position,' Sunny pleaded. 'The charges you've suggested won't keep him in jail. I assume he has no police record, so he'll undoubtedly get a suspended sentence, leaving him free to come for me again.' Sunny shook her head in horror.

'I'm sorry, Miss McGuire. If he had so much as grabbed your hand we could probably successfully charge him, but, as you said, he was comatose when you arrived home,' he nodded his head and grimaced. 'He most probably was planning on having sex with you, but I can't charge him for that. If it was illegal for men to contemplate, or plan to have sex with a woman, then there wouldn't be many men left walking around our streets. I apologize for what must seem to you as making light of the situation, but it's the best way I can describe my predicament.'

Chapter 10

The three of us had been traveling for a total of twenty-five hours. Our first stopover was in Kuala Lumpur in Malaysia, for three and a half hours and then an even longer one in Dubai.

Heathrow was hell, but at least it was our hell and great to be back on familiar soil, or more correctly, concrete. We had landed in London at 10 p.m. and we all felt completely second-hand and jet-lagged so we headed to our respective homes and slept as best we could.

I awoke the next morning in my own bed, in my own bedroom. Bliss. The day started with a big tick and a smile. I rubbed my eyes and admired the familiarity of it all. The sun was well and truly up as the room was bathed in a warm glow. Not quite as warm as the glow I'd become used to recently, but warmer in a cooler kind of way. There's nothing quite like home.

As I climbed out of bed I looked at my oak dresser and wished it had a big red bag sitting on top of it. Sunny had been in my thoughts most of the time I had been away, but the planning and action that had been required to make Gran's request happen had pushed her memory further from the surface than I wished. She had not helped things by being so ambivalent about our communications. *Bloody voice-mail.* I planned to talk to her about that, face to face, but after we had done other things face to face... a lot of times.

I have a jet lag cure, actually it's more like an exorcism, that I like to use. I go for a jog; it's a brutal way to force my body and brain to get their acts together. It's the same cure I use for a hangover, but I add aspirin and swallow half an hour before pulling on my shorts and trainers, for that ailment.

As I had arrived home in darkness and pretty much exhausted I had not given any attention to the place. It was still standing and my bed was inside - that was the beginning and end of my interest last night. The girls had mostly worked from their own homes so it had been left alone for the time I had been away.

Or so I thought.

I entered the kitchen to find a large tarpaulin stretched over one corner of the room with paint tins, buckets, thinners and brushes littering the top of it. Then I remembered Harry, my landlord, was going to *paint a black horse*. I smiled to myself at his scribble. Seems my first reading was correct; he was actually painting the back of the house. Thankfully it was the outside he was working on, which would be the reason I didn't smell the paint last night.

I went out the back door, which actually opens straight from the kitchen. I knew something was wrong as soon as I opened it. A ladder lay on its side, partially blocking the door. I eased my way around it, stepping and climbing where I could find a foothold, my apprehension rising with every step. Harry was lying half draped over the plank that he must have been standing on, between the two ladders, when things apparently went bad for him. A paint tin and a large splash of white paint lay beside him. What had remained after the tin's initial impact with the ground had pooled around him, partially painting one of his arms and the side of his body.

He was a mess. I rushed to him and felt his neck for a pulse. His skin felt firm and barely gave when I pressed my fingers below the bend of his jaw. He was cold. And when I looked closely I could see his skin had turned a blue color. His mouth was open as if he was trying to say something but Harry was never going to say anything ever again. I felt a strange pressure behind my eyes and before I could stop it tears poured from me. I blinked hard to stop them... but it didn't work.

I never cry. I didn't when my grandfather, Ed, died. I didn't when my first dog Chester died, when I was eight. But I cried when Harry Buxton died.

I warned the old bugger not to get kicked painting that black horse.

I went back inside and located my phone, which was still on charge in my office, and called the police. I must have sounded useless to the woman I spoke to because when I asked her who else I should call she told me not to worry, she would make all the emergency calls.

So much for my jog. I had found another way to get over jet lag, but I liked the jog method better.

The rest of the morning was spent with the police. I had watched as the coroner had examined Harry and decided that foul play was unlikely to be a factor. I had watched as Harry had been "bagged up" in what looked like a heavy black plastic sleeping bag and I watched as they wheeled him out to a nondescript brown, windowless Transit van and secured him in the back. Dignity and death do not seem to reside together at this stage of the journey.

After the police eventually left me I began to make

some phone calls. Sophie and Sky both loved the old bugger and were heartbroken by the news. Both blamed themselves for not coming in to work. I explained that the coroner suggested he had been dead for at least one whole day, which didn't ease either girls feeling of guilt. We had scheduled a meeting here for midday, but decided to postpone it until tomorrow. None of us could concentrate on anything other than Harry.

Maybe it was a premonition or maybe just an act of good faith, but about a year ago Harry had given me a key to his home. At the time he had suggested it was in case he lost his own key, but I wonder now if he was quietly assigning the task of one day discovering his dead body after his absence had become obvious. Harry lived alone and looked after himself. He cooked and washed and cleaned and shopped and, up until a day or two ago, did running repairs on two houses.

I parked in his drive and cautiously walked to his door. I knocked. Stupid? I really wasn't sure if Harry didn't have a friend staying with him. Anyway, he didn't, so I let myself in. The place had a musty, stale air about it. The blinds were drawn in most of the rooms. I suspect Harry only used a small number of the available areas. It was a large house on a good size piece of ground and the gardens and lawns were neat. I was looking for his telephone, which would be one of the old types that actually plugged into a socket in the wall. Harry had long ago given up trying to keep up with the changes in technology and locked himself into a time-warp - probably one that ended in the 1980's. His phone was in the kitchen and what I was looking for was sitting on the bench beside it. His teledex.

I just knew he would have one of these ancient

devices. I remember from my own childhood how the little plastic lid had fascinated me with its alphabet running down beside the little sliding button that ran through the middle. You could slide it to the letter J, or whatever, and instantly open to a list of all the people you knew whose name started with that letter. Very high-tech for the time.

I made my way through the list. I knew who I was looking for, Harry had mentioned her many times. I made the call using his phone thinking she would know the number and be more likely to pick up.

'Yeah! What do you want this time?' Came the blunt answer from a female voice I estimated to be middle-aged.

'Hello,' I said, a little surprised by her tone. 'Is this Angela Spencer?'

'Yes! Who the hell are you?'

'My name is Garrett Nixon, Angela and I'm calling regarding your father, Harry Buxton.'

'Yeah... What's the old bastard done now?'

Her tone was very annoying. A combination of aggression and disinterest which was anything but what I had expected. Harry had always talked in glowing terms about his daughter. Lamenting the fact that he never saw her because she lived in Manchester. I knew she was divorced and had two adult kids who did not live with her.

'I have some very bad news, Angela,' I said, ignoring her unflattering reference to Harry. 'I'm afraid Harry has passed away. We found him this morning.'

There was silence over the phone for a few seconds, then, 'Dead... you say?'

'I'm very sorry. Yes, Harry is dead.'

'Hot diggity-do. About fucking time,' she said, sounding cheerful for the first time since we had been speaking.

I was speechless. I couldn't believe this bitch was talking like this about her own father; a man who was as nice and generous as any person I had ever met. What could possibly be her problem? Eventually I managed to ask, 'Why are you pleased by this news?'

'Because at long last I'll get hold of the old pricks money. The bastard stopped giving me any a few years ago. It's been bloody difficult...'

I didn't hear any more because I had replaced the phone in its cradle.

I began a search of Harry's house. I was looking for his personal papers. I needed to find his will or at least the name of his solicitor. His paperwork eventually turned up, stored in an old shoe box in his wardrobe and after about an hour of reading I had, not only a picture of Harry's financial situation, but also the name of his legal representative. Ivan Stutzman of Stutzman and Jones, a local firm of solicitors.

I placed a call.

Stutzman was the opposite to Angela, he was actually saddened to hear of Harry's passing.

'Excuse me a moment, Mr. Nixon,' he said after I had explained my reason for calling. 'I'll get Harry's will out of our files and see what it says.' He disappeared for a minute then came back on the line. 'We need to make an appointment for you to come in to the office, Mr. Nixon. How about 10 a.m. tomorrow?'

'I don't understand Mr. Stutzman. Why do I need to come to your office?'

'Well, I suppose I can come to yours if it is a

problem for you,' he answered, in a slightly bewildered manner.

'No. You don't understand,' I said, 'I'm not related to Harry, I'm just his tenant. And also a friend.'

'According to this document, you are much more, Mr. Nixon,' he said. 'You are his executor and the major beneficiary of his estate.'

What the...

I drove the entire journey home from Harry's house with a look of shock chiseled on my face. My life had become like some kind of roller-coaster; first there was Ed's death and then I get compensated with part of his shareholding in Plutarch Resources. And now Harry dies, and I get compensated with a large part of his estate. It might seem wonderful that good follows bad, but I don't equate relationships in money terms and I would gladly give all my "good fortune" back for some more time with my two mentors.

The only thing I can do is accept my monetary gain gracefully and try and use it in ways my two elderly role-models would be proud of. I'm pretty sure Ed would be happy with the way things were going back in Australia.

That leaves Harry: *What would he want me to do?*

I was deep into pondering that question when my phone began to ring.

***

Sunny's apartment finally looked much like it always did. She had worked late into the night tidying up and cleaning. She had washed and replaced all the bedding in a vain attempt to remove any lingering

317

presence of Simon from her home.

She had retrieved the pictures from her neighbors rubbish bin and used her paper guillotine to completely destroy them. When she had shredded them to her satisfaction she throughly mixed them up and put them into a paper bag which she drove to the local shops and buried in the bottom of a rather full hopper behind a supermarket.

As she walked to her freshly repaired front door, she silently cursed Simon for dumping that considerable bill on her last night. She quickly diverted from her path to the pot plant where she had hidden her camera's memory card and retrieved it. Once inside she erased the pictures.

She had slept badly, tossing and turning, and waking frequently, even though she was totally exhausted from the nights activities. As a result she felt drained this morning. She decided to give work a miss, even though she knew it would be turmoil with both Simon and her missing. Instead, she ran herself a lovely hot bath and soaked for an hour. She brought her phone with her expecting the office to call, and sure enough, just as the bubbles had begun to work their magic, it rang.

'Hi. This is Sunny.'

'You fucking, drug addicted whore-bitch,' the female voice shouted down the phone into her ear. 'I hope you die with a needle sticking out of your eye!'

'What the...' Sunny spluttered. 'Who... who is this?'

'You piece of shit! It's the wife and mother of the asshole you've been banging for who knows how long.'

Sunny got it immediately. It was Suzie Sexton, Simon's wife and she had drawn some wrong conclusions. Sunny had met her a few times but they

318

had never bonded in any way. Suzie had always seemed wary of her, despite Sunny's attempts to convey her disinterest in the woman's husband.

'Suzie. You've got it all wrong,' Sunny said in an even voice. She would normally have responded to abuse like that with more strength, but she realized Suzie was in a state of turmoil and anxiety with the facts she'd been given, presumably by the police. 'Simon and I are not involved in any way. Never have been, and never will be.'

'That's bullshit, bitch...'

Sunny cut off Suzie's coming rant. 'I understand that you've drawn some conclusions because Simon was found naked, in my bed. But Suzie, he got there by smashing open the front door, and he was also found naked in his office that same morning. Simon is very sick. He clearly has a drug problem and mental issues that none of us in the office were aware of. I swear to you I have never had Simon in my bed, Suzie.'

She could hear the woman on the other end of the phone gently sobbing. 'What am I going to do?' she whispered softly, and followed it with a loud sniff. 'I'm not sure I can go on. Simon is only hanging on by a thread at the hospital. It's all too hard.'

'All I can say is that he needs you right now, Suzie. He's in a bad place and you need to be his rock: The strong one to guide him through this,' Sunny paused to give Suzie time to come to the same realization. 'You *have* to be strong Suzie. You're all he's got.'

'You swear there is nothing going on between the two of you?'

'No chance at all, Suzie. I have a boyfriend who I'm kind of crazy for. Simon is all yours.'

'Oh God! I'm so sorry I called you all those names, Sunny,' Suzie said, and she began to sob again.

'I understand what you're going through, Suzie. Now be strong and help Simon get better.'

That phone-call undid most of the therapeutic benefit the bath had provided, so Sunny topped up the heat with a healthy burst of hot water. The steam wafted gently from the surface and she slid down until only the parts of her face above her nose were still showing. She lay as still as possible and allowed the warmth to consume her body. Stillness was necessary because even a small wave threatened her ability to breath. The mention of the word *boyfriend* to Suzie caused her to think about Garrett. He wasn't her boyfriend, she had only just met him and she had only used that word to make it easier for Suzie to believe her. But there was a connection with him that was way out of the ordinary. She loved his sense of humor; she loved his face and his body. She loved his subtle, manly way of taking control, but still remaining totally aware of her feelings and needs. As she delved deeper into her feelings she realized she loved pretty much most of the things about him. And she especially loved "Little Gary" although she hadn't *formally* met him.

Her mind drifted back to the night she had undressed Garrett in his bed. That was wrong on so many levels but she was glad she had done it. He was totally out of it and he will never know that she couldn't help herself and gave Little Gary a goodnight kiss. That was the first and only time he had been unresponsive to her flirtations.

She laughed out loud which created a sudden, large air bubble to explode under the surface in front of her face, which caused a large splash of the water to end up inside her nose. The coughing fit that it caused forced her mind off Gary's body parts.

After she had settled into a normal breathing rhythm she allowed herself to relax and enjoy the warmth again.

Time passed slowly and she found her mind kept drifting back to Gary. She thought of all the calls he had made to her from Australia and she had always been busy, or preoccupied with her problems. She thought of all his sarcastic cracks about getting on better with her voice-mail than her and she realized he had a point. She had behaved badly. He had tried to keep the small amount of relationship momentum they had created, going, while she had been self-obsessed.

Well, there was no excuse for that now, the Simon problem had pretty much resolved itself and with it had gone her work problem. With Simon no longer in the picture the company would have to bring in a new Executive Producer and she would assess the impact on her, of that change, when it happened.

In the interim, she had little doubt they would ask her to fill Simon's role, it wasn't a career move she was aiming for but she knew she would give it a go. If they asked.

With that issue resolved in her mind she decided now was a good time to make up some lost ground. She grabbed her phone and dialed. It was answered on the third ring.

'Heidi!' He answered with a laugh. 'I'm almost speechless. Am I really talking to you or has your voice-mail taught itself to call out?'

'Stop it, Gary,' she chided him in a serious voice. 'I'm sorry I was so difficult to get hold of while you were away. I've had a few problems to deal with, but that is behind me now and I can give you the attention that I owe you.'

'From memory your last commitment was to offer me a banquet.' He laughed in her ear and she smiled at the familiar, lovely sound.

'I do recall offering that,' she said. 'The problem is that I'm in the bath at the moment and I really don't want to get out.' She gave a suggestive chuckle. 'Can we renegotiate?'

'So, you're saying you are too busy washing yourself to prepare my banquet?'

'Seriously, Gary, has standing upside down on the bottom of the earth caused the blood to bloat inside your head?' She paused, before adding, 'Maybe by washing myself... I am *preparing* your banquet.'

'Ha Ha!' He chuckled, as her meaning sunk in. 'Nicely put, Sunny. I can't tell you how much I've missed your cryptic take on the world.' His laughter tuned suggestive, slightly dirty even, then he said, 'A banquet in a bath, eh? That sounds more than a little tempting, I hope you have a big enough bath for the *three* of us.'

'No, it's just normal size,' It was Sunny's turn for a sexy chuckle. 'We'll probably have to work out the best way to squeeze in. It might take a while... and some trial and error.'

'Sunny, you need to stop talking immediately,' Gary said, urgently, 'Or, I'm going to have the banquet in my pants, right now...'

Sunny drifted peacefully into a mode that was just approaching sleep. She stayed like that for an indeterminate time. Her rest was suddenly broken by her phone ringing, yet again.

'Hello. This is Sunny.'

'Good morning, Miss McGuire. This is Inspector Brice. I'm sorry to have to inform you that Simon Sexton passed away a short time ago.'

'Oh my God!' Sunny exclaimed. Her free hand clutched at her mouth as if to hold back any further words.

If the Inspector could have seen the expression on Sunny's face he would have been very keen to use his interrogative skills to uncover the reason.

***

I drove like I was trying to qualify for an F1 race. I was pretty sure that this time Sunny and I would get to actually *race*. Continuing the race-car metaphor, I was a lock for pole position and Sunny would be in charge of the pit.

It amuses me the way my mind darts off on little tangents from time to time. I needed to do this right now because I definitely didn't want the exquisite feeling that was surging through my body to end. Hence, by deflecting my mind onto a similar, but different subject, I could maintain my arousal, and hopefully control it, until bath time.

Then it hit me - Bev! *Shit.. Shit!* I hadn't heard back from Hector in Australia with the results of my blood tests. That did it. Before I knew it my pole position had been replaced with a seat in the grandstand.

I was stopped at a set of lights, mouthing obscenities and thumping my fists against the steering wheel when I glanced sideways. I saw a little girl in the car beside me looking at me with a terrified expression like I was a madman. I changed expression and smiled sweetly at her and she turned to her mother and said something. Clearly I need to work on my smile because mom gave me a filthy look. Some situations just can't be retrieved so I conceded defeat and fixed my look straight ahead, although I could still feel the visual daggers being hurled from the car beside me. Then it occurred to me that perhaps I could retrieve my situation. I extracted my phone from my pocket and found Hector's number just as the lights changed to green. I dialed as I sped off, figuring if I got a fine for making a call whilst driving it would be worth it - if I could get the answer I hoped for.

I was still a few minutes away from Sunny's place so the situation was salvageable if Hector had some good news for me. Sadly, he didn't. Well, actually he didn't pick up, which left me in limbo. I had no quarrel with Hector for not answering; after all it was the middle of the night down there.

I knocked on Sunny's front door and immediately noticed the new raw timber around the lock. It seems she has had some trouble, I hope everything is alright.

After a slightly longer time than I had expected the door opens and Sunny is standing there, in front of me. I'd been anticipating this moment, urgently needing this moment for a long time. But all my fantasies evaporated as I looked at her.

Firstly, in my warped fantasy she was either naked or loosely draped in a towel, in reality she was fully dressed - in jeans.

Secondly, tears were streaming down her face. That alone is an erection killer but when you add the bunch of soggy tissues she's holding, it's game, set and match

324

for Little Gary; time to hang up the racket and balls.

Sunny rushes into my arms and buries her head in my chest. I hold her close and stroke her wet hair as I walk her backwards inside her apartment. I can feel my chest becoming wet through the shirt with her tears. I kick the door closed and maneuver her to the couch so we can sit.

She hasn't said anything so far, but being a perceptive, sensitive new-age guy, I realize she has a problem. A big problem if you measure problems by the number of tears they generate. I wait...

Eventually, 'Simon is dead,' she sobs into my chest,

This is big news. The guy who I suspected was responsible for my "lost" night a week or so ago is dead? *He was around my age so natural causes seem unlikely. If I was right about him trying to drug Sunny that night, it's a better bet that drugs might be involved in his demise. Or maybe some woman he tried to drug and rape, murdered him... Sunny? - Oh God, no!*

I ease her head away from my chest so I can look at her. 'How did he die, Sunny?' I ask, fearing the answer.

'A drug overdose, I think.' She is still sobbing, but talking about it seems to be helping her regain some control.

'Does this have anything to do with the damage to your door?'

'M..mm,' she nods, and the tears come again.

'Did he hurt you in any way, Sunny?' I ask, ready to kill him a second time if the answer is yes.

She looks at me and her face disintegrates. 'He broke into here and I found him naked on my bed...'

Sunny, in stuttered, broken sentences, slowly began to tell me the whole story. It took quite a while and almost a full box of tissues to get it out. She admitted that she wasn't going to tell me about her being raped, but decided to, because she wanted us to start with a clean sheet, so to speak, and ultimately she couldn't handle the burden of that knowledge alone, anymore.

I hated hearing what had happened to her, but I loved that she was prepared to share these horrible things that had come into her life... With me.

As her story unfolded towards the present time, she began to cry with more intensity. And then she said it. 'I killed him, Gary. I killed him.'

My mouth fell open and I gazed into her face. I couldn't believe what I was hearing, everything was spiraling out of control and heading for a massive crash and fireball.

'But Sunny, you told me he was unconscious when you found him. How could you have killed him?'

'I filled the syringe with whatever was in the bottle. I was going to put it in his arm. I wanted to make him pay for what he did to me. I wanted to hurt him...' She pulled another handful of tissues out and wiped her eyes and blew her nose. 'I couldn't do it. I held it above his arm, but I couldn't go through with it. I wiped my fingerprints off it and replaced them with Simon's, then I dropped it on the bed and went outside to wait for the ambulance.'

'Sunny, you didn't kill him. You didn't do anything. You just admitted that to me.'

'I wasted time, Gary. That's what killed him. A few minutes earlier and the doctors would have saved him.'

'You can't say that, Sunny. It's just not true. The way you told the story to me you had already called the ambulance before you tried to inject him. So, the time

326

you used up contemplating doing it meant nothing. The ambulance was already on its way.'

She finally realized what had happened, her guilt had prevented her from reasoning correctly and her tears began to dry. She looked at me intensely. I could see the weight had been taken away from her and her face slowly broke into a smile. She leaned closer and kissed me gently on the lips.

'Thank you, Gary,' she said, after the kiss. 'It seems I need you around to make sense of my life.'

'And don't you ever forget it,' I said as I grabbed at her and pulled her close and kissed her. I felt her hand slide up my leg, heading straight for Little Gary who was already doing his best to meet her half way. Sunny gently ran her fingers over the bump in the material she had created. Keen not to be left out of the fun my hands had found some nice soft things to play with.

We kept kissing for a minute or two and I knew where this was going to end up so I reluctantly eased myself back from Sunny.

'What is the problem?' She asked, with a bewildered, almost hurt look on her face.

'You've just had some terrible news and so have I. I think we need to wait until...' I stopped talking because my phone began to ring. I fumbled for it in my pants pocket which was stretched tight because something large was already taking up most of the available space in that area. Eventually the phone came out and I quickly connected the call, grateful for the opportunity to come up with a good excuse why I couldn't make love with this woman, even though that was the one thing I wanted to do most in the whole world.

'Sorry I missed your call earlier, Gary,' a familiar

Aussie accent said in my ear.

'That's okay, Hector. I apologize for calling you in the middle of the night.'

'I gathered what you would be calling about,' he chuckled. 'The results weren't in, so I called the lab and had one of the after-hours scientists give me what they had, over the phone. You're all clear, old son. No worries at all.'

'I love you, Hector.'

'Whoa! Back up soldier. I'm not that kind of girl,' Hector laughed down the phone.

'Seriously. Thank you for that. Your timing is brilliant. I've got to run, Hector, I'll call you soon. And by the way that thing I mentioned to you last time we spoke.'

'Yeah! I heard the news. It's gone badly pear-shaped, eh?'

'Hector,' I laughed, 'if I was you, I'd develop a massive taste for pears.'

I placed my phone down and turned back to Sunny.

She was looking at me like I'd been communicating in Russian. 'You joke about my cryptic take on the world...?'

I realized the half of the conversation that Sunny had heard would have made little sense, but there was no way I was sharing the meaning with her. 'That was Hector. A new Aussie friend I met on the plane. He has an ongoing joke with me. It would be too difficult to make any sense of it for you.'

She raised her eyebrows, questioningly at me. 'Before the call you were saying something about waiting...?'

I put my arm around her shoulder, then quickly

brought the other one under her legs and picked her up. Our faces were inches apart and I kissed her gently... and firmly... and every way in-between. Then I pulled back and said, 'That was me just being pragmatic and not wanting to take advantage of you while you were so vulnerable.'

She looked at me questioningly, again.

'What can I say, I gave you some time - and you got better,' I grinned at her cheekily. 'Plus, I was overruled. My vote seems to be unimportant.'

'What the hell are you saying, Gary?'

'I'm saying I was overruled by Little Gary. It seems he's keen for a game of Heidi.'

Still cradling her in my arms I headed towards her bedroom. I laughed raucously.

Sunny had already started unbuttoning her blouse.

Chapter 11

The sign at the front door of the ballroom advised that an "Extraordinary General Meeting of Plutarch Resources N.L." was taking place inside. This was the second smallest of the hotel's four ballrooms but still capable of holding up to 200 people. Inside about 100 remaining shareholders were sitting around enjoying the last of their free coffee and cakes. About twenty-five media people were packing up their camera gear and microphones. Print reporters were typing the final paragraphs of their stories into laptops along with any pictures they had taken, ready to email back to their editors and be in place in the Business Sections of their papers before the reporters had walked back to the car-park.

It had taken Truf and myself only a few minutes to take control of the meeting. Using the shares we controlled and the Proxy forms from Warra, Gran and Megan I called for the official vote for Chairman, Managing Director and Director. I was elected Chairman, and Truf and Tim were elected unopposed, as well. The remaining directors were left in place - for the time being. The Meeting was over in just a few minutes and was quite anticlimactic. The reporters had hoped for something explosive given the amount of media coverage Plutarch had received over the past few weeks.

330

The company was considered a national disgrace and the entire Coal Seam Gas industry had been given a massive black-eye.

I had taken the stage after my election and announced that I had been in unofficial negotiation with the Environmental Protection Authority over any penalties that Plutarch would face over the environmental damage. I relayed to the shareholders that a fine of one million dollars had been arrived at, plus they required the best possible restoration of the billabong to its natural state, at the expense of the company.

The former Chairman, Charlie Forman and another of his former Directors, Wesley Reynolds, were making a hasty exit from the ballroom through a side door. Felix Geyer remained, seated at the Directors table on the stage. He seemed reluctant to accept that he no longer had a job.

Truf approached him and leaned over the table placing his face only inches from Geyer's. 'You're done, Felix. As my first act as Managing Director I am advising you that you are fired... and the company will be seeking financial compensation from you for your actions.'

'English shit,' Felix spat the words at Truf. 'I should have cracked your skull open with the pool cue.'

'You should have done a lot of things, Felix,' Truf replied, nonplussed by Felix's outburst. 'Not the least would have been actually buying all those chemicals you have billed to the company and instead, pocketed the money. And the wages of the twenty-two extra employees on the payroll who don't exist and turned out to be you. You have a lot of Plutarch's money sitting in accounts somewhere. But don't worry we are well on the way to finding it.'

Felix's fist came out of nowhere and crashed into the side of Truf's face, sending him reeling back. But he didn't fall. The bulky German clambered over the table, smashing glasses and tumblers of water as he did, and crash-tackled him.

The room had suddenly gone deathly quiet, except for the noise of the fight on the stage. The cameramen quickly began to put their gear back into working order, but only one was already taping. Some shareholders had quickly activated their phones and were getting videos of the on-stage dramas.

When Felix crashed into Truf the two of them rolled on the floor. Truf brought up his knee as he fell and caught Felix in the stomach with it, driving the wind out of him, but not before he had connected with a second solid punch to Truf's cheek.

'Asshole, English shit,' Felix snarled like a wounded animal. He was still gasping for breath after his kneeing.

Both men weighed about the same, but Truf was considerably taller and had better reach, and, as it turned out, superior strength. Lying on his back with Felix draped over him Truf grabbed the German's jacket lapels and pushed him into the air, then he rolled him sideways. As Felix was falling, shoulder first to the floor, Truf was maneuvering his own body in the other direction. As Felix hit the wooden stage-floor with a boom, Truf's fist crashed into his nose, which exploded like a ripe grape into a red mist, accompanied with a satisfying crunch as the bone, along with the skin and cartilage, shattered and smashed.

'I warned you against this, Felix,' Truf said, grunting, as he lifted the stunned German to his feet, his nose pouring blood over his shirt and tie. 'Prepare for the worst pain of your life.' As he said it, he simultaneously crashed the side of both his fists into the German's ears. The resulting pressure wave instantly rammed down his ear canals, exploding both his eardrums.

The scream was heard at the end of the long hallway inside the hotels largest ballroom. It penetrated over the noise that the five hundred guests inside were making, causing a momentary lull in all conversations and curious, somewhat worried looks to be exchanged.

Truf stepped away from Felix, whose screams were causing his own ears to hurt. Hotel security people were scrambling onto the stage along with a host of others. Some keen to assist, some just curious to see what damage had been done. The cameras kept recording.

I looked beside me at Tim and said with a nod of my head, 'I guess we have just been promoted to lead story in the news.'

Sunny and Sammy were sitting beside Tim. Both women sat immobile, in stunned silence, their eyes were cringing at the ongoing screams that still came from the stage.

Sammy was first to react, jumping from her seat to run to her man. 'Oh Truf, you beautiful man. Did he hurt you?' She wrapped him in a bear-hug.

'I'm fine, sweetheart. But I think the cheek will heal quicker if you give it a little kiss.'

Sammy obliged and Truf smiled sheepishly at the cameras that were trained on them. This was all good PR for a company that had been kicked into the toilet for the past month. He could imagine the headlines, tomorrow. "Plutarch's new management disposes of the polluters." He found a lopsided smile forming on his face.

'You okay, Truf?' I asked as I patted him on the back. 'That was quite a show, pal. Remind me never to piss you off!' I grinned at him and watched as his cheek slowly swelled and turned a pale shade of blue.

The screams from Felix had begun to die down as the hotel's, hastily summoned resident doctor had just administered morphine to the belligerent patient.

A few minutes later the police arrived but as Truf had at least 50 eyewitnesses and numerous video versions of the event, he was allowed to go home with an assurance that Felix Geyer would face the full force of the law after he had recovered from his surgeries.

Sophie and Sky were flying in tomorrow and with the help of Sunny and Sammy we intended to do a complete forensic study of the financial state of Plutarch Resources.

Sunny had managed to get a bag of ice from the kitchen staff for Truf's face and he and Sammy left for their room on level 13. Sammy nursing the ice against his face as he walked off with his arm around her shoulder.

'They make a lovely couple,' Sunny said as she watched them leave.

'Not as lovely as you and me,' I quipped. 'And on that subject, young lady, you promised me a banquet which you still haven't delivered on. It's payday girl. I don't know if you noticed, but our room has a rather large Jacuzzi.' I leered, suggestively at her. 'I suggest we celebrate the fact that you are banging the Chairman of a Stock Exchange listed company, by downing a couple of bottles of Moet, some prawns and some Morten Bay Bugs - you'll love them.' I paused, then added, 'and quite a few mouthfuls of Sunny.'

'Ha!' she retorted. 'Banging the Chairman...' she made an unflattering raspberry sound. 'You've only had the job for five minutes and you've already got a swollen head.'

I smiled sheepishly at her, and said, 'As long as you are near me, my love, that can never happen. Remember where Little Gary gets his blood supply from?'

***

Three weeks later Truf and I called a press conference. Actually, it was called by our newly retained Press Consultant, a chap by the name of Frank Spiller. Because of Truf's new found status and media celebrity I happily handed the proceedings over to him. The event had a near capacity turn out, which according to Frank is as rare as hen's teeth for a penny-dreadful company. I need to talk to him about that reference, now that we run that penny-dreadful. It's more than a little offensive. Especially so, coming from our own PR man.

Truf began by welcoming everyone and got off to a rolling start by telling the assembled media that if they stayed until the end, he and I would have a punch-up for them after we had dealt with our business. They all laughed.

Like hell we would...

Sophie and Sky handed out media-kits to all the reporters that spelled out what was about to happen within Plutarch Resources.

Sophie had gone through the company accounts and had identified $4.89 million dollars that had been fraudulently stolen by Felix Geyer, using various means. She had been able to trace $3.96 million spread over three bank accounts. One in Zürich, one in Singapore and one in Lichtenstein. The three accounts had been frozen by our legal representatives and processes were being put in place to return the funds to Plutarch Resources. Felix also had some real-estate assets that were being investigated.

Given the strength of our case regarding ownership of these funds a local bank had supplied bridging funds to the company of $2 million dollars. The fine of $1 million levied by the Environmental Protection Authority had already been paid, and an environmental cleanup company called "Only Green is Green" had been contracted to rid the billabong and mining sites of as much chemical residue as is currently scientifically possible. OGIG have quoted a locked in cost to Plutarch of $500,000.

The final item of our press release pertained to our Coal Seam Gas exploration. Truf became agitated when he made this part of the announcement. 'I'm a geologist and mining engineer, but over and above that I'm a human being, just like the rest of you. All of us alive on this planet have a care of duty to pass the place on to our kids and grandkids in a state that we should be proud of. A state that will allow them to all live healthy, prosperous lives - as we have.'

He looked around at his audience, then he continued, satisfied that they were still listening.

'Coal Seam Gas extraction is a difficult technological process that involves introducing risk to the nations ground water that is buried well beneath the surface. This is a risk that we, the new managers of Plutarch Resources are not prepared to take on our children's behalf. GSG requires a well casing, or pipe if you like, to be drilled into the ground. Numerous highly poisonous chemicals, as you have just been made aware of from the clean up we have to undertake at the billabong, are then pumped into the earth. This causes the underground seam of coal to fracture a long way below the surface. It's called fracking. That releases the gas which is pumped to the surface and collected. Is everyone up to speed with this process?'

Once again he surveyed his audience looking for signs that he was loosing them.

'The well casing quite often passes straight through the layer of trapped ground water. I'm not going to bore you any more, pardon that pun by the way, with any more technical brief. I'm just going to say one thing, and this is the reason we are withdrawing from Coal Seam Gas exploration: It is an engineering fact that over the working life of well casings, 50% of them... fail. Put simply, that is an unacceptable risk to that ground water and the lives and livelihoods of our future generations.'

I couldn't believe it, but Truf's little speech got a round of applause. If they liked that, then they were going to love what was coming up.

'You may well think we have just committed financial suicide with that announcement. Plutarch shares are currently trading at just 2 cents each, which is arguably fair value for a company that drills holes and pours poison into the ground,' Truf smiled broadly at his audience but received only stunned glares back from his fellow shareholders. 'Plutarch's mining leases cover not only CSG exploration but also mineral exploration and with the help of the local aboriginal community we have begun some preliminary exploration of areas they have pinpointed to us. And the results are more than staggering. As a company executive I am legally forbidden to give false information that may effect the value of my companies shares. Instead I will show you something we have discovered and you can make up your own minds.'

Suddenly the side doors opened and four burly, armed security guards came into the room. They were wheeling a large stainless-steel trolley. It was covered in rocks. The men positioned the trolley under a special light and a cameraman moved over to film what lay on top. Six large screens were simultaneously turned on around the room and the camera zoomed in and began a slow pan of the rocks. There were gasps from the audience as some of them recognized what they were looking at when most of the rocks reflected back bright yellow flecks and lines of color.

'My God man, is that real?' someone shouted from amongst the crowd.

'Yes it is, sir,' Truf bellowed and laughed. 'For those of you who haven't worked it out those are quartz rocks and the yellow color that you can all clearly see is an element we call gold.'

'Good lord,' someone called out. 'They came from Plutarch Resources leaseholds?'

'They did indeed, and I can tell you that those rocks were collected by just three men in the space of about fifteen minutes.'

People were starting to stand to get a better view of the rocks, some even ventured to the edge of the stage but hard glares from the security guards kept them from coming closer.

As the audience collectively basked in the rich aura the sudden introduction of gold had created, Truf said loudly into the microphone, 'The original J.P. Morgan, who many consider a legend in the world of finance, once made a famous statement about the rocks you are looking at. He said, "Gold is money - Everything else is credit." Ladies and gentlemen, Plutarch Resources is going into the money making business.'

***

Within a week Plutarch shares were trading around $2 each. This guaranteed to make our jobs easier, as going from an exploration company to a mining company costs a huge amount of money. With investors keen to get on board we would be able to raise those funds by issuing more shares.

The weeks that followed brought a series of interesting developments.

Most notable was Ling Mein suing the Nixon Fund for $20 million. But our lawyers quickly got the problem dismissed. We had, after all, offered the shares back to him just after the bad news hit and included compensation, which he had rejected outright at the time.

Felix Geyer was released from hospital and placed straight into jail. He didn't collect $200. The Government have charged Felix with numerous offenses including fraud, Tax evasion, environmental vandalism, plus other company related offenses. They assured us that if Felix didn't get some decent jail time from those charges they would add common assault for his attack on Truf and if that wasn't enough then they would charge him with pool-table hogging. It seems the Australian authorities have quite a hard-on for Felix. His lawyers did manage to get him released on bail but he had to surrender his passport. Hopefully, the sneaky bastard doesn't have another one.

Plutarch's civil case against Felix for the return of the stolen funds was well advanced and our lawyers were confident a large proportion would be returned. Minus their fee which should take... I won't go there - I'm betting you already know what I was going to say.

Dr John Mackintime was offered a directorship in Plutarch Resources, and as an incentive to add his talents to the company, was offered an allocation of 250,000 options in Plutarch, exercisable any time within the next five years at 10 cents each. That meant he could exchange those options for full-priced shares at any stage within that time limit by paying $25,000. Not a bad deal when you consider the shares are worth about $500,000 at todays valuation and we haven't started mining yet. Ironically this was almost as much as Truf had paid the good doctor to part with his original share parcel a month or so back. He accepted the directorship.

The same option deal was presented to both Sky and Sophie. Both girls were keen to exercise their options and sell their shares immediately but Truf convinced them that in about three years time the company stood a good chance of producing at least $300 million worth of gold... every year for the foreseeable future, and the share price had a real chance of going a lot higher.

A certain doctor I know emailed me and thanked me for introducing him to the "pear" diet. His health was at least a million times better since he'd been on it, he told me. Who'da guessed?

Oscar Barrymore had accepted a job washing Bentleys at the local dealership. No, I'm joking. Oscar is still selling art all over the world. I should have asked for more money from him.

Warra's 67 paintings were placed in the hands of a reputable dealer in London and he had started to receive regular commission checks for large sums of money for the sales of those paintings.

He keeps them all in his bag in his hut.

Warra is without doubt the richest man in his part of Queensland. To celebrate his good fortune he bought each of his sons and daughters a second-hand caravan for their families to live in. Warra still prefers his hut. He also splashed out for a ten-seater van to get the kids to school. It is brown like all the family vehicles, but this one was actually painted brown. And only had 100,000 kilometers on the clock.

The whole point of this exercise was to protect the land that Warra and his tribe live on. So, with the CSG problem sorted I arranged some meetings with a few high level officials. I was able to secure a perpetual leasehold from the Government over an area of 20 square miles of the surrounding Crown Land for Warra's tribe to live on. My new found respect in the business world, as Chairman of a well known, and now respected company, opened many doors for me. I doubt I could have done that for Warra without the *big head* title.

Truf had explained that gold mining was just as dirty, in its own way, as CSG mining. We decided to run our mine as cleanly as possible. That made it more expensive to operate than other similar mines, but we could live with that. Our plan was to crush and mill the rock on-site and refine it as much as possible before the nasty chemicals, like cyanide, were required to extract the gold. That meant we needed to truck our concentrate about one hundred and fifty kilometers to an existing working gold processor. We negotiated a deal where we will pay all the refining costs and share a percentage of the profits with them.

By the way, we named the soon-to-be established gold mine "The Joey Nine".

Truf sold his business in London to his second-in-command partner and now spends most of his time in Australia - with his beautiful fiancée.

I troubled over Angela Spencer, Harry's daughter, for a long time. Needless to say she was pissed at not getting her hands on Harry's assets and money - and I was a little uncomfortable having it. I compromised and employed a private detective to check her out. He found that she wasn't doing drugs, but she drank a bit. It seems she had just had a pretty rotten time lately. Her problem with Harry was something personal that went a lot deeper and happened many years ago. A private matter that I instructed the detective to not delve any deeper into. *Families- Can't live without 'em - Can't shoot 'em.* The detective found out from neighbors that Angela had cried for days after Harry's death. That was the clincher for me. I assigned Harry's house over to her and all his other assets, except the house I had been renting, the one with the black horse Harry had been painting when his ladder and life came toppling down. I'll keep that as my London home and my connection with Harry. It is Sunny's home also, now.

Sunny and I are doing just fine. She's not only the

biggest part of my life, she's the only part of it that matters. I think she likes me too. There is only one problem at the moment - she just told me she's late.

Women. Always rushing here or there...

Go figga!

THE END

Oh! If you haven't worked out the paradox yet, don't feel bad. Truf and Tim haven't either. Let me recap and explain: The three men paid $100 each for the room, totaling $300. The receptionist should have only charged $250 for the room so he takes the $50 back to them. Realizing he can't split the $50 three ways, he pockets $20 and gives each man back $10.

So each man paid $100 less the $10 refund, equals $90. Three x $90 = $270. The receptionist has $20 in his pocket. That comes to $290. Where is the missing $10?

The problem is that you're still stuck on the original $300. Once they pay it over, it no longer exists. All that exists now is the $50 to be refunded, and that is accounted for: 3 x $10 to the men, and $20 to the receptionist.

Job done.

Also by Peter Butler

Womanhood

Kinky

Buy Me a Dream